Parkland

The Untold Story

By D.P. Conway

After Life Books
Book 2

Day Lights Publishing House, Inc.
Cleveland * Austin

"There is a demon inside my head, telling me to Burn. Kill. Destroy."

"Burn? Kill? Destroy... what?"

"Anything."

Nikolas Cruz, speaking to a detective after the shooting.

Published by Day Lights Publishing House, Inc
5498 Dorothy N. Olmsted Oh 44070
Austin Writing Location: 1901 E. 20th St. Austin TX

Author/Publishers Sources Note: The author of this work relied on hundreds of articles published by various newspaper and internet news agencies including, but not limited to, The Sun Sentinel, The Washington Post, The Wall Street Journal, The New York Post, The New York Times, The Florida Bulldog, The New York Daily News, Radar Online. Due to the works fictional nature, it was not possible to footnote sources without adversely affecting the nature and flow of the fictional story. Any inadvertently omitted sources will be added into subsequent editions and to dpconway.com.

Cover by Nate Myers, and key revisions consulted by Mary Egan.

Story Consultants: Angela Pensiero, Colleen Conway Cooper, Bridget Conway, Christopher Conway, Patrick Conway, Edward Markovich, Mary Egan, and Peggy Stewart.

Editing Team: Edward Markovich, Angela Pensiero, Colleen Conway Cooper, Peggy Steward, and Connie Swenson.

Dedications

For the families and friends
of the deceased,
May God hold you close
until the day you see
your cherished loved one again.

For those who were
wounded and traumatized,
May God continue
to heal you in every way.

For the school community of
Marjory Stoneman Douglas High School
Be the change you wish to see in the world.

Dear Reader

'Parkland' is an epic story, spanning twenty years of events, which ultimately led to the 2018 Valentine's Day Massacre at Stoneman Douglas High School in Parkland, Florida.

It is a compelling work of fiction, based on hundreds of newspaper articles that have been woven together into a dramatic narrative that tells the story of a tragedy, a tragedy that should have been stopped. In a world of natural and supernatural forces, and in my unique literary style, I weave Angels and Demons into parts of the story to vividly show the struggle of good versus evil. It is an attempt to bring order out of the chaos of this tragic historical event.

One of the reasons I wrote 'Parkland', is to hold the bureaucracy accountable. (the School Superintendent and District, the Sheriff, the Deputies, the Principals, the Professional and School Counselors, the FBI, the Security Monitors, Cruz's Mother, and the Lobbyist on both sides of gun and school security issues.) I hope this story sheds light on what they did do, and more importantly, what they did not.

I cannot imagine the pain of the families and friends of those who lost their lives. I, too, am grieved, as my research connected me with the seventeen dear souls in a way I had not anticipated. I hope this book honors them as it is the main reason that I wrote this story.

I encourage you to follow the lead of the students and parents of the Stoneman Douglas community. Contact your federal, state, and local officials and help usher in changes in law and policy needed to address not only gun violence but also school security.

And now let me tell you a story... the story of what happened in Parkland.

D.P. Conway
March 2019

Parkland: The Untold Story

Why Did You Let Him?

Why, Washington, did you use heavy handed tactics for social issues, while not doing the same to promote school security measures which might have stopped an active shooter?

Why, Congress, despite so many school shootings, did you do nothing and not hold a Judiciary Committee hearing on gun violence in over eight years?

Why, FBI, did you drop the ball twice, and why have you not been transparent with us in the aftermath?

Why, Sheriff Israel, did you allow the "may enter" policy, not train your people for mass shooters, not have proper communications, and have incompetent people working in your department?

Why, Sheriff's deputies, did you allow Cruz to harass his neighbors for so many years without stopping him?

Why, District Superintendent, did you stop reporting certain student offenses to law enforcement and not secure our schools, and why did you ask for teacher pay and benefit increases right after the tragedy?

Why, School Board, were there 104 million dollars allocated for security with only a fraction of that spent?

Why, Lynda, did you coddle your son, and why did you help him buy an AR-15 when you knew how unstable he was?

Why, neighbor, did you allow Cruz to bring his guns into your home while he lived with you?

Why, Principal, did you praise law enforcement when they utterly failed, and why did you praise the school district, and allow a culture of lax security, and why were you not notified of threats at the school?

Why, NRA, do you insist on positions that ignore common sense, including that AR-15's can belong in the hands of 18-year-olds. Why do you refuse to compromise in background check laws?

Why 911 operators, did you take so long to put out the alert when you heard shots fired?

Why, Social Workers and Mental Health Counselors, did you declare Cruz not a threat when he clearly was.

Why, School Counselors, did you have 140 contacts with Cruz and his mother, and still let Cruz stay at Stoneman Douglas and drop his special-needs status?

Why, Coward, did you not rush in when you were armed, a mere forty feet away?

Why, other Cowards, did you stay on the road, not rush in and drive away? They needed you. We all needed you.

Chapter 1

April, 2008
Lynda Cruz Home, Parkland, Florida

NIKOLAS RAN DOWN THE HALL into the living room, then turned and ran back to the front door, holding his hands over his ears, screaming, "Ahhhhhhh! Ahhhhhhh! Stop!!! Stop!!!"

His mother Lynda heard him and raced in from the back patio, "Nikolas, Nikolas!" She ran up to him, but he brushed past her, screaming, "Make her stop!! Make her stop!!"

Lynda saw her other son running down the steps and yelled, "Zachary call 911!"

Nikolas jumped onto the couch, writhing in agony. Lynda raced over and grabbed him, holding him close, rocking his shaking body back and forth, "What is it, honey? What is it?"

"Make her stop! Make her stop!"

"Who! Who, Nikolas!" she cried, as tears fell from her cheeks.

"Tira! Tira!"

Lynda had never heard him say this before and she was frightened. She shouted, "Zachary! Did you call 911?"

"Yes!" he said in a frustrated voice.

Lynda kept rocking his shaking body, hoping to calm him, when suddenly she remembered something she had seen her late husband Roger do. She slowly traced the Sign of the Cross on Nikolas' forehead.

Nikolas let out a long sigh, and the shaking began to lessen. Lynda kept rocking him back and forth, "It's ok, Nikolas. I've got you."

He shook his head, saying nothing, reaching up to wipe the tears from his eyes

Lynda heard the ambulance and began to feel nervous. She did not need another incident on his record. Now, she would have to explain everything to the paramedics.

The paramedics came in and examined the still shuddering ten-year-old boy in front of them. They asked numerous questions to which Lynda replied somewhat evasively.

One of them said, "Mrs. Cruz, we think we should take Nikolas in for an evaluation."

"No, he's fine. There's nothing wrong with him."

"Mrs. Cruz, your other son said Nikolas hears voices. That is not normal."

"No, I said he is fine."

Zachary interrupted them, "No, he's not fine, mom. He's crazy!"

Lynda turned in anger, "Zachary!!! Get up to your room, right now!"

Zachary turned in disgust and trudged away.

Lynda took a deep breath and allowed calm to instantly come over her again, "I'm sorry about that. No, Nikolas is ok. I will keep an eye on him. If anything changes, I will call a doctor." As soon as the words left her mouth, she knew she was lying. She would never allow them to label Nikolas as mentally ill. But it was more than that. Deep down, she knew there was something dark involved, something mysterious that her late husband Roger had hidden from her, and she was starting to get scared.

Chapter 2

February 14, 2018
TEN YEARS LATER

NIKOLAS SAT ALONE IN THE PARK with his backpack loaded with ammunition and his AR-15 in the canvas case next to him. He studied the map of the Stoneman Douglass Campus one more time. He would enter through the north gate parking lot, the one where he had been beaten up so long ago, and begin in Building 12 where many of the freshman classes were being held. He expected less resistance there.

In Building 12, there were 8-10 classrooms on each of the three floors, with as many as twenty students in each. He would move move from class to class in a zig-zag fashion, shoot all who tried to leave, go up a flight, then repeat, all the way to the 3rd floor. Then he would race outside with the fleeing students to start phase two, the battlefield phase, in which he would sweep across the entire campus to extract maximum casualties, and ultimately confront the sheriffs in a glorious showdown.

The Dark Angel Tira stood by, watching him think, worried the plan had been discovered. She nervously scanned the skies, but there was no one coming. All was a go. She whispered, "It's time Nikolas. It is time!"

Nikolas half smiled and pulled out his phone. He opened his Uber app and requested a ride. He turned his video camera on and told the camera what he was going to do, finishing with the words, "People are going to die!"

When the gold colored compact Uber arrived, Nikolas jumped in and calmly began the 12-minute drive to the school.

He texted J.T. Snead whose family he was living with, who he had seen just that morning. "Yo, J.T., what class are you in and who is the teacher?"

"It's one of the coaches. You know who."

"Ask the coach if he remembers me. LOL."

"Yeah, right, no way!"

Cruz stared at the phone. He was pretty sure what classroom that was, and he made a note of it. He then texted, "I am going to a movie. I've got something big to tell you!"

"What?"

"Nothing."

"I thought you said something big?"

"Don't worry; it's no big deal. Nothing bad."

Cruz saw the school in the distance. He went over his plan in his mind one more time as his hands began to perspire,

At 2:19 pm, the Uber driver came to a stop on Pine Island Road, not far from Building 12. Nikolas smirked and texted his friend, "Yo!"

Chapter 3

TWENTY YEARS EARLIER
Bamboo Tree Bar, Pompano Beach, Florida

BRENDA WOODLEY OBSERVED THE STRANGER as she picked up her bottle of beer, keeping her elbow pinned to the bar, and drained the final sip. The stranger was watching her too. He had been most of the night. It was getting late, and the beach side bar was thinning out, but it did not bother Brenda. She knew what the stranger wanted by his eyes, and she was all in. The only question was where. As she expected would happen, he got up and walked over. This was her first look at the whole of him, and she liked what she saw. He was tall, with dark brown hair that had a singed look to it. Coupled with his dark eyebrows, and leather shirt, he had a definite bad boy look to him.

She figured he was about five years younger than her, which would put him in his mid-thirties.

"Hello," he said.

"Hello to you. I haven't seen you here before."

"I don't come here that often, but I was in the area tonight." He paused, deepening his look into her eyes, "I noticed you, and I wanted to know your name."

"It's Brenda."

The man smiled, "I am Vesru."

"Vesru? That sounds like some Indian name."

"No, it is not an Indian name; it is an old name."

"You don't look very old."

"I am older than I look." The man looked around, "Why don't we go for a walk on the beach."

Brenda smiled and turned her head, peering into his eyes, wondering why they captivated her so. Perhaps it was because she felt buzzed, perhaps it was because she had not been hit on all summer. She glanced out through the open bar door at the warm summer night. The street outside the Bamboo Tree Bar was quieting down. It was only a short walk to the beach where they could find a quiet spot. She looked back at him, smiling, "Sure, I'll go for a walk with you." She pulled out ten dollars from her jean shorts, set it on the bar, and walked out with Vesru trailing just behind her.

They crossed the street and headed to a short access road and soon found themselves walking along the beach. It was a moonless night, and unbeknownst to Brenda, it was the only reason Vesru was with her. Dark Angels could only pursue the women of earth on such nights. To do so when the moon was visible, heightened the chance they could be caught.

Brenda knew wherever they did it; it would be quick, so she treated her walk as her time of foreplay, her time of letting things last a while. She asked, "So where are you from?"

"I am from far away."

"From where?"

"From up there." He pointed to the sky.

"What do you mean?"

"I am an Angel."

She stopped and looked at him. "You're putting me on, right?"

"Actually no."

Brenda decided to play along, "Well what are you doing here?"

"We Angels find you, women of earth, to be mesmerizing."

Brenda laughed. She was feeling pretty buzzed and a little more drunk than she realized, but she appreciated the entertainment. A small part of her fancied it was true though she knew it was a lie.

They reached a dark part of the beach. Brenda asked, "So where do you want to do it?"

"Right here."

"Here, in the sand?"

"No, here, on my wings."

Before her eyes, large dark wings came out from each side of him. He reached for her hand, and she took it, as the wings enveloped her. She felt a dark sweet flow of power in her hand and felt herself being laid down onto a pillow of soft feathers. In a moment, her jean shorts were off, and she felt him immerse himself in her. A dark swirling cloud enveloped her mind as she felt her body moving in ways she never imagined. A mounting feeling of ecstasy frightened her to the point that she screamed and then everything went black.

The sound of seagulls woke her, and she raised her head, noticing she was fully dressed. She said aloud, "Oh, my God, what the hell did I drink last night!"

She laid there for a few moments, exasperated, trying to remember the dream. It was a wild dream, she knew that, because it shook her to the core. She got up and looked around; she was alone. Her body shuddered, and it surprised her. *Was I dreaming or not?*

She was relieved that no one had seen her sleeping in the sand, and she began to walk away. But then she stopped and looked down. There was a clear imprint of an enormous set of feathery wings. "What the hell?" she said, suddenly feeling fear.

She looked around again at the desolate beach. There was no use telling anyone, no one would understand what the marks in the sand were. She sighed, shaking off the crazy notion, regretting at having drank so much and resolved she needed to stop. But then she saw something else, just a few feet away. Two dark brown feathers were laying in the sand. She picked them up and clutched them tightly. It was her proof. She had not been dreaming after all.

Chapter 4

December 19, 1997.
Our Lady of Lourdes Shrine, Pompano Beach, Florida
Four weeks later.

BRENDA WAITED SILENTLY IN THE PEW for what seemed like an eternity. Finally, the old nun returned through a door at the back of the altar and waved for her to come. Brenda got up and followed the nun through the sacristy, and through a door that led to a long, dimly lit hallway. They went through two ancient looking doors and into another hall, with carpet that looked very clean, and yet very old. They reached the doorway to a tiny room with two chairs facing each other and a large portrait on the back wall. The nun motioned for Brenda to enter, "Wait here, Sister Jane will be right over."

"Thank you," said Brenda, as she sat down in the chair and glanced up to her right at the picture of the Archangel Michael holding a sword standing over the fallen Angel Lucifer. She leaned forward, inspecting the picture, admiring the strength of the great Archangel while recollecting the strong masculine Angel who had laid with her only four weeks earlier.

It was eerily silent in the convent, and Brenda was wondering if she was doing the right thing. She thought about getting up and leaving, but as she was about to do so, Sister Jane appeared in the doorway, smiling. "Brenda?"

Brenda stood up, but the old nun protested, "Please, sit down." She waved for her to sit, while she lumbered in, leaning on her cane, and sat in the chair underneath the picture.

Sister Jane said, "I have not seen you in over twenty-five years. How is your mother?"

Brenda lowered her head, "She died about ten years ago."

"Oh, I am sorry to hear that. How did she die?"

"Cancer."

Sister Jane grimly nodded, she too had cancer, and the prognosis was not good. She asked, "And how are you doing?"

"Well, Sister, I have had a lot of trouble in my life. You know… with the law. But I am trying…"

"Well, I am glad to hear that." She grasped Brenda's hand in a warm, reassuring embrace, and asked, "What can I do for you?"

"Sister, I know this will sound crazy, but I met… an Angel. And um… it is crazy I know… but I laid with him."

Sister Jane stopped breathing for a moment; her senses suddenly on alert. "How do you know he was an Angel?"

"He looked like one, with wings and everything, almost like him." Brenda pointed up at the picture on the wall. She then watched as Sister Jane turned and looked up at the picture of the great Archangel Michael, but then lowered her eyes to the fallen Angel Lucifer.

Sister Jane slowly turned back to Brenda, "Brenda, is it possible you were dreaming?"

"No, and I have proof."

Sister Jane's face grew deadly serious. "What proof?"

Brenda reached in her purse and pulled out one of the feathers. "Here is a feather from his wings." She reached across to hand it to Sister Jane, but the old nun would not take it. Instead, she leaned forward to examine it more closely. A look of grave concern came over her face. "When did this happen?"

"About a month ago."

"Are you pregnant?"

She stuttered, "I am not sure. I might be."

Sister Jane let out a deep breath, and closed her eyes for a moment, mumbling a prayer to herself. While she was worried, she had run across this situation twice before in her long years. She knew that if a marked child was to be born, placing them with the right family would counteract the effects of darkness. She smiled, "Brenda, tell no one about this. But make sure you come and see me again if you are pregnant."

Brenda was more anxious than when she had arrived. She realized Sister Jane was also worried, and this scared her. She looked down at the feather again and then noticed it was not the white color of the feather in Michael's wings. It was brown, like the wings of the Dark Angel Lucifer.

Chapter 5

April 20, 1998
Vamorda's Plantation, Southern Shore of Hell
Four months later

THE DARK ANGEL VAMORDA sat on the portico of her palatial plantation overlooking the sea on the southern shore of Hell. She was feeling irritated today, as her last lover, a new arrival from Brazil, whom she had taken from her fields, had failed to satisfy her. He was paying the price now in the fields working under her most vicious Dark Angel overseer. But his punishment did nothing to quell her irritableness. She hated when she felt cheated.

Vamorda had been placed in charge of the Americas over 300 years earlier by the Dark Lord Legion himself. He was pleased with her progress, as she had overseen the steering of over a million men and women into Hell.

Still, she needed more to stay in power; being on top in Hell was never a secure place. As she sat looking out over the sea, a messenger bird arrived. It was from the Dark Lord.

Vamorda

I need to speak with you tonight at my villa. Come alone.

Legion

Vamorda cringed as she knew what this meant. Not only was she being dragged into another project, but Legion would have his way with her. He always did, and while a little part of her delighted in the dark thrill he alone could bring, the bigger part of her hated that he possessed her, as she was not her own when he was near.

~ ~ ~ ~

When evening came, she flew to his villa. Legion was waiting on his balcony overlooking the sea, wearing a long black robe with a V shaped neck that showed his gold necklace. She landed, and bowed, "Good evening, Lord Legion."

Legion looked angry, he snapped, "I have received word that your Angel Vesru has laid with a woman from the earth, and she is with child."

Vamorda was caught completely off guard. Vesru was one of her commanders, but she had over a hundred commanders. She knew the rules though, pregnancies from the unions between Dark Angels and human women were to be reported immediately. She stuttered, momentarily, then replied, "He should be punished, my Lord."

"Yes, and I want an example made of him. Do you understand what I mean by that?"

"Yes, I do, my Lord."

"Good," said Legion. "There is one more thing. The child is to receive the Dark Baptism."

Vamorda was confused for a moment. The Dark Baptism had not been given in centuries and had been long forgotten. It was said to be ineffective, and not worth the risk, but Vamorda knew truth.

She had administered the Dark Baptism once to Tomás de Torquemada, the bastard child of a Cardinal of Castile. She had personally overseen his growing up and rise to power as the leader of the Spanish Inquisition. Over 3,000 Jews and Muslims were sent by him to horrible, humiliating deaths and he imprisoned tens of thousands more. He was in Hell now, and one of 673,000 condemned men and women working her vast fields under the iron fist of her Dark Angel commanders.

But his case had so angered the Heavens that hundreds of Dark Angels were rounded up and cast into dark cages as a form of punishment. She narrowly escaped punishment only because she was careful. She was always careful. But from that time on, the practice of Dark Baptism stopped.

"But my Lord, as you know, we don't do Dark Baptisms anymore."

Legion seethed, "I will decide what we do, Vamorda!"

Vamorda froze, knowing she needed to tread carefully, she wanted no part of this. "My Lord, the wrath of the Heavens would be against the one who did it."

"Put Tira in charge of doing it. She is being assigned to watch over the child."

"Tira? She is nothing more than a lowly Dark Angel."

"Do not question me, Vamorda. I have chosen Tira because I can rely on her."

"Yes, my Lord." Vamorda already knew what that meant. Tira must be his latest conquest, his latest possessed, and she was enthusiastic about serving him. Something no one else wished to do any more unless they had to.

Legion then smiled, "Now, go inside, get undressed, and make yourself comfortable. I will be right in."

"Yes, my Lord." She bowed and turned, dreading what was to come.

~ ~ ~ ~

The following morning, Vamorda looked out the window at the 100 Dark Angel Commanders standing at attention in the compound outside her headquarters. She went out, making sure her face showed anger and walked down the steps stopping ten feet in front of them. "One of you has forgotten to follow the rules. You will answer to the charge now."

Silence gripped them all, as no one followed the rules in Hell, and every single one there knew they could be called.

Vamorda shouted, "Vesru, step forward."

Vesru tensed and walked up in front of Vamorda.

"Vesru, is it true you impregnated a woman of the earth, and did not inform me?"

Vesru lowered his glance, "Yes."

"Do you think my rules can be broken without consequence?"

"No, Vamorda," he grimaced, but expected no more than a slap on the wrist.

Vamorda stared at him, then said, "You will now receive your punishment."

Out of the corner of his eye, Vesru saw three guards coming across the compound carrying a dark cage. His eyes widened, "Wait... what are you doing!"

As the guards got closer, he tried to flee, but they apprehended him. They tied his hands and feet and brought him back in front of her.

Vamorda said, "Put him in the dark cage for the next five years."

A gasp went up from among the commanders as all knew even a short time in a dark cage was extreme torture for a Dark Angel.

Vesru pleaded for mercy, but Vamorda looked away, as they dragged him to the open door. They bent his head down as he let out a blood-curdling scream. They pushed him in, cut the rope tying his hands and feet, and slammed the door.

Chapter 6

May 25th, 1998.
Brenda's Temporary Apartment, Margate, Florida
One month later.

IN THE MUSTY ONE-ROOM APARTMENT she had rented three months earlier, Brenda tossed and turned, moaning, exhausted from the fear that had gripped her throughout the night. It was another night of nightmares, some brought on by the fear, but others brought on by the other-worldly presence growing inside her. She lurched up, yelling out, only to hear her plea for help answered by a neighbor shouting and pounding on the paper-thin walls.

Brenda was staying at the Comfy Inn Extended Stay. It used to be a beautiful Days Inn Motel, but that was over 60 years ago. Now, it was run-down, transient place, filled with drug addicts, prostitutes, and other neighborhood occupants who could afford to put up the money for a night, or a week, or perhaps longer, depending on how their luck was running.

Brenda was now in her sixth month of pregnancy, and she was becoming overwhelmed, not only because she was pregnant with no means of supporting herself but also because of the unrelenting thought that the child inside her was the offspring of an Angel, and perhaps even a demon. She had told no one, and truth be told, there was no one to tell. She had no friends or family. She was on her own. She had not gone back to see Sister Jane, hoping the nun's ominous warnings were nothing more than fantasies.

But as of late, she understood that Sister Jane was the only person who understood what was happening to her. She was thinking she needed to trust the old nun as her mother had trusted her before she died. She looked outside and thought of what was coming in three short months. She needed help.

~ ~ ~ ~

In the morning, Brenda got up, showered, and went to the nearby donut shop to have breakfast. After she was finished, she walked to the bus stop and waited for the bus. Within the hour she was walking up the hillside drive that led to the convent and church. She went to the convent door and rang the bell.

An older nun answered and invited her in. She was taken to the same sitting room she had been in the last time. Within a short time, Sister Jane came in, smiling.

"Hello Brenda, I am glad you came back." Sister Jane's eyes went to Brenda's stomach, and she half smiled. "So, I see you are pregnant."

"Yes, Sister, I'm scared. I can't afford this baby, and… and… I am afraid." A tear rolled down her face.

"There, there, Brenda. I understand. I will help you."

"How, what can be done? I'm afraid of who this child will be." Brenda wept.

Sister Jane sat down across from her, nodding. She already knew based on the feather she had been shown that a Dark Angel had sired the child. Throughout history, only Dark Angels had been bold enough to go against such a fundamental law of the universe. Yes, in the beginning, before the fall of Dark Angels, the male Angels of Heaven had relations with a fair number of human women, but the Lords had put a stop to it once it became known.

Sister Jane belonged to a secret order of nuns, privy to what could happen in the world. When a Dark Angel sired a child, the child would have the Mark, the Mark of Cain, and the old nuns knew what to do. "Would you like to give the child up for adoption?"

"Yes, I would," said Brenda.

"I can arrange for a special couple, one who can deal with the… child. They will help you get through the pregnancy, making sure you have a nice place to stay and making sure you have money and are under a doctor's care. But you can say nothing to them, nor to anyone, about the father, including your suspicion who the father might be. I will take care of that myself." Sister Jane stopped to see how Brenda was accepting things. She was.

Sister Jane continued, "They will compensate you so that you are taken care of afterwards. They are generous people. The only requirement I would ask is your silence as to the father."

"I would like that," said Brenda. "Will the child be ok? I mean, will he or she be normal?"

"I believe that the couple who will raise the child is well equipped, to make sure that the child has a great chance to grow up and have a normal life." Sister Jane smiled.

"Well, how do we arrange this?"

"I will contact them. But I must be able to contact you. Where can I reach you?"

Brenda gave her the number to the hotel where she was staying, and once more, glanced up at the image of Lucifer being held down by the foot of Michael the Archangel. She shuddered as her eyes were now drawn to the face of Lucifer.

Chapter 7

Memorial Day Weekend, 1998.
Roger and Lynda Cruz Home, Parkland, Florida
Two days later.

LYNDA CRUZ STOOD ON THE PATIO looking out at the small gathering of friends in her backyard. She and her husband Roger were hosting a cookout for Memorial Day. She called out, "Roger do you need anything?"

"Yes, bring me the extra bottle of barbeque sauce in the cupboard."

Just then Lynda heard the phone ring. "All right, I'll be right back." She picked up the phone. "Hello?"

"Is Roger Cruz there?"

Lynda hesitated, but only because the voice on the other line was that of an old lady, or else she would not have taken what appeared to be an unfamiliar phone call on a holiday weekend. "Uh… yes, he is. May I ask who is calling?"

"This is a friend of his, from the order."

"The order… okay, well hold on."

Lynda went outside. "Honey, you have a phone call."

Roger handed the cooking tongs to his friend and walked across the lawn to the house. "Who is it?"

"It's a little old lady who says she is a friend from the order." Lynda did not know what the order was, but she and Roger had married late, and there were always things, all good things, that would pop up about his past.

Roger half smiled and shook his head. "Okay, I'll take it in my study." Roger walked down the hall, showing no emotion, but he already knew this was no ordinary phone call.

Lynda waited a moment for Roger to get the phone in the study, then hung up.

Roger said, "Hello, this is Roger Cruz."

"Roger, did I get you at a good time?"

"Yes, now is fine. What can I do for you?"

"I have a special case, a marked case." The old woman paused, just to be sure she had not somehow called the wrong person. Roger's reply would tell her this.

"Yes, I understand. Go on."

"You are next on the list. Is this a good time for you and your wife?"

Roger was 61 years old, and a better time for him would have been twenty years earlier. He had waited a long time for this phone call, and part of him dreaded receiving it. His family name was Cruz, and they were a special family. His ancestor's hailed from Spain centuries earlier, and they had belonged to the Order of the Protectors of the Cross for just as long. Their name in Spanish meant Cross.

He looked out the window at Lynda. She was 49 years old, and she wanted a family with him. Their only hope though, because of both their ages, was adoption. They had married late in life and had no children together. But this call worried him. Although this would be a wonderful, fulfilling event in their life, because of his age, it could also mean hardship. Roger looked again at Lynda as she laughed, talking with the neighbors. She was strong, and he trusted her strength. He also sensed that if the Order was calling, God would provide.

"Mr. Cruz, are you still there?"

"Yes, I am sorry. Yes, this is a good time for us."

"Good, I want you to contact Sister Jane, at Our Lady of Lourdes Shrine in Margate. She has all the details."

Roger wrote down the name and phone number. He put "marked case" and the date below the number. "Is this a definite case?"

"Yes, it appears to be. We cannot be sure until the child is born. But the independent proof was obtained by the birth mother and verified, but when we see if the child bears the mark, it will be fully confirmed."

"Very well."

"Goodbye Roger and God be with you."

"Thank you."

He went outside and found Lynda waiting just outside the patio door. "What was that about?"

"Well, some news. It was someone from an order of nuns at the parish I belonged to a long time ago. There is a baby who needs to be adopted."

"Oh Roger, are you thinking we could?" Lynda gasped, jumping out of her chair.

He smiled, "Well, yes, I think we should."

"Oh honey, that is wonderful." Lynda threw her arms around his neck and hugged him.

Chapter 8

Aug 9th, 1998.
Brenda's Temporary Apartment, Margate, Florida
Two months later.

IN THE CORNER OF THE ROOM, watching Brenda sleep, the Dark Angel Tira stood perfectly still, immersed in deep thought. She was weighing all the risks. Legion had promised her vast riches, and a place next to him, as a ruler in charge of many things. She realized he might be lying, and yet his pull over her will was still deepening. She knew why. It was because he was such a dark lover, capable of rattling her cage as no one else could. She had heard the rumors of those possessed by him losing themselves, evolving into despair. But she was stronger than them, and in her mind, the prospect of wielding such power was worth playing with this fire, this sweet, dark, fire.

Tira shined the fake Heavenly glow around her and walked over next to the bed. "Brenda, wake up."

Brenda let out an extra loud snore, startling Tira. She grimaced, wanting to smack her. She hated unkept women and cared not if they were pregnant. She wondered what in the hell Vesru had seen in Brenda. She was no looker; that was for sure. Drugs and drinking and poverty had ravished her. Vesru said she had been drunk, and desperate. But why? Did he know more than he was letting on? Was Brenda special? Was this why the Dark Baptism was being given?

Another snore startled Tira out of her thoughts. She shook her head and said louder, "Brenda, wake up."

Brenda's eyes widened, she lurched up halfway, yelling, throwing herself back in fear, "Who are you!"

Tira wanted to smack her now; this was unneeded theatrics that was delaying her. "I am an Angel of Light. Heaven has sent me to tell you about the child to be born."

"Tell me what?"

"Because you have been chosen to bear a child born of Heaven, there are those who will seek to destroy the child. They will seek to destroy you, too." Tira was borrowing a theme from the ancient Christmas Story. Everyone knew the story, and everyone bought into it.

"What can I do?"

Tira felt like laughing and almost did because Brenda was taking the entire lie right in. "You must permit me to baptize the child as soon as it is born. In this way, they will protect both you and the child from the other side."

"From the other side?"

"Yes, from those who are against me, and you Brenda, and the child."

Brenda asked, "What do I do?"

"You must permit me to baptize the child with a Heavenly Baptism. The baptism will be secret, known to only you and me, and that is why we call it a Dark Baptism." Tira watched Brenda processing what she said, then raised her voice, "Do I have your permission, Brenda, to give the child a Dark Baptism, so you both will be protected?"

Brenda looked worried, she started to tear up, turning to look out the window. Tira wanted to shake her, and demand her 'yes,' but she waited a moment, then asked again, "Brenda, I need you to say yes. Heaven needs you to say yes!"

"Yes, yes, you can. When will this happen?"

"Right after the baby is born. I will be there with you in the delivery room. I will take care of everything. You will have a sign, as I will cause something loud to break in the delivery room, a signal to you that the Dark Baptism has taken place. From that moment, you will be safe."

"Thank you," Brenda said, still startled.

Tira smiled, "No Brenda, favored woman... thank you."

Chapter 9

September 23, 1998 9:30 p.m.
Northwest Medical Center, Margate, Florida
Six weeks later.

BRENDA LAY IN THE MATERNITY WARD at the hospital, fearful of what was to come. She had been brought in over an hour earlier after her water broke. Labor was upon her, and though the process had definitely started, it had now slowed, and she was drifting off, trying to calm her nerves by sleeping.

The Dark Angel Tira was there in the room too. Tonight, for the first time, she would perform the ancient ritual and administer the Dark Baptism, though she was unaware of its history, and of the risk it brought upon her.

She looked with disdain on the woman in front of her. Like most Dark Angels, Tira hated humans. They all blamed the humans for their being stuck in Hell. But Tira hated Brenda too. Because of Brenda, Vamorda would force her to spend ungodly amounts of time watching over a wretched human baby. But she knew this was her opportunity to please Legion, and to advance.

She was growing bored, and so she taunted Brenda. She walked up to her and whispered a fearful thought into her mind. "Your baby is a little demon child, Brenda."

Brenda stirred as her mind raced. She cried out, "Help me! Please, help me!"

Within moments a nurse came rushing in and turned on the light. "What's wrong Brenda?"

"Please, help me! The baby... I don't want to have a baby!" Brenda screamed, "Stop! Please!" Brenda wept, moaning, and muttering the words, "Stop this!"

The nurse ran down the hall and got a doctor who came in and assessed the situation. He gave an immediate order for something to calm Brenda, and within ten more minutes, Brenda was back to sleep.

Tira sat in the corner laughing to herself, "Maybe this will be fun. Brenda is easily rattled. I bet her baby will be too."

Chapter 10

September 23, 1998 10:30 p.m.
Northwest Medical Center, Margate, Florida

AN HOUR LATER, A DARK GRAY Ford Focus, driven by an elderly man, pulled up in front of the hospital. A young nun wearing a cross around her neck got out of the front seat. Two men came out of the back seat. The first, a taller man, was dressed in black, wearing the Roman collar. The second was a stocky man who looked to be of Spanish descent. He was wearing a brown pinstripe suit with a slender silver crucifix on a chain around his neck.

They were from the Order of the Cross, a secret order, with less than twenty members in the world, who dealt with the rare cases of Dark Angel offspring.

As their driver pulled away to wait for them, the three emissaries marched past the information desk to the elevators that would take them to the birthing unit. The man in the brown suit had been there earlier in the day and had already obtained all the needed signatures from the hospital administration.

When the elevator door opened, they walked out, went down another hall, and approached the nurse's station. The man in the brown suit smiled, and said, "We are here on behalf of Roger and Lynda Cruz, the adoptive parents of the child to be delivered tonight by Brenda Woodley."

The nurse looked at them, then held up her finger, signaling for them to wait. She picked up the phone, "Roberta, I've got people receiving their adopted child tonight? Do you know anything about this?" She paused, listening. "I see. That would be better for me. Thanks." She put down the phone, "Our supervisor will be right up. She was expecting you."

The man smiled and nodded, and the three stood still, waiting.

Tira heard the commotion and came out of the room to see what was happening. The sight of the priest and the nun enraged her. Still, she did not know why they were there. She walked over, unseen, and waited with them for the supervisor to arrive.

Within a few minutes, the elevator door opened, and the Nursing Supervisor came out. They all turned to face her.

"Hi, I am Roberta. I am the supervisor. They told me you would be coming." She looked at all three, and asked, "So who are all of you?"

The man in the brown suit said, "I am Tito Benavides, the attorney for Mr. and Mrs. Cruz. This is Sister Maria, and this is Father Ricardo. They are from the order that helped to arrange the adoption with Ms. Woodley."

Roberta smiled, "It is nice to meet all of you. Do you have all the paperwork?"

The attorney said, "Yes, I have the paperwork here. Your administration already has copies and here is a set of copies for you."

Roberta took them and said, "Please give me a moment to look everything over." Tira raced back into the room in a panic; everything was suddenly in jeopardy.

Chapter 11

September 23, 1998 9:30 p.m.
Northwest Medical Center, Margate, Florida

INSIDE THE HOSPITAL ROOM TIRA paced, "Those wretched priests and nuns. This will destroy me. Legion will put me in a dark cage. What can I do?" She felt panicked.

She looked over at Brenda who was half asleep, moaning. "If they baptize him first, I won't be able to do the Dark Baptism."

She turned and looked over at Brenda again. "It's Brenda or me at this point. Hmmm… tough decision. What are my options? I only have one, kill her and the baby, right now. I will smother her and then crush the baby. They will report it in the papers as a murder, and I will blame it on the Order. I will tell Legion I saw them leaving on my way in and found the mother dead. I will be Scott-free, and… free of this loathsome assignment."

She walked up to the bedside and slid Brenda's pillow out from behind her head. She then placed it on top of Brenda's face and pressed down. Within moments, Brenda struggled, but Tira held firmly.

The struggle continued, with Brenda kicking her legs, squirming. Tira heard a voice, "What is happening?"

Tira gritted her teeth and let go as the nurse ran in and pulled the pillow off Brenda's face. Father Ricardo came racing in behind her and walked over to the other side of the bed, followed by Sister Maria. He pulled the ancient oil from his pocket and traced the Sign of the Cross on Brenda's forehead. He held his hand over her head and said the ancient prayer. Brenda's breath burst forth, and she cried.

"What happened to you?" asked the nurse.

Brenda looked up, wide-eyed, "I don't know... someone was trying to kill me."

Brenda's eyes widened, and she looked up at the ceiling, "The Dark Baptism! Give it to me, now!"

Father Ricardo looked at Sister Maria with a puzzled, worried expression on his face.

~ ~ ~ ~

Tira screamed in the back of the room. Although no one had seen her, she had missed her opportunity to end it all. She could see the glowing Sign of the Cross on Brenda's head. She growled, with clenched teeth. Sister Maria turned and looked right at her, although Tira knew she was invisible, she could tell the nun sensed her presence.

Tira calmed her nerves, and a new idea came to her. Perhaps there was still time.

~ ~ ~ ~

For the next three hours, Tira sat in silence at the back of the room, plotting how she would find the moment to accomplish her deed. She watched Sister Maria keep vigil next to Brenda as she went through the pains of labor.

The doctor came in and examined Brenda, then said, "It's time."

Two nurses came in and wheeled Brenda to the delivery room. Sister Maria followed close behind. From in the hall, Mr. Benavides and Father Ricardo joined the troop, walking toward the delivery room. Tira pulled up the rear, confident of what would happen next.

When they reached the large automatic doors of the delivery room, a nurse turned and stopped them all. "You must wait here."

Sister Maria protested, but the nurse said, "I'm sorry doctor's orders."

Sister Maria glanced over to Mr. Benavides, who nodded, then said to the nurse, "It is important that as soon as the baby is born, Sister Maria is brought in to receive the child. This has all been arranged with Roberta, your charge nurse, and the hospital administration."

"Yes, I am aware. I will come for her as soon as the baby is born."

The three emissaries sat down, fully aware they were not "guarding" the child now, but there was little they could do, except pray. Sister Maria asked, "Why did Brenda say Dark Baptism?"

Father Ricardo replied, "I have been wondering that myself. I never heard of it." He turned to Mr. Benavides, who shook his head, signaling neither had he. Father Ricardo then said, "I will make a note in the report."

Inside the delivery room, Tira rolled her eyes as Brenda screamed, writhing in pain, lamenting she was having the child. "I don't want this baby! I'm going to die!"

Tira felt like picking up a pillow again and finishing her. But she composed herself instead, knowing her goal was in sight. She reached in the pocket of her tunic and pulled out the small vile of special oil the Lord Legion had given her. From her other pocket, she pulled out the folded piece of paper. She then looked around the room to see how she would accomplish the needed diversion.

After another fifteen minutes, the masked doctor reached his hands forward and grasped the head of the baby. "Here it comes!" As much as Tira and most Dark Angels resented women for their ability to bear children, Tira could not help but feel emotional. She could not believe the act of Creation was taking place again, right before her eyes.

She heard a loud slap, then a wailing cry and snapped into action.

She kicked the plug to the monitoring machine, sending an instant loud beeping noise throughout the room. Then she reached into the ceiling and pulled the wires to the overhead lights, immersing the whole room into twilight darkness.

"Get those lights back on!" snapped the doctor, as he held the baby over Brenda, still not having cut the umbilical cord.

Tira saw her chance, stepped forward and placed her hand on the doctor's forehead, uttering ancient evil words. The doctor froze, unable to think. She then steadied the baby and splashed the oil from the vial, tracing an upside down cross on the boy's head. She glanced at the doctor, who was still frozen, and she pulled the paper out.

"I baptize you in the name of the Dark Lord, and the Rebellion Leader, and the Dark Queen. I open your ears to hear the Dark Voice for the rest of your days."

Just then Sister Maria, Father Ricardo, and Mr. Benavides rushed in, with Mr. Benavides shouting, "What is happening?"

A nurse maneuvered an operating room light into position as the doctor called everyone back into action. "Get those people out of here."

Brenda was screaming, and so was the baby, in a frantic scene. The cord was cut, and the baby was swaddled. The nurse called Sister Maria back in. As she walked in, she glanced on the floor next to Brenda and saw something. It was a dark brown feather, she picked it up, and put it in her pocket.

The doctor ordered the baby to be kept for observation in the adjoining room because of everything that had transpired.

~ ~ ~ ~

At 4:30 A.M., after another hour and a half of making sure the child was ok, they handed him to Sister Maria. The three walked down the hall, but Sister Maria asked them to wait. She stepped into an unoccupied room and unwrapped the blanket the child was in to examine him. Then she froze. On the lower back, near the spine, was a black cloud shaped mark. It was the Mark of Cain, confirming the child was in the line of evil offspring. She wrapped the baby back up to prepare for the journey across town to the home of Mr. and Mrs. Cruz.

As they got into the waiting Ford Focus, she worried. Roger Cruz was a member of their order, yes, but he was old, older than most. The mark she had just seen was dark, and she feared what could happen should anything happen to Roger.

Chapter 12

September 24, 1998
Roger and Lynda Cruz Home, Parkland, Florida

AT 5:00 A.M., THE SMALL GROUP holding the swaddled infant rang the doorbell. Within moments, Roger Cruz opened the door, smiling, "Good morning and welcome."

Mr. Benavides asked, "Good day, Mr. Cruz. Are you ready?"

"Yes," said Roger. "Come in please and give me a moment to wake my wife. She nodded off a little while ago while we were waiting."

Everyone came inside, and Sister Maria held the baby as they waited in the living room for Lynda to come out of the bedroom. After a few minutes, Lynda emerged with a wide smile on her face, and greeted the three strangers.

Sister Maria smiled, and said, "It's a boy."

"A boy! Oh, how beautiful," said Lynda, "May I hold him?"

"Why sure you can," said Sister Maria as she handed the baby to Lynda.

Lynda pulled him close, looking in amazement at the new life in her arms. A tear fell from her eye as this was the moment, she had looked forward to for what seemed like ages. "Oh my, look at his beautiful dark eyebrows. They almost look like Angel wings."

Father Ricardo looked at the boy, then looked up at Sister Maria. He could tell she was alarmed too, but she was trying not to show it by holding a smile in place on her face.

Mr. Benavides asked, "Shall we baptize the child now?"

"Yes," said Roger, realizing he had forgotten to mention this to Lynda.

Lynda asked, "Roger, why would we baptize him now? Don't we do that later in church?"

Father Ricardo replied, "Mrs. Cruz, all the children adopted through our order are baptized as soon as we bring them to the adoptive home. That is why I came along, to administer the Sacrament."

She looked at Roger, who smiled and nodded.

"All right," replied Lynda.

Father Ricardo asked, "Have you decided on the name you will give the child?"

Roger smiled, and looked to Lynda who said, "Yes, his name shall be Nikolas de Jesus Cruz."

Father Ricardo then asked, "Mr. & Mrs. Cruz, will you allow Sister Maria and Mr. Benavides to stand in as temporary Godparents? You may still choose your own later."

"Yes, that would be fine," said Lynda, honored that a nun would be the little boy's Godmother.

"Great," said Father Ricardo, as he glanced one more time at the thick eyebrows that had a flare to them as if they were Angel wings, Dark Angel wings to be more precise. He pulled the holy water out of his vest pocket, raised his hand, and sprinkled it on the child's forehead, saying, "Nikolas de Jesus Cruz, I baptize you in the name of the Father, and the Son, and the Holy Spirit. I entrust you to the care of this family, and to Roger Cruz, whose family has been a part of the Order of Protectors of the Cross for centuries."

Father Ricardo put oil on his thumb and traced the sign of the cross on the baby's head. He felt an immense draw of his power as darkness began to swirl through his mind. Within an instant, Nikolas screamed, as if in pain. Father Ricardo kept still, waiting for the darkness to pass. He looked up and saw that Lynda had a growing look of alarm on her face. Roger saw what was happening, and he stepped forward and placed his hand on the baby's tiny chest, whispering, "There, there, little Nikolas, we are here. We are here to protect you." The baby quieted. With that, the three emissaries thanked the couple and left.

As they were leaving, an Angel Guard from Heaven arrived on the front lawn. He had been told that the child's baptism involved the order, but it was his first time seeing anyone, much less a small team from it. He smiled and marveled at the plain looking troop, out and about at 5:30 in the morning attending to the work of Heaven.

He walked over to the mother who was holding the child. "Hmmm... so this is Nikolas, my new client. Hello there Nikolas. I am Jordan, your Guardian Angel." To his surprise, Nikolas looked right at him, as if he could see him. Jordan stepped back, and ducked to the side, watching Nikolas' eyes follow him. "My, this is strange. I have heard children with the mark were special, but I've never heard of them being able to see us. This is odd."

Jordan made a mental note to talk with his Host Commander Rosie. He doubted Rosie would know anything, and he was sure they would have to send the question up to the big boss in the 3rd Heavenly Realm, the Archangel Michael. "Who knows," he thought. "Maybe it will go all the way to the Lords."

Jordan leaned closer and made his own Sign of the Cross on the boy's forehead. He then said a special prayer to bless the house and left.

Chapter 13

May 19, 1999
Roger and Lynda Cruz Home, Parkland, Florida
Eight months later

TRISH DEVANEY WALKED OVER to her new neighbor's home and knocked on the door. After a minute, a woman who looked old enough to be her mom answered the door with a toddler standing next to her. "Hello, can I help you?"

"Hi, my name is Trish, Trish Devaney. I just moved next door, and I wanted to introduce myself."

"Oh, hi Trish. I am Lynda Cruz, and this here is my baby Nikolas. Won't you come in?"

Trish walked into the luxurious, spacious house. "Oh, this is so nice." She looked down at the boy and was immediately startled by the eyes of the child. Something about them gave her pause, but then Lynda began talking, and she dismissed the feeling.

"Where are you from?"

"I am originally from New Jersey. I moved down here from the Carolinas."

"Well, that is nice. You will love it here in Parkland. We moved here about a year ago. I love it."

"Is your husband home?" asked Trish. She had seen him coming and going in the drive over the past couple days.

"No, I am afraid he is away on business. It's just Nikolas and me."

Trish smiled, glancing around at the beautiful home, then looked back at Nikolas. "How old is he?"

"He is turning eight months old on the 24th."

Trish nodded, smiling, still uneasy about his eyes. She remarked, "His eyes are, well... very unusual. Are they hazel?"

Lynda was growing a little tired of all the people who commented on her little boy's eyes and eyebrows. But she knew they were right. His eyes were unusual. She replied, "Yes, they are hazel. They have always been one of his little trademarks."

Nikolas turned and stared into Trish's eyes for a long moment, causing Trish to look away. She half smiled, dismissing the eerie feeling it caused.

Lynda interrupted her thought, "Come, sit down, I want to make us some tea, so we can get to know each other."

Trish smiled, "That would be nice."

After a little while of small talk, Trish said, "I am getting married in July."

"Oh, that is wonderful. Who is the lucky man?"

"His name is Noel. He lives in Orlando. He's moving down July 1st when his lease is up."

"Well, that is wonderful. Trish, if you don't mind me asking, 'How Old Are You?'"

"I am 25. How old are you, Lynda?"

Lynda smiled, "Well, it's hard to believe, but I am 50."

"Oh my, you're almost the same age as my mother!"

Lynda laughed, "Yes, and I have a feeling we are going to be great friends."

They both smiled and enjoyed the rest of their tea before Trish left.

Chapter 14

'December 7, 1999
Noel and Trish Devaney Home, Parkland, Florida
Six months later

ON AN UNUSUALLY WARM DECEMBER MORNING, Lynda walked across the lawn to Trish's house and knocked on the front door. Within moments the door opened, and Trish's smiling face greeted her. "Hey, Lynda."

"Hi Trish, I need to talk."

"Sure, come on in."

"I don't want to upset you, but I don't know who else to turn to." Lynda did not have many friends in Parkland. Not that she was unfriendly. She had just not been there long enough to establish herself, and with Nikolas being so young, she was home a lot.

"Oh, that's ok," said Trish, "What is going on?"

Lynda sighed, not sure where to begin, "Roger got a call last night from the nun who helped us arrange the last adoption."

"Is everything okay?"

"Yes, there is no problem, but she told him the birth mother is about to have another baby."

"Oh, I see." Trish paused, not sure how to react. She loved Lynda. They had become great friends from the time they met. Trish had even asked Lynda to be her maid of honor during her wedding last October when her friend had to back out. With Trish's mother living up North in New Jersey, Lynda had almost become like a mom to Trish. Trish asked, "So what is bothering you?"

"Well, she asked Roger if we were interested in adopting the second child."

"Oh, wow? What do you think?"

"It's complicated. Do you know Roger told me we had to pay $50,000 the last time? I mean, we have the money, but that was still a lot of money. I don't know if it's right for me to ask Roger to put up that kind of money again."

Trish's eyes widened, and she was about to say something when Lynda interrupted. "But there is more. She wasted that money. Roger said she is in jail right now."

"Jail?"

"Yes, I guess she is a real... well... criminal. I believe she may be a drug addict." Lynda already knew she WAS a drug addict. Roger had told her, but she felt uncomfortable admitting this to Trish.

"Does she know who the father is?"

"I asked Roger that. He said no. She didn't know who Nikolas's father was either, but she said it was not the same person. That helps! Right!" Lynda was being sarcastic, and Trish knew it.

"Lynda, I am a little concerned. You know nothing about either of these fathers. I mean... I know you are happy with Nikolas, but... well..." She stopped. Nikolas made Trish uneasy, and now she understood why.

Lynda interrupted again, already set on her course of action, "I keep thinking this is Nikolas's brother. They have the same mother, and... well... they are brothers. I think I want to do this."

"Well, I support you, Lynda. You know that."

Lynda nodded, "I am going to tell Roger that I want this child."

"Well, that's wonderful."

Lynda got up to leave, when Trish stopped her, "Oh Lynda before you leave, I have a little news myself."

"Don't tell me.... I think I already know... Are you... pregnant?"

Trish smiled, then burst out laughing. "How did you know?"

"Hey, us moms know these things. Congratulations Trish! I'm so happy for you! How far along are you?"

"I think a little over two months."

"That is so wonderful."

The two women hugged for several long moments and then Lynda went home.

Chapter 15

October 22, 2000
Roger and Lynda Cruz Home, Parkland, Florida
Ten months later

THE DARK ANGEL TIRA LEFT her hut in Hell and flew to the home of Roger and Lynda Cruz. She hated this assignment because of Roger Cruz. As a member of the ancient Order of the Protectors of the Cross, his presence limited her ability to affect Nikolas.

She was under no immediate pressure to perform. She had already informed Vamorda about the child's adoption. No negative effect accrued to her because of that revelation, still, she was frustrated. Her promotion to commander was a chance for her to shine. She had other clients, and she was doing well in working her evil intentions into their lives. But Nikolas was different.

He was the son of a Dark Angel. He bore the Mark of Cain. Everyone expected big things of him, or of her, one could say. This was her job, and Roger Cruz was in the way. But Roger was getting older, and Tira had nothing but time on her side.

When she arrived, it was a beautiful, sunny afternoon in October, with the temperature at 83 degrees. Trish and Lynda were sitting on the patio next to the pool. Trish's four-month-old son Gavin was laying on a comfortable towel, cooing and kicking his feet. Nikolas, now two was seated next to him, talking to him, as Gavin stared up looking into his face. Tira went over by Nikolas and sat down at the edge of the grass to observe everyone for a while.

Trish laughed at something Lynda said, then sipped her coffee. She turned to look at their two boys. "They are so beautiful. Lynda

I'm so happy we met, and now we are raising our children together. It's just wonderful."

Lynda smiled, "Yes, it's a blessing. Hey, why don't I get us all some lunch?"

"That sounds good. I am famished."

"Okay, I'll be right back."

Trish watched her friend disappear into the house, then glanced over at Gavin and Nikolas. She got up and walked over, squatting down between the pool and Gavin, and folded the towel to prop Gavin's head up. "Hello Gavin, how are you? You have a friend here. Do you have a friend here? Gavin, can you smile for me?" Trish got up and walked the ten feet back to her chair at the patio table.

Nikolas watched her, then resumed talking to Gavin.

Tira whispered, "Nikolas. Nikolas."

To her surprise, Nikolas looked up at her. Tira was amazed at his eyes. They were Vesru's eyes, and she knew there was no reason to be surprised, yet, they impressed even her. "Hi, Nikolas. Do you see me?"

Nikolas half smiled, revealing he did. Tira was again amazed. This was the first time she had contacted Nikolas, and she did not expect this to happen until Roger was out of the picture. Perhaps the fact he was away from home weakened his power to protect Nikolas.

Tira looked around to see what mischief she could accomplish. It wouldn't be much, but it would be a start, and it would be something she could report. Her eyes widened, as she glanced over at Trish, who was waiting for Lynda, with her view only partially on them, as they were to the side of her.

Tira began, "Nikolas, water... water... water Nikolas."

He looked up as a devious smile came over his face. He understood her. He got up, then sat down next to Gavin, placing his hands behind him and his feet by Gavin's side. Then he pushed. Then he pushed again. Gavin cooed, and rolled, as Nikolas glanced up at Trish who had just leaned her head back, taking in a moment of sunshine on her face. Nikolas smiled, as he heard Tira say, "Yes, that's it, Nikolas… now… water."

Nikolas pulled his knees close to his chest and gave one big push.

Trish heard the loud splash and jumped to her feet to see Nikolas seated next to the pool, leaning back on his hands with his feet a few inches in the air near the water. In the next split second, her eyes saw her baby sinking head first to the bottom of the 8-foot deep end of the pool. She screamed and dove fully clothed into the water. She swam downward, grabbed Gavin, and turned, panicking, racing against time, trying to kick back to the surface. It was taking too long.

She burst through the surface of the water, trying to hold Gavin above water.

Lynda came out, dropped the tray, and raced over, jumping in, swimming over to help hold Gavin up. They turned and swam the short distance to the shallow end.

Trish lifted Gavin and raced out, high stepping through the shallow water, screaming, "Gavin, Gavin, Gavin!" He was not breathing. She shook him, placing him on her shoulder and smacking his back.

Lynda ran up behind her, "Give him to me."

Lynda took Gavin and dropped onto the grass, laying him flat, pushing on his stomach. In a moment, Gavin spit up a mouthful of water and screamed.

Trish was already on the phone with 911, trying to talk through panicked emotions and sobs. "Please hurry, my baby fell into the pool." She looked down with a horrified expression on her face, seeing what Lynda was doing, "Yes, he is breathing now… He's… crying."

"An ambulance is on the way mam. I'll stay on the phone with you."

Trish dropped the phone and ran over to pick up Gavin. "Gavin, oh, Gavin," she said between sobs, "Are you all right, honey? Gavin? Mommy's here."

Lynda stood next to her, helpless, feeling the weight of the world on her shoulders, hoping nothing would be wrong with him. She asked, "What happened?"

Trish turned to her with an enraged look on her face, shouting, "He pushed him into the pool!"

Lynda turned to look at Nikolas, who was still seated in the same place, only now sitting with his legs crossed, facing them, looking at the ground. She screamed, "Nikolas! What did you do?"

Nikolas lifted his eyes to meet his mother's.

Lynda gasped, as she knew the look, and it bore the hint of a smile.

Sirens sounded in the distance as the ambulance raced down nearby Holmberg road to turn down the street to the family home at 6166 NW 80th Terrace.

Tira walked to the side of the house to get a look at Nikolas's face. She had never seen such a response from someone so young. She would keep this to herself though. She did not need to raise expectations which would only put pressure on her.

At this moment the Nikolas' Guardian Angel Jordan arrived. He knew he was too late to help, so he observed the child, wondering what had happened. Jordan now saw the Dark Angel Tira by the side of the house. It was the first time they had crossed paths. He went over to her, "What did you do?"

"Nothing, the ladies were talking about baptism, and Nikolas thought to baptize the little one himself."

Jordan reached for his sword, but Tira raised her hand. "Save it Jordan. It was an accident."

"Then what are you doing here?"

"Jordan, in case you didn't know, I have clients all over this county. You might say it's under my special care."

"Why would that be? You are nothing but a low-level Dark Angel."

"Well, in case you haven't heard, I've been promoted to Dark Angel Commander."

"Now I've heard it all."

Tira glared at him and reached her hand down to her sword. "Watch it Jordan; I'm not afraid of you."

Jordan leaned in. "Take your best shot, Tira."

Tira pushed him away, then flew off.

Chapter 16

November 10, 2000
Our Lady of Lourdes Shrine, Pompano Beach, Florida
Two weeks later

ROGER CRUZ SAT IN THE SMALL waiting room at the convent waiting for Sister Jane to come. He glanced up at the magnificent painting of Michael the Archangel subduing Lucifer, the devil. It was one of the most famous pictures of Michael and the scene had been duplicated all over the world for centuries.

After a long time of waiting in silence, Sister Jane appeared in the door. "Hello, Mr. Cruz. I am Sister Jane." Sister Jane already knew a great deal about Roger. The order had allowed her to see his file. He was a good man and was the 2nd generation in America from a proud family that hailed from Castile, Spain. They could trace their roots to several of the founding members of the Order of the Protectors of the Cross.

Roger stood, "It is nice to meet you, Sister." He waited for her to turn with her cane and close the door behind her.

"How can I help you, Mr. Cruz?"

It surprised Roger how feeble she was, and he understood why it had taken so long for her to arrive. "As you know Sister, I am a member of the order. We... well, my wife and I are having concerns about the child we adopted."

"Which child?"

"I am sorry, the first one, Nikolas. Zachary is fine. As you know, he did not come through the order."

"What is the problem?"

"He scares me… he scares my wife. He is… acting strange. I am afraid the mark is very strong in him."

Sister Jane showed no reaction, other than a slight look of concern crossing her face. "How old is the boy now?"

"He is past two."

"Are you praying the Rosary daily?"

"Yes, I am."

"Is your wife?"

Roger paused. Lynda had never been that religious, even growing up. Roger always felt funny asking her to pray the Rosary. He replied, "No, she does not. She knows what the Rosary is. She is Catholic, but she has never formed the practice of saying it."

"Well it is important you ask her to join you. You must say at least some prayers together daily although the Rosary is the best weapon against the forces of evil."

Roger nodded.

Sister Jane paused, thinking, then said, "Mr. Cruz, I am getting old and feeble. I would keep this, but I think it is best you have it." She reached in her pocket and drew out a cloth. She unfolded it revealing a dark brown feather that almost resembled the feather of an eagle.

"What is this?"

Sister Jane swallowed, "This is the feather of the Dark Angel that fathered the child. It is one of two the birth mother found. She has one, and now, you have one. I only share it with you to remind you how important it is for you to use the weapons at your disposal to keep the child safe."

Roger stared down at the feather with his heart racing. His knowledge of the order was extensive, and he knew of the tales of the Mark of Cain, and he knew the stories of Dark Angels interfering in the lives of Humans. But this was the first time he had seen something, anything from the dark side.

"There is one more thing you should know."

"What is it, Sister?"

"Mr. Benavides, the attorney that was there at the hospital has died. Something killed him in a freak accident at a construction site near his office in Atlanta."

"Oh my? What happened?"

"He was walking past a new building, and something fell on him."

"Oh, that's terrible. I am sorry to hear that."

"I am too. He did a lot of work for the order. I will miss him."

Neither said a word as Roger wrapped the feather in the cloth and slipped it into his suit coat pocket. He got up, bowed, and left.

Chapter 17

June 1, 2001
Devaney Home, Parkland Florida
Seven months later

TRISH DEVANEY'S MOM, NANCY, PULLED into the driveway of her daughter's home for the first time. A few hours earlier, she had landed at the Fort Lauderdale International Airport on an early morning flight from New Jersey. She parked her rental car near the end of the driveway, hoping to surprise her daughter.

As she got out, a little kid suddenly startled her. He was standing nearby wearing shorts and no shirt, and she wondered why she had not seen him. "Who are you?" she asked.

"I am Nikolas."

Nancy looked around and realized he must live next door. She bent down and asked, "Where do you live?"

"Right there." Nikolas turned and pointed to the house next door. He then turned back and stared at her.

Nancy felt uncomfortable for a moment, wondering again how he had appeared out of nowhere, but it was more than that. His eyes looked wild, and it unnerved her. She said, "Run along and go home."

Just then Nancy heard a voice, "Nikolas! Nikolas! You get back here right this instant! Do you hear me?"

Nikolas frowned and turned around to look. He took off running back to his house without saying a word. Nancy watched him and went to the door and knocked. She knocked again, and then the door opened.

"Mom?"

"Hey baby, I hope you don't mind me dropping in?"

Trish came out and hugged her. "I can't believe you're here!"

"I took time off work to help you with the baby."

Trish was nine months pregnant, and the baby was due in two weeks, but as things go in this late stage of pregnancy, the baby could come any time.

"Come on in, Mom. Noel is at work, but he will be home later. He'll be thrilled to see you." Just then Gavin came running around the corner, then stopped, unsure of who it was. He turned and ran back into the family room. "Gavin, come here." Trish laughed, and ran after him, then brought him back. "Gavin, this is Grandma. Remember Grandma?"

Gavin looked away, then smiled. Trisha looked at her mom, raised her eyes, and said, "Let's go sit down mom. You two must get reacquainted.

Two nights later Trish took her mom over to meet Lynda. Her husband Noel and Gavin also went along, but as was her custom since the incident, she would not let Gavin play with Nikolas. Nancy knew nothing of the incident, as Trish had been afraid to tell her. After the doctor checked Gavin and determined he was fine, she didn't feel it was necessary to worry her.

As the evening went on, both couples enjoyed hearing tales from Nancy of Trish's childhood. They all had an excellent time. But the evening was dominated by 3-year-old Nikolas running around wildly, while his younger brother, Zachary, close to 18 months, tried to keep pace.

It was a daunting evening for Trish, watching the frantic youth, and all the while having to keep Gavin away from them.

When they got home, they put Gavin to bed. Noel too went to bed, leaving Trish and her mom to sit in the living room talking. Nancy said, "They are a very nice couple."

"Yes, they are. Lynda has been like a best friend since I moved in."

"That's wonderful."

Neither said a word; both knew what had not been said. Nancy broke the silence. "Trish, listen. I don't want that boy Nikolas anywhere near my grandchildren. You must promise me that. He has crazy eyes. I am telling you; there is something wrong with that kid."

"I know there is. I promise I will not let Nikolas be alone with the kids."

Chapter 18

Thanksgiving Day, 2001
Roger and Lynda Cruz Home, Parkland, Florida
Five months later

ROGER CRUZ SAT IN THE family's spacious living room next to the new fireplace they had installed. It was a small unit, and they would only use it on select evenings during the winter. He had purchased it for reasons other than heating needs. Some months earlier, after thinking about his conversation with Sister Jane, Roger started a little tradition with his growing family.

Nikolas was now over three years old, and Zachary himself would be two in less than three months. Now, on many evenings, the family would gather once the sun was setting and have a small time of family prayer and story time. Roger's grandfather used to do something like it long ago when he was a child, and during the last year, it came to mind.

"Lynda, it's time for our story."

Lynda was in the kitchen making out a shopping list. She looked up, "Did you hear that boys, it's time for our evening prayers and story."

Nikolas jumped up and ran into the living room. Zachary followed behind, walking just about as fast as a two-year-old boy could. Nikolas jumped on the couch, turning around to face the pictures of Jesus and the Holy Family that Lynda had hung on the wall months earlier. Zachary ran into the couch and climbed up, almost falling back off, and sat next to his brother.

Lynda came in and took her seat on the couch with the boys. They were all facing Roger who then got up and lit a candle near the two pictures.

"Ok boys, it is time for our prayers. Nikolas, who do you want to pray for?"

Nikolas smiled, and nudged his brother, "For Zachary."

Zachary looked over and hit him on the arm.

"Boys," said Lynda.

Roger then asked, "Zachary, who do you want to pray for?"

"Mommy," came the innocent reply.

Roger and Lynda looked at each other and smiled. Then Roger led them in an Our Father followed by three Hail Mary's. Afterward, he pulled out the book "Peter Rabbit" and read three pages to the young mesmerized boys.

When he was finished, they were already yawning, as it was customary for them to go to bed after. Roger and Lynda each took one child and tucked them in for the night.

An hour later, Lynda saw that the children were asleep. She closed their bedroom doors and went into the living room. She leaned close to Roger, kissed him, took him by the hand, and said, "It's our time now."

Chapter 19

February 12, 2002
Legion's Villa, Southern Shores of Hell
Eight months later

VAMORDA WOKE TO THE SOUND of the waves crashing against the cliff outside Legion's seaside Villa on the southern shore of Hell. She looked out at the faint sun, then laid her head back down on the pillow, relishing the night of dark extravagance she had just experienced. As much as she hated Legion, she needed him, not only to keep her satisfied but to keep her in power.

"Vamorda, it is time for you to get up."

She sighed and turned her head toward the dresser. She had not noticed him, but he was standing by the mirror, naked, admiring himself. She watched as his reflection in the mirror turned to look at her.

He asked, "What is happening with the child of Vesru?"

It caught Vamorda off guard. Vesru was still in the dark cage. She had faced silent criticism from everyone under her command. Vesru didn't deserve what he had gotten, and in their minds, she was to blame.

"I don't understand, my Lord. There is nothing to report. I told you a long time ago that an order got involved. But we have power over the child because of the Dark Baptism."

"Is that so? I spent the night with Tira recently. She seemed to dance around the topic a little more than you did. I got the feeling she was lying."

Vamorda swallowed hard, trying not to let him notice. She got up and strolled over to the dresser, putting her arms around his waist, pressing her naked body against his backside. She was taller than him, and she knew that enthralled him. "You believe that little whore Tira?"

Legion stared at her eyes in the mirror, then smiled. "No, I don't Vamorda. I trust you will find out though. I have heard that his father is old. Move him out of the way. Do you understand?"

She swallowed again, "Yes, I do."

"Don't leave just yet, Vamorda." He turned and lifted her into the air as she wrapped her legs around him. He walked to the bed and laid down on top of her.

~ ~ ~ ~

The next day, Vamorda sat in her office waiting for the Dark Angel Tira. When Tira walked in, Vamorda stood, "What is happening with the son of Vesru?"

"Nothing, he is protected by that wretched order."

"You have made no progress?"

"No, none." Tira was lying, but that was Dark Angels did best. They lied.

"Why not?"

"I told you, the father is a member of the order. Our hands are as good as tied."

"Get him out of the way."

"But you know, as well as I do, we cannot interfere in the affairs of men and women."

Vamorda walked around her desk and stood in front of her. She picked her up by the tunic, lifting Tira off her feet. "Listen here, you little whore. Do whatever it takes and find a way."

Tira gritted her teeth. She was no fool. She would rather disobey Vamorda than break one of Heaven's explicit laws, and risk being hunted down by the Angels of Heaven. Roger was a member of the sacred order. Killing him would put her on the radar, and she refused to do that.

Tira mumbled, "We are NOT allowed to kill the humans."

Vamorda replied, "I did not say kill. Just do something and get him out of the way. Find a way."

"It will take time."

"I don't care. Just do it."

Chapter 20

February 14, 2002
Devaney Home, Parkland Florida
Two months later

"HAPPY VALENTINE'S DAY!" said Trish as she opened the door to her home. Roger and Lynda walked in first carrying Zachary, followed by Roger, holding the hand of Nikolas.

Lynda said, "Oh, happy Valentine's Day to you too." She handed them a small heart-shaped box of chocolate.

Noel took their coats as Lynda put Zachary down and took off his jacket. Nikolas was only wearing an oversized sweater, and he pulled away when Roger tried to remove it. "Ok, suit yourself."

Zachary ran across the room to find his friend Gavin, who was playing in the living room with some of his toys. Roger knew not to let Nikolas charge over, and he kept holding his hand, despite Nikolas' attempts to pull away.

"Come in and sit down. Noel made us some amazing appetizers, and I picked up the movie Sleepless in Seattle for us to watch."

"Oh, you found it! That's great," said Lynda. "I love that movie."

"Well, I don't know if the men will like it as much as us, but they'll just have to suffer along."

The couples went into the living room and sat down. Lynda asked, "How is little Kaitlyn?"

"She is sleeping right now. She was up all day."

"Oh, the little princess. How old is she now?"

"She'll be eight months on the 22nd."

"That's so nice."

The tension from Nikolas pushing Gavin into the pool had cooled down over the last year, in part because of Zachary coming into the family. Trish adored him and told her husband he was a loving little child, different from Nikolas. The birth of her daughter Kaitlyn in the summer also diffused things, as Trish now was occupied with two little children, and this kept her too busy to worry. But she kept her guard up and would never allow Gavin to play with Nikolas.

Lynda and Trish put Gavin and Zachary into the dining room and shut the doors to allow them to play. They gave Nikolas trucks and toys where he could play in the living room while they watched the movie.

About halfway through the movie, Trish heard Kaitlyn crying from up in her room. They paused the movie and Lynda and Trish went upstairs to change her and bring her down. Trish allowed Lynda to feed her then as they watched the movie. Nikolas kept looking over at them, and once or twice he came over to look at her. But he went back to his toys.

A short while later, Nikolas heard the voice. "She hates you, Nikolas. She hates you. Hurt her... hurt her."

Nikolas looked up at Trish. He knew she hated him. But then he looked down at Kaitlyn, asleep in the small floor bassinet they had set next to the couch. He looked up again at Trish and his mother sitting closest to him. They were engrossed in the movie. His dad and Noel were farther away, also watching. At one moment, Roger glanced over at him, but Nikolas pretended he was looking around.

As soon as Roger's eyes left him, he crawled over to the side of the bassinet. He lifted the baby's shirt, leaned over, and bit hard into her stomach.

Kaitlyn let out a shivering scream that erupted into a loud, painful cry. "Nikolas!" shouted Trish, and she raced over and knocked him away. She stared horrified looking down at Kaitlyn's stomach as the other adults all ran over. It had deep puncture wounds in the shape of Nikolas' teeth, and she was bleeding.

Roger grabbed him, shaking him, "What did you do?"

The baby screamed louder as Trish picked her up and ran to the kitchen sink. At that moment, Lynda fainted. Noel grabbed her and caught her from falling. He picked up the phone and dialed 911.

Roger glanced at the other room where the boys were playing. They were both standing by the French doors of the dining room, just staring at the mounting chaos.

Trish screamed, "Get out! Get him out of my house!"

Roger looked at Noel, then at Lynda.

Noel said, "Go, take him in the front hall Roger until the ambulance comes. I'll stay here with Lynda." Noel then ran to the sink. "Is she ok?"

Trish was dabbing the blood with a napkin, sobbing, "I can't take this… I can't take this… get him out of here!"

Noel heard the ambulance and thanked God they had come quickly. Lynda regained consciousness after they had put some salts under her nose. Noel helped her, Roger, and the two boys back home. On the way back over to his house, he vowed they would put the house up for sale. And the next day, before dinner the sign went up.

Chapter 21

February 28, 2002
Mount St. Joseph Convent, Loretto, Pennsylvania.
Two weeks later

SISTER MARIA WALKED down the quiet corridor of the mountainside convent in Loretto, Pennsylvania. She had been born in Mexico City 37 years earlier, but her parents had emigrated when she was five. She had lived in nearby Johnstown for most of her life. When she was 19, she joined the Sisters of Mount St. Joseph in Loretto, only a short drive from her parent's home.

Sr. Maria did not know why she had been chosen to join the secret Order of the Protectors of the Cross. But she loved her work with them.

She reached the office, and the secretary greeted her. "Good morning Sister Maria. How are you today?"

"I'm afraid I have a busy day. We are going to the clinic this morning."

"Oh yes, dress warm. It's a cold day."

Sister Maria nodded then got her mail. There was a letter with the address handwritten that was illegible. Sister Maria could barely see it was from Sister Jane, in Margate, Florida. She went back to her room, sat on the edge of her bed, and opened the letter. It was very hard to read, but after several passes, she had made it out.

Sister Maria

Order of the Protectors of the Cross

Dear Sister Maria,

I have failed in my duty to notify you sooner. Roger Cruz visited me, and he is very concerned. Unfortunately, right after he came, I was hospitalized with a severe infection in my leg. The infection became septic, and I spent over two months unconscious. After that, they sent me to a nursing home for a long recovery. It was only recently that I remembered he had visited me, and because of my feeble health, I thought it best to write to you, and notify you. The child is showing signs of influence by the Dark Side. It worried Roger, and so I thought it best to notify the order. I am very weak, and I trust you will notify Father Ricardo.

In the Name of Our Lord and Savior,

Sister Jane

Sister Maria set the letter down. During her 10 years with the order, there were four families she had taken part with in the placing of a child. She had hoped all were doing well. They were not to make contact unless there was a problem. But now, here was a clear indication of one. She knew she would have to speak with Sister Jane and see the child for herself. Just then the phone rang. "Hello?"

"Sister Maria, Tony and Marge Lavrisha are here to pick you up to go to the clinic."

"Thank you. Tell them I will be right there."

Chapter 22

March 8, 2002
Mount St. Joseph Convent, Loretto, Pennsylvania.
One week later

A WEEK LATER, SISTER MARIA JUMPED ON THE INTERNET and looked up the number to Our Lady of Lourdes Shrine. She dialed, and an answering directory answered. After listening to the myriad of options, the last of which was a dial by name, she entered the letters J A N. She heard a feeble voice say, "Sister Jane," then the system said, press 1. Sister Maria pressed 1.

After 6 rings Sister Jane answered. "Hello?"

"Sister Jane, this is Sister Maria, from the order. I received your letter."

"Oh good."

"I would like to come to see you, and perhaps even see the child."

"When?"

"March 20th is the earliest I can leave."

"That will be fine. You can stay here in our guest room."

"Thank you, sister. Don't alarm the family just yet. Let me speak to you first."

"OK."

"I will see you then, on the 20th."

"Thank you."

~ ~ ~ ~

On the morning of March 20, Sister Maria put her small suitcase and laptop into the trunk of the car assigned to her by the order. Her flight was leaving in 3 hours, and she had about an hour drive to the airport. It was a snowy day for the last day of winter, and the roads were slick.

She slowly pulled out of the convent drive and turned onto the long winding road that led down the small mountain that the community was built upon. As she neared the first curve, she applied the brakes, but they went all the way to the floor. She pumped them as she veered around the corner going faster than she would like.

The car picked up speed as it barreled down the icy mountain toward the next turn. "Jesus, Jesus, help me!" Sister Maria pumped the brakes as the next turn, the one overlooking the steep drop off was approaching. The car fishtailed right and left, sliding on the ice, and spun out of control. She gripped the wheel, trying to steady the car, screaming, "Jesus, Mary, and Joseph, help me!"

In the next instant, a car approaching from around the bend plowed into her with horrific force, sending her car toppling into the guardrail. It spun the other direction, then slid off the steep embankment at the end of the guardrail, dropping 35 feet. The car landed top down on the large mountain boulders.

The other driver was injured, and in a moment all grew silent.

From the top of the mountain, a blue Ford pickup truck drove up and came to a gradual stop. He looked at the man in the other car and saw he was unconscious. He then went to the guardrail and looked over the side. All he could see was the bottom of Sister Maria's car. He knew it was her car, he had expected it to crash somewhere, but this could not have been planned any better. He could tell the front seat had been crushed, and he doubted she could have survived. He wanted to go down to find out for sure, but it was too dangerous. He would have to wait until the authorities arrived to know for sure.

He waited another seven minutes, watching the road until he saw another car coming. He reached in his pocket and took out his phone and dialed 911, sounding frantic. "This is AJ, the maintenance man at

Mt. St. Joseph. There's been an accident on Mountain View road. Send two ambulances and hurry."

Chapter 23

March 21, 2002
Our Lady of Lourdes Shrine, Parkland Florida

THE NEXT DAY, SISTER JANE WOKE and sat in the lift chair in her room. She had nodded off to sleep waiting for news of Sister Maria's arrival the night before. She sighed and called the office. "Did Sister Maria arrive?"

"No one came yesterday, Sister."

"Oh, something has delayed her."

By the end of the day, Sister Jane was worrying. She took her cane and plodded down to the office near the front door of the shrine. A young woman was volunteering, watching the desk. Sister Jane asked, "Can you look up a phone number on the computer for me?"

"Sure, Sister Jane, what's the name."

"Mount St. Joseph Convent in Loretto Pennsylvania."

"Would you like me to get them on the phone?"

"Please."

The young woman handed the phone to Sister Jane. Moments later a quiet voice answered, "Mount St. Joseph."

"May I speak with Sister Maria? This is Sister Jane from Florida."

There was silence.

"Hello?"

"Sister Jane, I am sorry to tell you this. But our dear Sister Maria was killed in a car accident yesterday."

Sister Jane gasped and grabbed at her heart. She dropped the phone, steadying herself with her cane. The woman ran over and picked up the phone. "We'll call you back."

She hung up and helped Sister Jane head back to her room. As they walked past the waiting room, Sister Jane's heart was racing. *Mr. Benavides is dead. Now, Sister Maria is dead.* She stopped and looked into the waiting room at the large portrait of Michael the Archangel standing on the head of Lucifer. She shuddered and kept walking.

When she reached her room, she sat in her chair and picked up a note pad. She wrote a letter to the only other person left who had helped with the adoption, Father Ricardo.

Chapter 24

September 24, 2003
Orlando, Florida
Eighteen months later

"HAPPY BIRTHDAY TO YOU! Happy Birthday to You! Happy Birthday dear Nikolas! Happy Birthday to You!" The crowd of waiters and waitresses in black pants and red and white striped shirts finished their song then set down a cake filled with burning candles and clapped. Nikolas sat in the chair waiting for them to finish, knowing he was about to blow out the candles. "Make a wish!" shouted Lynda over the noisy gathering. Nikolas did not wish but blew as hard as he could, getting all five candles out.

Everyone clapped again, and the gathering of personnel at TGI Friday's in Orlando dispersed back to their duties.

"Happy Birthday Nikolas!" said an elated Roger.

"Thanks, dad."

Lynda exclaimed, "Oh, I can't believe you're five years old already. Happy Birthday, honey."

"Thanks, mom."

Nikolas picked up a french-fry from his plate and threw it at Zachary. Zachary laughed, and tried to duck, and nearly fell out of his booster seat.

"Nikolas!" shouted Lynda. "No throwing food. Do you hear me, young man?"

A devious smile came across his face, and he shrunk down a little, eyeing his brother. Zachary glanced at his mom, then threw a fry over at Nikolas. "Boys!" said Roger, "That's enough now. You heard your mother."

Roger waited, and said, "I have an announcement to make."

"What is it daddy?" asked Zachary.

"Yeah," said Nikolas. "What is it, dad?"

Roger looked over at Lynda, smiling. "Tonight, we are going to a hotel room that has a big pool and a slide!"

Both boys' eyes lit up with excitement.

"But that's not all. Tomorrow morning, after breakfast, we are going to visit Mickey Mouse at Disney World."

"What!" yelled Nikolas, "That's awesome dad!"

Lynda said, "Boys, isn't that great? Now finish eating, so we can go to the hotel. We've got a big day tomorrow."

"Thanks, mom!" said Nikolas.

"Yeah, thanks mom," added Zachary.

Chapter 25

Jul 16, 2004
Roger and Lynda Cruz Home, Parkland, Florida
Ten months later

THE ANGEL JORDAN SAT on top of the new apparatus in the backyard waiting for events to unfold. He had stopped yesterday to check in on the family and saw the workers. So, he found out what was happening and returned today. Jordan was very pleased with the progress Roger was making with Nikolas. His evening prayer and story time were having a positive impact on the boys. He only hoped that it could continue.

Roger stood at the back door of the couple's spacious home, holding the back door shut. Lynda had taken the boys away for the day, so he could manage the workers and plan the event. But now she was back, and it was time to take the boys out back to see what their surprise was.

"Are you ready boys?"

Nikolas would turn six years old in a few months, and he had just been diagnosed with attention deficit hyperactivity disorder, which only confirmed what Lynda had expected. In her mind, it explained away all the problems they had with him. Now medication would help him.

Zachary was four-and-a-half. He was a much more 'normal' boy, but as any four-and-a-half-year-old will show, he too possessed boundless energy.

"We're ready, daddy!" shouted Zachary.

"All right, go on out!"

Jordan saw the door opening, so he flew up into the sky to avoid being seen by Nikolas. In an instant, the boys ran out of the house into the back yard, wide-eyed, looking in all directions as they ran around the pool.

"Look," said Nikolas pointing to the enormous apparatus in the corner of the back yard. Zachary screamed, "What is it?" as he tried to keep pace with his older brother.

"It's a Jungle Gym!" shouted Roger, as he pointed the video camera, capturing what he and Lynda had imagined would be one of the most delightful moments for their boys.

Nikolas jumped onto the tire hanging from the rope and spun around. Zachary ran right up to him, jumping into him, and fell back, laughing. Nikolas jumped off and ran to the slide, running up it to the top, as Zachary followed him up, only to have Nikolas slide down into him, carrying them to the bottom in a tangled bundle.

Lynda yelled, "Nikolas! Be careful with your brother! Do you hear me?"

"They're fine Lynda. Don't worry. It's only boy's play!"

"I know. Isn't it wonderful Roger?" She grasped his hand, squeezing it.

Roger shut off the video. "It is wonderful honey. I love you."

She leaned her head against his broad shoulder, "I love you too."

After a while, they all went in, and Roger ordered a pizza.

Jordan hovered in the sky and watched the little family go inside. He had real hope for the first time in a long time. He flew back down and sat back on top of the Jungle Gym, taking in the evening sun, offering his evening prayer of thanksgiving to the Lords. He was finished visiting clients for the day, so he went back to his home in the 3rd Heavenly Realm.

Chapter 26

August 11, 2004
Roger and Lynda Cruz Home, Parkland, Florida
One month later

THE DARK ANGEL VESRU flew from his hut on the southern shore of Hell toward Parkland, Florida. Though she was not supposed to, Tira had briefed him on all that had been happening with his offspring Nikolas.

Vesru had no 'fatherly' interest in the child, none of the Dark Angels who had sired children with the women of the earth did. But as with all, he was curious. It was early in the evening when he arrived at the Cruz home. He entered through the back patio door, passing through undetected and invisible to all. Zachary who he couldn't care less about was watching TV in the living room. Lynda was sitting at the kitchen table having coffee and talking with one of her neighbors. Vesru heard voices, so he walked down the hallway toward the front of the house.

In the den seated on a couch, watching another TV, were Nikolas and Roger. Vesru walked in and sat down on a chair behind Roger's desk. Nikolas appearance stunned him. His thick eyebrows were clearly shaped like Angel wings. Vesru laughed, "Look at that little guy. He almost looks like me. Wow."

Neither Angels nor Dark Angels could reproduce together. It was why long ago, at the beginning of time, many took advantage of the women of earth. But it had been put to a stop, and the only ones who did it now were the boldest of Dark Angels. They took a great risk in doing so. Being found out by the Lords would mean probable arrest and certain punishment.

Vesru never imagined though being imprisoned by his own kind. The five years he had just spent in the dark cage was a horrific nightmare that still shook him to the core. He knew the effects on his mind would never pass.

Vesru had seen enough, and he was getting ready to leave when Nikolas turned and looked right at him. Vesru smiled at him, and Nikolas smiled back. *I can't believe he can see me.* Vesru glanced at Roger who was watching some game. Vesru then waved at Nikolas. Nikolas waved back.

Just then Roger noticed he was waving. "Who are you waving at Nikolas?"

"An Angel."

Roger looked over at the chair at his desk. It had turned from the customary position Roger always kept it in. "Where?"

"Right there, sitting in the chair. He has big brown wings."

Roger stood up with a horrified expression on his face. He suddenly grabbed for his chest. "Niko…" He fell back onto the couch, clutching his chest, gasping for air. "Nikolas, go get… mom… get mom."

Nikolas stood up and walked in front of his dad.

Roger motioned with his eyes toward the kitchen, wincing in terrible pain, "go… get… mm… mom."

Nikolas looked over at Vesru who sat still watching the child's reaction. Nikolas waited a few more moments, then turned and walked out of the den and down the hallway. He came into the kitchen and turned to go up the staircase that led to the bedrooms.

Lynda noticed him, and looked up, "Nikolas, what's the matter? Did daddy punish you?"

"Nope," he replied, matter-of-factly. "Daddy's dead."

Lynda's eyes widened, as she looked at her friend in a moment of frozen wonder. She burst out of her chair and ran down the hall, followed by her friend. "Roger! Roger! Oh my God! Call 911!"

She ran over to him, shaking him, but Roger was already gone.

~ ~ ~ ~

A week later Lynda stood in a drizzle at Forest Lawn Memorial Gardens with a small gathering of the few people who knew them in Parkland, along with two relatives who had traveled from New York. She was 55 years old, and she now had the sole care of two boys.

Chapter 27

May 13, 2006
Lynda Cruz Home, Parkland, Florida
One year and nine months later

LYNDA OPENED THE DOOR with a wide smile. The first guests for their party to celebrate Nikolas' First Communion had arrived. "Hi Mary, hi John, come in!" Lynda turned and called out, "Nikolas, your guests are arriving!"

"Hi Lynda," said her friend Mary. "I'm sorry we couldn't make the church. How was it?"

Lynda rolled her eyes, "It was nice, but it was hard. Zachary would not stand still."

More guests were getting out of their cars. Lynda pointed, "Help yourself to something to drink. Everything is out back." She turned again, "Nikolas!"

Just then Nikolas came running in from the back yard, wearing blue pants, a black belt, a white shirt, and a navy blue-clip-on tie.

"Hi Nikolas," said Mary, as she bent down to hug him, "Congratulations, honey." She handed him a large envelope. Nikolas took it and smiled, then ran away.

Lynda yelled, "Nikolas get back here and say, 'thank you.'"

In another instant, Nikolas raced back, "Thank you!" he then turned and ran into the back yard.

~ ~ ~ ~

Within the hour there were over thirty people, friends, neighbors, and people from church enjoying the food and drinks Lynda had catered in for the event. Nikolas and Zachary were occupying the Jungle Gym with the other kids at the party.

Lynda was seated by the back of the pool talking with Connie, one of her neighbors. Connie asked, "How have you been doing since Roger passed?"

"It's been a terrible challenge, and, I have been overwhelmed."

"I can imagine. Living alone and raising two boys cannot be easy. Have you thought about remarrying?"

Lynda laughed, "No not really. I don't think I could ever love anyone else besides Roger." What Lynda could not tell her, was that she missed him so much, she often cried herself to sleep. Roger was the only person she ever loved, and she had already vowed to herself that he would always be just that, her one true love. "But I have made other decisions."

"Like what?" asked Connie.

"I am getting a handgun, to help protect myself and the boys now that Roger is gone."

"What?" said Connie, in shock.

Lynda glanced back at the Jungle Gym for a moment. "Oh yes, I don't feel safe being alone anymore."

"But you know nothing about guns."

"Sure, I do. I've fired guns a hundred times when I was younger. My dad had a gun collection in his den. We always knew of them, and how much he valued them. He used to hunt wild boars with them. He'd always tell us we did not have to fear any intruders because he had the right to shoot anyone who came into the home unlawfully."

"Oh my gosh. Are you sure, I mean, with… your… well, with the boys?"

"I am sure. Enough about that, though, it's time to give Nikolas his gift."

Lynda signaled to her neighbor Paul, "It's time." She called Nikolas and Zachary. "Boys, come over here."

The boys and their friends ran over, and Lynda reached out and pulled Nikolas close. "Nikolas, I have a gift for you for your 1st Communion." Paul walked across the backyard from the direction of his garage, wheeling a brand-new mountain bike. Nikolas eyes widened, "Wow!" He ran over and took it, hoisting himself on it, and circled the backyard, with the other kids and Zachary chasing behind.

"Be careful!" yelled Lynda as they disappeared into the front.

Ten minutes later, one of the kids came running in the backyard. "Mrs. Cruz, Nikolas is hurt."

Lynda ran out front. Nikolas was sprawled in the driveway, face down, crying, while Zachary was standing next to the knocked over bike. Lynda screamed, "Zachary, what did you do?"

Zachary turned away as the crowd of guests gathered around. Lynda ran up and knelt beside Nikolas. She turned him over and saw the gash on his forehead. His eyes were on fire with rage, and he screamed, "Zachary pushed me down!" He gritted his teeth, and yelled, "Ahhhh it hurts! Dammit! Damn you, Zachary!"

Lynda tried to comfort him, "Oh, honey, I'm sorry." She lifted her head, "Someone get me a wet towel!" In a moment Paul was there to help stop the bleeding and clean the cut. Nikolas was helped into the house and onto the couch. Lynda screamed, "Zachary, go to your room!"

Nikolas was shaken, but he did not need stitches. Lynda sat next to him holding a bag of ice on his head, and the party ended early.

Chapter 28

April 17, 2008
Lynda Cruz Home, Parkland, Florida
Two years later

NIKOLAS RAN DOWN THE HALL into the living room, then turned and ran back to the front door, holding his hands over his ears, screaming, "Ahhhhhhh! Ahhhhhhh! Stop!!! Stop!!!"

His mother Lynda heard him and raced in from the back patio, "Nikolas, Nikolas!" She ran up to him, but he brushed past her, screaming, "Make her stop!! Make her stop!!"

Lynda saw her other son running down the steps and yelled, "Zachary call 911!"

Nikolas jumped onto the couch, writhing in agony. Lynda raced over and grabbed him, holding him close, rocking his shaking body back and forth, "What is it, honey? What is it?"

"Make her stop! Make her stop!"

"Who! Who, Nikolas!" she cried, as tears fell from her cheeks.

"Tira! Tira!"

Lynda had never heard him say this before and she was frightened. She shouted, "Zachary! Did you call 911?"

"Yes!" he said in a frustrated voice.

Lynda kept rocking his shaking body, hoping to calm him, when suddenly she remembered something she had seen her late husband Roger do. She slowly traced the Sign of the Cross on Nikolas' forehead.

Nikolas let out a long sigh, and the shaking began to lessen. Lynda kept rocking him back and forth, "It's ok, Nikolas. I've got you."

He shook his head, saying nothing, reaching up to wipe the tears from his eyes

Lynda heard the ambulance and began to feel nervous. She did not need another incident on his record. Now, she would have to explain everything to the paramedics.

The paramedics came in and examined the still shuddering ten-year-old boy in front of them. They asked numerous questions to which Lynda replied somewhat evasively.

One of them said, "Mrs. Cruz, we think we should take Nikolas in for an evaluation."

"No, he's fine. There's nothing wrong with him."

"Mrs. Cruz, your other son said Nikolas hears voices. That is not normal."

"No, I said he is fine."

Zachary interrupted them, "No, he's not fine, mom. He's crazy!"

Lynda turned in anger, "Zachary!!! Get up to your room, right now!"

Zachary turned in disgust and trudged away.

Lynda took a deep breath and allowed calm to instantly come over her again, "I'm sorry about that. No, Nikolas is ok. I will keep an eye on him. If anything changes, I will call a doctor." As soon as the words left her mouth, she knew she was lying. She would never allow them to label Nikolas as mentally ill. But it was more than that. Deep down, she knew there was something dark involved, something mysterious that her late husband Roger had hidden from her, and she was starting to get scared.

Chapter 29

April 18, 2008
Lynda Cruz Home, Parkland, Florida

THE FOLLOWING EVENING, Lynda took a long drag from her cigarette as she watched the evening sun begin its descent. In her hand, she held her second glass of wine. The recent events had shaken her, but they had only brought things to the surface. The past few years had gone wrong for her in almost every way. She was fine financially, but emotionally she was a wreck. Nikolas was almost ten years old, and Zachary had just turned 8, and they were at each other all the time. But it was more than that, there was something wrong with Nikolas, and Lynda knew it. It was as if something or someone possessed him or something.

Lynda was no stranger to cigarettes and wine. She had used them most of her life though she did it sparingly during the years of her marriage to Roger. But over the last year, with all the stress threatening to overwhelm her, she was not only smoking more but also having several evening glasses of wine.

She lifted the glass and finished it; then it hit her. She remembered Roger had gone several times to see the nun who had arranged the adoption. Perhaps she would know something about Nikolas father, something she was not telling them. Lynda got up and went to Roger's study which she kept locked, to preserve it the way it was when he was alive.

She opened the door and went to his large mahogany desk. She sat in the leather chair she had not touched since the day he died. She closed her eyes, remembering him, and remembering all the times he had loved her. She then opened the drawer on the left and looked through the files. One of the first ones was labeled, "Sister Jane."

Lynda pulled it out and read the notes. One prominent note said, 'Our Lady of Lourdes Shrine' and had the address. Lynda wrote it down on a piece of paper and put the file back. She locked the den back up and resolved to go in the morning.

She poured herself a third glass of wine and went back on the patio, waiting for the boys to come back from playing in the woods.

~ ~ ~ ~

The following morning Lynda woke with a throbbing headache. She showered, dressed, and got the boys off to school. She then drove to the shrine and parked her car in the lot next to the convent.

As she walked up the walk that led to the church and convent entrance, she marveled at the beautiful statues of the Blessed Mother and the Angels and Saints. She missed the days when Roger kept their family rooted, with his evening prayers and stories. Since he had died, it seemed all peace and order in the home had vanished.

She rang the tiny doorbell next to the mammoth old wooden door. A few minutes later and older nun, wearing a black habit opened the door smiling.

"May I help you?"

"Yes, is Sister Jane here?"

The nun paused, and a slight look of sorrow came over her face. "Won't you come in?"

Lynda walked in, and the nun walked to the lobby. On the walls were pictures, one of the Pope, and one of the local Bishop. There was also a picture of Jesus, and Mary, and another of the Holy Family. It all made Lynda feel peaceful. There was a stillness in the air, a holy one which Lynda had never experienced before. The old nun turned, "Won't you sit down."

Lynda sat in a comfortable old chair, and the old nun sat next to her. Close to them, a much younger nun, also wearing a black habit, was sitting at a desk in the office, looking at a computer screen. The old nun said, "What is your name?"

"My name is Lynda. Sister Jane helped my husband and me with an adoption."

"I see, I am Sister Louise. I am sorry to tell you, but Sister Jane succumbed to her cancer about a year ago."

"Oh, I'm sorry."

The nun nodded, "She lived a long and meaningful life, and we miss her."

"Well, I need to see someone about the..." Lynda paused and pulled the paper out of her pocket, "The Order of the Protectors of the Cross."

Sister Louise looked a little baffled, but out of the corner of her eye, Lynda saw the younger nun was listening, and began typing. She paused, then resumed.

The old nun replied, "I am sorry. I have never heard of it."

"Well, perhaps someone else has."

"I am the Superior here. I was fully aware of everything Sister Jane did. I'm afraid if I don't know, no one will."

Lynda noticed the young nun listening again, and she looked over, but the woman looked away.

"Well, can you take my number in case anything comes up?"

"Sure."

Sister Louise pulled a small spiral note pad from her pocket and a pen, and said, "Go ahead."

Lynda gave her the number and then left, feeling as lost and vulnerable as she had ever felt.

Chapter 30

July 7th, 2008
Lynda Cruz Home, Parkland, Florida
Three months later

NIKOLAS SAT OUTSIDE on a Saturday morning waiting for his brother Zachary to come out of the house. He was marveling at the new pellet gun his mom had bought him. She had set up a target practice area in the backyard, and Nikolas was under strict orders to only use it there. Also, Lynda laid down the rule that because Zachary was only eight years old, he could not touch it, though she promised him he would receive his own when he turned 10.

Zachary came outside, still half asleep. "What do you want?"

"C'mon. Let's go shoot squirrels!"

"Really!"

"Hell yes."

"Can Brody come?"

Brody was a neighborhood boy who was more friends with Zachary than Nikolas. He was closer in age to Nikolas, but he hung around with Zachary. "Yeah, that's fine. We'll stop on the way."

The boys took off down the street, then cut through Mrs. Begani's yard to the next street. Within minutes they were at Brody's house. Zachary knocked on the door, and within a minute Brody's mom answered, still in her nightgown. "What do you boys want so early?"

"Can Brody come out and play?" asked Zachary.

Brody's mom glanced over at Nikolas. She did not like him, none of the people in the neighborhood did, but he looked innocent enough standing there, and it was a glorious sun-shiny morning. She didn't imagine they could find any trouble that early. She glanced over at the wall, "What time is it?" She squinted, then said, "I guess so. Brody!" she yelled, waiting, "Zachary and his brother are here!" She paused again, listening, "He'll be out in a minute, boys."

Nikolas and Zachary sat on the steps, and Nikolas felt the pellet gun tucked in his pant leg. Neither said a word, and when Brody came out, Zachary said, "C'mon, we got somewhere to go."

As they walked, they heard Brody's mom say, "You boys stay out of trouble, and you be home before too long, Brody!"

Brody raised his hand, "Yes, mom." He turned to his friends, "Where are we going?"

"To kill squirrels," said Nikolas, with a wide smile on his face.

"What? With what?"

"With this!" Nikolas pulled out the pellet gun, and raised it, pointing it at Brody, "Pow, BAM! BAM!!"

"Hey, put that fucking thing down!" shouted Brody.

"Quit being a pussy. It's not loaded."

"You call me a pussy again, and I will kick your ass," said Brody, rattled at what Nikolas had done.

"Cool it, Brody," said Zachary, "He's only joking around."

None of them said a word. They reached Mr. Redmond's house which bordered the wooded area and long canal at the back of the development. "Hurry," said Nikolas, as he led the way along the side of Mr. Redmond's house, staying close to the bushes to minimize their chances of being seen.

When they reached the wooded area, Nikolas scanned all the trees, while Zachary and Brody scanned the canal. They were nervous, as there had been gators sighted there in the past, and they wanted to be sure none were there now.

Nikolas exclaimed, "There's one."

The other boys ran over, "Where?"

"Right there, on that branch." Nikolas gritted his teeth, raised the gun, and fired. The startled squirrel jumped to another branch and scurried up the tree. Just then Brody said, "Look, there's a gator! Damn, it's a big one."

They ran over to the edge of the canal, peering at the head and eyes resting above the water. "Don't get too close Nikolas!" screamed Zachary. Nikolas ignored him and stepped closer. He raised his gun, aimed, and fired. "Got him!" yelled Nikolas, as the gator lurched, then turned and went under.

"Did you see that? I shot that fucker right in the head!"

"Oh my God," yelled Brody. "That was amazing!"

Zachary said nothing; he was angry that his brother had gotten so close to the gator.

"Look!" said Brody, pointing.

They looked up at a lower hanging branch where a squirrel was chattering at them. Nikolas walked over, raised his gun, aiming, then pulled the trigger. The squirrel fell to the ground writhing in pain. Nikolas ran over, "Look at that little bastard!" the other boys came over too, laughing. Nikolas said in a low voice, imitating the movie the Terminator, "Asta Luego, Baby!" He put two more pellets into the writhing animal causing it to whimper, then die.

"That was sick!" said Brody, shaking his head. Nikolas picked up the bloodied squirrel by the tail, and twirled it, then thrust it at Zachary.

"Get that thing the hell away from me!" yelled Zachary.

Nikolas laughed, and Zachary ran at him, punching him in the face. They heard a voice. "What the hell's going on back here!"

The boys turned, it was the old man Redmond, walking toward them. Nikolas looked at the squirrel, then at Zachary. "Let's get out of here!"

The boys ran as Mr. Redmond shouted, "Stop you, kids, get back here!" He walked over and looked at the squirrel, then called the sheriff.

Twenty minutes later the sheriff knocked at Lynda's door. "Mrs. Cruz?"

"Yes?"

"I'm afraid your boys are in trouble. One of them killed a squirrel with a pellet gun."

Lynda screamed, "Zachary! Nikolas! Get in here!"

The sheriff's deputy threatened to arrest the boys, only Lynda's promising to seek counseling prevented him from doing so. He wrote up a citation, noting that someone would call Social Services, and that Lynda was to provide proof to the sheriff's office within 30 days that Nikolas was under a doctor's care for psychological counseling.

Chapter 31

August 10, 2008
3ʳᵈ Heavenly Realm, outside the home of Host Commander
Rosie
One month later

THE ANGEL JORDAN SAT on the bench overlooking the Heavenly Sea
outside the home of his Host Commander Rosie. He had arrived early
for their quarterly meeting in which he gave her updates on all the
Humans under his care. Jordan was troubled about a few of his
clients, for a myriad of reasons. The Dark Angels were winning. A
revolution was underway, one which was pushing the Lords farther
and farther away from people.

After a few more minutes, Rosie walked over, and sat down.

"All right, I'm ready, have at it."

Jordan accounted for each of his clients as Rosie listened.
Periodically, she would nod, or shake her head, or pause him to offer
counsel. Then he came to Nikolas. "I have one problem."

"It sounds like you have several on your hands. What's so special
about this one?"

"His name is Nikolas, and he is very, very troubled. He screams
a lot, and throws tantrums, running around yelling for the voices to
stop."

Rosie listened with grave concerns, "This is not sounding good."

"It gets worse boss. He has killed animals."

Rosie knew this was a terrible sign. Coupled with the other
symptoms he was having, she already knew he would need special

care. "Is this the young man who had the mark, the one you told me about years ago, who was able to see you?"

"Yes."

"But I thought they got the Order involved?"

"They did, but it's not working. His Dark Angel is around a lot too. It's the Dark Angel Tira, and, she makes me nervous."

Rosie shook her head. "I know who she is. She's trouble."

Jordan then said, "There's one more thing."

"What?"

"Sometimes, I can't find him."

"What do you mean?"

"I mean, I can't find him. I try to locate him with my senses, and it's a blank."

Rosie looked out at the sea with a confused look on her face. "I haven't heard of that happening for… for centuries. Are you sure?"

"Oh, I'm sure."

"All right Jordan, I know you have hundreds of clients, but keep a close eye on this boy. I will look into a few things."

Chapter 32

June 6, 2009
Sheriff Al Lamberti Office, Ft. Lauderdale, Florida
Ten months later

"LOOK AL, I'VE BEEN OUT on the streets for almost 25 years. I've paid my dues. Don't you think it's time I get to cash in for a better job?"

"What do you mean, better?"

"You know what I mean Al, easier."

Sheriff Al Lamberti sat behind his desk with a half- smile on his face. In front of him sat one of his longest-standing deputies. Scott Peterson was far from one of his best. He was overweight, and Al doubted he could chase a suspect over 100 feet. Still, they had known each other a long time, and Al knew that Peterson had earned something special after 25 years on the job. "How would you like to be a school resource officer?"

"Where?"

"Stoneman Douglas."

Peterson thought for a moment, "Do I still get my overtime?"

"Well, from what I've heard from Reilly, you can get as much as you want, and more."

"What's going on with Reilly?"

"He's retiring. Do you want it?"

Peterson thought for another moment, then smiled. "Yes, I want it. The way I figure, I've got about five more years, and I'm out of here." A worried look came over his face. "It's not too demanding, is it?"

"No, the job is to keep the students safe, and nothing ever goes on around there other than minor things. Can you handle that?"

Peterson smiled, "Yeah, I can handle that."

Chapter 33

September 16, 2009
Brody Phillips Home, Parkland Florida
Three months later

IT WAS A HOT DAY IN PARKLAND and one week before his 11th birthday. Nikolas got off the school bus and ran into the house, running right to the kitchen to make a few peanut butter and jelly sandwiches. He turned on the TV and chowed them down as he waited for Zachary's bus to come. Within twenty minutes Zachary, now 9, walked in. "Hey, Nikolas."

"Hey, Zachary."

"Man, school sucked today," said Zachary.

"Why?"

Zachary said, "I had this stupid math test. I think I got like two right."

"That blows."

Just then Zachary's phone rang. "Hello... hey Brody... yeah... in about twenty minutes... ok bye." Zachary ended the call and made himself a sandwich.

Nikolas watched him for a few minutes, "Where are you going?"

"Over Brody's to throw the football around."

"Can I come?"

"I guess."

It thrilled Nikolas. He had no friends, and he didn't know why. All the kids in the neighborhood seemed to keep their distance from him. The kids who should be his friends, kids near his age, were friends with Zachary instead.

They walked over to Brody's the usual way, cutting through Mrs. Begani's yard. When they arrived, Nikolas worried. Kenny Kirby and Scott Papes, a few of the boys in the neighborhood that for sure didn't like him were there. Papes' parents banned Nikolas from their house and yard at the beginning of summer, but not Brody's.

Kenny came running up, holding the football. "Nikolas, what are you doing here you little twerp?" Kenny was also 11, but he towered over the much shorter Nikolas.

Nikolas said nothing, as Zachary spoke up, "Leave him alone Kenny. We want to play football."

Scott Papes shouted, "Kenny, throw it long!"

Kenny reached his arm back and let it sail all the way into the backyard. Scott caught it, yelling "Touchdown!"

Just then Brody came out. "Man, Zachary, why did you bring Nikolas?"

Zachary shook his head, "I had to."

"Well, how are we supposed to play two-on-two?"

"I'll be official QB," said Zachary.

"Ok, that works. Me and Kenny, against Papes and Nikolas."

"Ok,"

The game started, and it was difficult from the start. Nikolas was smaller than the other boys, and they roughed him up every chance they had. When they finished playing, Scott Papes heard his mom calling. "Hold on; I'll be right back."

He ran over to his house, then came back. "My mom said we could go over to my house and chill and get something to eat."

"Sounds good," said Kenny, who threw the football down. "Let's go."

They all walked toward the narrow backyard cut through one could squeeze through to get into their fenced yard. Nikolas followed behind. He knew they had banned him from the yard, but summer was over. Perhaps Mrs. Papes had reconsidered. As they neared the cut through, Scott Papes stopped and turned around. "Uh, sorry Nikolas. You know you're not allowed over."

Nikolas sighed, shaking his head. He looked at Zachary, who smiled and went through the narrow passage first, leaving Nikolas to watch the others squeeze through. Then they were gone. Nikolas listened to their voices laughing at him as they walked to the back door and disappeared into the house. He cried, careful not to let anyone see him. He turned and walked back across the Brody's backyard, seeing Brody's mom eyeing him from the window.

He tried to hold back the tears as he cut back through Mrs. Begani's yard and headed down the street to his home. When he walked in, his mom was home.

"Nikolas, where is Zachary?"

He ran upstairs without replying. Lynda saw the redness in his eyes, and she went up after him. She opened the door to his room and saw him laying face down on the bed. "Nikolas, what's wrong?"

"Nothing!" came the distressed voice, muffled by the bedspread.

She sat next to him, rubbing his back, "What is it, honey?"

Nikolas was quiet for a long time, then said, "I have no friends."

The words broke Lynda's heart. A tear fell from her eye, "I'm sorry honey. Hey, you got me, I'm the best friend you'll ever have!"

Nikolas said nothing, but only let out a shivering breath. After a few moments, he said, "Thanks, mom."

"Hey, I will order pizza just for us. Let's watch a movie together."

Nikolas turned over, his eyes wet and red. "That would be cool."

"All right, now why don't you get those dirty clothes changed and come down."

"Ok, mom."

Chapter 34

October 31, 2009
Lynda Cruz Home, Parkland Florida
Six weeks later

IT WAS THREE IN THE AFTERNOON on Halloween, and a fresh Fall downpour was threatening to burst from the blue and purple clouds that hovered over Parkland. Lynda set out a plate of snacks for the boys and went outside to smoke a cigarette and retrieve the mail.

On her way back into the house, she rifled through the letters, then stopped. There was a peculiar looking letter, with the address handwritten in blue ink. It was from Our Lady of Lourdes Shrine. She opened it.

Dear Mrs. Cruz

You don't remember me, but I was at the front desk of the shrine when you visited inquiring about Sister Jane last year. Your mention of the Order of the Protectors of the Cross sparked my curiosity. I investigated the order on the internet, and, I could find nothing more than vague references to its existence, along with some stories that would appear far-fetched. However, I went through Sister Jane's personal effects, and I found a name and address I thought might interest you. Write to him at this address.

Father Ricardo De La Cruz

Guest in Residence
Holy Archangels Monastery
Kendalia, TX 78027

I wish you luck Mrs. Cruz. God bless you and your family.

Sister Shelly

Lynda felt a surge of hope, and, a surge of her feelings about Roger. She poured herself a glass of wine and went to unlock the door to his study. She went in, taking in the scent of the old desk he kept. She sat at the desk for a while, sipping her wine, letting a few tears fall, remembering him, wondering why he had to leave her, all the while looking down at the letter from Sister Shelly. She then pulled out a piece of paper and wrote a letter to Father Ricardo.

Dear Father Ricardo

I am Roger Cruz's widow. I need to know any information you might have as to the biological father of my son Nikolas. I am having terrible trouble with him, and I don't know what to do. All I know is that it is connected to you and your work with the order you belong to.
Can you please help me? I am desperate.

Lynda Cruz

When she had finished, she locked the study door back up and went into the kitchen to wait for the boys to come home.

Chapter 35

Feb 11, 2010
Lynda Cruz Home, Parkland Florida
Three months later

LYNDA STOOD AT THE KITCHEN counter, mixing the mashed bananas into the cake batter, and humming along to the music on the radio. Today was Zachary's 10th birthday, and she had a dinner celebration with a few of the family's close friends planned for later that evening. She heard the school bus pull up outside and smiled. She poured the batter into the greased pan, set the bowl in the sink, and put the cake in the oven.

Before she could turn around, both boys burst through the back door of the kitchen, greeting her. Lynda hugged them both, "Boys, go get changed. I have a special snack for you."

"What is it?" asked Nikolas.

"I made ham sandwiches, and... some chocolate pudding and... later tonight, we are having banana cake."

"Awesome mom, thanks!" said Zachary.

Both boys ran upstairs, then came down to eat. As they were eating, Lynda told them about her plans to have a small party later. Zachary said, "Cool mom, but I have to go over Kenny's house for a while. I'll be back in an hour."

"Zachary, the party is in two hours. You will be late."

"I won't be late!" yelled Zachary.

"Zachary, the answer is no. I want you to stay home."

"Mom, look, I have to go. Kenny is waiting for me."

Nikolas said nothing and only kept eating. He already knew he was not invited. Lynda said, "Zachary, you can go on one condition."

"What???"

"You have to take Nikolas with you, AND, you have to be back in an hour."

"Mom! I don't want to..." he stopped. He knew there was no point in arguing. "C'mon Nikolas, let's go."

The brothers talked very little on the way. Zachary had special plans with his friends, and he already knew they would be upset about his bringing Nikolas. They walked down the street to where the canal bordered the development, walked over the plank the neighborhood boys had put down years earlier for them to cross on, and headed to a poorer section of the neighborhood.

Kenny Kirby was an only child and lived with his dad who was divorced. Kirby knew nothing of his mother, as she had been gone for years, but his friends knew little of his father, as he was never around. Kenny said he was a truck driver, but the only thing his friends understood was that he was a prick, the mean kind, who often kicked Kenny's ass for little or no reason.

When the brothers arrived, they walked up the long driveway that led to the somewhat run-down double-wide home set about halfway back the deep lot. There was a broken-down pickup truck next to the house, and nothing else, letting the boys know the old man was not at home. Zachary walked around to the back of the house, followed by Nikolas, who was already having misgivings about coming along. Kenny and Scott Papes were sitting by a small fire not far from an old tree house.

Zachary called out, "Kenny! Yeah!"

Kenny turned, smiling, then stood up. "What the hell did you bring him for?"

Papes also stood up.

Zachary looked at his brother with disdain, "I had to, but don't worry. He's gonna stay the hell out our way!"

Nikolas glanced over at his brother and muttered, "You're a dickhead, you know that."

Kenny roared, "We got the bong ready in the treehouse. Let's do this."

Zachary looked at Papes, "You got the stuff, Papes!"

"Yeah, I do,"

They all began moving to the wide wooden treehouse ladder, and Nikolas followed. Kirby climbed half way up and stopped. "You wait here shit head. We'll be right down."

Nikolas waited till he turned, then popped the finger at him. He wanted to do it to his face, but Kenny was a lot bigger and stronger than he was. In a minute the three disappeared into the tree house some eight feet off the ground and closed the wooden entrance door.

That's when Nikolas heard the voice, "Nikolas, why do you let them hurt you. You are better than them. Show them... show them!"

Nikolas half smiled and looked up at the smoke coming from the open slats on the sides. He heard them passing the bong around, laughing, as they were getting high. He pulled out one of the cigarettes he had stolen from his mom, took out her lighter, and lit it. Suddenly he had an idea. He looked over at the nearby wooden shed.

He casually glanced up to make sure they were busy, then walked over and quietly opened the door. Once inside, his eyes widened, as he saw a can of lawn mower gas. Nikolas threw out his cigarette and picked up the can. He slowly walked to the tree house, trying to keep out of view. When he reached it, he quietly covered the wide wooden steps with gas.

He then stepped back, picked up his cigarette, took a few more puffs, then tossed the red hot cigarette onto the steps. There was a loud mini explosion, forcing Nikolas to leap back, as the ball of heat flushed his face. He sat on the grass with his heart racing as the steps exploded in flames.

The boys up top began yelling and screaming. Kenny started kicking out the back wall. When Nikolas could see they were going to get out, he got up and ran home.

Kenny landed and started to chase him, but he knew he had to put the fire out. A neighbor had seen the explosion and had already called 911. Kenny screamed at the others, "Help me!" and ran to get his garden hose. Within minutes, they heard the sirens and Kenny knew he was screwed. Papes and Zachary ran through the backwoods, leaving him to face the trouble alone.

A few minutes later, Nikolas walked into the kitchen, overhearing the fire truck racing down the street. Lynda came in, "Hi Nikolas, where is Zachary?"

"He's coming," he said, as he went up to his room.

Minutes later Zachary stormed in, "Where is Nikolas!"

"In his room, why?" said Lynda, with Zachary's tone causing sudden alarms to go off in her head.

Zachary gritted his teeth and ran past her, up the stairs. She froze for a moment, and turned the oven off, then took off after him.

Zachary raced into his room, "You little fuck head!" He ran to him, slugging him in the face. Nikolas tried to shield himself, and throw a punch, but Zachary grabbed him by the shoulders, and threw him onto his desk, knocking his computer and monitor against the wall. Zachary began wailing on his face as Nikolas frantically kicked his legs trying to push him away.

"Zachary!!!" screamed Lynda, as she ran over, grabbing him by the hair, pulling him off momentarily. He elbowed her in the chin, then dove onto Nikolas again. Lynda was in shock, she nervously fumbled for her phone, and dialed 911.

"911 what is your emergency?"

"Please! My son is trying to kill his brother! Please hurry!"

Lynda threw down the phone, picked up a chair, and hit Zachary in the side, knocking him off Nikolas. "Get out of here!" screamed Lynda.

Zachary stopped, unable to breathe. He got up and stomped out and went to his room. Within a few minutes more sirens were heard, this time it was a Broward County Sheriff's Office patrol car.

Zachary knew not to say anything about the fire because of the pot they had been smoking. He was sure the fireman had found the bong. The deputies reprimanded both boys and made them promise to knock it off. Then, they left.

Chapter 36

Feb 22, 2010
Lynda Cruz Home, Parkland Florida
One week later

LYNDA HEARD HER HOME PHONE ring, and she quickly picked it up. "Hello?" It was her neighbor, Paul. He was one of the nicer neighbors, one who seemed to like Nikolas or at least treat him with respect.

"Lynda, this Paul. You got a few minutes?"

"Sure Paul, what's up?"

"How about if I walk over?"

"Yeah, sure. I'll pour us some coffee."

"Sounds good. I'll see you soon."

Paul came right over. The kids were away, so they went into the kitchen and sat at the table. "What can I do for you, Paul?"

"Well, I saw the deputies over here last week. Marilyn heard the racket. I guess the boys were fighting."

"I don't understand them, Paul. They are brothers. How can they treat each other so hatefully? Zachary is the one always instigating."

Paul nodded, "Yes, I get it, Lynda. But you know, brothers sometimes fight, especially when there is no man in the house to stop them."

Lynda let out a loud exhale, and she put her head down. She folded her hands as her eyes began to water up, "I don't know how much more I can take." She glanced out the window, slamming her fist on the table, "Why did you die, Roger!"

Paul nodded, "I'm sorry Lynda. I know you miss him."

"You don't understand. I don't think I could love anyone else."

"I understand. But, you know, the boys would do well with a man around here. Have you thought about having a boyfriend? I mean, you don't have to love him like you loved Roger."

Paul already knew he was way down the rabbit hole, much further than he wanted to be.

"I don't know Paul, I mean, I've thought of it, maybe joining a dating site, but I keep backing out."

"Well, you'll know what to do. I wanted to encourage you."

Chapter 37

March 1, 2010
Lynda Cruz Home, Parkland Florida
Two weeks later

LYNDA SAT AT HER KITCHEN TABLE going through the junk mail. Her eyes widened, there was a reply from the Holy Angels Monastery she had written to 4 months earlier. She hastily opened it and began to read.

Dear Mrs. Cruz,

We are sorry it took so long to get back to you, but we tried to locate Father Ricardo and were unsuccessful. Father Ricardo was a guest with us for about a year. He left over a year ago, and no one here has been able to track him down.

I have forwarded your letter to the last known monastery where he stayed before this.

We are sorry we could not help further.

Sincerely,

Father Joseph Eddy

Lynda threw the letter to the floor in disgust, "Dammit!" She remembered Father Ricardo's commanding presence on the day they baptized Nikolas. She had been sure he would be able to help her. But now, she was at a dead end, and she had a feeling it was her last.

Chapter 38

March 20, 2010
Lynda Cruz Home, Parkland Florida
Three weeks later

LYNDA WAS READING A BOOK in her living room on a Saturday morning when she saw them.

Coming up the bottom of her driveway, having just turned in from the street, was a small group of her neighbors. "What the hell is this?" she said aloud, as she stood up and looked closer. "Nikolas! Zachary! Get down here!"

She peered out. It was Mr. Redmond, Mrs. Begani, Mr. Schmidt, Vi Matic, Georgette, a single woman who lived three doors down, and Mr. and Mrs. Papes, Zachary's friend's parents.

Zachary ran up next to her, looking out. "What are they doing here?"

Lynda looked down at him scowling, "What did you do now Zachary!"

"Blame Nikolas mom!"

"Nikolas!" she screamed.

Suddenly the doorbell rang. "Nikolas!"

Nikolas ran down the steps shouting, "What?"

"What are all these people doing here!" screamed Lynda. The doorbell rang again.

Lynda walked over and opened it wide, allowing Zachary and Nikolas to gather around her. "Yes?"

Mr. Redmond spoke first, "Mrs. Cruz. We want to talk to you alone, about the things your boys have been doing," he paused, adding, "Alone."

"I have no secrets from my boys. Go right ahead."

"Very well, Mrs. Cruz, we all feel your boys need help. That fire that Nikolas set was the last straw."

"What fire?"

Mrs. Papes spoke up, "Well surely you've heard that Nikolas set Kenny Kirby's tree house on fire a couple of weeks ago."

"I heard no such thing." She glanced down at Nikolas, who looked up, shrugging. She looked over at Zachary. He was shaking his head like he had no clue what they were talking about.

Mrs. Papes shot back, "Scott told me everything. You were there too, Zachary."

Zachary shook his head slowly, "I have no idea what you're talking about."

Mrs. Papes turned to her husband, "I told you this was a waste of time." She stormed away, followed by Mr. Papes.

Mr. Schmidt now spoke in his heavy German accent, "You boys better be careful. We will have them arrested!"

"For what?" exclaimed Lynda.

"Your boys threw seven eggs at my house. I had to have someone clean it. They are very, very, bad boys."

Nikolas stared at him, half smiling. He then mouthed the words, "Nazi," but only Mr. Schmidt saw him. Mr. Schmidt stepped forward, "I'll take care of you."

Mr. Redmond held him back, "Hold it, let the others say their piece."

Lynda said, "Mr. Redmond, I know why you're here. I do not condone what Nikolas and Zachary did to those squirrels."

"It was not Zachary; it was Nikolas."

"Well, whichever one it was, I punished them." Lynda knew she was lying, and so did the neighbors, as Nikolas and Zachary smiled at each other as soon as she said it.

Georgette then spoke, "Next time I see that little brat of yours looking in my bedroom window, I'm calling the sheriff. And you better hope my boyfriend doesn't see him. Because he carries a gun, and he gets nervous when people are sitting in my bushes, looking in my bedroom window."

Lynda was furious. "Maybe if you put some clothes on, you little hussy. I see you traipsing around your front yard in your skimpy bikini all day!"

"I'm warning you," said Georgette.

"No, I'm warning you. I have my guns, and I sure as hell know how to fire them. Now, all of you get the hell off my property!"

"Let's get out of here!" said Mr. Schmidt in his thick accent. "She is as crazy as them."

"You're damn right I am."

They left, and Lynda went inside, slamming the door. She went to her couch, sat down, and started crying, holding her hands in her face. After a few minutes, she got up and went to the refrigerator and poured herself a tall glass of wine, saying, "Get away from me boys. Get away from me!"

Chapter 39

August 9, 2011
Broward County School Board
Sixteen months later

ROBERT RUNCIE SAT OUTSIDE the meeting room where the embattled Broward County School Board was holding a private session. This would be his 3rd meeting with the Board, and he hoped it would be his last. This position represented a dream career move for him. It would enable him to give back and to help youth in a way he never imagined, but it was more than that.

It was Florida, and it was warm, and this job would be prestigious, as well as lucrative. If he succeeded here, he might just keep going all the way to the top. His friend and former boss Arne Duncan had done it, moving all the way up on the coat-tails of President Obama to become Secretary of Education.

He had spent the previous day at the home of Gil Donnelly, the school board president, who though under fire to resign, was still the most influential member of the board.

In their private meeting, Runcie stressed the reasons he should be chosen for the job. The district sorely needed money, and Runcie could deliver, including delivering education funds that would flow from Washington. Runcie had ideas, ideas that would fit well with the Obama administration initiatives to aid schools and teachers throughout the country.

He heard someone raise their voice and glanced at the door. Inside the room, the discussion was getting heated.

Gil Donnelly listened impatiently as his long-standing board members. Finally, he had enough. He waited for a moment, then stood, to address everyone, "Need I remind everyone of where we are at right now! Number 1, two of our esteemed members were on the front page of the paper and are facing bribery charges. As if that is not bad enough, the Sun-Sentinel is all over us." He picked up a couple of newspaper articles sitting in front of him and began waving them. Then he chose the top one, "Our class sizes are too large." He set it down, continuing to the next, "Our enrollment is dropping 2,000 students per year! We are shrinking folks! People are leaving!" He set it down, continuing, "Our school facilities are falling apart. Next, we just laid off 1,400 teachers, and the union is up in arms. Finally, our fund balance is dangerously low. Folks, we are broke!"

Beth Michaels, the newest board member who ran as an outsider to the burgeoning bureaucracy Broward Schools had become, said, "Mr. Donnelly, we are well aware of our problems, and may I remind you that you have overseen our descent into this state of chaos."

Gil Donnelly began nodding, "Look, Beth, that's a fair statement. But I'll tell you right now, we need a superstar, or every one of us is going to be out. The parents are near the tipping point." He paused, watching the reactions. His people were right behind him, they always were, but the new members were digging in. He continued, "Runcie's our guy. He's a rainmaker! He's going to deliver money we can't even imagine. He's been the chief of staff for the Chicago schools, and he's connected all the way to the President for God's sakes."

"But he's never been an educator!" said Beth Michaels, stealing his thunder.

Donnelly shot back, "We need way more than an educator! Now, it's time to vote. All in favor of hiring Robert Runcie say 'aye'" They went around the room. The vote was 7-2 in favor of Runcie.

Gil Donnelly turned to the secretary, "Please call Mr. Runcie in, we have some good news for him."

The following day Gil Donnelly called Beth Michaels. "Beth, this is Gil. Ok, first, sorry about getting heated yesterday."

"That's ok; I was too."

"Thank you. Secondly, we need to get behind this man. It's not going to go well for either of you new members being the only ones who voted against him. He is going to be against you from the start, and that is not helpful to anyone. Beth, I want to ask you to trust me on this, I've been doing it a long time."

"Well, what do you mean? We already voted."

"I can call for a formal vote at the next meeting. This way, it can be unanimous, and we can all march forward together."

There was silence.

Gil interrupted, "Trust me Beth, now is the time for us to be united."

"All right. I'm in, call the vote."

Chapter 40

August 29, 2011
Roger Stone Office 401 E. Las Olas Blvd
Three weeks later

SCOTT ISRAEL WALKED NERVOUSLY up E. Las Olas Boulevard accompanied by Ron Gunzburger, an attorney who was going to help him finally get elected. Israel had switched his affiliation from Republican to Democrat recently, and in his mind, their meeting today was not only risky, but it also made no sense.

As was Israel's custom, they were early for their appointment at the office of political strategist Roger Stone, located in the building housing the Royal Pig Restaurant and the Timpano Italian Chop House.

"I don't know about this?" said Israel. "Why in the hell would he want to help me when he defeated me only four years ago? Hall, he's a damn libertarian now."

"Look, I told you, he doesn't care about any party. He cares about money. He's going to cost a fortune, but he will help us to win."

"I don't know about this. Look, we have twenty minutes, let's grab a coffee at Starbucks. I need to discuss a few things one more time."

They stopped at the Starbucks located next to the Royal Pig directly below Stone's offices. Gunzburger asked, "So, what are your concerns?"

"I don't know; this seems too 'out there.' He destroyed me last time with those damn robo-calls. My family hates his guts. I'll tell you that."

"Scott, he's been in politics for decades. He earned his political chops working for Richard Nixon.

"I know, I know, believe me, I know."

Gunzburger laughed out loud, "That's a good one, Scott. They call him a dirty trickster that is for sure."

"He's a foul-mouthed son of a bitch too. Did you see that tweet he sent to the Sentinel about seeing them Next Tuesday? He lets the 'C' word fly at just about anyone!"

"I saw that. Scott, that's Twitter, and that's politics in Broward County. If you're not crude and vulgar and shocking, you don't get noticed. Hey, he helped Al Lamberti get past you in 2008, something no one expected."

"Still, he pisses me off." Israel was now letting his guard down. He hated Stone, and that was that.

Gunzburger glanced up at the awning of the Royal Pig Restaurant that offered Classy Cocktails. "Scott, see that awning?"

"Yeah."

"Well, that's what people think of Roger Stone. They either consider him a classy cocktail, or if you're up against him, they think of him as a royal pig. There is not much in between. Now C'mon, let's go up."

When they reached the office lobby, a beautiful woman stood up from behind the desk. Moments later they were ushered into a large spacious office where Roger Stone was sitting behind a large shiny oak desk. Nearby sitting on a couch was a young man with dark brown hair who looked no older than 30,

"Gentlemen, welcome. As you know, I am Roger Stone. This is my associate Andrew Miller." "Andrew is my Twitter expert, and a lot more. How do you describe yourself again Andrew?" Before Andrew could speak, Stone interrupted him, "Oh, yes, a political pirate, a provocateur, and above all, a street fighter. Does that sum it up, Andrew?"

Andrew smiled, "That sums it up nicely."

"So, Scott, you would like me to help you get elected?"

Israel took a deep breath, "Yes, I would."

"You both understand my fees then?"

"Oh, yes," said Gunzburger. "The fees will be paid. We have a sizeable war chest."

"Well working with me may make it even more sizeable. Now, what I have in mind is a very strong smear campaign against Lamberti."

Israel interrupted him, "But weren't you just in his corner a few years ago?" It was a rhetorical question, but Israel needed to know 'why?'

"Yes, but we've had a falling out. Now, I am up for grabs, and gentlemen, money talks. Politics in South Florida ain't beanbag. My activities are legal and protected by the First Amendment. When I do it, I do it better."

Gunzburger glared at Israel, telling him with his eyes to back down. "Go on Roger."

"Alright, I also have a new robocall campaign planned."

"Like the last time?"

"Oh, very much like the last time. My guy, as you found out last time, is the best."

Stone reached for the conference phone and spun it around. He hit speed dial and punched in a two-digit code.

A man with a funny voice answered, "Pizza on a Stone, may I help you?"

Roger Stone burst out laughing, "Gentlemen, meet Randy Credico, he... he makes pizzas."

"Would you like your pizza democrat or republican?"

Stone glanced over at Israel, "Gentlemen, this is Randy Credico, comedian, and impersonator. He is going to do the robo-calls."

Stone bent a little closer to the phone. "Randy, I've got a new gig for you. Remember last time you did those calls against Scott Israel. Well, he is sitting right here in front of me, and this time we will do the calls, 'for' Scott Israel."

"Well, I'll be a monkey's uncle," said Credico.

Stone looked up smiling. "It will be simple, remember the Al Sharpton message. Can you say it for us, Randy?"

"Uh, sure," there was a pause, and Randy put on his Al Sharpton voice, "Uh, this is the Reverend Al Sharpton. We can't afford to have Scott Israel, uh… running our sheriff department."

Israel's face grew angry. Stone held up his hand, "Ok Randy, we will say the same message, except, Old Uncle Al will say, "We can't afford NOT to have Scott Israel… uh… running our sheriff department. We need this man."

"I like it."

"I'd like a Bill Clinton one too."

Randy paused, "Ok, how is this? 'Hi… this is Bill Clinton… If you don't vote for Scott Israel, coming up this November… well there's no telling what dangers we will face.'" Suddenly Randy switched to a dark, sinister radio voice, "The preceding announcement is brought to you by Dewey, Cheatem, and Howe."

The men all started laughing. Stone stood up, "All right Randy, I'll be back with you." He pressed the disconnect button. "Gentlemen, welcome aboard."

Scott Israel and Ron Gunzburger stood up, shook the men's hands, and left.

Chapter 41

August 22, 2011
Mr. Schmidt's Home, Parkland Florida
Two weeks later

NIKOLAS, ZACHARY, AND BRODY knelt on the grass behind the neighbor's bushes eyeing Mr. Schmidt's house. It was almost dusk. "There he is," said Zachary.

"Where?" asked Nikolas.

"There, he just walked into the dining room."

"Look at that guy," laughed Brody, "He even walks like a Nazi."

All three of them started to laugh.

Suddenly the back door of Mr. Schmidt's house opened, and the boys crouched down lower. Mr. Schmidt walked back to his garage, opened the door, and pulled his large blue garbage can out, turned it, and began noisily wheeling it down the drive. Nikolas laughed, "Look at him, Nazi goose-stepping his garbage down the drive."

They all started laughing again, this time Zachary putting his hand over his mouth to avoid them being noticed. Nikolas smiled, loving he had made his brother laugh so hard, and whispered, "Heil Hitler, Herr Schmidt!"

Mr. Schmidt was nearly 80 years old. He was, a Nazi, though no one knew it. His father had died in Stalingrad, freezing to death during a brutal 3-day blizzard along with most of the soldiers in his troop. Only four survived the blizzard, and only of them ever made it back to Germany. He had visited Mr. Schmidt's mother after the war to let her know had happened. Mr. Schmidt was his mother's only son, and he joined the Nazi youth at the age of 12, very late in the war. During these last years of his life, he lamented the American youth, like Nikolas and Zachary who were so disrespectful. He wished Germany had won the war; it would be a different world. There would be no room for boys like Nikolas and Zachary. They would be in camps for unruly boys.

The boy's laughing got deeper, "Shhh," said Brody. "He's going to catch us."

Nikolas set the carton of eggs down and shuffled his feet to a more comfortable position. He thought for a moment Mr. Schmidt had heard them, but kept walking, and before long he went back into the house.

"Let's go," said Nikolas, as he picked up the carton of eggs and handed four each to Zachary and Brody.

They all crept out of the bushes, crouching as they went, getting to within fifteen feet of the house. "Now," said Nikolas.

One by one, they quickly hurled their eggs, giggling as they exploded on his house and windows, Nikolas saved the last one, and threw it right at the dining-room window, shattering the glass.

Suddenly they heard, "Get over here you hoodlums!" It was Mr. Schmidt, moving fast, coming around the corner of the back of the house, fast.

Zachary turned, and ran right into Nikolas, knocking him back. Nikolas took off toward the front, as the others headed to the side, but it was too late. In an instant, he felt his hair practically yanked out of his head. "Ah! Let go!"

Nikolas felt the side of his head absorb a wicked slap. "Ah! You fucking Nazi, let me go!"

Nikolas felt Mr. Schmidt's other hand grab his hair. Nikolas whirled around and kicked him in the groin, causing Mr. Schmidt to let go. Nikolas ran like there was no tomorrow.

"Next time I will kill you!" yelled Mr. Schmidt as Nikolas ran home.

He went straight to his room, sat on the bed, and watched the street. After an hour, he knew he was safe. Mr. Schmidt had not called the sheriff.

Nikolas began to calm down, glad he had gotten away. For a moment, with the strength and anger Mr. Schmidt had grabbed his hair with, Nikolas feared he was going to die. He began to breathe slowly, drifting off, and then he woke up. He was going to get back at Mr. Schmidt, and he would make sure it hurt.

Chapter 42

August 24, 2011
Lynda Cruz Home, Parkland Florida
Two days later

LYNDA WAS STILL IN BED when she heard the pounding on the front door. She looked over at her alarm clock and let out a deep sigh. Who the hell is here this early? "Just a minute," she shouted, as she reluctantly pulled the sheet off, put on her robe and slippers, and went downstairs.

The pounding came again, "Just a minute!" she said louder, now annoyed. It was only 8:30 in the morning, and it was Saturday.

She opened the door, and her countenance fell. It was Mr. Schmidt standing five feet back from the door with a very angry look on his face.

Lynda could not even start the conversation, nor greet him. She was too startled. "Yes?" she said in as polite a tone as she could, knowing he probably had a good reason for standing there.

Mr. Schmidt clenched his teeth , then said, "Your boys threw eggs at my house again two days ago. This is the last time. I will call the Sheriff next time."

Lynda sighed, "I am sorry Mr. Schmidt."

"Sorry doesn't help me."

"Would you like me to send them over to clean it up?"

"No!" he said in a loud tone, "Keep them away from me!" He turned and left.

Lynda watched him walk down the drive at a hurried, almost military style pace. She was sorry her boys were causing him all this trouble. She went into the kitchen, put on some coffee, and sat at the table thinking. She decided to call her neighbor Paul.

"Paul, this is Lynda. Do you have time for coffee?"

"Uh, yeah sure. Marilyn is asleep. I'll be right over."

When Paul arrived, Lynda poured him some coffee and recounted what Mr. Schmidt had told her. Paul listened, frowning. "Yeah, I heard all about that. Mr. Schmidt got hold of Nikolas and was pulling his hair, but Nikolas got away."

"He what!" yelled Lynda, now furious that he had laid a hand on her boy. "I'll be right back."

Lynda started to get up, but Paul said, "Lynda wait. Look, the boys are causing a lot of trouble, maybe they need something to keep them busy."

"Like what?"

"Like a dog… maybe?"

"A dog… hmmm, that might be good for them."

Paul thought for a moment, "My buddy Gary lives over in Ft Lauderdale. He's got a little farm, and he has some Jack Russell Terrier puppies. Would you like one?"

"I am afraid I need more than one. The boys will never share one."

"That's no problem. I'll call him today. I can drive up and pick them up. You want a male and a female?"

"Good gracious, no! Get me, two males."

"All right." Paul got up to leave, and Lynda extended her hand. "Thank you, Paul. I appreciate you and Marilyn always being so nice to us."

"You're welcome, Lynda. Talk to you soon."

Chapter 43

September 24, 2011
Lynda Cruz Home, Parkland Florida
One month later

LYNDA WAITED UNTIL 9:00 then finished her coffee and went to the bottom of the stairs, "Boys, get up! I have a surprise for you."

No answer.

"Boys!"

"What!" came the voice of Zachary.

"Zachary, get Nikolas up and come down. I made some pancakes... and I have a surprise for both of you."

Lynda went back into the kitchen and turned off the pancakes she had made for them. Within five minutes Zachary came down. Lynda poured him a glass of orange juice and called up again, "Nikolas?"

A few minutes later, Nikolas, now 13, came sleepily walking down the stairs. Lynda waited till he sat down. She then went into the dining room, lit the candles on top of one of the plates of pancakes, then walked in singing Happy Birthday.

Nikolas rolled his eyes and let his head drop back. He had been up most of the night playing video games and was exhausted. Lynda placed Zachary's pancakes down, then put the one with the candles in front of Nikolas.

"Happy Birthday, honey," said Lynda, "Make a wish."

Nikolas took a deep breath and blew them out.

Lynda said, "Boys, in honor of Nikolas' birthday, I got both of you a very special gift."

"What is it?" Zachary hastily asked, not expecting to receive a gift today.

"Come with me."

Lynda walked out the front door followed by both boys. They walked a few doors down to the home of Paul Gold. Paul was standing at the back of his drive by his garage, smiling. "What is it?" asked Nikolas.

"You'll see," said Lynda as they approached.

"Hi boys! Happy Birthday, Nikolas."

"Thanks."

"Are we ready?" asked Paul.

Lynda smiled and nodded, and Paul hit the remote opener button he had concealed in his hand. The garage door suddenly started to rise as the boys looked at each other with anticipation on their faces and stepped closer. In a moment they saw them, two beautiful Jack Russell Terrier puppies, only two months old. One was black with white markings, and the other was white with a great black spot covering most of his back.

The boys ran in, each of them cradling one. Lynda said, "Now Zachary, Nikolas gets to pick his first because it's his birthday."

Nikolas looked at Zachary, smiling, and put the white puppy down. "I want that one," he said, referring to the blacker puppy Zachary was holding. "Hell no, this one is mine."

"Zachary!" Lynda said in a gradually ascending tone.

Zachary grimaced, then put the puppy down. Nikolas scooped him up and began cradling him. "Your name is Nightmare. Do you like that little fellow? Do you like it, Nightmare?"

"Oh," said Lynda, "How nice. I like that. Zachary, what are you going to call yours?"

Zachary was still scowling, but he walked over and picked up the white one. He looked into his eyes, and said, "Cujo."

Chapter 44

March 24, 2012
Lynda Cruz Home, Parkland Florida
Six months later

NIKOLAS SAT AT THE SMALL DESK in his room scouring the internet. Today represented exactly six months since he had gotten the dogs for his birthday. Dates were important to Nikolas, and he knew it was time to begin moving his plan forward.

He had come up with a brilliant idea to help him train Nightmare and Cujo. The dogs were now largely his as Zachary had little interest in his dog after the first few weeks.

Nikolas laughed, as he began to type, "German command for sit." The results came up. He wrote down 'Sitz!'. Then he typed, "German command for no." The results came up. He wrote down 'Nein!'. Then he typed, "German command for a stand at attention." The results came up. He wrote down 'Achtung!'.

Then he typed, "German command for Attack." The results came up. He wrote down 'Fass!'. Lastly, a devious smile came over his face, and he typed, "German command for the kill." Nikolas stared at the screen, about to laugh, and wrote down 'Toten.'

He sat back looking at his list and began to recite the words out loud. "Sitz! Sitz! Sitz! Nein! Nein! Nein! Achtung! Achtung! Achtung! Fass! Fass! Fahs! Toten!!! Toten!!! Toten!!!" He shut down the computer and ran downstairs to begin teaching his dogs. He had not forgotten what Mr. Schmidt had done to him, and he had plans on exactly how to pay him back.

Chapter 45

August 22, 2012
Mr. Schmidt's Home, Parkland Florida
Five months later

NIKOLAS WOKE BEFORE DAWN and put the leashes on Nightmare
and Cujo. He quietly slipped out the door into the still dark morning
and headed over toward Mr. Schmidt's house. He went around to
the backwoods, crossed over a narrow stream, and drew closer.
Nightmare let out a bark, "Nein!" commanded Nikolas, as Nightmare
instantly obeyed.

Mr. Schmidt had three small pot-belly pigs he was raising. No
one knew why exactly, but the law allowed for it based on their breed.
Mr. Schmidt had built a crude shack near the back of his property and
had fenced in a small area in front of it so they could go in and out.

Nikolas had been training his dogs to attack and kill small animals
all summer. This was the big day though, the event he had been
working diligently toward, the day of his revenge. It was August 22,
exactly one year since Mr. Schmidt had caught up with him and
practically pulled his hair out. Nikolas had this date circled on his
calendar ever since he hatched his plan last November.

He reached the back of Mr. Schmidt's yard and stopped by the
edge of the woods, right near the shack. "Sitz!" he commanded, and
in an instant, Nightmare and Cujo nervously sat, anxious to move as
they sensed the other beasts.

Nikolas pulled out two snacks and gave them to the dogs. "Stay!"
he said, and he waited. He studied the house. Mr. Schmidt was
sleeping. Nikolas imagined it would not take too long for Nightmare

and Cujo to do their duty, but he had to get them back out and get back to the woods before Mr. Schmidt would see him, or worse, catch him.

The sun was cresting over the horizon. He could see his path through the woods to escape. It was time. He unleashed both dogs, commanding again, "Sitz!" Then he carried them both next to the fence. "Achtung!" he snapped, as both dogs sat still.

The small pigs had been inside the shack asleep, but Nikolas now heard them moving around, and making noise. They sensed the dogs. In a moment, Nikolas lifted both dogs and placed them inside the fence. "Sitz!" he commanded.

Then he waited. Inside the shack, the pigs were now making noise, but not enough to wake Mr. Schmidt. Nikolas smiled and gave each dog another snack through the fence, wanting to wait just another moment for the sun to get a little higher over the horizon so that he could watch them.

Suddenly one of the pigs lumbered out of the entrance, followed by another. Nikolas's eyes widened, and he said firmly, "Fass! Fass! Fass!"

In an instant Nightmare and Cujo barked and ran after the two pigs. The pigs began squealing and running in circles, desperately trying to evade the dogs. But it was in vain. In an instant, Nightmare and Cujo were on them. Nikolas now commanded, "Toten!! Toten!!"

Suddenly the back-porch light came on, and Nikolas heard Mr. Schmidt's thick German accent, "What's going on out there!"

"Toten! Toten" cried, Nikolas. Then he said, "Come, Snell! Snell!!" Both dogs let go and ran to the fence. Nikolas picked them up, glancing toward the back door. Mr. Schmidt was getting close, and he stared right at Nikolas, shouting, "I will get you!"

Nikolas turned to run, glancing back. Mr. Schmidt was gone. He stopped and looked again. Mr. Schmidt was not gone, he was laying in the grass not far from the fenced pigs. Nikolas walked back some, drawing close enough to see Mr. Schmidt holding his chest in agony, rolling on the ground. "Sitz!" he commanded. He watched for several minutes, then walked closer, occasionally glancing at the two bloodied pigs laying in the fenced area. Mr. Schmidt's arms fell to his side; then he stopped moving.

"Mr. Schmidt!" came a voice from the neighbor's back patio. It was his neighbor Georgette. "Mr. Schmidt? Are you all right?"

Nikolas turned and hustled away; he was not sure if she had seen him, "Come! Snell!" he said, and suddenly Cujo barked. Nikolas grimaced, "Nein!!" as he turned and took his dogs home.

Chapter 46

NIKOLAS CAME HOME, went into the shed and got out the hose. He carefully rinsed all the blood off both dogs, then got a scrub brush and some car wash and scrubbed the remaining remnants off them. He tied them in the yard to dry off. He then went up to his room and waited.

He picked up a ball and laid on his bed, throwing it in the air and catching it. His face bore a smile. He could not believe how smoothly his plan had gone. Not only had he probably killed the pigs, but Mr. Schmidt, his arch enemy, was probably dead too.

He heard the ambulance leaving, with its sirens on, which was not a good sign. Maybe the old man made it? Nikolas laughed, and said aloud, "Maybe they took the pigs to the hospital!" He began belly laughing and rolled over onto his stomach, then he froze. Pulling in the drive slowly was a Broward County Deputy's Patrol Car. This would normally not alarm Nikolas, other than the fact that today Mr. Schmidt had probably keeled over.

"Dammit!" he said, now waiting for his mother. It didn't take long.

"Nikolas! Zachary! Get down here this instant!"

Nikolas got up and walked into the hall as Zachary opened his door. "What the hell does she want?"

"I have no clue!" replied Nikolas.

When they reached the bottom of the steps, two very imposing deputies with serious looks on their faces were talking with Lynda. They all turned to look at the boys.

Nikolas felt disturbed. Two deputies entered who had never been inside the home before. Their looming presence and the sound of their dispatch radios made him nervous. He looked at their guns and handcuffs and imagined them hauling him away. But a small voice inside his head whispered, "stay calm Nikolas."

Lynda looked over scowling, "Zachary, Nikolas, did you have those dogs out this morning?"

Zachary said, "I've been in bed all morning."

Nikolas slowly nodded, "I was too."

Lynda instantly knew he was lying. She had heard him go out, and she had heard him come back.

Zachary asked, "What happened?"

The deputy spoke up, "What happened boys, is that someone let their dogs attack Mr. Schmidt's pet pigs, and now he's dead."

Nikolas said nothing, but he felt instant relief.

The deputy continued, "The neighbor said she thought she saw one of you boys and heard your dogs. Now, are you telling me the truth, because if you're lying to me, it's not going to go well? We have a dead man on our hands."

Nikolas shrugged his shoulders, "I couldn't care less about that Nazi."

"Nikolas!!" screamed Lynda. "Watch your mouth."

The deputy got angry, "You couldn't care less, huh? Where are your dogs?"

Nikolas looked bothered, and turned to Zachary, "Where are they?"

"How the hell do I know?" Zachary could also tell Nikolas was putting on a show.

Nikolas looked up, then turned around, "They are probably out back."

Both deputies went out into the back yard and over to the dogs. The taller deputy bent down and picked up Nightmare, examining him. Then he did the same to Cujo. Nikolas held his breath until the deputy set down Cujo. The deputies talked and walked back, shaking their heads.

"Well, I guess it wasn't your dogs that did this. So, sorry to have troubled you all."

As they were about to pass, the taller one stopped and looked down at Nikolas, "You'd be wise to watch your mouth young man. You got that?"

Nikolas slowly nodded, "Yeah, I got that."

Chapter 47

Nov 12, 2012
Scott Israel Home, Ft. Lauderdale, Florida
Three months later

SCOTT ISRAEL SAT IN HIS Ft. Lauderdale home, nursing a headache from drinking too much champagne the night before. He was sipping his coffee and staring proudly at the headline in the morning Sun-Sentinel he retrieved moments earlier from his front lawn. The headline read, "Israel Elected Sheriff."

Scott Israel had just been elected as the 16th Sheriff of Broward County. It would be the biggest job of his life. He was now in charge of a budget surpassing 450 million dollars and responsible for the policies, direction, and leadership of 5,400 employees charged with serving and protecting the residents of Broward County.

It was a hard-fought election. Israel's unusual stance against gun ownership along with his opposition to conceal and carry put him at a distinct disadvantage. Somehow, though, his charisma along with the fact he was a Democrat, now, carried him to victory. The phone rang.

"Hello?"

"Scott, it's Roger. Congratulations."

"Thank you, Roger. You guys did a great job. I'll be calling you again in a couple of years."

"No problem, Scott. We'll be ready to help."

Scott hung up and finished his breakfast. He then dressed and went into the offices Ron Gunzburger had set up for him to begin planning the transition that would take place within a few short months.

Later that afternoon one of the new men he would be bringing into a new specially created position with him, and who was charged with reviewing key policies that they would consider changing came into the conference room they were working from.

"Scott, I think we should look at this policy. It is right at the heart of the change we want to bring here."

"Which policy is that?"

"Well, it says here, that right now, law enforcement "may" confront a threat. Scott, to be honest with you, I've never seen such a policy. Anywhere else I have ever worked has clearly stated that law enforcement "shall" confront a threat."

"I don't understand, what are you saying?"

"It says 'may confront' instead of 'shall confront'. That's a hell of a distinction if there is a shooting."

"Yes, I agree. Let me think a moment." Scott put his hands behind his head, and leaned back in his chair, thinking, "You know George, I think we leave it alone. I want my deputies to be empowered. I want them to have the discretion to make their own call. I don't want them trying to act like heroes and end up engaging in suicide missions."

"Well that's our job, going in to confront a threat, don't you think?"

"I understand but leave the policy alone for now. Let me see how my leadership and management style can influence them."

Chapter 48

November 20, 2012
Lynda Cruz Home, Parkland Florida
One week later

LYNDA DREW A LONG DRAG from her cigarette and blew it out into the brisk air, watching it ascend toward the cloudy skies. It was 1:30 in the afternoon on Tuesday. Nikolas, now 13, and Zachary who just turned 11 were both in school. Lynda took another drag, then stamped her cigarette out in the patio ashtray, as she held the smoke in for one final second.

She exhaled once more to clear her lungs, so as not to bring the smoke into the house, then went inside. She had just finished lunch and was about to sit down and do some reading before the boys got home when the doorbell rang.

"Just a minute," said Lynda, as she walked toward the front of her spacious home. She opened the door to see a tall man with dark black hair and a beard sprinkled with steel-silver gray. "May I help you?"

"Mrs. Cruz, I don't know if you remember me."

"I'm sorry, I... I don't think so."

"It has been many years, I'll admit, and I am older."

"Where do I know you from?" she asked.

"I am Father Ricardo."

Lynda's eyes widened in shock. "Father Ricardo, oh my gosh, I didn't recognize you. I mean... you're not... "He finished her sentence, "Not wearing my uniform?" he smiled a warm smile, the kind that can be trusted. "I will explain Mrs. Cruz. May I come in?"

"Absolutely Father, please come in. I was hoping I would hear from you."

Father Ricardo walked in and glanced around. "Is Nikolas here?"

"No, both boys are at school. Here, Father, let's sit down in the living room." Lynda directed Father Ricardo to sit on the armchair while she sat on the couch. "I am glad you came, Father."

"Well, I finally got word of your letter."

"I did not think I would ever find you."

"I am sorry Mrs. Cruz. As part of the order, I travel the world. And, as you have found out, not many people know of the work we do. Mrs. Cruz, how is the boy?"

"He's terrible. Father, I love my son, but he is very troubled. Sometimes I am afraid of him."

"I see," he replied. "How is his brother?"

Lynda grimaced, she blamed Zachary for many of the Nikolas problems. "He is just as bad, but differently. He bullies Nikolas, and they fight all the time. If he would just help his brother, I am sure Nikolas would be different."

Father Ricardo half smiled, nodding. He knew that this was not true, and from what he could gather, Zachary was probably just a normal child — misguided perhaps, unruly perhaps, but nothing out of the ordinary.

"Mrs. Cruz, did Roger ever mention anything to you about Nikolas's father?" He wanted to ask her if she had ever heard him say anything about a Dark Baptism. This was his way around it.

"No."

"Did he keep files, or records anywhere?"

"I thought you had all this information?" Lynda was getting upset, and it showed.

"We do Mrs. Cruz, normally. It's just unusual circumstances I am afraid."

"Like what?"

"The other people who helped with the adoption have died. So, I have no access to their information."

Lynda thought for a moment; her racing thoughts were threatening to overwhelm her. "Come into my husband's study. You can look at his files."

Father Ricardo followed Lynda down the hall and watched her take out her keys and unlock the door. "I keep it locked and keep everything the way it was when he died so that I can remember him better."

"I see."

Father Ricardo entered and went to the desk. He knew of course, the origin of the father, but he knew virtually nothing of the birth mother. Once adoption had been arranged, the only thing that mattered to the order was the child. Sister Jane had all the records about the mother, and she was dead.

Lynda pointed to the drawer, "I found the file with Sister Jane's information in there. But that was all I found." As soon as she said it, Lynda realized she had not dug deeply enough. She had stopped as soon as she found Sister Jane's file.

Father Ricardo rifled to the back, then lifted out all the files, peering inside. He smiled, "I may have found something."

He set the files down and reached in, pulling out a file that had been neatly placed on the bottom of the back of the file drawer. It read, "Brenda Woodley." He knew this was the birth mother's name.

Father Ricardo held it up, smiling. He opened it and saw one piece of paper with a few notes. "What does it say?" asked Lynda.

"It does not say much, but it has an address."

Father Ricardo took out his phone, snapped a picture, and gave it back to Lynda. "I will try to find her Mrs. Cruz. When I do, I will find out what I need to know and report back to you."

"Thank you, Father. Can I write a letter to…"?

He interrupted her, "It's best if you don't Mrs. Cruz. I need to find some things out, and I am afraid we will spook her.'

Lynda nodded, then escorted Father Ricardo out, pausing to lock the door, and continuing to the front door. Just then the back door opened, "Mom, I'm home."

Lynda turned to Father Ricardo and asked with her eyes, he nodded, signaling he wanted to see Nikolas. "Nikolas, come here, there is someone who wants to meet you."

Nikolas came around the corner, then stopped. Something told him to stop. Something warned him to stop.

"Nikolas this is Father Ricardo. He is the priest who baptized you."

Nikolas stared at him, "He doesn't look like a priest."

Father Ricardo smiled, he was not amused, though he pretended to be. He felt the darkness surrounding the boy. He reached into his pocket and pulled out his small bottle of holy water. "Hello, Nikolas. I have not seen you since you were a baby."

Nikolas replied guardedly, "Hi."

Fr. Ricardo asked, "May I give you a blessing?"

Nikolas stood perfectly still, not sure how to answer.

Lynda said, "Nikolas, come over here and let Father Ricardo bless you."

Nikolas walked forward, as Father Ricardo sprinkled holy water on his hand from the vial and then waved his hand over the boy's head, making the Sign of the Cross. He then held his hand above Nikolas' head momentarily, causing Nikolas to back up, and duck out of the way.

"I'm sorry, Father," said Lynda.

"That's ok. All kids do that." But all kids were not surrounded by darkness and Father Ricardo worried. He thanked Lynda, assured her he would be in touch and left.

Chapter 49

November 23, 2012
Broward School District - Fort Lauderdale, Florida
Three days later

ROBERT RUNCIE SAT AT THE head of the small round table with his four most trusted advisors. More than anyone else, they helped develop the policies governing the nearly 31,000 employees and 230,000 students in the district. Whether his advisors agreed or disagreed with his ideas, he could count on them to hash them out before they were made ready for public consumption.

Runcie began, "I have been wrestling with some ideas to reduce the high number of student arrest rates we have. Last year we had over 1,000 arrests inside our schools, and 700 of them were for minor juvenile offenses?"

He paused, "Since we are the 6th largest district in the country, if we can find a way to bring down that number, we will accomplish a couple of things. First, we will help a good number of those kids avoid getting their first offense in the justice system. Secondly, it will look good in the eyes of Washington. Third, if we can generate success, it will help us to attract more funding."

Stan Michaels, his most conservative advisor, commented first. "Bob, that sounds good, but how are we going to do that. We can't wave a magic wand and get the kids to change."

Runcie listened, trying to be patient. Stan was a thorn in his side. He constantly questioned his initiatives. Runcie put up with it for one reason: Stan's voice often represented the opposition that Runcie needed to be ready for. In modern high schools, changing tradition always faced opposition. A skilled superintendent knew how to traverse those waters. He shot back, "Stan, nearly 90% of these kids are black. Now it begins to look a lot like racism if we do nothing."

Stan leaned back in his chair, "Forgive me, Bob, but I don't see how race has anything to do with it."

"Stan, we have our first black President, and Obama wants to address these injustices. He and Arne Duncan both know all this inequality starts in schools."

"Bob, an offense is an offense, no matter who commits it. If 90% of these kids are black, then that is just the way it is. We can't change that."

Runcie replied, "Stan, your point is noted."

There was silence as all felt the uncomfortable feeling still hanging in the air.

Julie Evans, one of Runcie's favorite advisors, asked, "How do you propose doing it, Bob?"

Runcie replied, "We can lower the bar."

"I don't follow," replied Julie.

"We can launch a new program where, instead of calling in law enforcement, the school handles many of these offenses in-house."

Stan looked puzzled, "I don't understand?"

Runcie said, "It's simple, we will handle a good number of these situations internally, through counseling, through warnings about juvenile court, through suspensions and measures like that. I am thinking of calling it the PROMISE program." He gave a brief handout to each of them. "As you can see, PROMISE stands for Preventing Recidivism through Opportunities, Mentoring, Interventions, Supports & Education."

Runcie watched their reactions, and added, "I believe this will go a long way in helping many of these 1,000 kids who get arrested each year."

Runcie looked over at Stan who was leaning back in his chair, tight-lipped, with his arms folded in front of his chest. Runcie dreaded it, but he knew he needed to hear what Stan was thinking. "Stan, you look like you're not sure about this. What are you thinking?"

Stan sighed, "Bob, look, I know we want to help these kids, I mean, a thousand kids is a lot, right? But what is this going to mean for the other 269,000 kids in the system? Do we endanger them, for the sake of the 1,000? What is this going to mean when students are not confronted properly when they commit juvenile offenses? My vote is no."

Runcie honestly felt Stan was wrong. Important social change always needed to push the majority to move off the status quo. "Stan, my job is to ensure the well-being of all students. I cannot ignore injustice for one thousand, just because it may inconvenience others."

Stan closed his mouth. He had stated his opinion; now, it was out of his hands.

Chapter 50

April 19, 2013
Lynda Cruz Home, Parkland Florida
Five months later

ZACHARY CRUZ WOKE UP and glanced out the window, thinking about his friends. He got out of bed and went into the hall. *What the hell?* He took a few more steps, covering his nose, and shouted, "Close the damn door when you're in the bathroom, Nikolas!"

"Screw you!"

Zachary grabbed the door, smacked Nikolas in the head, and violently pulled the door shut.

He started walking back to his room when he heard the door suddenly open behind him. Nikolas ran at him, screaming, "Why did you hit me!" With fists flailing, Nikolas charged him.

Zachary leaned back and caught his flailing fists, twisting them, and throwing Nikolas to the ground. Nikolas would not stop, he lunged at Zachary's legs, wrapping them, tackling him as Zachary crashed into the wall behind them, putting a large hole in it with his head. Zachary screamed, "get the fuck off me!"

Nikolas punched him, landing a rare hard punch to Zachary's face. Now suddenly enraged, Zachary stood and grabbed Nikolas by the hair on the sides of his head and drove him down the long upstairs hall. Nikolas fell back into a picture at the other end of the hall, knocking it off the wall, sending it toppling down the stairs where the glass overlay shattered all over the tile floor.

Lynda Cruz ran out of her room screaming as Nikolas turned and ran down the stairs with Zachary in close pursuit. As they entered the kitchen, Zachary dove on him, sending them both careening into the kitchen table, knocking it over, and everything on top of it onto the floor. They continued struggling, trying to land punches.

Lynda finally arrived, screaming, and pulled Zachary off. "Get away from him! Go, go outside now!"

Zachary shook her off and went outside. Lynda helped Nikolas up, "Are you ok, honey?"

"Yes, I'm fine!" he said, as he pushed her aside and went up to his room.

Lynda went into the living room and started to cry. Within the half hour, at different times, they both came into the kitchen, saw her crying, grabbed something to go, and went to school.

~ ~ ~ ~

Later, after school, Nikolas was the first to arrive home. He saw his mom was still sitting in the living room, now quietly reading. On the counter was a note. It read, "Zachary, Nikolas, if you do not take your medicine you are NOT allowed to go out anywhere tonight!" Next to the note were two pill dispenser paper cups with each boy's medicine, meds they were supposed to take daily for their ADHD and other mental disorders they were diagnosed with. Nikolas said nothing, grabbed something from the refrigerator and went up to his room.

Two hours later, Nikolas got up from laying on his bed and went down the hall to Zachary's room. "Hey, let's get out of here."

"Where are we going to go? Mom will have a fit!"

"I don't care, but I'm not staying here. Are you coming or not?"

Zachary smiled, "Yeah, I'm coming."

Zachary followed Nikolas into the hall, then Nikolas waved him into his room, "This way."

"What are you doing?"

Nikolas headed to the window, "This way!" He turned, smiling and opened the window. They climbed out onto the roof, ran over to the downspout, lowered themselves down, and took off into the woods.

It was late before Lynda decided to make dinner. She cooked a few hamburgers, then called upstairs, "Boys! Come down for dinner."

After a few more attempts, and no reply, she went up. She looked in Zachary's room, then opened the door to Nikolas's room, "Boys?" Then she saw it, the opened window. She looked out as dusk was settling over Parkland.

In a sudden panic, she ran downstairs and grabbed the phone and dialed 911. "Help, please. It's Lynda Cruz. My sons have run away from home, and they haven't taken their medicine! I'm worried!"

"Ma'am calm down, please. How old are your boys?"

"15 and 13! Please hurry."

"Ma'am, are they in any danger?"

"Yes! They must take their medicine. They haven't in four days!"

The dispatcher was silent for a moment. She could tell Lynda might not be entirely stable. But they had numerous calls from the home before. "All right ma'am, I am sending a deputy car out."

Fifteen minutes later a sheriff deputy car pulled in. Two deputies Lynda recognized came to the door. They took all the information and determined there was no real danger, noting that the boys were probably just out playing. "Mrs. Cruz, we will check back with you later. Please call if they return home."

The deputies left and sat in their car filling out the report. One, fairly new to the department, said, "I'm looking at the history of this house. Someone's been called out here like 35 times in the last four years."

"Yeah, it's crazy over here. This woman's sons are out of control."

"Well, is there something we should do?"

"What can we do? It's all just juvenile nonsense. No real laws are being broken."

"Well, that sucks. I feel sorry for this lady."

"Yeah, me too. But what are we gonna do?"

Chapter 51

April 21, 2013
Lynda Cruz Home, Parkland Florida

THE FOLLOWING MORNING Lynda woke on the couch in the living room. She had been up most of the night waiting for the boys to return but had fallen asleep in the early hours of the morning. She immediately went upstairs and looked in their rooms. They were both asleep, and Lynda noticed Nikolas window was ajar again. She imagined they had snuck back in the same way they went out, and thought, *At least, they are safe.*

She went downstairs and saw her note from the previous day, the one about the medicine, and she realized she had to put her foot down with them. She waited for them to get up, then said, "Boys where were you last night?"

Zachary answered, "We were out. What do you care?"

"The Sheriff's Deputies were here."

Nikolas said, "Oh, why the hell did you call the sheriff?"

"Watch your language, Nikolas."

"I'm sick of this!!" he screamed, holding his head, walking back upstairs. Lynda followed him, "Listen here Nikolas, I am going grocery shopping, and neither of you are allowed to turn on the TV or anything else until you take your medicine!"

"Shut up, mom! Shut UP!"

She turned around to look at Zachary, "That goes for you too, Zachary! You take that medicine; do you hear me?"

"Yeah, right mom!"

Lynda grabbed her purse and stormed out.

Chapter 52

April 21, 2013
Lynda Cruz Home, Parkland Florida

AN HOUR LATER LYNDA PULLED IN the drive. She opened the trunk and grabbed the few bags of groceries. When she opened the door, she heard the blaring noise of the Xbox. Nikolas and Zachary were sitting on the couch playing a game. Lynda stormed over to the medicine holders on the counter. They had been knocked on the floor, and the pills were scattered all over the kitchen floor. She marched over to the TV, slammed the power button, and stared at them with her arms folded.

"What the fuck!" said Zachary, as he got up, threw down the controller, and stormed off to his room.

Nikolas did not move, he only glared at her, as rage started to build in his mind. He slowly got up, walked right up to her, and violently shoved her backward.

Lynda screamed and fell into the wall, hitting her head hard.

Nikolas then grabbed the vacuum hose sitting nearby and smacked her over the head.

Lynda covered her head, screaming, now crying out, as Zachary ran down, yelling, "Stop it you asshole!"

Nikolas walked away as Lynda frantically pulled out her cell phone and dialed 911.

Within minutes the sirens could be heard, and moments later two deputies came in through the front door without knocking. They hustled back to the kitchen and saw Lynda laying next to the TV against the wall crying and holding her head.

"Who did this to you, Mrs. Cruz?"

"My son Nikolas."

"Where is he?"

She pointed, "Upstairs!"

One deputy ran upstairs while the other attended to Lynda. In a few minutes, the deputy came downstairs holding Nikolas by the shoulder. Behind them walked Zachary.

"You want to tell us what happened, Mrs. Cruz."

She began to weep, then said, "He pushed, and hit me with the…"

The deputy spun Nikolas around and reached for his handcuffs.

"No, no, no!" cried Lynda, getting up immediately. "No, I am not going to file a report!"

"Mrs. Cruz, I strongly suggest you do. Otherwise, our hands our tied."

"No, he's… he just forgot to take his medicine."

The other detective went to the car and brought in a file. He opened it, "Mrs. Cruz, after last night, I did some digging. Just in the past year, we have been called out here for: A complaint that Nikolas killed squirrels with a pellet gun. A complaint that he stole neighbors' mail. A complaint that he tried to get his dog to attack someone's pet piglets, and that man died of a heart attack. You also told us on several occasions that both boys pick fights with other kids constantly, and that Nikolas bit one kid's ear. There is another complaint, by another neighbor, that he threw rocks and coconuts, breaking two of her windows."

He looked up, with an upset look on his face, then continued, "Another neighbor, said he was lurking at late hours along the drainage ditches that run behind the backyards of every house on this block. Another neighbor complained that she caught him peeking into her bedroom window."

He paused and looked at Nikolas, who had a half smile on his face as if he were proud of his accomplishments. "Mrs. Cruz, I am afraid we have to report this to social services. We have looked the other way for far too long."

The deputy had Lynda sign the waiver form and gave her notice of their referral to Social Services. "Expect a phone call, Mrs. Cruz, and be careful."

Chapter 53

February 13, 2014
Westglades Middle School – Coral Springs, FL
Ten months later

ON THE DAY BEFORE VALENTINE'S DAY, Lynda arrived at the school counseling offices at Westglades Middle School in Coral Springs. Nikolas had been there for a year and a half, and now, at the age of 15, he was finally going through the 8th grade. "Mrs. Cruz, hello my name is Todd Carson, I am one of the counselors here. Please come with me."

Once they arrived at his office. He sat behind his desk and motioned for her to sit on the other side. "Mrs. Cruz, I need to speak to you about Nikolas. He is very abusive toward other students as well as his teachers. Some of them have raised concerns about their safety." He pulled a piece of paper from the file and slid it to her. It was an email to him from Nikolas' language arts teacher. The key sentence was highlighted. "I feel strongly that Nikolas is a danger to the students and faculty at this school. I do not feel that he understands the difference between his violent video games and reality."

Lynda read it and put it back down in disgust. She looked out the window and suddenly began to cry. "I don't understand why he is like this. Nothing I do is working." She turned to him, "He misses his father. I know that's what it is. It's been ten years now." She lowered her head, with more tears flowing, then collected herself. "I'm sorry, it's just so hard."

"Mrs. Cruz, Nikolas is being transferred to Cross Creek. It is a special school that has programs for emotionally and behaviorally disturbed children."

"He will hate that."

"I am sorry, but it is not up for discussion. The principal has made his decision after consulting with Nikolas' teachers. I am going to call him down now so he can be informed. He begins Monday."

When Nikolas was told the news, he went ballistic. He jumped up and pounded his fist into the wall. "Nikolas!" screamed Lynda, "Stop that!"

"I don't want to go there. It's for dumb kids!"

Mr. Carson waited until he calmed down. "Nikolas, you begin Monday. If you do well there, you will have a chance to come back to the main school, and by then that will be Stoneman Douglas."

~ ~ ~ ~

That night, Nikolas laid in bed wide awake staring at the ceiling. He had no friends, and now he was being thrust into a new school full of people who did not know him. He sat up in the dark and started screaming in his mind, but without allowing any noise to come from his mouth. "I hate myself! I hate myself! I hate my fucking self! I hate myself!" He then gritted his teeth and punched himself in the cheek. He then punched himself in the other cheek. He kept going, alternating fists, punching his own face as hard as he could. Suddenly Lynda opened the door. She had heard him, and when she opened the door, she saw him. She ran to his side stopping him, holding him next to her, as he repeated in a trance-like voice several times, "I hate myself."

Chapter 54

June 6, 2014
Lynda Cruz Home, Parkland Florida
Four months later

IT WAS 3:00 PM ON A SATURDAY afternoon, and Nikolas sat at the computer in his room looking at pornographic websites. It was his new favorite pastime. Zachary was downstairs playing a game on the Xbox, and Lynda was at the store. Nikolas heard the familiar voice in his head. "They hate you, Nikolas, they all hate you."

Nikolas began to feel afraid, scared because he knew the voice was right. Everyone in the entire neighborhood did hate him. He had no friends, and he had no girl-friends, even though many other boys his age did, some of them even going all the way with them. It seemed like something that would never happen for Nikolas, and it angered him.

He got up and went downstairs and out to the back yard to retrieve his dogs. He was about to unleash them when he remembered the Pape's daughter's new rabbit. He left the dogs, went back up to his room, and got his pellet gun. As he was coming down, Zachary asked, "where the hell are you going?"

"None of your fucking business!"

"Fuck you."

Nikolas raised the pellet gun, "Say that again and I'll blow your head off."

Zachary picked up an ashtray and pretended he was going to throw it, and Nikolas quickly left. He went down the street and cut through Mrs. Begani's yard heading toward the Papes. Nikolas had an eye for the Pape's daughter, Cindy. She was two years younger, but he thought she was beautiful, initially. That was before she and her friends made fun of him when he was over Brody's house with Zachary. Now she was on his enemy list.

He circled around the back to the woods that bordered all the homes and hid behind some trees. Both of the Papes' cars were gone. He carefully watched the house. There was no movement. The doors too were all closed.

Nikolas moved closer until he could see the rabbit cage set up next to the garage. He crept into the backyard, careful to stay on the side near the bushes between Brody's house and the Papes. When he reached the cages, he peered inside. There was not one, but two rabbits. He smiled, he had only heard about one.

"Hey, you little beast, what should I do with you? Should I hurt you?" The voice in his head urged him on, "Yes, Nikolas, yes, hurt it, kill it."

Nikolas opened the latch to the cage door, then opened it. He put his hands on the fur of its back, as if he were going to pick it up, but then let his hand drop lower around its neck. He squeezed, slowly tightening his grip. The other rabbit began jumping wildly around the cage while Nikolas held the other one firmly.

Wham! Nikolas went flying. It was Scott Papes.

The rabbit cage fell over, and in a moment, Scott was on top of Nikolas wailing on him. Nikolas kicked him off and ran back into the woods, racing now back into Brody's yard. But Scott was too fast for him. He leaped onto Nikolas back, tackling him. He turned Nikolas over and began punching his face.

Nikolas frantically tried to push him away, but he couldn't. Finally, Nikolas heard Mrs. Brody screaming, and she pushed Scott off him.

"What are you boys doing?" she screamed.

"He tried to kill Cindy's rabbit."

"No, I didn't," sniveled Nikolas, crying, shaking at being so badly beaten, "I was... was just petting it."

"Bullshit!" cried Scott.

"Go home Scott!" said Mrs. Brody. She helped Nikolas up and took him inside wiping the blood off his face. When she was sure Scott was gone, she sent him home.

Nikolas went home and straight to his room. He cried most of the night because he felt so utterly alone. All that mattered to him was that he was hated, and now things would only get worse, and he dreaded what Cindy Papes and her friends would say the next time they saw him.

Chapter 55

July 23, 2014
Bamboo Tree Bar, Pompano Beach, Florida
Six weeks later

IT WAS AN UNUSUALLY COLD summer night in Florida. Brenda Woodley sat at her familiar place at her favorite bar in Pompano Beach. She was old now, but she clung to the memory of the night she had encountered the Angel from Heaven. On numerous nights, when she had too much to drink, she had shared her story with whomever would listen. No one believed her, of course, but Brenda needed this story, and she needed to remember because it was just about all she had going for her. Addictions had plagued her life, and she was tired and afraid that death would come soon.

Then she saw him. A middle-aged man with black hair, sprinkled with gray, was standing at the other end of the bar, looking at her. He looked away, trying not to be noticed. Brenda kept drinking and periodically glanced over at him. At one point the bartender said aloud, "Brenda, are you ready for another one?"

"No, I'm good now, Charlie."

Within moments the stranger came over, "Excuse me, are you Brenda Woodley?"

"Who is asking?"

"My name is Ricardo. I am a friend of Roger and Lynda Cruz."

Brenda looked down at the bar, set her drink down, and looked up at him, "What do they want?"

"Can we grab a booth and talk?"

Brenda looked behind her at the sparsely filled bar. "Sure."

They walked over to one of the booths against the side wall and sat down. Fr. Ricardo asked, "Can I get you something to drink?"

"Sure," Brenda said, smiling.

Fr. Ricardo raised his hand and got the attention of the bartender, "Can I have two coffees over here please?"

Brenda reached out her hand and touched his arm, "Make mine a screwdriver, Ricardo."

He half smiled, "Uhh… make that one coffee and one screwdriver." He turned to her and got right down to business. "Brenda, I am a priest. My name is Fr. Ricardo; I was there at the hospital long ago when your son was born and was given for adoption to Mr. & Mrs. Cruz. Do you remember me?"

Brenda began nodding, "Oh, yes, I do remember you."

"Can you tell me about the boy's father?"

"He as an Angel from Heaven. I met him right here in this bar." She pointed, "He was standing right over there." She paused, and Fr. Ricardo nodded, signaling she should go on. "We went for a walk, and somehow he wrapped his vast wings around me and well, the rest is history I guess."

"Did he ever mention a Dark Baptism?"

"No, but another Angel did?"

"Another Angel visited you?"

"Yes, her name was Tira. She said I was highly favored among women, and I needed to give her permission to let Nikolas have the Dark Baptism to protect us. She was right, Father. Someone tried to kill me that night in the hospital."

Fr. Ricardo remembered her being smothered, but why?

"You say her name was Tira?"

"Yes, Tira." She looked down, somewhat embarrassed, "How are… my boys?"

"They are doing all right, Brenda. How are you doing?"

"Not so good, Father, to be honest."

He asked, "May I give you some money, to help out?"

"Sure."

He handed her an envelope from his jacket. She opened it, and her eyes widened, "There's a lot of money in here. I don't..." she started to tear up and looked toward the wall.

"It's ok; I know you need it. There is $2,000." He paused, then asked, "Can I give you a blessing?"

Brenda wiped her eyes, "Yes."

He pulled out his holy water vile, sprinkled her, and made the Sign of the Cross over her. "It is nice to have met you, Brenda. Take care of yourself."

"I will. Thank you, Father."

Chapter 56

December 19, 2014
Lefty's Bar & Grill, Parkland Florida
Five months later

DEPUTY SCOTT PETERSON, the Resource Officer at Marjory Stoneman Douglas High School, was the first to arrive at Lefty's Bar and Grill. He had organized the gathering in appreciation of some of his fellow deputies in the Broward County Sheriff's Department.

"Hi Lefty, are you ready for us?"

"I sure am, Scott. Just to confirm, you've got seven other people coming, right?"

"Make it eight. Deputy Fugate decided to join us."

"No kidding! I haven't seen Bob Fugate in a few years."

"Well, you'll see him tonight."

"All right, Scott. Go on back. We've got the back party room all set up."

"Thanks, Lefty. I'll settle the tab once everyone orders dinner. They're on their own after that."

"Got it."

Peterson went back to the small party room they had set up for his annual Christmas dinner. It had nothing to do with Christmas, other than he did it right after school ended for Christmas break each year. There was a large round table set with a nice blue table cloth, and Christmas colored plates and napkins. In the center of the table were a few bottles of wine, already opened, ready to be poured as soon as everyone arrived.

First in was Deputy Arthur Perry, the newly appointed School Resource Officer at nearby Park Trails Elementary School. No one doubted he had the most cushy job of all who would be attending. He had a master' degree in criminal justice and was considered a neat freak.

Next in was Deputy Bob Fugate. He was a big mouth and not liked by more than a few deputies who would be attending.

Deputy Michael Kratz walked in behind him, followed within moments by Deputy Brian Goolsby. Long ago, Goolsby had won a marksmanship badge in the Army, and he frequently bragged about this fact, considering himself a kind of badass because of his Army days.

A few minutes later, Deputies Brian Miller and Edward Eason arrived. They had driven over together right from work.

Deputy Joshua Stambaugh then walked in, and when he saw Deputy Fugate, he stopped, "Bob Fugate, what the hell are you doing here?"

"Hey, Merry Christmas to you too, asshole."

Stambaugh began laughing loudly as he walked over and grabbed Fugate by the shoulders, "It's good to see you, Bob. Where the hell have you been?"

"I've been doing mostly street patrol on 3rd shift. That's probably why we haven't seen each other."

"Well it's good to see you."

Last in was Deputy Richard Seward. "Scotty!" he yelled at the entrance to the party room.

"Come on in, Seward. You're the last one, so you can close the door behind you."

All nine men gathered in the makeshift bar Lefty had set up for them in the corner. After a half hour of talking and having a few drinks, they sat down to eat. Scott Peterson called everyone to attention, "Before we eat, it's time for our annual "who got the 'mostest' award. Does everyone have their final pay stubs?"

All nodded.

Peterson asked, "Who's going to start us off this year?"

"I will," said Seward, "because this year, I win!" Seward unfolded his stub, "$152,023, even."

"Oh, bullshit!" said Peterson.

"It's right here!" He leaned over and handed his stub to Peterson.

"I'll be damned!" said Peterson. "All right, keep going guys, food's getting cold."

Eason said, "I got only $118,431, but I'm happy."

Goolsby said, "I got $108,030, but keep in mind, I was on leave for seven weeks."

"Who gives a damn about your leave?" said Fugate.

Everyone laughed, and Peterson said, "Keep going."

Next was Kratz, "$123,362; I'll take it."

Perry said, "$99,677."

Peterson then said, "$119,666."

Fugate said, "Watch that number, Peterson! It's a devil number."

"Screw you! What do you got Fugate?"

"I got $139,435, and I worked my ass off for it."

Peterson glanced down at his paper he was writing the amounts onto and said, "Hold it, that's only eight." He looked down and back up, "Stambaugh, what's your number."

Stambaugh smiled widely and slowly unfolded his final pay stub for the year. "152,857." He turned his stub around and passed it around the table.

"Well, I guess Stambaugh wins."

Fugate raised his glass high, "Here is to the taxpayers in Broward County, may you prosper, and keep paying your taxes!" He paused, and stood up, "Because it keeps me fat, dumb, and happy!"

Everyone laughed. Seward stood up, with his belly hanging out, "Hell Fugate, you can't even catch me in a damn race!" Seward often complained about the rigors of his cushy job, though they were not rigorous.

Fugate said, "All I know is I'm retiring in a few short years. And do you all know what my motto about retirement is?"

Everyone waited, and Fugate proudly said, "Fake it till you make it!"

Everyone howled.

Chapter 57

February 5, 2015
Washington DC
Two months later

ROBERT RUNCIE AND HIS FOUR ADVISORS walked up the broad sidewalk toward the Department of Education building in Washington DC. They were there by special invitation to tout the successes of the PROMISE program. The program was delivering on its promise to lower arrests though nothing was changing inside the schools. Students were misbehaving at the same rate they had always misbehaved. The only difference was that law enforcement was no longer being summoned. Kids were being sent to the office and sent to counseling or suspended.

During the day-long conference with leading districts invited by Arne Duncan, Runcie's PROMISE program was showcased as a model of success worthy of replication throughout the country.

As Runcie listened to how they had reduced student arrests by 70%, as well as drastically reduced repeat offenders, he knew the numbers did not tell the whole story. The bar had been lowered, and in addition, the program erased a student's record at the start of each year, making it difficult to become a repeat offender. But Runcie truly believed, like Secretary Duncan, that keeping these kids records clean, and giving them access to counseling and mentoring, would give them the best chance to succeed.

Despite all the praise from above, some of Runcie's chiefs were hearing complaints from the teachers, that they were losing control of classrooms. Students knew they could get away with a more than they used to. It was the underbelly of the program no one wanted to talk about because Washington was watching.

That night at dinner Julie Evans, Runcie's favorite advisor, got a call from one of her direct reports. "What? Are you kidding me? How much?" she listened for a few moments. "That's not going to fly. It's too much."

She hung up, and Runcie asked, "Who was that?"

"It was Danny DiRuggiero. He said the proposal to put metal detectors in all the schools is coming in at 26 million."

Runcie shook his head, "We don't have that much money for metal detectors. Tell him to get more quotes."

Stan chimed in, "Well if we don't spend the money on security, we will be in default of our promises to the public. Just let some incident happen where some kid gets hurt, and we will have a lawsuit knocking at our door."

"Thank you for stating the obvious Stan," said Bob. "Julie, call him back and tell him to keep getting quotes."

Chapter 58

Jun 15, 2015
Trump Tower, New York, New York

ROGER STONE SAT in the lobby outside the office of his long-time friend, real estate mogul Donald Trump, when his phone rang.

"Hello?"

"Roger, this is Scott Israel. How are you doing?"

"I'm doing well Scott. How about yourself?"

"Just fine, but I have to get ready for another election. Will you and your crew be able to help me get elected again?"

Stone smiled widely, "I'm afraid not, Scott. Don't take it personally, but I have something far more important to do."

"Oh yea, what is that?"

"Well, I can't say right now. But turn on your TV tomorrow around noon. There is going to be a press conference."

"About what?"

"Let's just say, presidential politics."

"Really, well that sounds exciting."

"It is Scott. I can't say anything more, other than, it's going to be a wild ride and something I could have only dreamed about."

"Well, no problem, Roger. Hey, is your guy a Democrat, or a Republican?"

"Can't say, Scott, got to go."

Roger hung up, just as a secretary came out. "He is ready to see you now, Roger."

Chapter 59

August 29, 2015
Brandon Phillips Home–Coral Springs Florida

BRANDON SAT IN HIS ROOM thinking about what his mom might say, and worse, what his dad would say. The senior student who had given a talk in class was so brave, not worrying about what others thought, but staying true to who he knew he was. Brandon admired this, and he was tired of hiding and pretending to be who he was not.

He got up, went downstairs, and peaked around the corner into the family room. His mom was reclining on the couch watching 'Dancing with the Stars.' He started in, then stopped and went back upstairs. He could not muster the courage. *You must do this. Remember what the kid at school said. 'It's better, to be honest at as young of an age as you can.'*

He looked up at the clock. In ten minutes, the show would be over, and it would be a better time to get her attention. He waited, then went back down again.

"Mom, can I talk to you?"

Megan Phillips had been divorced for almost six years now, ever since Brandon was nine. She had thought about dating but had instead focused her attention on raising him. "Sure, honey, what is it?"

She sat up on the couch making room for him to sit down.

Brandon took a deep breath, "Mom, um mm... I am gay."

"You're what..." she stopped, as her heart began racing through an enormous range of emotions. "You're gay? How... how... are you sure?"

Brandon half smiled, "I am sure."

"Well, whew… come here." She pulled him close to her hugging him against her chest, staring off into the distance, not letting him see the growing worried look on her face. Megan was not against anyone who was like that, but she never imagined it would be her son. Concern after concern raced through her mind, but then she stopped. Her first duty was to Brandon. "Brandon, I am glad you told me. It's ok. We will get through this together."

"There is nothing to get through mom. It's just the way it is. I heard a speaker at school today who told us his story. He said most parents won't get it."

"At school? What do you mean?"

"One of the seniors gave a talk in class of how he found the courage to tell his family and friends that he was gay. He was really brave." Megan wanted to scream. She was outraged her son would be listening to something like that at school. But she could not do that to her son, not now, at this important moment in his life.

"Brandon, I love you, and it doesn't matter to me if… if you are gay." Just saying the words crushed her, but she held him closer trying to hide her moistening eyes. She knew very little about any of this, but she remembered she had a cousin who was gay, and his life had been very difficult.

"Mom, I don't want to hide anymore. I am going to join a group at school."

"What group?"

"The Gay-Straight Alliance."

Everything was moving way too fast for Megan to fathom. People didn't talk about things like this in her day. She quickly thought of her high school best friend Jody who had confided to her that she might be a lesbian when they were 16. Megan had promised to keep her secret. Two years later Jody met a boy, and that was the last Megan ever heard of their secret.

Megan was very uncomfortable realizing the schools were encouraging kids in matters like this. Their job was to teach. "Brandon are you sure you want to join now. Maybe you should give it some time?"

"I am sure, mom. I... I am tired of hiding."

"Oh, Brandon... oh, Brandon." She held him for a few long quiet minutes, grateful he had told her. She got up. "Hey, lets you and I go out and get some pizza."

"What about dad? How am I going to tell him?"

Megan let out a long sigh, "I think you should let me tell him. Give me a little time. I need just to think how to tell him. But it will be fine. Don't worry."

Brandon nodded. He knew she was right.

Chapter 60

September 1, 2015
Little Havana Bar & Grill, Coral Springs, Florida

DEPUTY PETERSON PULLED UP in his patrol car and parked outside the Little Havana Bar and Grill. He was meeting a few of his fellow deputies for lunch to discuss their recent evaluations. As he walked toward the restaurant, he could see Deputies Eason, Perry, and Seward, already seated, looking over menus. Peterson was relieved to see they had a table in the back, and that it was not crowded. They would be able to talk more freely, and they needed to; they were all angry.

Peterson walked up to the table, "Well, I guess I will be ordering a salad, cause according to my evaluation, I need to lose some weight!" He put his hands on his round stomach and laughed.

"Welcome to the Club, Peterson!" said Seward, "I got the same bullshit thrown at me. Like I've got to be in shape to be a school resource officer. It's a bunch of bullshit! I'll tell you what I'm going to do. I'm going to retire, and they can have their younger, faster, stronger, and DUMBER new deputies!"

Eason laughed, "You're hilarious, Seward... and I like your plan."

Seward asked, "What did they say to you, Eason?"

"I brought a copy so that I could remember the exact words. Oh, gentlemen, let me tell you, they were inspiring. Here it is. 'Deputy Eason has displayed deficiencies in the areas of work performance, customer service, critical decision making, planning, and organizing, as well as following policies and procedures.'" He put down the paper, "What kind of crap is that!"

Perry laughed, "Well guys, I guess you just gotta know what the boss is looking for. Let me demonstrate my point." He pulled out his evaluation, smiled, and said, "Deputy Perry's uniforms are always clean… and the trunk of his car is organized very neatly." He looked up smiling, then looked down again, "and… Deputy Perry even takes his own time to wash and wax his car by hand."

He put his hand in the air to signal the waitress, "You see guys, you just need to know how to handle your boss."

"Hell, Perry," said Eason, "It sounds like you just gave the guy a blow job!"

Seward and Peterson burst out laughing, while Perry swiped the menu to crack Eason on the head, but missed, and then they all burst out laughing.

"One thing they did say," said Perry. "They wanted me to get my stupid active shooter training done."

"Oh yea," said Peterson, "They've been after me on that for a couple of damn years now. What the hell are we supposed to do in a situation like that? Run in, guns blazing, on a damn suicide mission."

"No," said Perry, "Israel's got our backs on that one. His policy, or the one he kept in place, says we 'may' engage a shooter. It doesn't say we must. It's up to us, and frankly, I like that. Leave the decision to the man closest to the action. It's good management policy if you ask me."

"Good management policy or not," said Peterson, "I heard the training course is a big waste of time."

"I heard that too," said Perry.

Then Seward interrupted them, "Speaking of bosses, do you know I just heard that those assholes that Israel hired are making almost $200,000 each? He hired five of them, all newly created positions, costing my 'available raise money fund' over a million dollars a year."

"What?" asked Peterson, "How do I get some of that money?"

"Who are you talking about," asked Perry in an angry tone.

Seward replied, "Kinsey, Dale, Adderly, Harrington, and Pusins, they are called the FOI."

"What the hell is FOI?" asked Peterson.

"Friends of Israel," said Seward, "And it's well over 200k each when you add in benefits. These guys are worthless if you ask me."

Peterson said, "Isn't that the way things always are? The big wigs do nothing and get all the money, while us peons do all the work, and struggle to make ends meet. Well... I guess we do ok... but still, we are the ones out here on the front lines facing danger every day... even if some of us are just school resource officers."

Eason chimed in, "It's the same damn thing at the school board. Runcie's got so many damn chiefs down there, all making well over 200k when you add in benefits. There's more of them than you can count, and if you're one of the lower paid chiefs, yes, that's right, they even have lower paid chiefs, a whole giant level of them, you only are making about 150k with benefits. That money should be going to us. Now, with this stupid PROMISE program, they want school resource officers to start taking care of all their problems, instead of calling in the department. We're supposed to work with the counselors to keep everything nice and neat and swept under the rug. I'll tell you, here and now, it's not gonna work!"

Peterson replied, "I tell you something else, things are so damn far gone in this damn county, they will never get better. Give me a few more years to pad my pension, and I am out of here."

"Sounds like a good idea," said Seward.

Chapter 61

September 4, 2015
Parkridge Church—Pompano Beach, Florida

SKYLAR DUNBAR STOOD ALONE at the side lectern strumming the last part of the closing song at her Church service. Before her, a congregation of over 300 people heartily sang along. When the song was over, she took off her guitar and put it into her case, then looked for her parents.

Her mom found her first, "You played wonderfully today, Skylar."

"Thanks, mom."

As they made their way out the front door, Pastor Eddie was there greeting everyone. "George, Mary, you've got a special young lady here."

"Yes, we do. Thank you, Pastor," said George Dunbar. Skylar was their only child, and George could not be any prouder of her. She was starting her sophomore year and was a straight-A student. But the thing he liked most about his daughter was her quiet spirit. Like her mom, Skylar possessed a natural gentleness about her, and George just knew she was going to be a great person in the world.

As they were nearing their car, one of Skylar's friends came up to them. "Hey, Skylar."

"Hi, Cody."

"Are you going to First Priority tomorrow?" First Priority was one of the clubs at Stoneman Douglas High School. It was a Christian group whose purpose was to bring the light of Christ into the schools. There were only about twenty kids who attended meetings regularly, but Skylar liked them all, and she looked forward to attending the weekly meeting. She replied, "Yes I am going. Are you?"

"Yeah, I will see you there. I might bring a friend."

"Ok, see you later."

Chapter 62

September 17, 2015
Stoneman Douglas High School

NIKOLAS LOOKED OVER his shoulder and then back down the other direction of the hall as the student before him examined the large pocket knife. "How old is it?"

"I got it two weeks ago. Look do you want it or not? I've got to go."

"I'll give you $10 bucks."

"$15 is as low as I will go."

"It ever been used?"

"Just once. I killed a rabbit with it."

"Gross, all right, I'll take it."

Suddenly Mr. Jenkins stepped in. Nikolas had taken his eye off the hall behind him for too long. "What the hell is going on here."

Nikolas tried to close the small lunch container he kept his knives in, but Mr. Jenkins grabbed it. "Give me my fucking bag!" screamed Nikolas.

Mr. Jenkins pulled it away and grabbed Nikolas by the sleeve, "Come with me, now!"

Nikolas was hauled to the principal's office and given two detentions and ordered to see a school counselor.

Two days later, he was sitting before a Maurice O'Grady, a school counselor at Stoneman Douglas. Though Nikolas was still a student at Cross Creek, but this semester, he was allowed to attend 2 classes a day at Stoneman as a way of seeing if he could make the transition back to the regular high school.

Today, by coincidence, his Dark Angel Tira was also checking on him, so she went along. Nikolas sat at the desk in front of him and put his hands on his lap. Knowing that Mr. O'Grady could not see his hands, he extended his middle finger, in a perpetual popping of the bird.

O'Grady looked at his file, "Nikolas, I see you have had a lot of suspensions over the last few years. I have to warn you, if this behavior continues, you will have to leave Stoneman and only attend Cross Creek for the rest of high school."

"I hate that fucking school!"

"Well that doesn't matter. You may have to anyway." O'Grady was surprised at his brashness. It was as if he had no remorse.

"Nikolas, we found small amounts of marijuana in your bag. Why are you smoking marijuana?"

The Dark Angel Tira smiled, and whispered into his mind, "Tell him why Nikolas."

Nikolas grinned, "Because there is a demon in my head. It tells me to do bad things, but… I don't want to do bad things, and when I get high, the demon shuts up."

O'Grady did not know how to react. It was one of the most unusual responses he had ever heard, and he did not know if Nikolas was indeed crazy, or just putting him on. "A demon? Really?"

"Yeah, an ugly fucking female demon."

"You've seen this demon?"

"When I was little, I did a lot. Now, I just hear her."

O'Grady could not believe how far down the rabbit hole he had gotten. "All right, Nikolas, you have been warned. Keep up with all of this behavior, and you will be leaving Stoneman Douglas and back at Cross Creek full time for good."

"Oh, I understand," Nikolas said, now extending his other middle finger.

"One more thing, Nikolas."

"Yes?"

"You can put your fingers down now."

Nikolas face grew sullen, but then he raised his eyes, smiled, and left.

Chapter 63

September 22, 2015
Stoneman Douglas High School

DEPUTY PETERSON picked up the phone and dialed the number of Deputy Stambaugh who had worked at the same school Nikolas Cruz attended before coming to Stoneman Douglas. "Stams, this is Peterson. I got a question about some kid named, uh, let's see here... Nikolas Cruz."

"Oh yeah, he's a piece of work."

"Can we talk about him now?"

"Sure, I'm driving."

"Well, I got this report from his counselor that says they are worried about his explosive tendencies? What do they mean by that?"

"You know those school counselors; they sit around all day talking to kids and typing up reports that never amount to anything. Everything is a big deal to them; it's how they justify their jobs."

"Yeah, I get it, but what about this kid?"

"The kid is a punk, and he's a little runt of a punk. You know what I think. I think we should get Miller or Goolsby to have a 'talk' with him. That will straighten him out real fast."

"Yes, they have a way with words."

They both laughed.

"Do I have to worry about this kid?"

"I don't think anything more than normal. He's a punk, comes from a broken home. From what I hear, his brother is not much different. He's a few years younger."

"All right, what are you doing the rest of the day?"

"Not much today," said Stambaugh, "But tomorrow I have my session of 'active shooter training.'

Peterson said, "Hey, you know what Goolsby said we need to do in an active shooter situation?"

"What?"

Peterson chuckled, "Bring in an Army marksman like him and blow his head off. He calls it the 'one-shot' method."

"Yeah, that's funny. That would take care of that, wouldn't it?"

"All right, thanks for the update, I'll catch you later."

Chapter 64

September 26, 2015
Stoneman Douglas High School

THE CAFETERIA WAS BUSTLING with the noise only a group of hundreds of high school kids could make. Skylar Dunbar sat at the table with her friend Randi eating some breakfast. Their friend Cody walked up along with someone. "Hey girls, this is my friend Parker." They all said 'Hi', as Cody and Parker sat down. They were talking some when Randi asked, "Who is that kid?"

They all looked over. Cody said, "That's Nikolas Cruz. I went to middle school with him. He's bad news."

"Why do you say that?" asked Skylar.

"He is psycho in about every way. He loves shooting like squirrels and birds and stuff. He's weird."

"Watch this," said Parker. Parker got up and walked over and bumped into Nikolas intentionally, "Oh, I'm sorry."

Nikolas turned and glared at him as all of them watched.

Parker shrugged his shoulders and looked over at them, laughing. Nikolas too looked over at them all, and Skylar felt as if he had just stared into her soul.

"He looks scary," said Randi.

Skylar said, "Cody, tell your friend to leave us out of his antics. That was wrong."

She got up, and walked away, glancing over her shoulder, only to see that Nikolas was watching her.

Chapter 65

October 22, 2015

Bamboo Tree Bar, Pompano Beach, Florida

FATHER RICARDO SAT IN THE BACK of the cab driving from the airport to Benedictine Abbey in Cleveland, Ohio. He was thinking about how long every step had taken, and he knew dark forces were at work. After finding Brenda, and learning of the circumstances of the Dark Baptism, he wrote to the only person who might know the matter, his old friend, Father Guardi, curator of the Vatican Archives

Fr. Guardi was a very old priest, and it took him a long time to write back. In his letter, he said he had checked all his sources and found there was only one priest who possibly understood the subject matter. His name was Abbot Clement.

Fr. Ricardo arrived and walked into the office attached to the church. He was escorted into a large room filled with pictures of saints. A few moments later, a side door opened and an old monk walking with a cane hobbled out. "Hello, I am Clement."

"Hello, Abbot Clement. I am Father Ricardo. I am a member of the Order of the Protectors of the Cross."

Clement nodded, "I am familiar with the order. Come with me; we will talk in my room."

They walked down the long ancient looking corridor until they reached the modest room. Clement motioned for him to sit and sat across from him. "What can I do for you?"

"Abbot Clement, have you ever heard of the Dark Baptism?" Father Ricardo watched the old Abbot's mind turning; he knew something.

"No, I have not."

"Are you sure?"

"Yes, of course, I am. Why do you ask?"

Father Ricardo shook his head, "I guess it does not matter."

Abbot Clement asked, "Is there anything else?"

"No," said Father Ricardo, sighing. He knew the old Abbot was not being forthright. But there was nothing he could do. As he was walking out, he saw a picture with light shining down from Heaven. Underneath the inscription said, "What is hidden must not remain hidden."

He stopped, and turned, "Abbot Clement, perhaps you should follow this motto.

"What motto?"

"'What is hidden should not remain hidden.' I sense you are not telling me everything."

"Sit down for a moment please." Abbot Clement picked up the phone. "Doris would you come in?"

A minute later an elderly secretary came in, "Yes, Abbot?"

"Doris, what does it say on that picture?"

She looked at the picture of the light shining down. "What do you mean?"

"What words are written on the inscription?"

"There are none," she replied, looking confused.

"Thank you, Doris."

The secretary shrugged her shoulders and left.

Fr. Ricardo seemed puzzled. "I don't understand?"

Clement smiled, "You, Father Ricardo, are one of the prophets, just like I am. Only a prophet could have seen those words. Now, listen carefully. I will tell you everything."

Father Ricardo leaned forward, and Clement began. "When John the Baptist was beheaded by King Herod, his body and his head were given to his followers for burial. Herod placed the head in a bronze box. John's followers buried him, but they clipped some of his bloodied hair and kept it in the box.

They eventually learned that a single strand of this hair could exorcise any demon, and the early Christians used this. But it was eventually lost and forgotten until the box showed up at the Vatican hundreds of years ago. No one knew what it was, and it was stored deep in the bowels of the archives."

"How do you know all of this?"

"When I was a young priest, I spent two years in Rome and studied the archives. I knew of the box, but it was only a few years ago that I found out what it actually was."

"I don't understand? How?"

"John the Baptist was a member of the Essenes. Have you heard of the Dead Sea Scrolls?"

"Of course, they were..." Father Ricardo's eyes widened, "written by the Essenes."

"Yes, and I have been studying the scrolls online. They refer to the strands of hair from the Baptist and later mention the box. So far, to my knowledge, only I have understood what they were referring to."

"That is absolutely fascinating."

"Yes, but it is also all true. Go there, get one of the strands of hair with the Baptist's blood on it from the box. It will undo any effects of a Dark Baptism."

"Are you sure? How can they still be intact?"

"Miraculously, they are intact. The bronze box is in the room on the lower levels where unknown items are stored. Wait here. I still know the old archives curator and I will write to him asking if he will allow you to view the room."

"But I thought only scholars were allowed to view those rooms in the archives."

"I am not talking about those rooms. I am talking about a secret room."

Chapter 66

Jan 9, 2016
Mr. Cooney's Algebra Class, Stoneman Douglas HS

NIKOLAS NERVOUSLY WALKED down the crowded hallway towards Mr. Cooney's Beginner's Algebra class. It was his first class of the day in the new semester. He had just been given permission to leave Cross Creek and attend Stoneman Douglas full-time.

Despite the happiness he felt, he was nervous as hell. He could feel the pressure; he could feel the noise in his head; he wanted it to stop. When he walked into the classroom, it was already half-filled with kids turned in their desks, talking to each other, catching up on their life since leaving for winter break three weeks earlier. He went to an open seat about halfway back and began doodling in his notebook.

When he looked up, he saw a beautiful girl with medium length brown hair and hazel eyes walking down the aisle next to him. To his surprise, she sat next to him. Nikolas watched out of the corner of his eye as she took out her algebra book, along with a notebook and some pens. Then she turned to him and said, "Hi."

Nikolas smiled, "Hi."

"What's your name?" she asked.

"I'm Nikolas, what is yours?"

"I am Kaylee."

Nikolas was not sure what to say, so he asked, "What's your last name?"

She giggled, "It's Loftus."

"Great, my last name is Cruz."

"Well, it's nice to meet you, Nikolas Cruz."

"Thanks." Nikolas was trying to think of something else to say, but he could not.

Just then, Mr. Cooney, a tall, athletic man who was also a coach on the football team called the class to order. Throughout the class, Nikolas could do nothing but think about the girl he had just talked to. There was something about her smile that mesmerized him.

Chapter 67

February 9, 2016
Meeting of the Gay-Straight Alliance Club

MARILYN CULVERT, the teacher responsible for facilitating the Gay-Straight Alliance club at Stoneman Douglas, sat to the side of the room. Karen, one the students who was questioning her sexuality, stood in front of the group, talking about the struggles she was facing at home with her parents. Each week any of the students were allowed, and indeed encouraged, to talk about the difficulties they had, whether at home or school.

Marilyn herself was part of the LGBTQ community and knew first- hand how hard it could be, especially in a school where kids often made immature rash judgments.

Though years of progress and great strides had been made since President Obama was elected, still, there was an unspoken stigma on a person who professed to be anything other than straight.

When Karen had finished her talk, everyone applauded, and Marilyn stood to address the group of seventeen students in front of her. "Thank you, all, for sharing your stories. I'll see you all next week. If you need anything, you all know you can email me, and I will get back to you right away."

Brandon Phillips picked up his backpack and left. He walked alongside one of his friends, talking about nothing important. Just then the kids from the Christian group also entered the hall. As Brandon went down the steps, he looked up and saw his neighbor Parker walking down the next flight of steps staring at him.

Parker was a bully, and Brandon knew this, but he had managed to stay off his radar. He was surprised to see him with the Christian group, but he ignored him and looked away. At the next turn of the steps, he noticed Parker staring at him again, this time, Parker raised his eyebrows. Brandon looked away and kept moving.

He exited the door and walked out the front towards the front of the school then crossed the main street and began the long walk home. Suddenly he felt a violent jolt, "What the…"

"Hey, little gay boy. Was that you with all your faggot little friends!" It was Parker.

Brandon felt his heart racing. Parker was much bigger than he was. "Leave me alone, Parker."

"Why should I?"

"Just… just… leave me alone."

Parker gritted his teeth, stepped forward, and quickly put his leg around Brandon's legs and pushed him backward, sending him down hard. Brandon slammed his head on the sidewalk and started to wince.

"Take that, you little gay boy."

Brandon laid on the sidewalk, trying not to cry, as Parker walked away, kicking his backpack as he did.

~ ~ ~ ~

For the next three weeks, Brandon left his weekly meeting and went down the opposite stairwell. In this way, he managed to avoid Parker. But in the fourth week, Parker saw him. Brandon had about three blocks to go when Parker came riding down the street behind him on his bike. Brandon instantly began to run, as Parker raced up beside him, dismounting on the fly, and the chase was on. Brandon was indeed faster, and he was pulling away, but then he stumbled, and in a moment, Parker jumped on him and punched him in the back of the head twice. "Get the fuck off me!" screamed Brandon.

Just then someone came out of their house, "Get off him!"

Parker got up, ran back to get his bike, and took off. The woman helped Brandon up. Brandon looked at her with his red eyes, and said, "I'm ok. Thank you."

Brandon walked the remaining two blocks home, trying not to cry, but he was unbelievably upset. He thought about turning Parker in, but he feared it would only mean worse trouble. He was so deeply frustrated, he uttered a prayer, "God, please help me! Please help me!"

Chapter 68

Feb 14, 2016
Stoneman Douglas High School, Building 7

EVERY DAY SINCE HE HAD MET KAYLEE LOFTUS, Nikolas could do nothing but think about her. While he hated all his classes, the one class he could not wait to come to every day was Algebra. It was because of her smile and her voice. They soothed his mind like nothing else ever had.

But ever since the calendar turned to February, Nikolas began to feel the pressure mount. It meant Valentine's day was coming, and since he in his mind, he thought he was her boyfriend, he would be expected to buy her a gift.

He and Kaylee had never talked about being boyfriend and girlfriend, but Nikolas knew that it was their destiny. She was made for him; he was sure of it.

A week before Valentine's day he followed her at a distance from Algebra class and saw where her locker was. He was planning his big event, and he needed to be sure of every detail.

One thing he did not like. She seemed to be friends with a few of the kids from the school Christian club. There were other friends too, lots of them, as Kaylee was very popular. But the girls from the Christian group scared him. Nikolas didn't know why, but he hated them. He had no reason to hate them, but when he was near them, or when he saw them, his anger began to mount. Their names were Skylar and Randi.

On the morning of Valentine's day, Nikolas left home early and stopped at Walgreens. He waited for some kids from school to leave the store, then nervously walked to the aisle where they had Valentine's day items for sale. He scanned the store again to make sure no kids were inside, and quickly picked up a small heart-shaped box of chocolate. He paid for it and put it in his pocket.

During Algebra he thought of giving it to her, but he was afraid, so he decided to wait. Later that day she was in the hall of Building 7, putting some books in her locker. Nikolas watched from a distance, scared to death she would reject him. He felt for the box in his pocket and thought about turning away. But he gathered his courage and walked over.

"Kaylee?"

"Oh, hi Nikolas."

"Hey, I have something for you."

"Oh really," she said, smiling. "What is it?"

"This." He pulled the box out, and nervously handed it to her, almost dropping it. "Uh… Happy Valentine's Day."

"Oh, that's so sweet, thank you, Nikolas."

Kaylee reached over and hugged him. For Nikolas, his entire world just turned right side up. Kaylee was indeed his girlfriend. Out of the corner of his eye, he saw a group of five girls standing in a group about ten feet away. They were some of Kaylee's friends, and Randi was among them. They were giggling, watching Nikolas and Kaylee.

Nikolas felt his rage began to boil. He looked back at Kaylee and saw her smile at her friends and wave. Nikolas suddenly felt foolish, so while he had imagined having a long talk with her, perhaps even about how much they liked each other, instead he said, "I'll see you tomorrow."

"Thank you again, Nikolas. I like it."

Nikolas walked away in the other direction from the girls, but as he did, he heard them laughing.

Chapter 69

March 5, 2016
Broward County Sheriff's Department, Ft. Lauderdale

"SHERIFF'S DEPARTMENT, MAY I HELP YOU?"

"Hi, yes, I am a neighbor to a very disturbed boy named Nikolas Cruz. He posted on Instagram earlier today that he plans on shooting up the school."

"Hold for one moment ma'am."

"Hi, this is Deputy Eason. May I help you?"

"Yes, I am a neighbor of Nikolas Cruz. I just told the other lady that he posted on Instagram earlier today that he plans on shooting up the school. He put a picture of a gun there." She raised her voice, "I am telling you, this kid is nuts, he is like the devil incarnate!"

"Ma'am, please calm down. What school ma'am?"

"The High School, Stoneman Douglas."

"Thank you. Now, what is your name?"

"I can't give you my name. He will find out, and I will be on his list. No, I've told you what I saw, now please do something about it."

"Ma'am, kids do things for attention all the time."

The woman asked in a frustrated tone, "Did you even hear what I just said?"

"Ma'am, he has a First Amendment right to make the post on Instachat or whatever it is."

"Well can't you stop him from buying guns!"

"Ma'am, that is covered by the Second Amendment. If he is over eighteen. And I believe the Cruz kid is over 18." Eason was guessing, he had heard he was close to 18, but he didn't know for sure.

"What's wrong with you! Are you listening to me!"

"Ma'am, we are going… Ma'am? Ma'am?" He looked over at the deputy at the desk next to him, "She hung up!"

Deputy Eason looked at the phone for a moment. "Damn!" He hung up and called over to Stoneman Douglas. "Scott Peterson please."

"Hello, this is Scott Peterson, School Resource Officer for Marjory Stoneman Douglas High School in Parkland, Florida. Please leave your name, the time you called, and the reason for your call. I will get back to you as soon as I am able."

Eason shouted into the phone, "Goddammit, Peterson, can you put a shorter message on your phone! This is Eason. I've got a call from some lady about a Nikolas Cruz with some Instagram post or something, talking about shooting up a school. Get back to me as soon as you check it out." He slammed down the phone. "These goddam kids and their social media."

The deputy next to him asked, "What's that all about?"

"Ah, probably just some kid trying to get attention."

"What did he say?"

"He said he's going to shoot up a school. I'll just called Peterson over at his school. I'll wait to hear from him." Eason made a note on a yellow post-it and put it in his desk. "You ready for lunch?"

"Yeah, I am famished. Hey, why don't we take a ride over there after lunch and see what's going on?"

"All right, let's go."

Chapter 70

March 5, 2016
Broward County Sheriff's Department, Ft. Lauderdale

FOLLOWING LUNCH, EASON and the other deputy drove to Stoneman Douglas. They went to the principal's office and walked up to the long counter behind which sat what looked to be over twenty secretaries and other personnel. A woman got up from her desk and approached the counter, smiling, "May I help you?"

Eason said, "Yes, we need to speak to Principal Thompson."

The woman smiled, "Sure, what are your names?"

"I am Deputy Eason; this is Deputy Jones."

"And... may I ask what this is regarding."

"We have some kid on Instagram, or one of those sites, who talked about being a school shooter someday."

The woman's eyes widened some, "I see. I am going to get one of our assistant principals, Jeff Morford."

"Well, why not just go get Principal Thompson? He's the one we want to talk to." Eason was feeling the depths of the bureaucracy, and it was way worse than even at the sheriff's office.

The woman smiled, "He has Jeff handle things like this, it will just be a minute."

Eason looked at his partner, "That makes no sense."

A few minutes later a tall, athletic-looking man with gray sprinkled throughout his hair approached the counter. "Hello deputies, what can I help you with?"

Eason was growing impatient. "We need to pull Nikolas Cruz from class and go to his locker. We have a threat against the school."

"What is the threat?" asked Morford.

"You mean your secretary didn't tell you?"

"Gentlemen, first, she is not my secretary. She is an administrator here. Secondly, no, she did not tell me."

"Nikolas Cruz posted something on Instagram about being a school shooter. Now, we need to see him now."

"I see," said Morford. He turned around and walked back a few desks and asked someone, "What class is Nikolas Cruz in right now?"

"One moment Mr. Morford. He is in biology, on the 3rd floor of Building 12."

Morford thanked her, and casually walked over and picked up a Radio, "Joan, we need to get Nikolas…" Eason interrupted. "No, hold it. We are going over there together right now. Tell her to do nothing."

Morford sighed, "Cancel that Joan." He turned to the bullpen of people behind him, "I'll be right back."

The three marched silently down a long hall, out some doors into an expansive courtyard where various staff and students sat at picnic tables, into another building, then back outside. None of them spoke as all of them were brooding as to the other's attitude. They crossed a wide sidewalk and entered the furthest building, Building 12. As they entered the stairwell, Morford turned to them, "Deputies, you'll forgive me for not being too alarmed. We get an average of two threats a day here at this school. With 3,300 kids to watch over, there are always emotions running high."

Eason put on a fake smile, "Yeah whatever. Let's keep going."

Morford led them to a third floor classroom. "He should be right in here."

Morford was about to walk in, when Eason grabbed him by the arm, "I'll go first."

Eason unlatched the strap on his gun, then walked in, followed by Morford and Deputy Jones.

"Nikolas Cruz?" he announced in a booming voice.

Cruz raised his hand.

Eason walked over to him, "Stand up please."

Cruz looked angry as he stood.

"Where is your backpack?"

Cruz pointed.

"Ok, let's walk over, and you show it to me."

Cruz did so.

Deputy Eason picked it up and unzipped it. He nodded, "All right, come with us."

When they got outside the classroom, Morford asked, "What did you find?"

Eason pulled out three large pocket knives followed by a black pistol-style BB gun. He turned to Cruz, "What is this post on Snapchat all about?"

Cruz started to smile; he knew adults had no clue about social media. "It was Instagram, and it was a joke."

"Well, it's not funny. You can get in a lot of trouble saying things like that. Where is your locker?"

"It's in building 4," replied Cruz in a low cool voice.

"Let's go."

The four marched over to building 4, and Cruz opened his locker. Inside were some more pocket knives, and on the floor of the locker, wrapped in bathroom paper towels, was a small dead bird.

"What the hell do you have this here for?"

Cruz half smiled, and coolly replied, "No reason."

"All right, turn around." Deputy Eason reached for his handcuffs, but Jeff Morford stopped him. "Deputy, with only a BB gun, and a couple of fishing knives, this is an internal matter. Nikolas will receive an in-school suspension, during which he will meet with one of our counselors, along with a meeting with the school resource officer."

Deputy Jones said, "What kind of bullshit policy is that?"

"Deputy," said Morford, "This is our policy. If you don't like it, you will have to take it up with our District Administration and our School Board. They are the ones who set it up."

Jones looked at Eason for guidance since he was the senior deputy. Eason said, "It's this ridiculous Promise program they have in place." He shook his head.

Morford said, "Deputies, thank you for following up. I will take Mr. Cruz to the office now."

Eason shook his head, and asked, "Where is Peterson's office?"

"He is in building 5."

Deputy Eason motioned for Jones to follow him. "Let's go talk to Peterson. We have to let him know."

Chapter 71

May 12, 2016
Broward County Sheriff's Department, Ft. Lauderdale

ROBERT RUNCIE WALKED IN TO JOIN HIS four advisors in the conference room. "I just got word from Arne Duncan. The Department of Education is issuing guidelines to treat a student's gender identity as the student's sex. This means that a school must not treat a transgender student differently from the way it treats other students of the same gender identity."

Stan asked, "So what does that mean?"

Runcie looked up, "Hold on, Stan; there's more."

He continued, 'A school may provide separate facilities by sex but must allow transgender students access to such facilities consistent with their gender identity. A school may not require transgender students to use facilities inconsistent with their gender identity or to use individual-user facilities when other students are not required to do so. A school may, however, make individual-user options available to all students who voluntarily seek additional privacy.'"

Stan jumped in, "All right, I am confused, I think. Are you talking about kids using whichever bathroom they like?"

"Yes, and not just bathrooms, the rule is going to include locker rooms too."

Stan shook his head, "Locker rooms? Do you mean the ones with the open area showers? This is insane."

Julie Evans face grew cross, "Why Stan? The transgender kids need to be protected."

"This is not about protection! You forget Julie; I am involved directly in this matter. The person who heads up our LGBT support oversight reports to me. Hell, there is only a very small number of our 230,000 students who are transgender."

Julie Evans replied, "There is way more than that. There are thousands who question their gender."

"How do you know that? How could any of us know that? It's called adolescence, Julie. Kids are naturally confused at this age."

Runcie would normally have stopped the argument, but he decided to let them go on. But he realized Stan had missed one important facet to what Washington wanted. "Stan, this is not just the kids who are already identified as transgender. It is for any student who questions their gender identity, and it applies from K-12."

"K-12! That's outrageous!"

"That's what Washington wants, and that is what Washington is going to get."

Stan stood and walked toward the window, then turned, "You are telling me a mere child can just decide to change their gender, and poof, they can? Do you have any idea how many of our troublemakers will take advantage of this?" Stan paused, knowing he needed to clarify, "Let me be clear, I am not talking about the kids out there who have not dared to come forward. I am talking about the wide berth this gives to every single kid. We all know that there are kids who will abuse this. It is going to disrupt everything."

"I disagree with Stan," said Julie. "We can have policies that allow a student to come to the office and declare their intention. At that point, we must support them. This is our job, Stan."

Stan replied, "Julie, I know all about supporting the kids. Marcia Marconi is in Jefferson Middle School. She is a transgendered person. She experiences gender dysphoria, real stress about her gender if you will. Marcia feels like she is a boy. She knows she can use the bathroom in the nurse's office if she wishes to. We support her, and we accommodate her needs as well as we can. Why? So, she can have a positive education experience. That is our job. This... this policy the Obama Administration is shoving down our throats is not that. This is going to be a source of division for the entire school community."

Julie shot back, "I don't understand why. Is it because bigots won't accept the needs of those who are different?"

"Bigots? Reasonable people can disagree, Julie. What about the privacy concerns of everyone else? Do I want my ten-year-old daughter in the bathroom when any boy can walk in? No, I don't think so. What if it's an older boy? What if something happens?"

Julie tightened her lip; she hated when Stan tried so hard to find an angle to justify his bigoted thinking. "There is no link to crime and transgender people using bathrooms, Stan. You know that."

"Yes, of course, I know that. We are, though, talking about a disruption of the learning environment, and confusing children, especially young children. That is the worst part of all this."

Runcie had heard enough. "Look, the bottom line is we are moving forward with full and immediate implementation in all schools, K-12. I am holding a press conference tomorrow. My text will state, "We have a moral obligation and a responsibility to protect all students from discrimination, bullying, and harassment. The bottom line is we will continue to respect, value, and support the needs of our diverse students."

Stan asked, "And why are we not taking more time to evaluate this? Why are we not getting the parents involved in crafting this policy?"

"Because Stan, Obama wants this! Arne wants this! And our funding depends on this!"

Stan nodded, "Look, Bob, I am telling you right now, we are opening Pandora's box with this one, for us, for the community, and for young kids."

"Noted!" said Runcie. "Let's get back to it. Have a good day, everyone. Julie, stay here, I need to go over a few things with you."

Chapter 72

June 3, 2016

Marjory Stoneman Douglas HS - Last Day of School

NIKOLAS WAITED NEAR the hallway of Building 7, not far from Kaylee Loftus's locker. He needed to catch her and talk to her. It was already 2:30 in the afternoon, and she had not been in Algebra class for the last several days. Now he was worried he would miss her and not be able to talk with her all summer. But then he saw her.

She was walking down the hall talking with a small group of girls. There was one guy in the bunch, and Nikolas knew who he was. He had gone to middle school with him. His name was Rick Polito; he was a jock and a pitcher on the middle school baseball team. Nikolas didn't know if he was on the high school team or not, but he suddenly didn't like him. Nikolas waited until Kaylee got to her locker. To his dismay, while the other girls said goodbye and kept walking, Rick stayed and chatted with her by her locker for a few moments. Then he left.

Nikolas saw his chance and nervously walked up to her. "Hi, Kaylee?"

"Oh, hi Nikolas. I haven't seen you in a few days."

"Yeah, I noticed you haven't been in Algebra."

"Yes, I tested out of the final, so I didn't have to go last week."

"That's great. So, what are you doing all summer?"

Kaylee wanted to be nice to Nikolas, but by now she had heard all the rumors about him, and it all alarmed her. Still, he was always nice to her, so she felt she owed him the same. "My friend Skylar and I are traveling to a summer study session in Italy for a month; I can't wait. Besides that, I am going to be working at my uncle's marina and laying out by the pool as much as I can."

"You're going to Italy! Wow! Skylar is that Christian girl, right?"

"Well, yes she is Christian," Kaylee giggled, "Most of us are, I guess. But yes, she told me about the trip, and my parents looked into it and... I am going."

"That's great. Hey, are you on Snapchat?"

"Yes,"

"Can I friend you, so you know... you can send me some pictures."

"Sure, that sounds good."

Nikolas was about to leave, when he said, "You live over by Pine Hollow Farm, don't you?"

"Yep, you should stop by sometime this summer. We've got a nice new pool. Find me on snap chat."

Nikolas was elated; he had just been invited over by her. He wanted to hug her or kiss her, but it all felt so awkward, so he smiled, "Bye, Kaylee, Uh... have a nice summer."

"You too, Nikolas."

Chapter 73

Aug 22, 2016
Marjory Stoneman Douglas HS – First Day of School

NIKOLAS GOT TO SCHOOL early on the first day of school. Over the summer he had tried to message Kaylee on Snapchat about going over her house. But by the time he had gotten up the courage, she had already gone to Italy. During her trip, she had sent him some pictures, mostly after he reached out to her with pictures of his own. He knew they would be boring to her, but it was his only way to stay connected with her. He had inquired about coming over about a month into her trip, knowing she would be coming home soon, but she informed him that she and Skylar had extended their trip two weeks, and she would not have time.

He waited by the west gate of the school parking lot, as he knew that was where she usually parked the year before. As he was watching for her car, Nikolas saw Rick Polito pull up into a not too distant parking spot in a blue Camaro. Within moments he jumped out, and on the other side of the car a girl got out too. It was Kaylee. Nikolas' heart dropped. He quickly turned around and walked far enough away so he would be out of sight. He turned and watched.

Rick walked alongside Kaylee as they talked, both laughing, and then they stopped. It was apparent they were going in opposite directions. But then Rick leaned down and kissed her. Nikolas mind screamed in anger as he watched her put her arms briefly on his shoulder, accepting his kiss.

Nikolas walked further away, then went home. He was not going to school today.

Chapter 74

September 20, 2016
Marjory Stoneman Douglas HS — West Entrance Parking Lot

ON WEDNESDAY MORNING, Nikolas waited by the same parking lot. He knew Rick Polito parked there, and while the last two days he had brought Kaylee to school, Nikolas also knew there were days when he did not. At 8:40 he saw Rick pull up and his passenger side was empty. Nikolas put his back pack on and secured it. He pulled the handful of bullets out of the pocket and put them in his pants pocket. He would use these to further intimidate Polito after he kicked his ass. Polito was about the same size as Nikolas, and though he was an athlete, Nikolas felt sure if he surprised him, he could have the advantage.

Nikolas crept into the parking lot, crouching down, angling over to near Polito's car. When he was close, he waited for Polito to begin walking across the lot. When he did, Nikolas ran at him, leaped into the air, kicking Polito in the lower back. Polito fell, and Nikolas jumped on him and began wailing on him. It didn't take long for Polito to gain the advantage. He flipped Nikolas over and began punching him in the face, causing Nikolas to scream as his head pounded into the blacktop.

Suddenly someone grabbed Polito and pulled him off. It was Mr. Cooney.

"Get the hell off him," he said, as he pulled Polito aside.

Polito yelled, "He jumped me?"

Mr. Cooney picked up Nikolas, and two bullets fell out of his pocket. Cooney looked at him and picked them up. He then grabbed

Nikolas backpack, pulled it off him, and opened it. Inside were three more bullets and several large pocket knives. "What the hell is all this?"

"Nothing!" Nikolas screamed.

Mr. Cooney smacked him across the head, "Shut the hell up. You two, come with me."

He grabbed the defiant Nikolas and ushered him forward as Polito followed behind. Many students were now gathered, and suddenly Kaylee came running up.

She took one look at Nikolas and scowled at him, then ran to Rick. "What happened?"

"He jumped me!"

Nikolas turned and gave them both an evil smile.

Chapter 75

September 20, 2016
Marjory Stoneman Douglas HS — Principal's Offices

NIKOLAS AND POLITO were taken to the principal's office, where they were put into separate rooms to await their fate. Denise Reed, one of the assistant principals, went in to speak with Polito. Assistant Principal Winifred Porter was sent in to get Cruz's side of the story, and more importantly, find out why he was carrying bullets and knives in his backpack. After a short time, Assistant Principal Reed came out and called in a few students who had witnessed the events. In her mind, Polito was not in any way to blame. She waited for Principal Porter to finish.

He finally emerged with a grim look on his face, shaking his head. He said to her, "That kid is disturbed."

She replied, "Well it seems to me he may be the instigator here. What do you think?"

"Oh, he is. The question is what are we going to do about it? Let's go talk to Morford."

"Don't you think we better let Principal Thompson know? After all, the kid was carrying bullets."

"No, absolutely not. Remember the last time I tried to tell him about some threat? He made it quite clear these things are to be handled by us. Let's see what Morford thinks."

They walked across the large administrative office and knocked on Assistant Principal Morford's door.

"Come in."

"Hey Jeff, we got a problem. This kid Nikolas Cruz started a fight, and he had some bullets in his backpack."

"Bullets?"

"Yes, four of them."

"Was there a gun?"

"No, but he had some knives."

"Oh, I remember this kid. He was the one with the BB gun and the dead bird last year."

"That kid?" remarked Assistant Principal Reed.

"Yes, that kid. He's a real trouble maker. In-school suspend him for three days, request a conference with his mother, and send him downstairs for counseling."

Reed asked, "Don't you think we should refer this to the Sheriff?"

"You know the drill Denise; we handle these things internally now. Washington is watching."

Chapter 76

Oct 3, 2016

Broward County Sheriff's Department, Ft. Lauderdale

IT WAS MONDAY AND BRANDON had so far, during the first month of school, stayed off the radar of Parker. He went to his locker and opened it. Laying near the bottom on top of his books was a folded up piece of magazine paper someone had slid through the locker vent.

He picked it up an unfolded it. It was a naked woman from some playboy magazine. Across the picture was written in black marker. "Want some Pussy Brandon!"

Brandon crumpled it and threw it onto the hall floor. It was then that he saw him. Parker and another boy were watching him, laughing. Brandon knew he could take no more. He ran at Parker as fast as he could, flailing with his arms, punching Parker in the face. Parker grabbed him and threw him to the ground, just as a teacher stopped them both and took them to the office.

Parker denied having put the paper in Brandon's locker, and so they were both suspended and sent for counseling.

Brandon didn't care. He had stood up for himself. He had fought back.

It didn't stop Parker though. Three days later Parker had chased him all the way home. Brandon made it safely, but it was clear that Parker had it out for him.

Two weeks later, Brandon was coming out of the weekly meeting when he saw Parker standing in the hall talking to one of the girls from the Christian group. Brandon knew her name, but that was all, though he had seen her talking with Parker before. He assumed she might be his girlfriend. Brandon looked at her as Parker turned and glared at him. Skylar half smiled, not noticing what Parker was doing until Brandon had turned away.

Brandon thought, *So, she thinks it's funny too. Idiots!* He kept going and headed to the stairwell.

"Why did you glare at him like that?" Skylar asked Parker.

"He's just some little gay boy from the gay club."

"Parker, what are you talking like that for. Those kids don't deserve that."

"Look, he's a punk from my neighborhood. I give him a hard time sometimes."

"Well, that is not what we stand for in First Priority, Parker. I suggest you find a new club."

Skylar walked away, and Parker was furious. He had been attending the club in hopes of going out with her, and now that was suddenly shot to hell.

Chapter 77

September 24, 2016
Lynda Cruz Home- Nikolas 18th Birthday

NIKOLAS SPENT HIS BIRTHDAY alone with his mom. She made him a special dinner and rented a movie for them to watch. Turning 18 years old seemed daunting to Nikolas. He was suddenly expected to be an adult, and he had no idea how to. He had no girlfriend, no driver's license, no job, and no real hope for the future. He was sinking deeper into depression.

After watching the moving, he went to his room and began to cry. Losing Kaylee, when he loved her so much, was destroying him. Being hated by almost everyone he knew was destroying him. He went to his drawer and pulled out a razor he used on some animals he had killed. He then logged into Snapchat. He sat on the edge of his bed and started his video feed. Slowly, he drew the blade down his arm, grimacing as the blood began to roll out along the length of the cut. He yelled, "I hate myself!" then stopped the video and sent it to everyone on his friend's list.

He then went downstairs and out to the shed with an empty glass. He grabbed the lawn mower gasoline and filled the glass halfway. He went back to his room and turned the video on. He was going to show them all how he felt. He was going to let them know they were hurting him. "Hi, this is Nikolas. I will let my actions speak." He picked up the glass, swallowed hard, then exhaled loudly. He lifted the glass near his mouth, held his breath, and gulped down three sips. He began to gag, then set the glass down. He glanced over at his lighter sitting next to his cigarettes and realized the video had gone off. "Goddammit!" he screamed.

A few moments later, Zachary pounded on his door, shouting, "Shut the fuck up, Nikolas. I'm sleeping."

Nikolas glared at the door, then back at his lighter, then he started to gag, and ran to the bathroom vomiting. After that, he posted the video showing himself ingesting some gas, then went to sleep.

Chapter 78

Oct 2, 2016
Lynda Cruz Home—Parkland, Florida

MARCIA STEPHENS of the Florida Department of Children and Families pulled her car into the driveway of Nikolas Cruz's home. She knocked on the door, and within a few moments a tan, slightly older looking woman answered. "May I help you?"

"Are you Mrs. Lynda Cruz?"

"Yes."

"I am Marcia Stephens from the DCF. We are investigating the well-being of your son Nikolas."

"I don't understand?"

"May I come in? I would rather not talk out here."

Lynda invited her in, and Marcia took out a folder and showed Lynda pictures someone had downloaded of Nikolas with his arms bloodied. Then she played the video.

"Oh, my God," said Lynda. "What is that?"

"That is called cutting. And what is in the glass appears to be gasoline. Were you aware of this, Mrs. Cruz?"

"No, I mean, I know he has been very depressed, oh, my God!"

Marcia unfolded her notebook and took out her report along with the clipboard and began taking notes. "Did he say why he is depressed?"

"I know why; he broke up with his girlfriend recently."

"Did he tell you this?"

"No, not at first. Her mother called over here and said neither she, nor the girl wanted Nikolas contacting her anymore." Lynda rolled her eyes, shaking her head, "She said Nikolas was unhealthy for her daughter's well-being."

"Did you ask Nikolas about this?"

"Yes, he told me she was cheating on him. It's no wonder he attacked that other boy."

"I'm sorry?"

"He got in a fight with her new boyfriend. They suspended Nikolas, but he's back in class now."

Marcia paused, trying to catch up her notes.

Lynda felt emotional as she looked out the window into the distance, "My poor Nikolas, he has such a hard time making friends. I think losing this girl really hurt him."

Marcia looked down the report at the other boxes she needed to check, "Mrs. Cruz, are there any guns in the house?"

"Yes, I have one, but I keep it locked in a secure case. There is a combination and only I know it."

Marcia began to write, but then Lynda interrupted her, "Oh, Nikolas has a pellet gun, or had a pellet gun I should say. I took it away from him because he broke the rules."

"What rules?"

"He is only allowed to shoot it in the yard, at a target area I set up. But he kept taking it out, and we had complaints from neighbors he was shooting, well, at squirrels and birds and things."

Marcia looked up, "Does that alarm you?"

"Of course, I mean, my father was a hunter, but this is different I guess, right?"

Marcia was alarmed slightly. She wondered for a moment if Mrs. Cruz had a completely firm grip on reality. "I have two more questions, Mrs. Cruz. Is Nikolas receiving regular counseling?"

"Yes, I take him every two weeks. He is on medicine for some disorders." Lynda listed them as Marcia wrote them into the report. "He also receives lots of counseling at school. I get letters and calls from them every few weeks."

"Is Nikolas home?"

"He is up in his room?"

"Please call him down." When Nikolas came down, Marcia asked him about the pictures and why he had cut himself. He said nothing. Then she asked, "Was this gasoline?"

"Yeah, so what."

"Were you trying to hurt yourself?"

"Yeah, I was going to light a match next!" Nikolas grinned.

"Nikolas! Stop this!" Lynda screamed.

"I am just kidding."

"But why did you do this?"

"I wanted her… them… to see that they hurt me!"

Marcia shook her head. "I see. Nikolas, would you go get your backpack?" She had not mentioned it to Lynda, but the person who called in the complaint noted that Nikolas had Nazi symbols and some occult symbols scrolled on his backpack.

When he brought it down, she looked at the back of it. There was writing about Nazi's, and the other symbols the caller had mentioned. Marcia asked, "Nikolas, do you have problems with people of other races?"

"No?"

"Where did you see these symbols?"

"I saw them in my mind."

"Why did you write them down here?"

"A voice told me to."

Marcia glanced over at Lynda who was shaking her head and wrote down his answers. She checked the remaining boxes for the home visitation portion of the report and left.

Chapter 79

Oct 4, 2016
Stoneman Douglas High School later

Two days later, Marcia Stephens walked into Stoneman Douglas High School and was directed to the administration offices. She needed to speak to school counselors as well as the school resource officer, if there was one at the school, to gather more information. It was one of the steps outlined in the DCF protocol for an investigation to a child's wellbeing. Marcia was diligent about her job; all the boxes needed to be checked. "May I help you?"

"Yes, I am Marcia Stephens from the DCF, here to see James Jenkins."

"Please have a seat." Marcia watched the woman call down to the counseling offices. She then picked up a radio, "Monica, I need an escort."

In a moment a woman carrying a radio arrived. "Monica, please take Ms. Stephens down to the counseling offices.

Monica took her down and moments later Marcia walked into the bustling center that looked like an administrative disaster. Papers and files were everywhere. There were about 13 students also sitting in a waiting area, some talking, others looking at their phones, as they waited to be called into the offices that lined the back and sides of the room.

Marcia was directed to have a seat. A few moments later an older man came out. "Marcia Stephens?"

She raised her hand and followed him into his office.

"So, you are here to talk about Nikolas Cruz."

"Yes," she said, as she pulled out her form and clipboard. "Has he shown any tendencies toward violence?"

"Some, yes," said Jenkins, perusing the file, not looking up, "He's been suspended recently for fighting."

"When was that?"

"Let's see here, oh, it was just two weeks ago. His 'girlfriend' got a new boyfriend, and Nikolas didn't like it."

"I see. What else?"

"He was suspended late last year for having fishing knives, or pocket knives, and a BB gun in his backpack. Oh, yes, I forgot," he said as he looked toward the bottom of the report. "He had a dead bird in his locker."

"A dead bird?"

"Yeah, you know kids these days, they'll do anything to get attention."

"Hmmm, interesting."

"Let me look at a couple more things." Jenkins perused the computer record. "It says here he has been suspended nine times in all district schools combined. And it says, he has been referred to counseling um... well, this is a lot... One hundred twenty-two times since kindergarten."

"Since kindergarten?"

"Yes, the first few instances took place then."

"Sounds like a troubled youth to be sure."

"Oh, he is. I've talked to him. I think he has Autism or something like that. He doesn't fit in very well."

"Mr. Jenkins, here is a copy of the complaint against Nikolas. He cut himself on a video posted online, and he also ingested gasoline, which, could have been fatal. I think the school needs to keep a close eye on him."

Marcia checked off another box. "Ok then, can I speak to the school resource officer?"

"Sure. It was nice to meet you. You can wait in the lobby."

"Thank you."

A few minutes later Marcia was escorted into the neatly organized office of Scott Peterson. He was seated at his desk with his hands folded, waiting for her. He stood up, "Hello Ms. Stephens; I am Deputy Peterson."

"Nice to meet you, I have a few questions about Nikolas Cruz."

"Shoot," he said.

"What can you tell me about him?"

"Not that much. He's in trouble a lot, minor stuff, but a lot of it." Peterson was not going to say anymore. He was under pressure from above, not pressure specific to any administrator at the school or the district, but pressure, nonetheless. Everyone across the entire Broward County School District knew Runcie's Promise Program was being touted by President Obama and Arne Duncan as a model of success for the nation. The unspoken message was, 'Washington is watching, so don't rock the boat.'

Marcia asked, "Can you tell me about the incident with the BB guns and the dead bird?"

Peterson laughed, "Kids these days. There were concerns about some post about a shooting, but it turns out it was only a BB gun. I guess that won't get you very far."

"I see? But that does not alarm you?"

"Not really."

"Mr. Peterson, here is a copy of the complaint against Nikolas. He cut himself on a video posted online, and he also ingested gasoline, which, could have been fatal. I think the school needs to keep a close eye on him."

"Look, this kid is a punk who wants attention. That's my assessment. Uh… do not quote me on that."

Marcia looked up, half smiled, made a small note, and checked the box. "Thank you, Deputy Peterson."

"You're welcome, any time."

Chapter 80

Nov 1, 2016
Lynda Cruz Home, Parkland Florida

LYNDA NEVER HEARD BACK from the Department of Children and Families, so she assumed the matter had been closed. But in her mind, something was desperately wrong with Nikolas. She saw the cuts he gave himself. She was worried that now that he had lost his girlfriend, he had nothing to live for. His brother Zachary was no help. They argued constantly, and Lynda had to keep them separated most of the time.

She sat quietly in her living room one evening thinking. She went to the steps, "Nikolas?"

"Yeah?"

"Come down; I want to talk with you."

A few moments later he rumbled down the steps. "What's up, Mom?"

"Come over here and sit by me. I want to talk with you."

Nikolas sat down, and Lynda asked, "How are you doing... you know, after losing your girlfriend?"

He frowned, "Not too good."

"I am sorry that happened to you."

"What will make you happy, Nikolas?"

"I want to learn how to shoot a rifle."

"What, since when?"

"I've been thinking about it. You said your dad used to be a hunter. I want to do the same thing."

Lynda smiled. She knew how much hunting had meant to her dad throughout his life, and she was impressed that Nikolas had been thinking about it. She began to nod, "Would you follow all the rules?"

"Yes, I would."

"Well, let me think about it some more. I might want to wait until the Spring. But... I think it might be good for you."

"Thanks, mom." He reached over and kissed her.

"You're welcome, honey. Now get up to bed."

Chapter 81

Nov 22, 2016
Vatican – Rome, Italy

FATHER RICARDO WALKED ACROSS the vast grounds of the Vatican toward the library to meet the old curator, Mr. Lodi. When they met, Lodi brought him into the library, and they went into the back operations area where Mr. Lodi introduced him to the current curator. Lodi was then handed a key, and he waved for Father Ricardo to follow him.

They opened a tiny room where there was a door in the back. Lodi unlocked the other door, and they went down an old staircase surrounded by unfinished walls. Two flights down another door was unlocked, and they stepped into a dark hallway. Lodi turned on a dim light revealing a fifty- foot long hall that had several old wooden doors on each side. "It is down here, at the end."

They went down the hall, and Lodi opened the keyed bolt lock on the last door. It was dark in the room, but there was a single very dim bulb already lit, apparently tied to the hall light.

"Does anyone ever come down here?" asked Father Ricardo.

Lodi smiled, "No, no one is allowed."

Lodi pointed at the bronze box near the back wall. "It's over there."

Father Ricardo anxiously walked across the 10-foot wide room and examined the box. He carefully lifted the lid and saw a tuft of black hair with dried red blood. He could not believe he was looking at the hair of John the Baptist.

Suddenly the door shut behind him, and he heard the bolt lock. He raced over, and within moments of pounding, the lights went off.

Lodi closed and locked the hall door. As he ascended the stairs, the faint knocking completely faded away. He went through the small room, locked both doors, and then found the curator. "It wasn't what he was looking for."

"Did he leave?"

"Yes, he had someone else to see. Here are the keys."

Lodi went outside and walked into an alley. He waved his hand in front of his face, and his appearance changed to that of a youthful looking middle-aged man. It was Legion.

Chapter 82

Nov 22, 2016
Florida Department of Children and Families

AT THE DEPARTMENT OF CHILDREN and Families, Marcia Stephens read through the report from Henderson Health. They were providing counseling and psychiatric services for Nikolas. She went down to the conclusion of the report, where the physician stated that Nikolas posed no risk to harm himself or others because he is on a treatment plan for ADHD, Depression, and Autism. The report further stated Nikolas has been coming to his appointments consistently.

Marcia paused, thinking, then began nodding.

She put their report down momentarily and pulled out her report and checked a few more boxes. She then inserted the report from Henderson Health into her report and looked everything over once more.

All the boxes were checked.

She thought back to the other people surrounding Nikolas, like Lynda, like the school counselor, like Deputy Peterson, and now the physician, and they all had one thing in common. They all felt confident that Nikolas did not pose a threat.

Marcia checked the final box on the report, the one closing the case, and signed her name.

Chapter 83

Dec 5th, 2016
Stoneman Douglas High School — Language Arts Class

TEACHER TINA MARVIN WROTE A QUESTION on the board then turned to face the class. She called out, "Nikolas? Can you answer this question?"

Nikolas looked up as a smile slowly came over his face. He had not been paying attention, and now all eyes were on him. "How the fuck would I know?"

The class burst out laughing as Tina tightened her lip and marched down the aisle toward his desk. "Pick up your things and go to the office right now."

"Why!!!" Nikolas screamed, alarming everyone. Tina left the room. Moments later, she returned with one of the hall monitors carrying a radio. "Let's go, Cruz; you are going to the office."

Nikolas stood up and flipped his desk over, screaming, "I hate this fucking place!"

Tina and the monitor approached him, but Nikolas pushed Tina back. The monitor radioed "Security monitors to room 2102."

Nikolas stood nervously waiting as the uneasy standoff ensued. Within moments a husky, heavy-set man wearing cut-off jean shorts and a baseball jersey named Andrew Medina walked in. He was one of the security monitors on campus.

"All right Cruz, come with me."

Nikolas hesitated, but then a second security monitor, David Taylor, arrived. They took him by the shoulder and led him away to the principal's office.

Assistant Principal Jeff Morford was waiting. "Put him into conference room A."

Morford grabbed Assistant Principal Denise Reed, and they went in together. "So," said Morford, "You pushed a teacher."

"No, I didn't. She tried to grab me, and I just pushed her hand away. That's my right."

Reed asked, "Don't want to graduate, Nikolas?"

Nikolas smiled, "Actually, I would rather be out killing small animals. I hate this fucking place! And I hate everyone in it!"

"Well, you are suspended again," said Morford. "Three days starting today. You will meet with a counselor on Monday, and you won't be allowed back in classes until you and your mother meet with one of our counselors. We will be calling her to notify her after this meeting. Now report to detention."

Chapter 84

Dec 11th, 2016
Stoneman Douglas High School — Counseling Office

NIKOLAS FINISHED HIS SUSPENSION on Friday, and Monday morning he reported directly to the counseling office. After waiting in the waiting area for 10 minutes, a sharp looking middle aged woman came out and called him. Nikolas followed her back to her office and sat down. She closed the door.

"Nikolas, my name is Mrs. Osgood, I am an exception student education specialist here. I wanted to talk to you about what is going on. Now, before we start, Nikolas, it is being recommended that you return to Cross Creek." Cross Creek was the place for troubled students, as well as those who were not bright enough to attend regular classes.

Nikolas shook his head, "I can't go back there."

"Why not?"

"Don't you understand? That is where all the dumb kids go. I won't be able to handle it... I just won't." He began to break down, sobbing in front of her.

"I'm sorry, Nikolas. But it's not true!"

"I was there. I know. Please, I need another chance. I... I can do better. I promise."

"Nikolas, why did you say you would rather be killing small animals?"

"Because I like hunting. Right now, I only have a pellet gun, so that is all I can do. But my mom is going to get me a real gun I can use to go hunting with."

Mrs. Osgood's husband was a hunter, so she knew all about hunting, still, Nikolas was in no mental state to own a gun. "I will talk to your mother about that Nikolas."

"Nikolas, perhaps you should give Cross Creek a try for a while, maybe a semester." Mrs. Osgood knew it was more than a suggestion. The decision to transfer him, due to his special-needs status, had pretty much been made.

Nikolas began to weep. "Please give a little more time to prove myself. I have nothing. I don't have any friends. I don't have anything. I just need another chance."

Mrs. Osgood felt sorry for him. She looked over his file and saw a young man, without a father who did not know how to fit in. She also knew there was no way he would be allowed to stay unless perhaps one thing occurred. "Nikolas, there is one way. Do you still see an outside counselor?"

"Yes."

"You are eighteen, right?"

"Yes."

"Well, technically, you are old enough to revoke your status as a special-needs student. In that case, they could not transfer you without your permission. You could stay here. It would give you a little more time to prove yourself as you say."

"I want that."

Mrs. Osgood pulled out a form from her desk. "Sign this form." Nikolas hastily signed.

She then said, "Nikolas, return to detention until I see what time your mother can arrive. We can speak to her and then you are free to return to classes."

An hour later, Lynda Cruz arrived at the counselor's office. Mrs. Osgood ushered her in, and explained what had happened in the classroom. Lynda's only response was, "Nikolas needs something positive in his life. He is miserable, and he is taking it out on others. 'Hurt people, hurt people.' Isn't that what they say?"

"Mrs. Cruz, Nikolas has elected to revoke his special needs status so that he can stay at Stoneman Douglas. They wanted to transfer him back to Cross Creek, but now the decision is in his hands."

Lynda looked a little confused, "I know he hates that school. So, I don't know..." Lynda stared out the window for a few moments, tired of it all, "I guess I am fine with that."

"Mrs. Cruz, there is one more thing. Nikolas said you were going to buy him a gun. I would strongly advise against that at this time."

"Listen, the kid needs something. He wants to get into hunting. If he wants a gun, I think I am ok with getting him a gun. But I am still thinking it over."

With that, Lynda signed the form verifying she came in and left.

Chapter 85

Dec 13th, 2016
Lynda Cruz Home

IT WAS 5:30 IN THE EVENING. Lynda laid on the bed in her room in the darkness, holding her eyes shut. She had been battling worsening depression for a few years now. The darkness of December and the never-ending troubles at school were pushing her into a very dark place.

Nikolas knocked on the door, "Mom, are you ok?"

"Go away."

He tried to open the door, it was locked, but he knew how to jimmy it, so he did. He opened the door and saw Lynda laying face down in her pillow.

"Mom, what is wrong?"

"I can't take it anymore Nikolas. I am selling the house. I can't keep up. I can't... I can't handle you boys anymore..."

"Mom, c'mon it's ok."

"It's not ok. I am very depressed."

"Mom, I will change. I promise."

"Nikolas go. I already sold the house. We are moving... in a month."

"You what! I don't want to fucking move!"

Lynda started to scream, "Nikolas, get out! I told you I can't take it anymore! Get out, please!"

He closed the door.

~ ~ ~ ~

Christmas time came, and for the first time, Lynda did not put the Christmas Tree up. She was too depressed. The house was dark that year as Lynda went to bed almost every night very early in the evening. By January it was nearing time to move. Lynda paid for a moving company to come in and pack up the house. Half of their things were taken to storage while a much smaller amount followed them to their smaller home on the other side of Parkland.

~ ~ ~ ~

Moving day was one of the saddest days in Nikolas life. He hated leaving; he hated the feeling that his neighbors had won. They got to stay, but he had to leave. Lynda drove them to the new house. When they arrived, Nikolas and Zachary watched the movers bring all the boxes and set up all the furniture wherever Lynda directed them to. Nikolas watched his mom carefully. Something was very wrong with her. She was growing weaker by the day.

As soon as the movers left, Lynda went into her room and collapsed on the bed.

An hour later she woke to hear Nikolas and Zachary arguing loudly over who would get the first bedroom at the top of the stairs.

Holding her eyes shut due to the emotional anguish she was feeling, she screamed, "Nikolas, please stop Nikolas. Please!"

Nikolas heard the desperation in the plea, and he stopped.

~ ~ ~ ~

The Angel Jordan was watching in the hallway. Something new was happening. Nikolas was listening to Lynda for the first time. It was as if her illness was weakening whatever dark power held sway over him. But it didn't make any sense. It also didn't make sense that Jordan was able to find Nikolas lately. No longer was he mysteriously hidden from his view. This too did not make sense. The only thing that was different was Lynda was growing weaker. *But how does all this connect?*

Chapter 86

Jan 10, 2017

Stoneman Douglas High School—Reading Class

SKYLAR AND RANDI walked into their first day of second-semester reading class. They sat down and waited for the other students to come in. Nikolas also walked in, alone, and sat across from them. Skylar remembered him, but she had not seen him in a very long time. She remembered Kaylee telling her that he was crazy. She leaned over to Randi, "That is that Nikolas kid who gave Kaylee a hard time."

"Oh yes, I remember him. He's strange."

Skylar thought about the sermon she had heard just yesterday, the one about welcoming the stranger and trying not to judge others. She looked over at Nikolas and gave him a half smile. Nikolas looked at her, and she could feel as if he were staring into her soul, but not a stare of goodness, nor evil, but a stare of emptiness. She looked away as class began.

Halfway through class, Nikolas leaned over and turned toward Randi, "Can I borrow your I-pad for a minute to look up the assignment."

Randi hesitated but acquiesced.

A little while later, after giving the I-Pad back to Randi, Skylar noticed Nikolas fidgeting with something in his hands. He was holding it near his crotch. She looked more intently and saw feathers. It was a dead bird. She shrieked slightly, putting her hands over her mouth.

Mr. Bova heard her, "What's going on back there?" He started down the aisle. "Skylar, what is it?"

She looked up at him, and over at Nikolas, who was holding very still. Mr. Bova saw him. "Nikolas, what is that in your hands."

Nikolas glared at Skylar for a moment, pulled his clasped hands up, then opened them to reveal a dead bird.

Mr. Bova said, "Let's go."

He escorted Nikolas out and down to administration.

Chapter 87

Feb 5, 2017
Stoneman Douglas High School – Principal's Office

NIKOLAS SAT IN THE WAITING ROOM seething. He had just got into a shoving match with a kid in his Biology class. He watched as School Resource Officer Scott Peterson walked in and went directly to Assistant Principal Jeff Morford's office. Moments later Peterson came back out and approached Nikolas. "Come with me, Mr. Cruz."

They walked into Morford's office to see Jeff Morford leaning against the credenza behind his desk with his arms folded. Next to him was Principal Thompson. Deputy Peterson closed the door.

"Mr. Cruz," said Morford, "We have warned you repeatedly, and I am afraid your assault on Tom Runyon in Biology Class today was the last straw. You are expelled from Stoneman Douglass High School. So, you know, we will be placing a call to your mother to inform her, and to let her know of your options at this point."

"What do you mean options?"

Morford glanced over to Principal Thompson who nodded, signaling it was ok to tell him. "There are three Alternative Schools in the district where you can conduct a hybrid of online and on-site programs to obtain your diploma. You will 'never' be allowed back at any of the district schools, including Cross Creek. Deputy Peterson will escort you to your locker, and then escort you off campus. Goodbye Mr. Cruz. We wish you luck."

Deputy Peterson escorted Nikolas out and down to his locker.

Nikolas wanted to scream as he felt the eyes of everyone staring at him. Then he saw Kaylee walking with Skylar. He felt so embarrassed. First it was his neighbors who he had imagined were laughing at him, now he imagined all the students were laughing at him. They had destroyed him, and he would get them back.

~ ~ ~ ~

As soon as Nikolas got off campus, he called Uber and raced home. His mom was not at home. He ran to the answering machine and hit 'play'. It was from the school. "Mrs. Cruz, this is Melanie Stapleton, the secretary for Jeff Morford. Please call me."

Nikolas thought for a moment. If his mom knew he had been expelled, she would never recover. He picked up the phone, and talked in a feminine voice, "Mrs. Stapleton, this is Lynda Cruz."

"Yes, Mrs. Cruz. I needed to inform you that Nikolas was expelled for fighting today. Would you like a meeting with Mr. Morford?"

"No, I... I understand."

"I am sending a letter home today that will outline Nikolas's options for getting his high school diploma."

"Thank you. I have to go."

"Very well Mrs. Cruz, good luck."

Nikolas hung up. He now only had to do two things. First, convince Zachary to keep his mouth shut, and second, intercept the letter. Within two days, both had been accomplished.

Chapter 88

Feb 12, 2017
Gun World of South Florida, Deerfield Beach

THE DARK ANGEL TIRA stood in the corner of Nikolas room whispering into his mind. "It's time to get your rifle, Nikolas."

Nikolas got up and went to his mom's room. Mom, you said I could get a rifle. I want to learn how to hunt and how to shoot."

Lynda was well into her third glass of wine, sitting on her bed watching TV. "Nikolas, I told you we had to wait."

"Mom, I am sick of waiting. I've done what you asked. Now let's go."

She went to put her drink down and almost spilled it. "Dammit!"

She put her hands over her face, "You know what? Fine, I promised you a gun, and I will get you one."

"Can we go tomorrow?"

"Yes."

The next day, Lynda woke up with a headache. Her and Nikolas got into the car and drove for 15 minutes to Gun World of South Florida in Deerfield Beach. The clerk greeted them and asked for identification. Nikolas had no record of any kind, so he was cleared to do whatever he wanted. As he gazed around the vast store of guns, he felt a surge of power and confidence. The clerk said, "Let me show you our state-of-the-art firing range." They followed him back, and he picked up a pistol and fired, and then he picked up and semi-automatic weapon and fired.

"Wow!" said Nikolas. "Mom I want one of those."

"Nikolas for what? No! You just need a rifle for hunting."

"Mom, did you ever think I might want to join the army? I want one of these. Please?"

The clerk said, "We have sold a fair number to younger patrons. We have lessons every week here at the firing range."

"Mom, please I promise this will make me happy. Nikolas knew he was old enough to decide for himself, but he needed his mom to pay for it. He did not have the money."

"Do you promise you will come to lessons every week?"

"Yes!"

"And you have to have a locked case in the house. I hold the key!"

"Mom, that's fine."

Lynda smiled, "All right. I guess you are serious about this. I will let you."

The clerk said, "It will take a few days for all the background checks to go through. I will call you."

~ ~ ~ ~

Two days later Lynda woke up with her eyes widened. It was 11:00 in the morning. She had been unable to wake earlier as depression was holding a tight grip on her.

Then she thought of Nikolas and his gun. She looked up the number and called, "This is Lynda Cruz. Was my son's gun approved?"

"Mrs. Cruz, yes, I was just about to call you. Everything went through."

"Would you please not give it to him unless I am there with him?"

"I don't understand."

"It's just because he's young, and I just want to make sure he's safe and everything,"

"Ma'am, Nikolas is over 18 years old, and he is legally allowed to pick up the gun himself, that is unless you for some reason do not feel he is fit to own one."

"No, no, he's fine. I just… I want to make sure he's safe, you know, he's young. It's his first gun,"

"Well, as I said, if he comes in, he is allowed to pick it up himself."

Nikolas came home from school, and Lynda took him to purchase the gun and a case in which to lock it up. When they got home, she locked it in the case and told him he could attend the first class on Saturday.

Lynda took him to his lessons every week. After each lesson, he practiced at the shooting range. Before long Nikolas convinced Lynda to purchase a few more guns, all of which were kept locked away at home.

Chapter 89

Feb 26, 2017
Stoneman Douglas High School

THE SECURITY MONITOR SAT in the tiny office, he and the other security monitors shared, staring at his emails. There was an email addressed to all staff from Assistant Principal Winifred Porter.

To: All Staff
From: Winifred.Porter
Subject: Nikolas Cruz

One of our students, Nikolas Cruz, was expelled yesterday. Mr. Cruz has carried various weapons such as knives and a pellet gun in his backpack in the past. He is not allowed on campus anymore. Anyone who sees him should notify the appropriate personnel immediately.

Medina chuckled and turned to his associate David Taylor. "Look at this. They expelled crazy boy Cruz."

Taylor looked up from reading the latest edition of Sports Illustrated. "It's about damn time they got rid of that troublemaker. He has always spooked me."

"Well, he won't be spooking you no more!"

"That's good."

Medina got up, and Taylor asked, "Where are you going?"

"I'm going to go take my walk around seeing how everyone is doing today."

"Hey, don't forget. The team's got indoor practice tonight."

"Yeah, I know."

~ ~ ~ ~

A half hour later, Kaylee, Randi, and Skylar sat at the cafeteria table having breakfast together when security monitor Andrew Medina walked over to them. "Hello ladies, you're looking pretty this morning."

Only Skylar looked up, half smiling, "Good morning." She noticed Kaylee and Randi going to great pains not to look at him, so she looked away. After the uncomfortable silence, Medina bent forward and whispered to Kaylee, "You look wonderful." Then he walked away.

Randi eyes widened as she said, "That guy gives me the creeps."

"Me too," said Kaylee, "Did you hear what he said to Meadow?"

"Yes, I already heard," said Randi.

"What did he say?" asked Skylar.

Randi frowned, "He told her she looked fine as F…!"

"What!" fumed Skylar, "How can he get away with that!"

"Oh, he is not," replied Randi, "Meadow already reported it to the office."

Skylar did not know Meadow that well though she had heard her name before. She was about to ask more when the bell rang, and everyone got up to go to the next class.

Chapter 90

Feb 26, 2017
Stoneman Douglas High School

LATER THAT DAY ASSISTANT PRINCIPAL Jeff Morford placed a call down to security and requested that Andrew Medina come to the office. Medina was an assistant baseball coach though he did not resemble one. He was an out of shape, middle-aged man who offered little in terms of help to the athletes. The only reason he was still active with the team was his long-held connection to the head coach. He arrived in shorts, a baseball jersey and a ball cap.

"Medina, we have a report here that you made inappropriate, lewd comments to one of our students."

"I did no such thing," Medina knew he was lying, he made comments to lots of the girls. He also knew he had recently crossed the line with one of them, going beyond what might be considered debatable. The young woman was named Meadow, and she was the first one to have the courage to report him.

Morford said, "That will be determined during the investigation. Unfortunately for right now, you are being placed on administrative leave until the district can gather the facts."

"Will I still get paid?" asked Medina.

"Yes, you will, but as you know, if these allegations are proved to be true, this is an offense that could result in termination."

"This is bullshit."

"Well, maybe so. We shall see. Anyway, leave the building at once. Your union steward has already been informed, and they will be in touch."

~ ~ ~ ~

Within a month the district finished its investigation. He was informed it would be put to a full vote by the committee in early October.

His union steward, Sheila Johnson delivered the news. "Andrew it is not looking good. You are now to stay on administrative leave, with pay until the vote, but I must tell you, it is not going to go in your favor. There have been a lot of complaints about your job performance, and frankly, you were on thin ice even before you made these comments."

"What comments? What did they say?"

Sheila Johnson looked up at him with a serious look on her face. "First of all, they have a video of you following the girl and confronting her in the hall, alone, and talking for over a minute and a half. Secondly, the girl, and I believe you know which one, stated that you asked her where she worked and when she told you, asked if you could stop by there and flirt with her. She said she called in sick that day. She also said three weeks later you asked her if she wanted to have a drink with you but said she would have to keep it low key. Her friend reported that when you saw them, you lowered your sunglasses and said, 'damn Mami.' Shall I go on?"

"That's all bullshit. I asked her to come to a baseball game to support the team, not go on a date."

"I am afraid that minute and a half video looks like a lot more than a simple invitation to watch the school baseball team play."

"Ok, look, maybe I was a little too friendly, but I swear, I would not put myself in a compromising position with students."

"Andrew, I have to be honest. This girl is very credible."

Medina grew defiant, "Look, I've been a member of this union for a long time. I have helped more than a few of the people in high places around here, and they know it. I need those favors called in."

"Andrew, I do not think that..."

He interrupted her, "You remind Julie Evans of what I did for her. She will know. Tell her I need this chip cashed. I can't afford to lose my damn job right now."

Sheila said nothing. She knew that Julie Evans was one of the people who had tried to help him behind the scenes. But she also knew the nature of his comments had thus far kept her from doing anything substantive. "I will let her know."

"You make sure you tell her, that this is the chip she promised me I would be able to cash in someday."

Chapter 91

Jun 26, 2017
Lynda Cruz Home, Parkland

NIKOLAS FELT THE CHILL in the air that he now knew accompanied her arrival, and he knew for certain she was there. He closed his eyes trying to listen, but he could not hear her voice. It was the Dark Angel Tira standing before him frustrated. She glanced over her shoulder and walked down the hall. Sitting up in her bed, holding a rosary in her hands was Lynda. Tira winced as she felt the shooting pain race through her chest. She backed away and went back to Nikolas's room, thinking, trying to understand what was happening.

Some force for good was blocking her, and it was coming from the mother. Perhaps it was because her health was failing, perhaps she was nearing the end of her life. "Dammit!" Tira said aloud.

She knew the prayers of a dying person held great power over the work of any Dark Angel. Neither Vamorda nor Legion would be pleased if she failed. And now she was being blocked. But she had an idea. Saturday was coming and Nikolas would take his weekly shooting lesson. She would test her idea then.

The following Saturday Tira arrived early and waited for Lynda to load up the locked gun cases into the car. Nikolas came out, and they drove to Dunkin Donuts on South Powerline Road. Tira grew angry as she had no time for delays. To make matters worse, Lynda took Nikolas inside, and they sat at a small booth, taking their time eating. Finally, they arrived at Gun World

Tira watched closely as Lynda helped him carry his gun cases inside. She gave Nikolas the keys to the cases, told him she would return in two hours and left. When he was in class, Tira whispered "Nikolas, can you hear me."

She watched his face and saw a smile creep across it. She knew she had made her connection. She had been right. When his mother was not around, she held sway over him, but when she was around, she was blocked. She needed to work fast. "Nikolas, go make a copy of the key."

Nikolas left class and went to the front desk. "Where can I get a key made?"

"There's a key duplicator at Walmart over on South Military Trail."

"Ok, can I leave my cases here? I want to go make a set."

"Sure."

Nikolas pulled out his phone and opened the Uber app. Within 5 minutes Uber arrived, and Nikolas went over to Walmart, made a duplicate set, and took Uber right back. The entire trip took only 22 minutes.

Chapter 92

Aug 19, 2017
Stoneman Douglas High School — Main Lobby

PETER, ALAINA, AND MARTIN sat in the school cafeteria excitedly talking, getting to know each other. Alaina had just joined the Junior ROTC of which Peter and Martin were already members.

Peter asked, "Why did you join?"

"I am not sure. I saw the poster, and I've seen students walking in their uniforms, and I thought that I would like that."

Peter replied, "Cool, you will enjoy it. It's a really good group."

"Yeah, I met someone who was part of their school's ROTC when I was down helping out in Everglades City after Hurricane Irma."

"You were down there?" asked Martin.

"Yeah, my parents let me go. It was amazing to be part of such an amazing effort to help those people."

Peter nodded, "Wow, that is really cool. I would like to do that sometime."

"You know who I met down there. A lady whose son was wounded in the Las Vegas shooting."

"No kidding?" said Martin.

"Yes, I guess he nearly died. But he is ok now. She lives in Everglades City."

"Wow," said Peter. "These shooters are all cowards."

"They sure are," said Ailana. "I wonder if it could ever happen here?"

"I'm sure it could."

"I wonder what I would do?" asked Ailana. "I mean, would I run away, or would I try to stop him?"

Peter replied, "I guess you will never know unless it happens."

Chapter 93

Aug 19, 2017
Stoneman Douglas High School — Main Lobby

TODAY WAS THIS FIRST DAY of school after the break, and Brandon had just spent the most wonderful summer of his life. He was 17 years old now and beginning to understand himself finally. The club at his school was helping him in ways he didn't dream possible, and now he was on the road to his destiny. He was not gay. He understood this now. He was transgender; he was a female trapped in a male body. Late in summer, he decided he would transition to becoming a woman, eventually. He needed more time to embrace the idea. He had not told his mom yet, only because he had no way to figure out how to explain it. But he would take small steps, so he went to the counselor's office during the first break in his classes.

Counselor James Pesta took his walk-in appointment and escorted him back to his office. "Please sit down, Brandon. What can I do for you?"

"I... well... I am a transgender person. I wanted to report that, register, you know."

"I see, Brandon, are you a boy?"

"Yes, but I am transitioning to a girl."

"Ok," Pesta pulled out a form from his desk. "Brandon, I am glad you came in. The school is here to support you in your transition."

"Thank you," said Brandon nervously.

Pesta explained, "So, you know, now that you have let us know, you can use any bathroom you like if you are more comfortable using the girl's bathroom that is your perogative.

Brandon's face grew a little worried, "So, I can just go into the girl's bathroom."

"Yes, and, you can still use the boy's bathroom too, and if you prefer, you can go to the nurse's office bathroom. You can use any one you like."

"What about the locker rooms, like for gym class?"

"You are entitled to go into the girl's locker room if you prefer."

"But, well, where will I shower?"

"They have set up some private stall showers in both locker rooms."

Brandon was thinking to himself how weird that would feel. He felt more confused than ever now.

Pesta looked down at the form, checked a few boxes, and asked, "Brandon, there is one more thing. Do you have a new name?"

"Yes... well... not really, not yet."

"Ok, when you do, let us know, so we can ask your teachers to begin using it."

"Ok."

"Brandon, have you told your mom yet?"

"I am going to, very soon."

"All right, well, we have to send a letter home notifying her of this meeting. Is ok to do this now?"

"Yes, it's time. I will tell her tonight."

Chapter 94

September 3, 2017
FBI Headquarters Washington DC

THOMAS MERTON ANSWERED his phone, "FBI, Merton."

"Mr. Merton, as I just told the woman, my name is Chris Sommers. I have a video blog I maintain. Some person named Nikolas Cruz posted a comment." He said, 'I am going to be a professional school shooter.'"

"Ok, Mr. Sommers, what is the address of your blog." Merton took down the information and logged on. He confirmed he had the right sight, then set about getting as much information as he could. The comment had already been deleted, but the FBI had ways to trace history.

"Mr. Sommers, thank you for the call. We will follow up."

"Will someone get back to me?"

"I am sorry Mr. Sommers. We may not be able to, but we will if the details of our investigation permit."

Merton waited a moment, then hung up. He pulled up an incident report and began filling out the information. It would be sent to another department which would be able to dig into the details and determine the source of the comment.

Fourteen days later the report came back to him. They were unable to track down who had commented. Merton wondered for a moment how deep they had gone.

He thought about picking up the phone to find out if they had called Google who owned YouTube, which was something he would have done when he worked in that unit. But his case load was backed up as it was, and he had their report, which was what he needed to sign off and close the case.

So, he did.

Chapter 95

September 29, 2017
Stoneman Douglas High School — Main Lobby

SKYLAR AND HER FRIEND RANDI walked out of the chemistry class and went straight to the girl's bathroom located just off the main lobby. Skylar went into an open stall, closed the door, pulled down her pants, and sat down. "I can't believe he's not going to curve the quiz."

"I know. That was funny," said Randi, as she lowered her voice, mimicking their teacher, "Skylar, we cannot curve the quiz just because you want me to."

Brandon was listening in to their conversation from a nearby stall. It was only his third time using the girl's bathroom, and it was empty when he had come in.

Skylar laughed, "I thought he was going to have a cow! That was so funny!"

Randi also laughed. Skylar glanced down at the backpack on the ground in the next stall. It seemed odd to her, but she quickly thought about something else.

Skylar said, "I don't know why boys don't have to deal with these stupid periods every month!"

"I don't think they could handle it," said Randi. "It is why they are the weaker sex."

They both laughed again. Someone else too commented, and more laughter could be heard.

Brandon quietly got up, flushed the toilet, and opened the door. He wanted to get out quickly. He turned to pick up his backpack and as soon as he stepped out of the stall, Skylar also stepped out.

Her eyes suddenly widened in shock, and she screamed, "What are you doing!"

Brandon was caught off guard. "I'm allowed in here. I am... I am transitioning."

"You're what! You, idiot. Get out of here!"

"I said, I am allowed in here!"

By now a crowd was gathering outside. Skylar raced over to the sink, quickly washed her hands, and stormed out. Outside the door, a crowd of almost 30 students was gathered, and she began to wade through them, embarrassed, with Randi right behind her. There was subtle laughter from a number in the crowd.

She stopped in her tracks. She wanted to scream and desperately needed to get away from the eyes staring at her, hoping to see her reaction. No sooner had she gotten past them all when she turned to see Brandon walk out. Everyone cheered, and Brandon nervously raised his hand in the air, waving, not knowing what else to do.

Down the hallway, Randi asked, "Are you ok, Skylar?"

"No, I am not. I need to be alone."

"All right. I'll see you at lunch." Randi looked over her shoulder, "That jerk."

Skylar walked away and over to a side entrance where there was a bench outside. She had never felt so humiliated in her life. She went over to the bench and began to cry.

Brandon was high-fived by a few of the kids outside in the hall. He was nervous but felt good the other students had accepted him. He pushed through the crowd and headed to his next class.

As he walked past a side entrance, he saw Skylar. She had her back to him, but he could see she was crying. Suddenly, his heart dropped. He watched her for a moment and began to feel lousy. He realized, though he had not meant to that he had embarrassed her, and he regretted what had happened. He quickly left, not wishing for her to see him.

Chapter 96

October 4, 2017
Home of Scott Beigel and Gwen Gossler

GWEN GOSSLER AND TEACHER SCOTT BEIGEL sat glued to their TV screen, overcome with emotions, as the lives of the victims of the Route 91 Festival Shooting in Las Vegas were being shown on TV.

Gwen wiped a tear from her eye, "I can't believe those poor people were killed like that. They were out having fun, and... it is senseless."

"I can see it happening more and more. It seems one of these monsters inspires the next. But what I can't figure out is why? Why did he do this?"

"I don't think we will ever know," said Gwen.

"I'll tell you what, I wouldn't be surprised if something like this happens in the Broward Schools. With this new PROMISE program, the place is a lot less safe. Kids know they can get away with anything they want."

"Why are they allowing it?"

"Don't ask me. The powers that be think it is good for the students. I don't agree."

Neither said a word for a little while as the lives of several more of the victims played on the TV. Scott then turned to Gwen and said, "If that happens to me, If I get shot, make sure people at my funeral know that I was a jerk."

"Don't say that," Gwen said. "You are a wonderful man and a wonderful teacher. Let's turn this off."

"Thanks, Gwen, yea, this is just too sad." He turned the TV off, and they went to bed.

Chapter 97

October 4
Broward Country District Offices

JULIE EVANS PICKED UP her office phone and dialed Chief Human Resources Officer Craig Nichols. "Craig, this is Julie. Look, we have been talking about this vote to fire the security monitor Andrew Medina. Bob wants you to overrule it."

"Why?"

"Well, it's simple. There is no direct evidence of sexual harassment against him, nor is there any evidence of physical contact."

"I don't know about this, Julie. Who wants this?"

"Look, we have discussed it. This is what Bob wants." Julie was not telling the whole truth, and she knew it, but she also knew Craig would never challenge her.

"I don't want to be held accountable for the decisions of a group, Julie."

"Craig, just do your job. There is no evidence. The guy does not deserve to be railroaded out of here."

"Fine."

~ ~ ~ ~

Two hours later, Craig Nichols sat in the room and watched the committee unanimously voted to fire Andrew Medina. When they were about to finalize their decision, Craig Nichols spoke up.

"Committee members, I am here to represent the wishes of Superintendent Runcie. After consulting with our legal department as well as our school police department, we have decided to lessen the discipline of Mr. Medina. The primary reason is the lack of any direct evidence."

Craig could see the anger, as well as suspicion, come over some faces of the committee members. But it was his right to override such decisions, and he had done so.

One committee member asked, "This girl is a minor. Shouldn't this be referred to Child Protective Services so law enforcement can get involved?"

Nichols replied, "No, under our new guidelines this is an internal administrative matter."

"Well, what good is it to have these hearings if "designees" of Mr. Runcie keep overturning our verdicts?"

Nichols did not reply but closed his dossier and left.

Chapter 98

October 29, 2017
Lynda Cruz Home

THE ANGEL JORDAN sat, reclining on the grass with his arms behind him in the backyard of the Cruz home. He was observing Lynda and praying for her. She was seated on the patio, dressed in a robe, with a glass of wine and a cigarette in her hand. She coughed again, louder this time. She had been doing so for the last few months.

Jordan was worried. While Angels did not know the future any more than humans did, anyone could see Lynda was dying. He had been transferred to her care over a year ago. When she began getting ill, his Host Commander Rosie felt it expedient to have him watch over Lynda as well as Nikolas.

Jordan wondered why she would not go to the doctor. Her former Guardian Angel said it was because of two things. First, she could not take the heartache of knowing Nikolas was headed for a life of misery. Secondly, it was because she longed to be reunited with Roger. She often talked to him in her prayers as if he were just beyond the clouds. The feeling of love between them was very much alive in her heart.

As Jordan sat in the grass, he saw Nikolas come outside. He had just come home from school. "Hey mom," he said as he walked up and sat across from her.

"Hi, honey... how was... school?" Lynda asked as she started coughing incessantly for a few moments.

Jordan raised his eyes. Nikolas had been lying about school for over six months now. He attended the alternate schools sparsely and was nowhere near getting his diploma. He was destined to become a dropout. "It went well today, mom."

"Is Zachary… staying at Jake's house?"

"Yeah, he said he would be there until Thursday."

Lynda closed her eyes nodding, thinking, trying to reserve her strength.

Jordan heard something behind him. He turned. It was the Dark Angel Tira.

"What are you doing here?" he asked.

"You know me, Jordan. I like to keep a close eye on my clients. Poor Nikolas, he is going to lose his mother soon, and then there will be no one in his way."

"I will be in his way. I will be standing right between you two." Even as Jordan said it, he knew it would be fruitless. He had no idea why, but his influence over Nikolas was not working. Tira was winning in a big way, and all he could do was sit back and wonder how.

Tira said, "I hear you had a client who was killed in Las Vegas at the shooting."

Jordan looked up, "How do you know?"

"I was there. Legion invited me to watch." Tira smirked.

"Legion invited you? I doubt Legion talks to a lowly Dark Angel like you."

Tira kicked his arms out from behind him, and he fell back onto the grass. "Why should he not talk to me? He is my lover."

"Oh, you mean you are one of his latest concubines."

Tira swung her foot to kick him in the face, but Jordan caught it with one hand. He twisted it hard and threw her to the ground. "Watch it, Tira. You may be winning, but you are no match for me."

Tira jumped to her feet, pulled her dagger, and began to circle, "Get up you wretch. I'll show you right here and now."

Suddenly he heard, "MOM!"

Tira and Jordan turned just in time to hear a wine glass shattering. Lynda was laying on the brick patio face down. Nikolas ran to her side, yelling, trying to lift her, then pulled out his phone and called 911.

Chapter 99

October 29 - November 1, 2017
Northwest Medical Center, Parkland Florida

NIKOLAS FURIOUSLY TEXTED his brother Zachary.

"Zachary, mom is on her way to the hospital. Get your ass home."

"What the hell happened?"

"Something is wrong!"

"What?"

"I don't' know. She passed out."

"Well, what the hell did you do now?"

"You idiot! Get home. Hurry, I am calling Uber to take me there."

"What hospital?"

"Northwest."

"I'll get a ride there."

Twenty minutes later Uber arrived and drove Nikolas to the hospital. He got out at the emergency room and went inside. His mom was being attended to by several nurses who were putting IV's in her arm. A breathing mask was over her face. Nikolas was afraid.

He stood in the back of the room watching them work on her. Her eyes were closed, and her breathing was labored. He noticed the nurse kept looking up at the vital signs. Soon a doctor came in and listened to her heart. He ordered a scan of her chest. Soon, they all finished, and the nurse told Nikolas to sit down in a chair and left.

~ ~ ~ ~

Two days later Nikolas sat in the back of the room watching Lynda's breathing continue to slow. It was evening, and Zachary had already left to go back to his friend's house. Nikolas had not left the room since he had arrived at the hospital, sleeping in the chair each evening and buying his food in the cafeteria. He walked over to the bedside and brushed the hair out of Lynda's face. She looked pale and thinner than he had ever seen her. He was scared. "Mom, please don't die. I need you. Mom? Can you hear me?" Tears began forming in his eyes.

The Dark Angel Tira was present. She could see that he truly loved his mom, and while she normally hated such displays, something about this lost soul crying for the only person who ever loved him touched her. Tira had known love only a few times in her thousands of years. Now she was being used as nothing more than a sex slave, or as Jordan had put it, a concubine, and she hated it.

Suddenly a light appeared by Lynda's bed, and Tira cringed. In a moment the Angel Jordan appeared accompanied by another tall Angel, a female dressed in white who carried a torch. Tira recognized her. It was the Angel of Death. Jordan whispered, "Lynda, your troubled days are over. The Lord has granted you grace to die on this holy day."

Lynda opened her eyes slightly and looked up at Jordan. Nikolas saw this and drew closer to her, "Mom, can you hear me?"

Lynda turned her head to look at Nikolas. Her eyes were full of sorrow, and she slowly smiled, nodding. Then she looked to the foot of the bed and glared at Tira. Tira was startled. She had no connection with Lynda, and it was seemingly impossible that she could be seen. But Lynda deepened her glare and mouthed the words, "Leave… him… alone!"

Tira felt a jolt of pain rip through her, and she knew this was a warning, not from Lynda, but from the other side. It caused her to shudder. She swallowed and saw Jordan glance over at her. He knew what had just happened, and his eyes showed not anger, but rather a pity as if he knew some darkness was coming for her.

Nikolas cried, saying, "Mom, I'm sorry,"

Lynda turned to look at Nikolas, and a tear rolled down her cheek, then another, then another, then she stopped breathing and grew still.

In a moment the Angel of Death took her by the hand and helped her to stand. Lynda walked with her peacefully away from her human body out the hospital room door with Jordan trailing behind. This was the way every person left the world. But Lynda stopped, she resisted, pulling away, trying to go back. "He needs me!" she cried. But Jordan gently turned her back, "Your time is over Lynda. We must go."

The beepers next to Lynda's dead corpse started going off, and Nikolas started to scream, "Help! Please! Someone, help!"

Tira should have been elated, but she had already left. She was sitting on the roof of the hospital breathing heavily. Whatever had just happened to her had scared her. It was as if her sins, all her sins, were suddenly being cast on top of her head. She thought of long ago when she was an Angel of Light when she foolishly followed them all to their own 'promised land.' She thought about the day she found out that they could never go back. Then she thought about the years sealed in by the dome, and she began to cry.

Chapter 100

October 29 - November 1, 2017
Forest Lawn Memorial Gardens, Parkland Florida

NIKOLAS STOOD BY THE COFFIN sitting atop the large straps that would later lower his mother's body into the ground. "Nikolas?"
He turned, it was their former neighbor Roxanne Deschamps. "How are you, honey?"

Nikolas shrugged his shoulders.

Roxanne said, "I spoke to your brother Zachary. I want you to both come live with me in Lantana Cascades. My son Mark has moved out, and I have a bedroom for each of you."

"I don't know," he said, turning to look back at the coffin.

"It will be good for you both, Nikolas. I am a very good cook."

"Ok."

"Your uncle told me they are selling the house so you may as well get your things and come over later today. Would you like that?"

"Ok."

"All right, honey. Would you like me to give you a ride to get your things?"

"No, I'll take an Uber."

"All right, here is my phone number and address. Call me when you are leaving, and I will cook up some hamburgers. Zachary is coming over now."

"Ok."

"I'll see you later then." She turned and left, and Nikolas pretended to walk away, but when he saw she had left, he went back to the graveside and stared at the coffin for over an hour.

Chapter 101

November 29, 2017
Roxanne Deschamps Home, Lantana Cascades

A MONTH LATER, NIKOLAS STARED OUT THE WINDOW at the steady rain from the backseat of Roxanne Deschamps Ford Explorer. He shouted, "Just take me to my fucking friend's house!"

"Watch your mouth, Nikolas!"

"This, sucks!" He began punching the interior ceiling of the car. "This sucks! This sucks! This fucking sucks!"

"Stop it!" screamed Roxanne as she pulled into the short drive next to her mobile home. She got out and stormed into the house and called her son Mark. Nikolas walked in and went straight to his room. Within minutes Roxanne heard things being thrown against the walls, breaking. She ran down the hall. "Get the hell out of this house!"

"Fuck you!" he screamed, holding his hands against his head, "Stop! Stop! Stop!"

"Who the hell are you talking to!" she screamed.

"It's her! It's them! It's Legion!" he yelled, as he picked up the alarm clock and smashed it into the window, cracking the glass.

Within a minute, her son Mark pulled in, screeched to a stop, and ran inside, going right past his mother and into the bedroom, yelling, "What the hell are you doing?"

Nikolas turned to him, and his eyes glowed like fire. In a low groveling voice, he said, "Get away from me! I will kill you!"

Roxanne felt fear shoot through her veins. She frantically fumbled her phone in her hands and dialed 911.

"911, what is your emergency?"

"Help! My name is Roxanne De...." She heard rumbling in the room and ran to the door to see Mark and Nikolas wrestling and punching each other. "Stop it!" she yelled. She dropped the phone and ran over, kicking Nikolas in the back, knocking him off Mark. Nikolas got up and turned toward her. He froze and smiled. He grabbed his wallet and opened his top drawer, withdrawing a single bullet and holding it up in her face. Then he left.

Roxanne helped Mark up and picked up the phone.

"Please send the sheriff right away."

"Deputies from Palm Beach are already on the way ma'am. Stay on the phone. What happened?"

"It's this crazy kid, Nikolas Cruz. He just threatened to kill my son. He just bought another gun. I think he is going to get it and come back and kill us."

"How do you know him, ma'am?"

"I took him in because his mother just passed away," she said. "That's all he wants is his gun. That's all he cares about. Wait a minute!" She raced to the window and looked out the back at the hole Nikolas had dug the day before, the one she had planned ongoing to look at when he was not home but had not had the chance yet. She ran back to the phone, "He dug a hole in the backyard, and I think he has a gun buried in it."

"Stay inside the house, ma'am."

"This kid already owns eight guns. He keeps them at his friend's house in Parkland... and he has a bullet-proof vest!" Roxanne was feeling more panicked by the moment.

"Ma'am, has he been known to be violent?"

"Yes, God yes! He put the gun to his own mother's head back in June. His brother Zachary told me. He said he did it to him too, just three weeks ago." Roxanne could not believe her own words. She could not believe she knew all this and had allowed her concern for his welfare to override her judgment. It all started to become clear. She heard the blaring sirens, and she let out a great sigh of relief. "They are here."

Chapter 102

November 30, 2017
Roxanne Deschamps Home, Lantana Cascades

ROXANNE SAT UP ALL NIGHT piecing things together. Both Zachary and her son Mark had talked with her much of the night, both decrying how crazy Nikolas was. When Zachary told her about all the incidents at school, and about Nikolas Instagram post over the summer, she realized she had to warn the Sheriff's Office. She fell asleep, woke early, and immediately picked up the phone and dialed the Broward County Sheriff's Office.

"Hello, may I help you."

"I need to report an incident that may occur."

"That may occur?"

"Yes, I believe there is a dangerous person who could be a school shooter in the making."

"One moment ma'am."

She was on hold for over ten minutes, and she muttered to herself, "They tell us if you see something, say something, and then they put us on hold."

On the other end of the line, Deputy Guntis Trejos, a nineteen-year veteran of the department, poured his coffee and grabbed one more half of a donut. A secretary in the bullpen smiled, and shouted over, "That lady is still on hold!"

"Oh, shit. Hold on Jim; I gotta take this call."

He and Jim were taking a ride out for lunch to a special restaurant. Today was Jim's birthday.

"Hi, this is Deputy Trejos, how can I help you?"

"Yes, Nikolas Cruz, he used to live there in Parkland, and he used to go to Stoneman Douglass High School. I am telling you, this kid is angry. He is a school shooter in the making! He owns like eight guns."

"Slow down man. What is his name?" He motioned up at Jim who was standing in the doorway to wait a minute.

"Ok, can you spell that?"

Roxanne spelled it out, "N I K O L A S   C R U Z."

He wrote on a yellow sticky note, N I C O L A S   C R U Z.

"Ok ma'am, I've got it. Now why do you say this?"

"He's collecting guns and knives, and he's been talking about killing himself. He hates everyone at that school!"

"Ok, slow down ma'am, let me write this down..." He wiped the glaze from his fingers on the back of the sticky note.

She waited for him, and he said, "Ok, you said he used to live here?"

"Yes!"

"Where does he live now?"

"He lived with me here in Palm Springs County until yesterday. He may be going back to Parkland."

Trejos looked up at his partner again and signaled another minute. "Ma'am, I am going to refer this over to the Palm Springs County Sheriff's Department since that is his most recent address."

"I am telling you he is a Parkland resident. He was only here temporarily."

"Hold on, ma'am."

Trejos pulled up his computer and typed "Nicolas Cruz." Nothing came up because he had used 'c' instead of 'k'. He paused for a few moments, thinking, then said, "Ok, ma'am. I am going to investigate this. Thank you for the call."

He hung up, "Let's get going I am starving."

His now placed the not-so-sticky note on his desk. As they went to leave, the note fell unnoticed to the floor at the back of his desk.

Aloof to it all, Officer Trejos returned from lunch, got busy with something else, and never made the call.

Chapter 103

Dec 9, 2017
Snead Home, Parkland Florida

J.T. SNEAD HUNG UP THE PHONE. He had just talked to Nikolas. He now dialed his mom's cell phone, "Mom, remember my friend Nikolas?"

"Of course, I do. His mom just passed a month ago."

"Can he live with us for a while?"

"Why?"

"He said that he and his brother were living with some lady and she was using his credit cards. He said he is supposed to inherit $800,000 but not for a year or so."

Kimberly Snead was a compassionate woman, but she did not need another headache. The fact that Nikolas stood to inherit money meant that he would not become dependent on them. She remembered him as always being quiet, strange too, but quiet. "Well I have to talk to your father, but it sounds ok to me, but only for a short while."

That night Kimberly spoke with her husband, James. James was a decorated army veteran and a former military intelligence analyst who served stints in the Middle East. He knew how to raise successful children.

"I know who Nikolas is. I don't know why we couldn't give it a try."

"There is one catch."

"What is that?"

"He has guns, and from what J.T. tells me, he has a lot of them."

"I don't have any problem with guns, but they have to be locked up, and we have to have the key."

James and Kimberly had their own collection of guns. A robbery a few years earlier had pushed them to the point of having them in their home for protection, but the guns were stored in a locked case to which only they had the key.

The following day Nikolas pulled up in an Uber and unloaded several large duffel bags on the lawn. J.T. and Kimberly were waiting for him. "Hi Nikolas, welcome. Wow, you have a lot of stuff."

Nikolas smiled, nodding.

Kimberly asked, "J.T. told me you have a number of guns and knives. Where are they?"

"In those two bags."

"All right, we will put those into the garage until my husband comes home. He wants you to purchase a gun locker, and they will have to be locked up."

Nikolas nodded, and said calmly, "That's fine."

"Why do you have so many guns, anyway?" asked Kimberly.

"I am learning how to hunt."

"Oh, ok," she turned to her son, "J.T. help him carry those into the garage and then you boys can take everything else into Nikolas' room."

"Thank you, Mrs. Snead."

"You're welcome."

Nikolas put his stuff away then called Uber. He went to the Gun World of South Florida, Deerfield Beach and purchased a gun locker large enough to fit his guns. It came with two sets of keys. He then took Uber home, stopping at Walmart to have a duplicate key made.

When James Snead came home, he was surprised to see Nikolas had already set up and locked up his gun case in the garage. Nikolas handed him both sets of original keys.

James said, "Well, let's see what you got here."

James opened and immediately his eyes widened at seeing the AR 15. "Whoa, what do you have this for."

"I've been learning how to shoot all kinds of guns. I want to be a hunter like my dad was."

"All Right here are the rules. This case stays locked, and you must ask me for permission to unlock it. I will hold both keys. Is that understood?"

"Yes," Nikolas said quietly.

Chapter 104

December 17, 2017
Stoneman Douglas High School

IT WAS EARLY MORNING when Assistant Principal Winifred Porter picked up the phone and dialed his fellow principal Denise Reed.

"Yes?" Denise said.

"Hey, I forgot to tell you. Julie Evans is sending over some security expert today to meet with us."

"What! Right before Christmas! Well, this is great timing. I am so busy. I don't think I can take on one more thing."

"I know; I had to schedule it. They've been after me to show some progress. They said we've been putting it off for too long."

"Well that's not true. It's their job to direct us. We don't really have a say. By the way, why doesn't Principal Thompson handle this himself? He's more in touch with district."

"Don't ask me. But as you know, he has put me in charge of campus security."

"I still don't know how we are supposed to afford all of this security?"

"From what I've heard, the district got over 104 million dollars from the bond levy Runcie got passed a couple of years ago. I also heard they've only spent 5 million of it so far."

"104 million dollars! That is outrageous. That's so much money."

"Oh, don't worry. I bet Julie Evans and the rest of them down at district wish the money could be put into salaries and benefits for personnel. You know how Runcie feels about fighting for our pay. I've got to give him credit."

"Well, I know they can't do that, but I tell you one thing, we could all sure use a raise. I wish they would pass a bond levy for that!"

"Yeah, right? Listen, I've got to go. I'll see you at the meeting later."

~ ~ ~ ~

Former Secret Service Agent Steve Wexler was sitting on his patio sipping coffee and jotting down some notes about his upcoming visit later that morning when the phone rang. It was his boss, Eli Coury.

"What's up, Eli?"

"Are you going down to Stoneman Douglass today?"

"Yes, I am. I am getting ready for the meeting now."

"We've got to break through. This dance around security has lasted long enough."

"I don't follow."

"They keep saying they don't have any money. These schools are a security nightmare. We have got to show them how vulnerable they are."

"I have an idea."

"What is it?" asked Eli.

"When I was in the secret service, we used to use yellow sticky notes to demonstrate just how at-risk people in a situation were. I would place one onto people who would likely be shot. It had a pretty dramatic effect."

"Well, let's hope it has a dramatic effect! They are so slow in that county! It seems to me that they are dragging their feet on purpose. I've been trying to get them to spend more money on security with us for two years. All we get is a dribble."

"All right. I will try that today, and we will see if it does not send a message."

"Document this, so I can send it to Julie Evans, not that it will do any good!"

"Yea, right? Ok, I'll talk to you later."

~ ~ ~ ~

That afternoon, Wexler circled the block once, then drove unchallenged through a wide-open security gate at the west end of the building. He parked his car in a no-parking zone near the entrance, walked into the school and asked for Assistant Principal Winifred to be called down. When Winifred arrived, Wexler said, "Follow me."

He proceeded to approach people nearest him, hand them a yellow post-it note, and ask them to stay in place for two minutes. When he had handed out twenty, he turned to Winifred and said, "These 20 people have just been shot."

Winifred looked puzzled, "I don't understand."

"I just drove unopposed through that gate over there. I walked in, unopposed, and if I am a trained shooter, I began firing my weapon right away. Those twenty people I handed yellow post it notes to, would have been shot within the first 30 seconds."

"All right, you made your point. Let's go upstairs."

~ ~ ~ ~

Later that day Assistant Principal Winifred called Administrator Julie Evans at the Broward County Schools District Offices and relayed what had happened.

"That's ridiculous!" she said.

"I know. It scared more than a few people."

"What did Principal Thompson say?"

"He was pissed. He felt it was an overreach."

"I will talk to Wexler's boss. All they want is for us to spend more money."

"Hey Julie, is it true we have 104 million to spend?"

"Yeah, on paper it's true. But you know how it goes. It's priorities. Runcie's focus is teachers' salaries and benefits."

Julie then asked, "Hey, by the way. We have already allocated money to keep those gates closed. Why aren't they being attended to? Who is supposed to handle that?"

"That's our wonderful security monitor team. They open all the gates every day an hour or so before dismissal."

"Well, why?"

"Because they're too lazy to do it the right way. Does the name Andrew Medina or David Taylor ring a bell?"

"I remember Medina. Look, Winifred, these people get paid plenty of money to do a simple job. Tell them to start doing it right."

"I'll try, but to be honest, there seems to be a whole culture of lax security around here. I am trying to change it."

"Welcome to my world," said Julie. "I've got to go. Merry Christmas."

"Ok, bye. Merry Christmas."

Chapter 105

January 5, 2018
FBI Headquarters – Washington D. C.

A TALL RED-HAIRED AGENT in his mid-fifties swung around in his swivel chair and picked up the phone.

"This is Agent Demeter."

"Hi, I am calling about a neighbor of mine. This kid is trouble, and I just know he's going to explode."

"Ok, what is your name?"

"I am not comfortable giving my name."

"Ok, that is fine. Tell me his name please."

"His name is Nikolas Cruz."

"All right, what else can you tell me about him?"

"I am afraid he is going to slip into a school and start shooting the place up. He hurts animals. He is obsessed with guns. He is constantly posting disturbing pictures on social media. He may be involved with ISIS."

"Where does he live, ma'am?"

"He lived in Parkland, Florida and moved when his mom died. But I am pretty sure he is back in Parkland. I think he is staying with a friend."

"Do you have their address?"

"No, but I believe the kid's name is J.T. Snead."

"All right, thank you for the call."

"Wait! What, are you going to do?" she asked, anxious at the perceived laxity in the agent's voice.

"We are going to do what we always do with tips like this, mam. We are going to look into it."

"Will I be notified?"

"No, mam. That is not our policy."

"Ok, thank you."

~ ~ ~ ~

The following day, Agent Demeter was assigned onto the growing task force investigating the mass-shooting in Las Vegas. Two weeks after that, under the mounting pressure from his supervisor of his growing case backlog, Agent Demeter spent an entire day going through all the calls he had received over the past month. At one point, he picked up his notes related to the phone call regarding Cruz and looked them over. He determined there was no need to contact the Miami Field Office, and he closed the case, checking the box that stated, "no lead value."

Chapter 106

January 20, 2018
Vamorda's Villa, Southern Shores of Hell

LEGION ARRIVED AT VAMORDA'S VILLA. He walked in and found her sitting on a couch. He said, "I am worried about our plans for the son of Vesru. Tira is too inexperienced; I am afraid she will fail us."

Vamorda said, "I will go and make sure!"

"No, you fool, you cannot go. It will be noticed. I need someone else, someone I can trust."

"Who, my Lord."

"Sansa."

Vamorda laughed, "You put her in a dark cage for failing to keep Thaddus occupied during the Las Vegas Shooting. Why would you trust her now?"

He sneered, "Do not question me, Vamorda. Before that, she served me well for a very long time. I think she has something to prove, and certainly a reason not to fail again. Bring her to me."

Vamorda immediately summoned two of her Dark Angels and instructed them to retrieve Sansa from the dark cage she had been hanging in for over 100 days. They went to the cage and slowly lowered it to the ground. When they opened the door, she fell out onto the ground in a fetal position, shaking uncontrollably. They picked her up as her body continued to shudder from the trauma.

They flew her back to Vamorda's villa and threw her down in front of them. Legion bent down next to her, "Sansa, have you learned your lesson?"

She began to shudder as several tears fell down her cheeks. In a quivering voice she whispered, "Yes… yes, I have…, my Lord." Sansa was lying. Being inside the cage had changed her in a way she could have never imagined. She was emptied of every ambition she ever held.

"Good, because I will give you another chance to prove yourself. You will see that a young boy who is the son of a Dark Angel is going to do something very sinister. You will oversee Tira make sure that everything goes according to my wishes." Legion brushed her hair out of her face, "Can you do that for me, Sansa?"

Sansa began to nod quickly, "Yes."

"Good. Vamorda, get her cleaned up and fed. Summon Tira and put everything in motion."

Chapter 107

January 31, 2018
Parkland, Florida

SIX DAYS LATER, THE DARK ANGEL SANSA FLEW alongside Tira toward Nikolas' home. She still felt weak and struggled to keep up. Sansa asked, "Why are we not being opposed more by the forces of Heaven in this case?"

Tira coyly smiled, "He has been given a Dark Baptism, and they do not know about it."

"I have not heard of a Dark Baptism being given in a very long time."

"That's why he is so special. We can use him for something very dark. Legion and I know this. We have been working with this child for a long time."

"Aren't you afraid of getting punished by the Lords?" Sansa was grimly aware of what it meant to be in a dark cage, even if only for a day. It was a horrible experience that would haunt anyone. She was also quite aware of the hundreds of Dark Angels who were imprisoned currently in dark cages for carrying out atrocities that went well beyond the normal battle for the souls of men and women.

Tira laughed, "Why should I be afraid? They can't even find Nikolas half the time. Besides, I have plenty of alibis."

Nikolas was not at home, but Tira knew where he would be, and they flew to the shooting range. Nikolas was there practicing shooting, firing off hundreds of rounds. When they were leaving,

Tira said, "I will begin putting the seeds of the plan into his head. Legion wants this to be big, very big."

"How big?"

Tira smiled, "Hundreds."

Sansa was struck by the evil, unfeeling way Tira said it, and she instantly knew that being inside the dark cage had changed her. Something was different, something had been lost forever.

Sansa asked, "Why have you not acted sooner. From all you told me, this could have been done years ago."

"It was his wretched mother standing in the way. Her prayers during the last years of her life blocked my power."

"Really?" asked Sansa, surprised to hear this.

"Yes, Nikolas treated her horribly many times, but he always listened to her, and until she died, I could not connect with him."

Sansa nodded, wondering about all she had said, including wondering about that age-old mystery neither the Angels nor the Dark Angels understood: The power of a mother's love.

Tira then said, "The plan is set for February 18th. I will meet you here on the 15th to begin the countdown and make sure he goes through with the plan."

"Don't you want my help before then?"

"Help, for what? I am busy before then and nothing needs done. The seeds have all been planted not only in Nikolas but in everyone surrounding this as well. Besides, I have plans with one of my lovers. Don't you have a lover, you must after being cooped up for three months."

Sansa felt confused, and it was a feeling she had not felt in centuries. She would normally take command of the situation and be angry with Tira, but she wasn't. She would also have any lover she wanted, but she didn't want any. She wanted to be alone.

Sansa replied, "Fine, I will see you on the 15th."

~ ~ ~ ~

That evening Sansa flew to the western side of Florida and picked the beach near the Marriott Resort on Marco Island. She sat in the sand taking in the setting sun, marveling at all the tourists enjoying the beach. Normally she would be loathing their very presence, but now, in some way, they didn't bother her.

When the sun went down, she nestled into the sand, covering herself with her dark wings, and tried to sleep, but she couldn't. Her conversation with Tira kept running through her mind. *How could Tira be so bold?* There was good reason to be afraid of what the Lords when planning something like this.

Sansa looked up at the lights of the Marriott and it reminded her immediately of Las Vegas. She had escaped the wrath of the Lords there in October, only because of her distant connection. She needed to stay far away from this event too. But how? If Legion found out, she would be destroyed. If the Lords were to find out of her involvement, especially after Las Vegas, she would be locked away in a dark cage. She was damned either way.

Feeling completely overwhelmed, she began to weep softly, and fell asleep.

Chapter 108

February 3, 2018
Snead Home, Parkland Florida

KIMBERLY SNEAD said to her husband James, "Nikolas has been so aimless lately. I think he is depressed."

"Really?"

"He asked if he could take his gun to the shooting range."

"Well, I think that is ok. Maybe it will help him."

Later that morning Kimberly took him to the range.

The Angel Jordan had been watching and went along. He sensed trouble was brewing, and despite his ineffective influence over Nikolas, he was determined to keep a close eye on him.

Nikolas stood in the outdoor firing range, methodically shooting round after round with his face showing no emotion. It was if he were some kind of infantryman.

Just then Jordan saw her arrive. It was Sansa, landing in the nearby woods, also watching Nikolas. He stepped behind a wall to hide. *Sansa, what is she doing here? It has been so very long.* He waited a little while, then circled and came up behind her. "Sansa?"

Sansa immediately knew the voice. She wheeled around, "Jordan? What are you doing here!"

"I am Nikolas' Guardian Angel. I think the question is, 'What are YOU doing here?'"

"I... I am a friend of Tira's. She asked me to keep an eye on him."

"Oh, I see." Jordan knew she was lying, but somehow, he did not mind. He had loved her since the first time he laid eyes on her thousands of years earlier. She was the one, the one who broke his heart when she left during the mass exodus of the Angels who left Heaven.

Jordan asked, "How have you been?"

She wanted to tell him. She wanted to tell him everything. He didn't know about Las Vegas, nor about her role, or the punishment in the dark cage. She softly replied, "I've been better. But... I hope things will improve. UMM... look I must go now."

"Ok." Jordan was surprised at her demeanor. It was devoid of the typical edgy animosity all Dark Angels held.

All the way home Sansa had one thing on her mind: Jordan. Jordan was her first lover in Heaven before she followed the rebels who foolishly left for their own land, and ultimately, the Dark Side. Jordan was the one she could never forget. She never sought him out, for her own reasons, though she had heard he was happy.

When she was in the dark cage, the memory of him, for some strange reason, had come to her mind, and it helped her to get through.

Chapter 109

February 8, 2018
Dollar Store, Parkland Florida

NIKOLAS WALKED DOWN the dirty carpeted floor toward the back of the Dollar Store. He opened the closet next to the customer service room, pulled out a vacuum, and began vacuuming. He felt good having a job although he was a little embarrassed that it was there. He wanted to do something important, to be someone important. He heard the door signal go off.

He left the vacuum and went up front. It was two girls from Stoneman Douglas. He had seen them around and was pretty sure they were freshmen. One of them he had noticed before and thought she was pretty.

They asked for some birthday balloons to be blown up. Nikolas asked, "So... um... you go to Stoneman?"

"Yes," the one he thought was cute replied.

"Whose birthday?" he asked, as he began blowing up a balloon.

The other girl replied, "It's her boyfriend's. Oh look," she said pointing, "Valentine's day balloons. Let's mix some in."

Nikolas frowned. He wanted a girlfriend in the worst way, but he did not know where to even begin.

The girl Nikolas liked said, "That's a great idea."

She turned to Nikolas, "Can you blow up some of those too?"

Nikolas walked over to the giant red balloons, "Sure. How many?"

"Oh, three or four, hey, didn't you used to go to Stoneman?"

"Yes, I did," Nikolas felt a glimmer of hope like he was a person worthy to talk to.

The girl asked, "Did you graduate already?"

Nikolas smiled, and would not answer. He was too embarrassed. He turned and began blowing up the balloons. He finished the birthday balloons then began blowing up Valentine's Day balloons. He heard the girls talking and giggling, and it made him mad. He hated Valentine's Day. He remembered in vivid detail the day, two years earlier, when he tried to give Skylar the box of chocolates and her friends laughed at him.

Nikolas finished blowing up the balloons and rang them out without saying a word. He watched them leave, embarrassed he was not doing more with his life. But he didn't know what to do, and he didn't know even where to begin.

When he got home, Kimberly Snead was cooking dinner. She said hello and watched him go straight upstairs. She could tell he was despondent, so she went upstairs, "Nikolas, can I come in?"

"Yes,"

"What is wrong?"

"A lot. I have a lousy job... and I don't have a girlfriend."

"Oh, don't worry about that." Kimberly sat on the bed and put her arm around him, "You're a good-looking young man. Some girl is going to be happy to meet you someday. It will happen."

"When!" he said in a tone that alarmed her. She stood up, "Well, someday."

"I can't stand it! All those kids... they laugh at me!"

"What kids?"

He leaned his head back, grimacing, "Those stupid kids at school!"

"What school?"

"Stoneman! They all did!"

She sighed, "Nikolas, I'm sorry!"

He said nothing.

"Hey, Nikolas, I have a really good therapist. He's a young guy. Do want to come with me and maybe talk to him?"

Nikolas did not respond, but he was thinking.

Kimberly said, "It might be good for you."

"Maybe, but I'm not taking any fucking medicine!"

She was alarmed, this was the first time she had heard him swear so vehemently. "Ok, that is fine. We will go in the morning."

The next day Nikolas accompanied her and spent a few minutes talking to the therapist, discussing if he should start seeing them. He took a business card and told them he had to figure out what his insurance would allow. On the way home, he seemed excited.

"What is it?" Kim asked.

"I know what I want to be?"

"What?"

"An Army Infantryman. I want to carry a gun and shoot people!"

"When... when did you decide that?"

"A long time ago. A recruiter came to our school. I just forgot about it."

"Well, we can look into that. You let me know when you are ready, and I can drive you down to the recruiting office."

Nikolas sat looking out the window, firing his AR 15 in his mind, "BAM! BAM! BAM! BAM!"

~ ~ ~ ~

It was now the fifth day since Sansa had seen Jordan and the old feelings of love, she had for him were back. All day long she could think of nothing else but him. She lamented the day she had left.

She had to explain to him, to let him know how sorry she was. She needed to spend time with him. She went to a stationery store and got a piece of parchment looking paper and a pen, then sat down.

Dear Jordan,

I need to see you and talk to you. Long ago, I did something foolish that I have regretted my entire life, and I feel like I can't go on anymore unless I have the chance to spend some time with you and tell you how I feel.

Could we carve out a few hours and just meet and talk?

Sansa

She wiped the heartfelt tears from her eyes and rolled up the letter. She then summoned a messenger bird and told it to take the message to the Angel Jordan.

Chapter 110

February 11, 2018
Vamorda's Plantation – Southern Shores of Hell

TIRA STOOD ANXIOUSLY in Vamorda's spacious parlor waiting for her meeting. She was taking a big risk, and she knew it, but she also knew she was never going back to the obscurity of being nothing more than a rank-and-file Dark Angel. This was her moment to shine, not Sansa's and certainly not Vamorda's.

Vamorda walked into the room, towering over the much shorter Tira and glared at her, "Where is Sansa?"

"She is with her lover, but we are meeting tomorrow." Tira was lying, but that was what Dark Angels did, they lied.

"What is your report?"

"Everything is going exactly as planned. Now that the mother is out of the way, there are no obstacles."

Vamorda face grew sinister, "You two best not foul this up, or I promise my wrath will be severe. Do you understand?"

"Of course, I do."

"Good, then as soon as you leave here, go find her and start the final steps."

~ ~ ~ ~

Sansa woke to the sound of the gently washing surf. It was her third consecutive night sleeping on a beach in the Florida Keys. Despite the beautiful sunrises and sunsets, she was growing despondent. Jordan had not written back, and for reasons she could not fully understand, she felt lost. She got up and waded into the morning surf to bathe, then flew to a nearby orchard to pick a few oranges she could eat for breakfast.

While she was sitting on the beach, a messenger bird arrived. Her heart leaped as she anxiously opened it. It was from Jordan.

Dear Sansa

How nice of you to write to me. As you know, as an Angel of Heaven, I am not allowed to have any meeting with an Angel from the Dark Side, but I will make an exception, because I too, wish to spend time with you and talk.

Meet me at Upolu Island in the Pacific Ocean in two days. I will be there at sunrise.

Jordan

Sansa shook her head for a moment; she suddenly recalled how Jordan always carefully followed the rules to the 'T.' She didn't mind, it was never her way, but Jordan's attention to this had always amused her. The truth was though; she was excited to see him. But at the same time, she felt risk. Should Legion discover her meeting, it would be trouble, perhaps trouble that would finally destroy her. She folded the letter up, kissed it, and put it into the pocket in her tunic.

Chapter 111

February 11, 2018
Anne's Beach – Florida Keys

SANSA WOKE UP on the beach feeling excited. She washed up then looked to the East. She would fly in that direction to the Island of Ulopu. She set out, flying into a strong prevailing wind. While flying over the African Continent, she flew lower to see the vast herds of animals beneath her. She remembered the day it all changed.

It was the day Eve ate from the forbidden tree. On that day, the animals became vicious, and not only turned on the Angels but turned on each other.

Soon she was back out over the Pacific Ocean when the other fateful day came to mind. It was when she left Heaven with over 200,000 Angels. It was a decision every one of them would forever regret. She wiped a few tears from her face and kept going.

Finally, the Island of Ulopu came into view. She landed, feeling nervous, and she knew 'why'. It was because Jordan was the only Angel she ever truly loved. The months in the darkness of the cage had reminded her of that.

A short time later, Jordan arrived, dressed in his typical uniform of the 3rd Heavenly Realm. "Hi Sansa, how are you?"

"I am... well... to be perfectly honest... I am hungry!"

Jordan laughed, "Well, that figures. You were always hungry. Why should anything have changed."

Jordan looked around, "Well, I suppose we better start by gathering some food. Let's go."

They flew up towards the middle of the island and gathered some fruits and nuts. They sat eating together on a hillside overlooking the sea.

When they had finished, Sansa asked, "Jordan, do you still enjoy swimming?"

"Oh, yes, just as much as ever."

"Good, catch me if you can!"

Sansa leaped up into the air and raced toward the ocean as Jordan followed. She plummeted downward, piercing the ocean surface, shooting through the refreshing clear waters. She glanced behind her and saw Jordan smiling, right on her tail. She laughed and started to zig zag, trying to lose him, but it was fruitless. Finally, she slowed and waved for him to come alongside.

Soon, they headed for the shore, and Jordan snagged two fish which would be their lunch. On the beach, they built a fire, cooked the fish. As they quietly ate, Sansa wondered what Jordan was thinking. She wondered if he still loved her. She wondered if he was still attracted to her. She wondered if there was someone else, and perhaps this magical day was just a courtesy to her.

After lunch, they went on a hike around the island. There were some homes along the South Ocean Road and in front of one of the homes were several bikes. Sansa ran up, hopped on one and said, "Let's go for a ride Jordan." She took off, riding down the hillside road.

Jordan yelled, "Sansa, you can't just take someone's bike!"

He waited a moment, and when she did not stop, he jumped on the other bike and took off after her. He was laughing to himself watching her race ahead down the ocean-side road. Behind him, he heard someone shouting, and he saw the homeowner bewildered as to how two of his bikes had driven off by themselves.

Jordan laughed loudly as the breeze blew across his face. He had just stolen his first bike, and it was because of Sansa, and he realized how empty his life had been without her.

Sansa raced past a sign that said To-Sua Ocean Trench, and she stopped. She threw the bike down and ran down the path. Jordan jumped off and raced after her.

Suddenly Sansa saw the most amazing ocean inlet she had ever seen. She ran to the cliff edge and dove into the pristine waters. She bobbed up to see Jordan looking down.

"Come on in! The waters warm!" she yelled, laughing.

Jordan walked back ten feet, then ran full speed, leaping off into a magnificent swan dive, piercing the water next to her. He reached the bottom, then turned and swam upwards. When he saw Sansa's legs paddling in the water he could not resist, and he zoomed toward her, grasped her ankles, and pulled her under.

"Ahhh!" she screamed as she flailed her arms in the air and quickly closed her mouth just before going under. Under the water, Jordan rose upwards behind her, put his arms around her, and hugged her tenderly. Sansa let herself surrender to him, then turned to face him. They looked through the clear water into each other's eyes, both remembering the love that was seared into their hearts so long ago.

Sansa then pushed him away and swam up to the surface, flying out onto a plateau on the side of the cliff. Jordan flew up next to her.

Sansa could do nothing but smile and stare into his eyes, seeing his face illuminated with the love he felt. It all came rushing back, and she asked, "Jordan, may I kiss you?"

Jordan eyes lowered for a moment, as the hint of a smile came over his face, "Yes."

Sansa leaned forward and gently touched her lips to his. Jordan closed his eyes, and stayed still, taking in her warm, innocent kiss. They pulled away.

Jordan looked out at sea, silent for a few moments, thinking, then said, "I want you to know, Sansa, that right now, I cannot kiss you the way I want to kiss you. But I have a feeling that someday I will be able to, and... well, when that day comes, you better just watch out."

Sansa loved him; she pointed at him, "No, Jordan, when that day comes, you better watch out."

"Uhh, no," said Jordan smiling, and as he stood up on the plateau, and pointed down at her, "You, young lady, better watch out."

Sansa stood up, stepped forward, put her hands playfully on his neck, and pushed him into the cliff, "No, you better watch out mister, because when I am able to kiss you like I want to, it's going to be all over."

Jordan laughed, feeling his head pressing slightly against the rock, "Ok, ok Sansa, you win." He started laughing and watched her playfully glare at him until she smiled and let him go.

"C'mon, let's go," he said. "We can watch the sunset together before we leave."

They walked back towards the bikes, saying nothing, then pedaled down to the beach.

Chapter 112

February 11, 2018
Island of Ulopu

IT WAS TIME TO GO. Sansa and Jordan sat quietly, knowing their magical day together was ending soon. Jordan turned to her, "Why did you leave?"

The words crushed her. "Jordan, at that time, our love was drifting. I was bored, tired, and I felt aimless. Then, the news that so many were leaving came. I didn't know what to do, and... you wouldn't talk to me."

Jordan remembered he had been angry with her because she had said that the leaders had every right to question the Lords. He did not talk to her for weeks, and suddenly, he heard she had gone with them, something he never expected she would do.

"I'm sorry," he said.

"For what!" said Sansa, "I am the one who left."

"You know, Sansa, it crushed me. I never got over it."

She nodded, but it was all too late.

They were quiet for a while, when Jordan asked, "Why are you involved with Tira, and Nikolas?"

"I am not really. I just... you know... I was helping her out."

Jordan said, "Something is happening, I know it. But I can't put my finger on it. It is like nothing I have ever experienced. I can't get through to him. It is like I am blocked."

"That's strange," Sansa replied.

A tear rolled down Sansa's cheek. She knew why. She was lying to the only one she ever loved.

"Why are you crying?" he asked.

She turned away.

"Sansa, what's wrong?"

She wiped her eyes, but more tears fell.

"Sansa, talk to me."

"It's a lie!" she said loudly.

"What?"

She turned to face him, "I am lying to you. It's all a lie. It's been a lie since the first day when we followed them out of Heaven, and ever since, there has been nothing but lies. I'm done lying."

"What, what lie?"

"Nikolas. I have been assigned to watch over Tira, to make sure she succeeds."

Jordan looked perplexed, "Succeeds in what?"

"They want him to kill hundreds."

Jordan froze. "What! When?"

"In five days."

"Where?" asked Jordan.

"Where else. At his former school. But there is more; you need to know that Nikolas received the ancient Dark Baptism. That is why you cannot find him half the time. It is why he cannot hear you. When his mother was suffering, and praying for him, there was a chance, but now…."

"I knew it!" said Jordan. "We have to tell the Lords. They… they must know about the Dark Baptism. It could change everything. Come with me."

"I cannot go to Heaven! I am not allowed."

"My commander Rosie can get us into the Throne Room without any questions."

Sansa protested, "I cannot face the Lords!"

"Sansa, there could be mercy for you. They had mercy on the Dark Angel Thaddus just four months ago."

Sansa cringed. Jordan did not know she had been involved in that terrible massacre. "I can't go there, Jordan."

"Please, for the sake of love, for the sake of everything good, please come with me."

She looked into his sincere eyes and knew she had to trust him now. Something inside her was beckoning for her to move toward her destiny. She said, "Ok, let's go."

Chapter 113

February 13, 2018
Outskirts of the 3rd Heavenly Realm

IT WAS NOW NEAR DUSK as Jordan and Sansa raced towards the border of the 3rd Heavenly Realm. When they arrived, Jordan pulled up in the air, "Wait here, I will get my commander, Rosie."

Sansa watched him race off, and she could not help but feel scared. Everything inside her wanted to turn around. There was still time to avoid Legion finding out. There was still time to save herself. But deep inside she knew it was already too late. She had already chosen her fate. She had to stop Tira.

But seeing the Lords and going before them as the Dark Angel who had helped keep Thaddus away from Stephen Paddock during those last fateful days of his life was filled with danger. Within mere hours she could be back in a dark cage, and this time, not for months, but for years, or even decades, a fate worse than death.

She waited. In the distance, she saw Jordan flying toward her with another taller Angel next to him. Rosie flew right up to her, "I know who you are, Sansa. This better not be a trick."

"It is no trick."

Rosie turned to Jordan, "Bringing a Dark Angel to the Throne Room could cost me dearly, Jordan. Are you sure about her?"

"I am," he said resolutely.

"Then let's go."

~ ~ ~ ~

At once the three flew to Holy Mountain. When they landed on the portico, the guard noticed she was a Dark Angel, "What is she doing here?"

"She is with me," said Rosie. "We need to see the Lords. It is urgent."

"Wait here."

A moment later the guard returned. "They will see you."

A few minutes later the doors were opened, and Rosie, Jordan walked in with Sansa walking behind them They crossed the vast marble Throne Room floor to the three thrones set up in the back as the final rays of the setting sun illuminated everything around them.

They stood before the empty thrones until suddenly the back doors opened, and the three Lords emerged from their living quarters. They quietly walked in glancing at Sansa as they did.

The older Lord, Adonai spoke first, "Rosie, we were told you have an urgent matter. What is it?"

"My Lords, there is a young man, who has received the Dark Baptism."

Adonai looked at the other two Lords, "This has not happened in centuries, are you sure?"

"Yes, my Lord. This Dark Angel here, Sansa, has told us. Something very terrible is about to happen. There is to be a mass shooting."

Adonai said, "Sansa, step forward."

She did, and Adonai asked, "Is this all true?"

"Yes, Lord Adonai," she said, keeping her head down.

"Weren't you involved in what happened at Las Vegas last year?"

"Yes, I was, Lord Adonai."

Jordan looked over at her, puzzled.

Adonai looked at the other Lords whose faces now bore grim looks. Adonai asked, "What do you want us to do Rosie?"

Jordan spoke up, "My Lords, because of the Dark Baptism, we would have a reason to intervene. That was an outlawed practice. It's not a fair fight."

Adonai said, "Jordan, the law of Free Will can never be suspended. You must find a way to stop this if you can. But we cannot stop it. We cannot stop anything a human being decides to do."

Sansa spoke up, "But Lord Adonai, surely this is different."

Adonai thundered, "Sansa, you should consider yourself lucky that we don't arrest you for what you have already done."

Sansa closed her mouth and stepped back.

Rosie knew their answer was final. She bowed, as did the others, and they left.

Outside the Throne Room, they all stopped on the portico. Jordan asked, "How were you involved with what happened in Las Vegas?"

Sansa's countenance fell. "Jordan, I will tell you soon, but not now. It is a long story, and something Legion forced me to do. Will you trust me for a little while?"

Jordan nodded, "Yes, I will." He then asked, "What are we going to do now?"

No one said anything.

Rosie asked, "Can't you stop him, Sansa?"

"I don't know."

Jordan said, "Legion will punish you if he finds out."

"I don't care anymore."

None of them said anything. Rosie and Jordan both knew to cross Legion in this fashion would mean dire trouble. There would be no mercy for her from the Lords either as Yeshua had just made clear; Sansa was a marked Dark Angel.

Chapter 114

February 13, 2018
The Eve of Valentine's Day - Parkland Florida

NIKOLAS SAT UP IN HIS BED holding the video controller as Call of Duty lit up the screen. He was firing fast, accurately, more efficiently than he had ever done before. In his mind, he imagined what he would someday do to all of them that hurt him. They had rejected him, and now they would pay the price.

James and Kimberly walked past his room on their way to bed. James stopped, "Hey, you better turn that off soon. It's getting late."

"I will soon."

"Do you go to the alternative school tomorrow?"

"No, besides, I never go to school on Valentine's Day."

James didn't want to get into it, so he nodded. "Well, do you need a ride to work in the morning?"

"No, I am going in later. I'll take Uber."

"Ok, have a good day."

Nikolas looked up, smiling, "I will. You too."

Tira stood in the corner of his room worried. Nikolas was her ticket to fame and power or misery. She thought back to Brenda, his real mother, and thought about how gullible and weak she was. She thought about the Angels on the other side. They were clueless as to what was going on, but would they catch on somehow? Would they find a way to stop him?

She only had a short time left, and her deed would be accomplished. The key now was to remain blameless, and yet, take all the credit.

Chapter 115

February 13, 2018
The 3rd Land of Reform

NIGHT HAD FALLEN UPON THE HEAVENS as Rosie, Jordan, and Sansa flew back toward the 3rd Heavenly Realm. Suddenly Sansa stopped. "Wait, I have an idea."

They turned to her, "What is it?" asked Jordan.

"Where is Nikolas' mother?"

Jordan said, "She is in the Land of Reform."

"We must go to her. She may know something, some secret... something, anything we can use to get through to him."

"That's brilliant," said Jordan. He looked over at Rosie. Rank and file Angels were not allowed into the Land of Reform. If caught there, they faced stiff punishment. But as a Commander, she could gain entrance and easily find out where Lynda Cruz was.

Rosie said, "Let's go."

They flew to the Land of Reform. The frontier guard flew out, "Halt, who goes there?"

"I am Rosie, Commander in the 3rd Heavenly Realm under Michael."

"You may proceed."

They flew immediately to the offices of administration. Rosie said, "I am here to see Lynda Cruz."

The attendant pulled out a large book, "She is in house 7918."

They flew to the large white old hotel like house that held 144 people and spoke to the administrator. Moments later, Lynda Cruz walked down the stairway from the third floor with a bewildered look on her face. "Who are all of you?"

Jordan spoke, "Lynda, we are Angels. Your son Nikolas is in trouble. He is about to do something very evil, and we need to convince him to stop. Is there anything you can tell us?"

"What is going to do?"

Sansa replied, "He is planning on killing hundreds of students at his school!"

"Which school?"

"Stoneman Douglas."

Lynda's eyes rolled upwards, and she fainted. Jordan quickly caught her preventing her from hitting her head. Sansa knelt next to her and took charge, "Lynda, please I need your help. What can I say to Nikolas to get him to stop?"

Lynda closed her weary eyes again. Sansa shook her slightly, "Lynda; you have to help us. Please!"

"He won't listen to anyone. He has the Dark Baptism."

"We know this, Lynda. There must be another way."

Lynda's eyes widened. "Take me with you. He will listen to me."

Sansa looked up to see Rosie shaking her head back and forth. The answer was no.

"Why not?" Sansa asked.

"Sansa," said Rosie. There is an ancient law that was put in place on the day the Lands of Reform were created. It says, "Any Angel or Dark Angel who removes a person from the Land of Reform and brings them to earth, will surely die."

"It's just a law. What if they don't find out?"

"It's not like that, Sansa. It's more than just a law. Other Angels, good and bad, have tried, and as soon as the human they were transporting touched the earth, the Angel died. There have been no exceptions."

Sansa turned back to Lynda, "There must be something you can tell us."

Lynda suddenly remembered, "Yes, there is something. There is a priest named Fr. Ricardo. He was going to find out how to reverse the Dark Baptism. Find him, and you may find the way."

Lynda's face suddenly grew fearful, "Please, please stop him. He is a good boy! He is just lost!"

Sansa brushed Lynda's hair out of her face, "I will try my best Lynda. I promise."

She looked up, "We have to find Fr. Ricardo."

They helped Lynda stand and left. Outside the boundary of the Land of Reform, they pulled up in the sky, and Jordan asked, "How do we find him?"

Rosie said, "Whether he is dead or alive, we will be able to find him. We just have to do some checking. Sansa, when is this going down?"

Sansa said, "In four more days."

Rosie replied, "Good that gives us time. Sansa, you go back and stay with Nikolas. Jordan go home, get some shut-eye, and report to my office in the morning. We will track down Fr. Ricardo."

They all went their separate ways, determined to find a way to prevent this disaster.

Chapter 116

February 13, 2018
The Eve of Valentine's Day – Elsewhere in Parkland Florida

SKYLAR DUNBAR SPENT THE EVENING at choir practice for her church. When it was over, her mom and dad took her out for tacos. They laughed and talked for over an hour about life. She had no special plans for Valentine's day but had a big day at school, and she was looking forward to the inevitable excitement and fun that always accompanied Valentine's day. After they got home, she texted her friend Randi, then went to bed.

~ ~ ~ ~

Brandon Phillips and his mom spent the evening watching the movie Toy Story 3 together. It was one of their favorite movies and the one they both felt was the best of the Toy Story movie. They ordered in some pizza and had a wonderful night laughing hysterically together.

~ ~ ~ ~

Meadow Pollak sat at the kitchen table finishing her Algebra homework. "Oh shoot."

Her mom, Julie, who was nearby making popcorn asked, "What's wrong, honey?"

"Oh, I'm just stuck on his problem."

"Well call your father, I know I am a doctor, but I am not great at Algebra anymore?"

"Mom, you're funny. How come you don't like Algebra?"

"Well, when I was growing up, me and most of the girls I knew agreed that we did not need Algebra to live life. Granted, I had to figure it out in college, but... as for now, we were right?" she smiled and shrugged her shoulders.

Meadow laughed and called out, "Dad, can you help me?"

Her dad, Andrew, came from the living room. "Sure honey, what is it?"

"I can't figure out this Algebra problem."

"Let me see that." Her dad said as he sat down looking it over, he then said ever so slowly, "Oh I see the problem."

Meadow could tell by his funny voice that he was kidding her, she looked up, smiling, "I see the problem too, dad. Now, what's the answer?"

"Ok, ok," Andrew said, as he focused back in. He looked for a few more moments, and pointed, "Here."

"Oh, yes, I see it now too. Thanks, dad."

"You got it, honey." He looked up at his smiling wife and winked.

~ ~ ~ ~

Coach Aaron Feis sat on the edge of the bed finishing up talking with his daughter Arielle about school. He leaned over and kissed her good night. "Good night, honey!"

"Good night, Dad."

As Aaron was about to shut the bedroom door, Arielle called out in a loud whisper, "Dad, did you get mom anything for Valentine's Day?"

Aaron laughed and tip-toed back over and stood next to her, saying in a low voice, "Well of course I did."

Arielle looked over at the door, "What did you get her?"

Aaron's eyes widened, and he whispered back, smiling, "I can't tell you!"

"Dad!!! Tell me!"

"Ok, ok. I got her chocolate hearts."

Arielle's eyes widened. "Oh, that's good. She'll like that."

"I got something for you too."

"You did!" she said excitedly. "What is it?"

"I can't tell you!" He smiled.

"Dad!" she protested.

He kissed her again on the forehead. "Good night, sweetheart. I love you."

"Good night, dad. Happy Valentine's Day."

Aaron chuckled, "Happy Valentine's Day Arielle."

Coach Feis went downstairs and packed a few snacks away. He was due to be on campus early in the morning where he would drive the bus and then act as a security monitor in the north parking lot. He did this before school every day. It was one of the myriads of jobs he held around campus. His passion though was what he did after school most days, working as an assistant coach on the Stoneman Douglas football team.

~ ~ ~ ~

Peter Wang quietly finished eating with his parents Hui and Kong. His brothers were outside already playing. His mother, Hui, asked him, "Peter, how are you doing with your grades?"

"I am doing good, mother."

Kong nodded, and smiled, "That is very good son."

"Thank you, father."

Hui and Kong were immigrants from China and worked very hard to make sure all their three sons did well in school. Peter got up and went to his room. He closed the door and plopped down on the bed. He could not get the Rockets game out of his mind. Harden had lit up for 40 points in their win over Phoenix only two nights earlier. Peter called his friend Steve.

"Hello?"

"Stevie, what's happening?"

"Nothing, just doing my stupid Geometry homework."

"Did you see what Harden did the other night?"

"Yeah, that awesome."

"I know, I can't believe he went for 40 points. Man, he is amazing."

"Wow... yea, unbelievable. Hey, are we playing tomorrow?"

"Yeah, right after school. Jimmy's coming too."

"Ok, cool. Hmmm... we should have eight. That will be enough."

"All right, I'll catch you later."

~ ~ ~ ~

Gwen looked up from reading as Scott Beigel come out of their bedroom wearing shorts and carrying his running shoes. "Are you going for a run, honey?"

"Yeah, I need to run tonight!" Scott said to the love of his life. They had gotten engaged not long ago, and he was excited about his future with her.

Gwen said, "That sounds good. By the way, what are all those uniforms in the washer for?"

"Oh, yes, I almost forgot. We had so many kids turn out for track that there weren't enough uniforms. I am letting them borrow the cross-country ones. They are practically the same. Can you toss them in the dryer?"

"Sure," Gwen said as she watched him sit down to lace up his shoes. She loved Scott, and she loved how much he cared about his students. She said, "Hey, don't forget, tomorrow is Valentine's Day!"

"I didn't forget. I was planning on picking up some strawberries and some chocolate after school. We can make some chocolate covered strawberries together."

"That sounds fun."

Scott finished tying his shoe then walked over to hug her, "It may turn out to be even more fun than you think."

"Is that so?" she said, smiling, as she reached up and kissed him. "Scott, but I didn't get you anything." She was not exactly telling the truth, but feigned disappointment.

"Oh, that doesn't matter," said Scott. "You are my gift. I'll see you in a bit."

Gwen waited until he went out the door, then quickly retrieved the Valentine's Day card she had made for him out of pink construction paper. She laughed at the little red hearts she had drawn, knowing he would be laughing when he saw them. She read her message of love once more, and sealed it with a kiss. She ran out to his car and put it on the dash where he would find it on the way to school in the morning.

Chapter 117

February 14, 2018 10:30
Snead Home, Parkland Florida

SANSA FLEW OVER the Florida Keys taking in one of the most beautiful days she could ever remember. She was in love for the first time in ages, and despite the difficulties that lie ahead, everything felt right today. Deep down she knew there was a chance she would never fulfill the promises she and Jordan's unspoken words had said to each other's hearts. But in some strange way, it didn't matter to her. She had been redeemed. She had been found worthy of love again, something she never imagined happening to her.

As she headed toward the home where Nikolas was living, she wondered how it would all play out. She was trying to think of a way she could stop him and still escape. It upset her that the Lords would not intervene. It was obvious that they did not believe in her, nor understand her. No one from either side would understand her actions, but it didn't matter, because Jordan understood. Because of this, she was resigned to do whatever it took to stop Nikolas, no matter how it might seal her fate. She owed that much to Jordan. She owed that much to herself.

She spotted the house, flew down, and went in the back door. It appeared that no one was home, so she went upstairs. Nikolas' door was ajar, and there was talk coming from inside. It was the voice of Tira.

Sansa peaked inside, and her eyes widened. Nikolas was standing next to his bed dressed in all black. He had on a bulletproof vest and a baseball cap. He was packing box after box of rounds into a gym bag. Next to the bag lay an opened gun case. On top of the case was his AR-15 gun.

Tira was standing behind him, taunting him, coaching him, whispering into his mind. "Nikolas, these are the kids who bullied you. They are the ones who made fun of you. They think they are better than you. You must kill them all Nikolas. You must kill hundreds today, hundreds! Today is your day Nikolas! Be fast, be quick, kill hundreds."

Sansa gasped, desperately trying to remain quiet, "Today! Oh my God!"

She watched Nikolas' reaction. He was taking it all in with a growing smile coming over his face.

Tira then said, "I am going now to instill fear among the guards so they will be afraid of you. I will be back Nikolas. Today is the day Nikolas; today you become important Nikolas. Today they will know that you are better than them."

Tira subtly turned then went out the window. Sansa bent down and watched her fly up and away, then went in. She walked up to Nikolas and began to try to speak to his mind, "Nikolas, no, you cannot do this. Nikolas, your mother, wouldn't like this. Nikolas you don't have to do this." He was not hearing her. Something was blocking him. He reached down and picked up his gun and began saying, "BAM! BAM! BAM!."

He wheeled to the mirror and said it again, "BAM! BAM! BAM!"

Sansa tried again, "Nikolas, don't you understand, you will only…"

Suddenly Sansa felt a piercing pain in the side. "Ahhhh!" she screamed as Tira jammed her sword blade deep into her side. Sansa desperately reached to pull it out, cutting her hand open. Tira then pulled the long blade out and knocked Sansa to the floor.

Sansa's eyes rolled behind her head, Angels could not die of wounds like this, but the pain was as great as any human would feel. She passed out, bleeding all over the floor.

An hour later, the stabbing pain in her side woke her. She lifted her head. Nikolas was gone, so was the gun.

Chapter 118

February 14, 2018 10:30
3rd Heavenly Realm

SANSA GOT UP and limped to the bathroom. She took two washcloths and held them tightly to put pressure on the large slice in her hand, then pressed her hand onto the wound in her side. She said aloud in a panicked voice, "What should I do? I won't be able to stop him alone, not now, not with so little time. I have to get help." She bolted out the bathroom window and flew straight to the 3rd Heavenly Realm. When she was near a frontier guard intercepted her.

"Stop! You are not allowed here."

"Please, I have to speak to Commander Rosie or the Angel Jordan. It is urgent!"

The guard looked at her bloodied clothing and her wound. "What is this about?"

"Please, there is no time. Something very terrible is about to happen. They know about it. I... I was here last night!"

The guard had heard there was a Dark Angel there last night. "Wait here." He turned, then stopped, "On second thought, come with me."

They raced to the headquarters of the 3rd Heavenly Realm. The place looked practically deserted. "Sit down," said the guard as he raced up the stairs into the offices. Sansa anxiously looked around. She knew things were taking too long. Time was running out. Not far away some uniforms were drying on a line. She had an idea. She casually walked over and took two of them down, rolling them in a tight ball, tucking them under her arm with the towel she was holding.

The guard returned, "I am sorry. Rosie and Jordan left over an hour ago to find someone. There is no word as to when they will return."

Sansa sighed and closed her eyes as a tear fell down her cheek. There was only one thing left to do.

"Are you ok?" asked the guard.

She looked up through tearing eyes, "Yes, I am. Listen, you must get a message to Jordan and Rosie. It is urgent. Tell them it is today! Tell them Nikolas is doing this today!"

"I will send out a team to find them right now."

"Thank you, I have to go," said Sansa.

"Hold it, before you go, I brought you something," he said, holding out a small dish containing a mixture. "It's some healing balm for your wounds."

She took it with her other hand and started to leave. The guard said, "Hey, I don't know who you are. But good luck."

"Thank you," she said, as she flew off.

Chapter 119

February 14, 2018
Park in Parkland, Florida

NIKOLAS SAT ALONE IN THE PARK with his backpack loaded with ammunition and his AR-15 in the canvas case next to him. He studied the map of the Stoneman Douglass Campus one more time. He would enter through the north gate parking lot, the one where he had been beaten up so long ago, and begin in Building 12 where many of the freshman classes were being held. He expected less resistance there.

In Building 12, there were 8-10 classrooms on each of the three floors, with as many as twenty students in each. He would move move from class to class in a zig-zag fashion, shoot all who tried to leave, go up a flight, then repeat, all the way to the 3rd floor. Then he would race outside with the fleeing students to start phase two, the battlefield phase, in which he would sweep across the entire campus to extract maximum casualties, and ultimately confront the sheriffs in a glorious showdown.

The Dark Angel Tira stood by, watching him think, worried the plan had been discovered. She nervously scanned the skies, but there was no one coming. All was a go. She whispered, "It's time Nikolas. It is time!"

Nikolas half smiled and pulled out his phone. He opened his Uber app and requested a ride. He turned his video camera on and told the camera what he was going to do, finishing with the words, "People are going to die!"

When the gold colored compact Uber arrived, Nikolas jumped in and calmly began the 12-minute drive to the school.

He texted J.T. Snead whose family he was living with, who he had seen just that morning. "Yo, J.T., what class are you in and who is the teacher?"

"It's one of the coaches. You know who."

"Ask the coach if he remembers me. LOL."

"Yeah, right, no way!"

Cruz stared at the phone. He was pretty sure what classroom that was, and he made a note of it. He then texted, "I am going to a movie. I've got something big to tell you!"

"What?"

"Nothing."

"I thought you said something big?"

"Don't worry; it's no big deal. Nothing bad."

Cruz saw the school in the distance. He went over his plan in his mind one more time as his hands began to perspire.

At 2:19 pm, the Uber driver came to a stop on Pine Island Road, not far from Building 12. Nikolas smirked and texted his friend, "Yo!"

Chapter 120

February 14, 2018
3rd Heavenly Realm

SANSA STOPPED IN THE AIR outside the 3rd Heavenly Realm. She took off her tunic, letting it drop down into the Heavenly Sea below her. She put the healing balm over her wounds and unfurled one of the rolled-up uniforms she had stolen from the line. She brushed her hair back as good as she could and headed east.

After a while a vast land appeared in the distance and as she drew nearer two guards flew out. "Halt, who goes there?"

"It is me, Commander Rosie of the 3rd Heavenly Realm. I need to see someone."

"Do you know where they are."

"Yes, I was here yesterday."

They let her pass, and Sansa flew down to the community home where Lynda Cruz was staying. She walked in and saw the administrator she had met the day before. She signaled for her.

The woman came over, "Can I help you?"

"I was here yesterday with Commander Rosie and the Angel Jordan. I have to speak with Lynda Cruz."

"Very well, one moment."

Sansa looked around and saw a back entrance out onto a large lawn. It would have to do. Lynda then came out with a surprised look on her face.

"Lynda, I have to speak with you. It is urgent. Let's go out back."

Lynda quickly hurried out back with her, Sansa immediately turned, "Nikolas is on his way to the school to kill hundreds."

"What can I do?"

"Do you trust me?" asked Sansa.

"Yes, I do."

"Put this on. I am taking you to him."

Lynda's face grew somber, but then a look of determination came over it. She took the uniform and slipped it over her tunic.

"What will I say to him?" asked Lynda.

"You have to convince him not to do this. I am just worried we may be too late."

"Where is he?"

"I believe he may already be at the school."

"Oh my God," Lynda cried. "Wait. Yesterday, your friends said any Angel bringing someone back to earth would surely die."

Sansa suddenly felt scared because she knew it was true. She put on a fake smile, "It doesn't apply to me, because I am a Dark Angel."

"You are! Then... then... why are you doing this?"

The words pierced Sansa's heart, as all her sins and all her mistakes came rushing back a lifetime of regret hitting her in a single moment. She coolly replied, "Because, I've got some making up to do."

Sansa grasped Lynda by the hand, and they flew up into the sky. They only had one hurdle, and that was to get past the guards in the sky surrounding the Land of Reform. Sansa was afraid, as it would not be as easy taking someone out, as it had going in alone. She knew too, they were running out of time.

Chapter 121

February 14, 2018
Marjory Stoneman Douglas H.S. – Parkland Florida

2:19 P.M.

Nikolas got out of the car on Pine Island Road and walked through the wide-open pedestrian gate heading directly for Building 12. Classes had not let out yet, and virtually no one was in sight.

Andrew Medina, an assistant baseball coach and un-armed campus security monitor, couldn't wait for this day to end. He felt exhausted from checking out the many beautiful girls all day, and he wanted nothing more than to get home and have a drink. He was driving in his golf cart along Pine Island Road heading toward Building 12 when he saw Cruz walking. "Holy shit, the crazy boy is here. What the hell is he carrying?"

Suddenly, Nikolas saw Medina in the distance, cruising in his golf cart.

"Shit," said Nikolas, as he kept walking, unable to conceal the gun case that held his AR-15.

Tira whispered in his mind, "Keep going, Nikolas. Keep moving."

Nikolas didn't care anymore what she said, this was his show. He paused, thinking about pulling it out and making Medina his first victim, instead, he pretended not to see him and continued at his hurried pace.

2:20 P.M.   **1 MINUTE HAS PASSED SINCE CRUZ'S ARRIVAL**

Medina eased up a bit, but kept moving forward, watching Cruz, wondering what he was doing there. He remembered the email they had all gotten only a few months earlier warning them that Cruz was not allowed to bring a backpack on campus. He also knew Cruz had been expelled since then and was not to be on campus.

Medina slowed down even more now, watching from his golf cart as Cruz headed toward the east entrance of Building 12. Medina pulled out his radio and pressed the transmission button. He thought about calling Code Red, the lockdown code, but that might come with consequences.

If he were wrong about the need for it, he could get into even more trouble. He was on thin ice as it was. It was no small matter to lockdown a school of over 5,000 students, teachers, and personnel, especially when it was almost time to go home on Valentine's Day.

So, he let go of the transmission button, then pressed it again, and instead called his fellow security monitor David Taylor who was inside Building 12. "Taylor, this is Medina, there is a suspicious kid headed your way. I think it's crazy boy Cruz."

2:21 P.M.   **2 MINUTES HAVE PASSED SINCE CRUZ'S ARRIVAL**

David Taylor, another un-armed campus security monitor, hired mainly so he could be a part time baseball coach with Medina, was walking down the hall of the 2nd floor of Building 12 when he got Medina's call. He listened, then said, "Cruz is here? Ok I'll check it out." He put his radio back on his belt feeling annoyed.

Taylor was aware of all the trouble Cruz had caused over the years, and he didn't need it today. The school day would be over in a half hour, and it was Valentine's Day. Everyone had plans, including him. But deep down for some reason, he felt fear. He said aloud, "This damn kid is a nuisance."

Taylor went down the stairwell at the west end of the building and walked down the first-floor hall toward the east entrance where

Cruz would be coming in. That was when he saw Cruz. He was wearing a black hoodie and a black cap and carrying a long case and a backpack. But what struck him was the deadly serious nature of his stride. Cruz looked like he was on a mission.

Taylor felt fear that he did not understand. He watched as Cruz walked in through the wide doors and turned out of sight into the east stairwell. Taylor turned too, and walked the other way, trying to decide what he should do. He went to the other end of the building and up to the second floor. He thought about calling Code Red, but he was not sure he was authorized to do so, and he worried that, perhaps, it would be premature,

Once in the stairwell, Cruz stopped and quickly unpacked his AR-15. His mind was racing, but he was ready. Suddenly the door opened and Chris McKenna, a student Cruz had seen before, came in. McKenna stopped, startled and unsure of what he was seeing. Cruz did not look at him but held his AR-15 aloft, and said, "You better get out of here, something bad is about to happen." McKenna said nothing but walked out the door and ran to get help.

Cruz watched McKenna leave and for a moment regretted letting him go for help. He wanted no witnesses. He put the rifle up to his shoulder in firing position and raced around the corner into the hallway.

In a moment, he saw the first students through his scope: Martin, Luke, and Gina. He knew them all. They were only twenty-five feet away, laughing about something when suddenly Martin turned. He was wearing his ROTC uniform. Martin instantly knew what was happening and did not hesitate. He immediately charged at Cruz. In a frightening moment, two loud shots shattered the silence at Stoneman Douglas. Luke watched Martin fall and instinctively jumped in front of Gina, trying to shield her and push her into the classroom, but Cruz fired four loud shots in succession, hitting them both.

Cruz moved past the three wounded students, just like in the countless video games he had played. He kept his rifle at shoulder level, peering through the scope, sweeping back and forth for more targets.

Outside the security monitor Medina was watching Building 12, thinking about what to do, when suddenly he heard gunshots. His heart began racing, and he knew he should go in, but fear gripped him, and he turned his golf cart around and drove back towards the office to get help. He did not signal Code Red for lockdown.

From the 2nd floor, security monitor Taylor also heard the gunshots. He raced down the empty hallway, opened a janitor closet, moved some things aside, and hid. Inside the dark closet, he heard his radio transmitting. He quickly turned it down so the shooter would not find him. He did not signal Code Red either.

On the 1st floor, Cruz crept slowly to the other side of the hall. The Dark Angel Tira screamed into his mind, "You are going too slow!! Nikolas, hurry!" Nikolas ignored her, everything felt slow in his mind, and his mind liked the feeling. He suddenly felt like he was in a slow-motion video game, as he stepped toward room 1216.

He peered into 1216 through his raised scope and fired. "BAM! BAM! BAM! BAM!" Seven methodical shots went off, hitting four unsuspecting students as the remaining fourteen frantically bolted out of their seats, screaming and scrambling to find cover.

Cruz slowly turned away, keeping his rifle pointed in firing position. Tira screamed again, "What are you doing Nikolas, kill them all." But Nikolas was deep inside his own video, and he ignored her and kept moving.

2:22 P.M.   3 MINUTES HAVE PASSED SINCE CRUZ'S ARRIVAL

Chris McKenna ran as fast as he could for help. He saw Coach Aaron Feis driving in a golf cart and frantically waved him down, "Coach, coach! Stop! Nikolas Cruz has a gun. He is shooting up the 1200 building."

"What! Go... go get help now!" Feis whipped around the golf cart.

"Where are you going?" McKenna shouted.

"To try to stop him!" Feis was worried, and his heart pounded furiously. He wished for a moment he had his firearm, but this was no time for wishing. He didn't have it with him because he wasn't allowed, and it didn't matter, because right now he needed to save his kids.

He fumbled with his radio, thinking to call a Code Red, but then he heard the shots ring out, "BAM! BAM!, BAM!," and he floored the golf cart gas pedal, racing to Building 12.

School Security Administrator Kevin Greenleaf heard Medina's radio transmission and walked out of his office to find Broward County Sheriff's Deputy Scott Peterson. Peterson was the designated deputy on campus and was the only armed person among the 5,000 students and personnel on campus. "Peterson, Medina just said shots may have been fired!"

"Where?" asked a startled Peterson.

"He said Building 12."

"Let's go," said Deputy Peterson, and they started running. They immediately saw Medina racing toward them in his golf cart and flagged him down. "Move over," said Peterson, as he and Greenleaf jumped in and the three men now turned to go back toward Building 12.

On the 1st floor, Cruz ignored the growing chaos and inched toward room 1214. He heard the screams and frantic voices from within the classroom. He stepped into the doorway with his rifle raised. The screams of those inside grew louder and Cruz immediately fired. BAM! BAM!, BAM! Eight shots rang out, many finding their mark in the frantic, chaotic scene. Cruz slowly backed away from the door.

Suddenly he felt lost. It was as if the game was ending. Students nearby began running away, screaming, and stumbling in every direction. Cruz stood still for a while, confused. The Dark Angel Tira was livid as she was suddenly beginning to feel the pressure. This day was not going like it was supposed to, and Legion would not be pleased. She screamed, "You idiot! You're going too slow. There are more in there! Kill them!"

Cruz took a deep breath, put his rifle back into firing position and turned back toward room 1216. "No!" screamed Tira, "Go the other way!"

Cruz ignored her and stepped back into the doorway of room 1216, firing several more shots into the panic-stricken classroom, as more students fell to the ground wounded.

At the City of Coral Springs 911 call center, a call from a terrified female student came through.

The 911 operator picked up, "911, what is your emergency?"

"Hello, I am at Stoneman Douglas High School, and I think there is a shooter."

In the background, the dispatcher heard gunshots and screaming, but nothing else. He asked, "Hello? Are you still there? Talk to me please."

The female student hung up.

The dispatcher also hung up, and he immediately dialed the Broward Sheriff's Office 911 Center. They were responsible for handling law enforcement at Stoneman Douglas even though the school was located right next to Coral Springs.

The operator at the Broward Sheriff's Office, also called the BSO, answered. "911 what is your emergency?"

"Yes, I just got a call from Stoneman Douglas High School, a female on the line advised me she believes there is a shooter at the school."

"Ok, at Douglas High School, in what city?"

"In Parkland, 5901 Pine Island."

"5901 Pine Island?"

"Yes."

"Ok... let me see if they're working anything there."

2:23 P.M.   **4 MINUTES HAVE PASSED SINCE CRUZ'S ARRIVAL**

Coach Chris Hixson sat in his office inside Building 13, thinking about what he would get his wife for Valentine's Day. Like most guys, he was risking a lot by waiting until the last minute. But he wasn't worried, he had successfully maneuvered these marital waters countless times before. Suddenly he heard gunshots. He knew because he owned a gun, and he suddenly wished he had it with him. He instantly bolted from his office, sprinting out Building 13, and across the narrow grassy area toward Building 12. He had one thought on his mind. He needed to stop the shooter. As he ran across the lawn, the loving words he and his wife had shared that morning came into his mind, somehow, he knew destiny was calling, and he hoped he would see her again.

Coach Hixson burst through the double doors into the wide hall, and there was Cruz, with a grim half smile on his face. Cruz turned and lifted his gun, and Hixson charged. The sickening sound of thundering shots echoed through the hall, and the screams grew louder, as Hixson fell hard, suddenly unable to breathe, with excruciating pain gripping his badly bleeding chest. Cruz turned away momentarily, and Hixson slowly crawled to a nearby alcove. He was alive, and everything in his life he ever regretted not doing suddenly mattered.

At the BSO 911 center, the dispatcher was still checking to see if there were any reports. She asked, "And it's second-hand information... about a shooter?"

The Coral Springs dispatcher grimaced. He hated dealing with BSO because everything moved like molasses. But no one could say anything because the bureaucracy was so entrenched. He repeated, "A female called in... it sounded like possible shots... in the background."

"Ok..."

He sighed, even more frustrated, adding "I think I heard 5 or 6 shots, in two different bursts."

"Ok… and you're calling from where?" asked the BSO dispatcher. "I'm the 911 dispatcher from Coral Springs."

Seven seconds of silence ticked by as he waited for her. Finally, she came back on and asked, "Do they have a specific location?"

"They just said its Stoneman Douglas. It looks like the line is still open. I'm going to try to ping it to see where the girl called from."

"Ok, thank you."

Inside Building 12, Cruz now moved through the chaos, smoke, and noise to room 1213. He felt a rush like he had never felt before. He leaned into room 1213 and peered at the mass of students trying to crowd behind a single desk and file cabinet. He began firing. BAM! BAM! BAM! BAM! He then turned and headed toward the stairwell.

Outside Building 12, Deputy Peterson, Greenleaf, and Medina arrived in the golf cart. Peterson knew what he was supposed to do. He was the only person on the entire campus who had a firearm. He unlatched the safety strap on his holster as he and Greenleaf jumped out of a golf cart. They cautiously walked towards the east entrance of Building 12. Suddenly they heard gunfire, and they retreated several steps to assess the situation, hesitant to go in.

The BSO 911 dispatcher patiently waited 15 more seconds while the Coral Springs 911 dispatcher pinged to see what tower the call had come from. Finally, he came back on the line, "She doesn't seem to be on the phone on anymore. I'm going to GPS it."

"Ok," replied the BSO dispatcher, also asking, "And your operator # is?."

"It is #9233," he said hurriedly, "We just got another caller advising someone was shot in the 1200 building."

Several more seconds passed, until the BSO dispatcher asked, "You guys have ambulances going out, correct?"

The Coral Springs dispatcher replied, "We have rescue, but they won't be able to go in until they are cleared to enter." Coral Springs was right next to Parkland and responsible for Fire and Ambulance.

But Broward Sheriff's Office was responsible for Police services, and everything concerning law enforcement had to be transferred to them.

"Right," she said, trying to determine how she could make sure this whole thing was not a hoax.

The Coral Springs dispatcher said, "And we are still hearing of gunshots from multiple calls."

"So, you're getting multiple calls at this time?" asked the BSO dispatcher.

"We're getting multiple calls, yes."

The Coral Springs dispatcher shouted to a coworker, "I am on the phone with BSO, trying to relay the information."

The BSO 911 operator asked, "They have one confirmed patient at this time?"

The Coral Springs dispatcher said, frustrated, "We have one confirmed.... one confirmed patient currently. A person at the 1200 building is the only one we have so far?"

Based on other calls coming in, a supervisor at the BSO 911 call center finally understood what was happening and put out the alert, "Attention all units in District 15, possible shots fired at 5901 Pine Island Road at Stoneman Douglas High School, possible shots fired at Stoneman Douglas High School."

Deputies cruising in the area got their first news of trouble.

Inside an alcove on the 1st floor, Coach Hixson tried to get up, but he could not. His breathing had slowed, and the bleeding was bad. Suddenly Cruz stepped into the alcove, looked at him with demonic eyes, and lifted the gun. Hixson closed his eyes, "Oh, God, help me..." Cruz fired again.

On the other side of Building 12, as more gunshots echoed, Deputy Peterson and Greenleaf turned and ran backward to take cover by the wall of the nearby building. Medina jumped back in the golf cart and drove away. Deputy Peterson grabbed his radio, "Please be advised, we have possible... uh... could be firecrackers, uh...

could be shots fired, possible shots fired 1200 building." He was frightened more than he had ever been in his life.

One by one, several Broward County Deputies acknowledged the alert. Virtually none of them had trained for a mass-shooter scenario, though they were all supposed to have done so.

Inside Building 12, someone activated the fire alarm. It did not affect the first floor. On the second floor, the teachers had heard the gunfire and were busy locking down their classrooms. But on the third floor, mass chaos erupted as hundreds of students emptied into the crowded hallway unaware of what was happening on the floors below them.

.

2:24 P.M.   5 MINUTES HAVE PASSED SINCE CRUZ'S ARRIVAL

Coach Aaron Feis raced his golf cart around Building 13 toward the sound of the gunfire. As he neared Building 12, he leaped off the cart and ran toward the nearest entrance. Feis saw two girls outside, crying, looking inside, and he knew the trouble was inside Building 12. He charged toward the entrance.

From the hallway near room 1213, Cruz glanced over his shoulder and saw Coach Feis racing across the lawn, coming to stop him. Cruz quickly ran backward toward the entrance as if defending the rear of a fortress.

Feis ran toward the opened double doors. Suddenly Cruz stepped into the doorway. Feis stopped dead in his tracks. He saw Cruz glance at the girls, so he quickly moved between them and Cruz, and stood facing him and the AR-15 rifle pointed at him. He raised his hands, trying to connect with Cruz. "Nikolas, Nikolas please… stop. You don't have to do this. Put the gun down. You don't need to hurt these…"

"Bam! Bam! Bam!"

Coach Feis grabbed his chest, "Uhh… Niko… please… stop!" He stumbled back as the searing, jolting pain of the bullets pierced his body, knocking him backward onto the grass. He was unable to breathe and realized his life was suddenly ending. This was not supposed to happen. He needed more time. He was only 37. The love of his life, Melissa, and his daughter Arielle passed through his mind. He tried to shout, to stop what was happening, but couldn't. He needed more time, for them, for his students. Everything grew dimmer. He regretted he had been unable to stop Cruz. Tears rolled down his face as his heart pumped in vain, trying to keep going, but he closed his eyes and slipped into darkness.

Nikolas Cruz numbly moved back into the stairwell. He was done on the first floor. He looked up and headed to the second floor.

Deputy Peterson knew that even from his hiding spot, he could be inside Building 12 in 20 seconds, but he was frozen in fear. He peered around the corner, and waited another 30 seconds, listening to the gunfire coming from inside the building, trying to convince himself to go in. Instead, he picked up his radio, "Be advised all units we need to shut down Stoneman Douglas… and the intersection."

Nikolas Cruz entered the second floor and immediately knew something was wrong. Though the fire alarm was blaring, there was not a single person in the hall. The windows of the doors of all classrooms were also covered. He tried the first door, then the next. They were locked. He screamed and begin firing at one of the door windows, shattering the glass. He peered in the narrow window opening with his scope.

"What the hell!" he screamed, as he stared into the empty room, not seeing the seventeen students and teacher silently cowering behind a single line of tape the teacher had wisely laid down months earlier after a security memo had been circulated. She had urged other teachers to do so, but hardly anyone at Stoneman Douglas nor in the entire district for that matter had done so. Behind that line, no one could be seen from the door window. It was meant to save them.

Cruz screamed loudly as pain shot through his mind. "No, no! I'm not done! No!"

The Dark Angel Tira grimaced in anger. Nikolas had been too slow. She raced up to the 3rd floor. The fire alarm was still blaring, and almost two hundred confused students were in the hallway, unaware of the shooting going on below. Many wondered if it was really a fire drill. Tira knew there was time, and she raced back down to find Nikolas.

On the second floor, hiding inside the unlocked janitor closet, security monitor David Taylor held his breath and watched from the vent in the closet door as Cruz's walked by.

Just then, Tira found Cruz aimlessly patrolling the empty hallway. She screamed, "Nikolas! Go up to the third floor!"

Cruz stopped. He had heard her clearly. He paused, then ran down the hall toward the stairwell.

In his classroom on the third floor, Geography Teacher Scott Beigel was sitting alone in his empty classroom grading papers. It was his prep period, and he had no students at this time of the day. He heard the fire alarm and paused, annoyed by the timing. He sighed and glanced over to see students already filing into the hallway to go downstairs.

At this moment, Code Red, the shutdown code, that would have sent students back into their classrooms to be locked inside, away from Cruz, had still not been called. Instead, the students were all crowded in the hall, like sitting ducks, unaware of what was coming up the stairs.

Beigel opened his door and peered into the crowded hall. He didn't understand why, but he sensed something was wrong. Chaos began to spread as the students who had been filing down the stairs started running back up to the third-floor hall. Others started getting texts from their friends and began yelling as the realization that a shooter was headed their way spread.

Beigel glanced at one of his fellow teachers and their worried eyes met in a moment of dire awareness. They bolted into action, yelling, "Get back into the rooms! Get back into the rooms!" Immediately, all the teachers on the floor began racing to herd their students back into classrooms, not knowing that Cruz was only moments away.

Outside the building, Deputy Peterson was still only 20-30 seconds away, but was afraid to go in. He picked up his radio to begin another transmission, "We're talking about the 1200 building uh... the 300 building... uh, we're talking about the building off Holmberg road."

In his patrol car, fellow BSO Deputy Kratz, the closest deputy to the school, had been listening and driving at a normal pace. He was near the middle school and very close to Stoneman Douglas. He casually picked up his radio, "Any description?" he paused, "I'm coming up on the middle school now." He took a deep breath and listened. He too suddenly felt fear.

Deputy Peterson replied, "We don't have any description yet. We just hear shots, appears to be shots fired."

Kratz hung up his radio.

2:25 P.M.   6 MINUTES HAVE PASSED SINCE CRUZ'S ARRIVAL

Cruz reached the top of the 3rd floor stairwell as the chaos unfolded.

Teacher Scott Beigel was still in the hall outside his classroom, located nearest to the stairwell, and he sensed he was running out of time. "Hurry, hurry," he yelled as the last of the eight students raced past him into his classroom. He glanced over at his associate, Stacey Lippel, the teacher in the adjacent classroom who was frantically pushing kids in. Their eyes met, and both held fear, not for themselves, for the students.

Suddenly shots rang out and Cruz burst into the hall firing back and forth in front of him, filling the hall with smoke. There were still over fifty students in the hall. Cruz fired down the hall and everyone began running.

Beigel, with his back to the shooter, pushed the final students into his class, "Go, go, go, go!" he yelled. He reached out to grab the door and close it, but Cruz stepped in front of him only five feet away. Beigel looked up at the evil eyes staring at him from behind the raised rifle. Neither spoke, as Beigel paused, then tried to pull the door shut.

Cruz fired three shots that ripped into Beigel's chest and shoulder. But he held his ground, knowing he was the only thing between Cruz and the screaming students behind him.

Beigel clung to the door and pulled it toward his body as he began to fall. Cruz fired three more times. Beigel instantly knew it was the end of his days, but he would not let go of the door. He needed to hold on for his students.

Losing consciousness, but needing to save those behind him, Beigel fell forward in a last gasp effort to grab Cruz's legs.

Cruz stepped back, then turned and walked away down the hall. Beigel saw stars as his heart slowed. He thought of his fiancée Gwen as tears rolled down his cheek. He wanted to tell her one more time that he loved her, but all went black.

Cruz looked to the end of the hall and saw over thirty students. He shot a rapid-fire volley down the hall. Everyone screamed. Several were hit.

Meadow Pollack had been helping direct some frightened freshmen when more shots rang out. "This way! This way!" she yelled. She learned how to be strong from her mother, an ER physician. Suddenly she felt several jolts, followed by a piercing pain in her side. She had been hit several times. She tried to run but fell, unable to breathe. She looked ahead and saw a boy named Brandon duck into a closet. She looked over and saw a freshman girl curled up in a fetal position, crying uncontrollably. Meadow closed her eyes, trying to preserve her strength.

Deputy Peterson stood safely just outside. He radioed, "I'm over on the south side of 700 building." He closed the transmission, then looked up at the third floor where he heard more shots.

Skylar Dunbar ran down the third-floor hall. She had just seen Meadow fall, and she was scared to death. Everyone around her was running and screaming as shots whistled past. Suddenly she felt a jolt and fell screaming in pain. She had been hit in the calf. She tried to get up but could not. She crouched down, shaking, frightened, as tears ran down her cheeks. She peered back down the long hall. Cruz was looking the other way.

Suddenly, more shots rang out and Skylar held her hands in front of her face. She couldn't take anymore. She watched some students run from a classroom toward the stairwell. She wished she could join them, but she was too hurt. She was trapped, and it was too late. She glanced behind her and saw Cruz was moving slowly.

Inside the nearby closet, Brandon sat perfectly still. He was staring out the vent in the lower part of the door. It was then he saw Skylar. He was safe. She was not. He opened the door and called out, "Skylar!"

Skylar looked over, and their eyes met. It was Brandon Cousins, the boy who had humiliated her in the bathroom so long ago. She could see the fear in his face, and the urgency too in his gesturing for her to come. She quickly crawled to the closet and somehow got in. Brandon closed the door. There was barely room for both of them.

Skylar said, "Brandon, I'm so scared."

"I am too! It's Nikolas Cruz."

"I know, I saw him." Suddenly shots rang out. Cruz was coming closer.

Skylar grasped Brandon's hand tightly and whispered, "Please pray with me."

Brandon squeezed her hand.

Skylar began to whisper, "Jesus, please help us. We're so scared, Lord give us courage."

Outside the building, another campus security monitor, Elliot Bonner, raced in his golf cart toward Building 12. As he rounded the corner, he saw Coach Feis laying on the grass. He backed up his cart and began driving away. He picked up his radio and signaled for Code Red. Stoneman Douglas was finally on lockdown.

Not far from the stairwell at the other end of the hall, freshman Peter Wang, still in his ROTC uniform from an earlier event, hid with a large group of students inside a classroom. They watched another student race past them, stopping to push on a locked door. He could not get in, and tried to run, but was shot before their eyes.

Peter turned to the others, "He's coming. We've got to get out of here."

"I'm too scared!" said one girl.

"Don't worry. I'll lead the way. Is everyone ready?"

Fifteen students nodded. Some made the sign of the Cross. Some began to cry. Some began to pray. Peter held up his finger as he peered down the hall. He could tell Cruz seemed confused, angry, arguing with himself.

Peter saw their chance. "Now!" he said, "Follow me!" He raced into the hall followed by the rest. He yanked open the stairwell door and began waving the students past, keeping his eye on Cruz who now turned and saw them. Their eyes met as Cruz raised the rifle. Peter waved the last two students past him as Cruz fired. The last girl, named Jaime, was hit in the back. Peter caught her and pushed her through the door, then he felt the jolt. He was hit bad, and he fell through the doorway into the stairwell.

Outside, Deputy Kratz drove cautiously to the nearby football field and stopped. He looked at Building 12. He was only a thousand feet away, a distance that could be driven in less than 20 seconds. He put his vehicle in park, picked up his radio, and said, "Shots fired by the football field."

Deputy Peterson radioed to his fellow deputies who he knew must be near, "Keep the school locked down, gentlemen."

Deputy Kratz radioed back, "Someone said it was firecrackers, but we are not sure... by the football field."

2:26 P.M.   7 MINUTES HAVE PASSED SINCE CRUZ'S ARRIVAL

Up on the third floor, Meadow opened her eyes. She knew she was very badly wounded, yet she felt a sense of destiny like never before. She thought of her mom and her dad and her brothers. She thought of all they had taught her about faith, about strength, about love, and above all about courage. She was bleeding badly, and yet she held onto hope that she would be going home today.

She looked at the young girl frozen on the floor next to her, crying uncontrollably, and glanced down the long hall. Cruz was still at the other end, but he was finishing up. He would be coming. She weakly said to the girl, "Hey... don't... be afraid."

"I... I can't help it," said the girl, "I am so scared!"

Meadow swallowed, trying not to show her pain, and crept over to the girl. "Lay still... play dead... I will cover you."

The girl stayed still as Meadow crawled on top of her and acted like she was already dead.

Inside the closet, Skylar tried to stop the bleeding on her calf by applying pressure, but the pain was unbearable. The bullet inside felt like hot molten lava within her.

Suddenly she heard more shots directly outside the door. She peered out of the door vent and saw Meadow laying on top of another girl. She knew Meadow was gone and now realized the girl she was covering was gone too. She whispered a prayer, crying, "Brave Meadow, brave, brave, Meadow, go with God."

Brandon asked, "Is he close?"

Skylar said, "I don't know."

Suddenly Skylar saw Cruz thuggishly walk past. He walked out of sight, but then suddenly reappeared, shouting, "I saw you run in here. Did you think I would not find you?"

Skylar almost screamed, but she quickly put her hand over her mouth, stopping herself.

Brandon looked over at her with wide eyes, knowing that Skylar was now a target. Brandon suddenly felt a fear he had never felt.

He whispered, "Skylar I am so scared. I don't want to die!"

Skylar grabbed his shoulders, "Brandon, we are going to be ok. Don't worry!"

Brandon replied in escalating fear, "You don't understand, he hates me!"

Suddenly shots rang out above them, piercing the door. Brandon grabbed Skylar, and clutched her tightly, "I'm sorry for everything! I'm sorry."

Through a tear-stained face, Skylar whispered, "I forgive you. I'm sorry too Brandon, please forgive me."

He pressed his forehead against hers, "Thank you."

Skylar said, "You take care of yourself! For me!"

She quickly stood up inside the closet, Brandon gasped loudly, "What are you doing?"

She looked down, tears streaming down her face, and opened the door. Brandon tried to stop her, but she brushed him off and quickly stepped out to face Cruz, trying to shut the door as she did, but Brandon's foot was in the way, and it stayed ajar.

Brandon listened, "Oh, look, the bible thumper! You think you're better than me, don't you?"

Brandon could now see Skylar backing up, past the door, then he saw the muzzle of Cruz's weapon pass the door, then Cruz, backing Skylar up for some reason, seemingly afraid to shoot her. At that moment, Brandon knew Skylar had given her life for him.

He thought about that day long ago in the bathroom, he thought about seeing her cry and how it broke him. He wasn't going to let it end like this. He jumped up and stepped out of the closet, shouting, "Over here you jerk!"

Cruz wheeled and fired, hitting Brandon in the chest, dropping him. Skylar screamed and raced to tackle Cruz, but he wheeled and fired, hitting her in the shoulders and neck. Skylar winced in pain, and fell to the ground, with blood gushing from the gaping hole in her neck and pouring into her mouth. She looked up and saw Cruz step over Brandon and walk away.

Skylar closed her eyes, and whispered a prayer, as she then felt a hand grasp hers. It was Brandon's. He had crawled over to her. Skylar felt him squeezing her hand, then everything went black.

Deputy Scott Peterson watched as the deputy cars flew around the corner and raced down Holmberg Road. These were his buddies, every one of them, and they were there to save the day. He proudly picked up his radio, "We are locking down the whole school right now. Make sure there is no pedestrian traffic anywhere on Holmberg road."

2:27 P.M.   8 MINUTES HAVE PASSED SINCE CRUZ'S ARRIVAL

On the third floor, Cruz was now nearing the end of the hall, and teacher Ernest Rospierski was trapped in the hall, waiting for what might be the end. He and several other students were still hiding in two shallow alcoves half way down the hall. They had seen others make a run for it, and they had seen many get shot. They knew a similar fate could await at least some of them if they tried to make a run for it. So, they waited.

Ernest looked again and saw that Cruz was now walking toward them, but Cruz suddenly stopped and began to reload, fumbling in his backpack.

Ernest saw his chance, he bolted, grabbing the students from the alcoves, pulling and pushing them toward the stairwell. He turned and saw Cruz running toward them, finishing his reload on the fly. Ernest pushed the students ahead of him through the door, turned, and slammed it shut. They were now in the stairwell. He yelled at the top of his lungs, "Run!!!"

He leaned toward the wall, away from the window, hiding, but holding the door closed with his body and foot. Cruz pounded furiously on the other side, trapped, pushing as hard as he could on the door, wanting to follow them down, to kill them, and to get outside. He was only part way through with his plan. Phase two was about to unfold. The phase where the most killing would begin, outside, out in the crowd of thousands fleeing. He would die there too, but only after mowing down hundreds.

Cruz now stepped back and fired several shots through the steel door. Ernest closed his eyes, waiting for the pain, but nothing. Cruz had missed him. Ernest stayed put, holding the door until he heard Cruz walk away. He then ran down the stairs to safety.

Outside on Holmberg Road, along the north side of the north parking lot, a good distance away from Building 12, five deputy cars converged and pulled up on the road adjacent to the school grounds. Deputies Eason, Goolsby, Perry, Miller, Seward, Fugate, and Stambaugh all got out of their cars and assessed the situation. One asked, "Should we go in?"

Fugate said, "How the hell do I know. We haven't been trained in these damn situations. What did Peterson say?"

Stambaugh said, "He just said to keep all pedestrian traffic off Holmberg."

"Hell, there must be a sniper," said Fugate. "We better take cover. Where is Peterson?"

"He must be in there," said one, pointing at Building 12 a mere 400 feet away.

Inside Building 12, Cruz heard the sirens approaching, and lamented that the stairwell door was jammed. "Shit," he said, as he went across the hall into the teacher's lounge with Tira following him in.

From there Nikolas could see Holmberg Road, and from there he could see all the deputy cars and ambulance sirens. Going back down the hall was too far, and he did not know what was outside the other side of the building.

He glanced out the window to the left and saw the hundreds of kids running, easily within range. He had practiced for this, and he was ready. He glanced right and saw a group of deputies cowering behind their vehicles, way out on Holmberg road.

"Look at those pussy deputies!" he said, laughing, closing his eyes, dropping his head back in ecstasy. He was feeling the rush like he never felt in any game before, it was as if his mind wanted to fly. Tira smacked his head and screamed, and his face grew deadly serious. "Nikolas, it's time for phase two! Kill them! They are getting away!"

"I'll do it from here!" he yelled into the air. He gritted his teeth and fired three shots at the window, hoping to break it so he could fire down on the hundreds of fleeing students, but the hurricane glass would not break. "Dammit!" He needed to get downstairs. He needed to start phase two.

Suddenly he heard the stairwell door close. Someone had just gone out it. "It's open. It's showtime!"

Outside Coral Springs Police Dept Sgt. Reid was driving when he was waved down by a Fire Truck. Sgt. Reid, asked, "What's going on?"

"There's an active shooter situation at Stoneman Douglas."

"What!" he yelled, "Why the hell weren't we told!"

He jumped on his radio, "Dispatch, is there shooting at Stoneman!"

"Yes, there is!"

"Why the hell..." He switched frequencies. "All units, all units get to Stoneman Douglas now! Active shooter, I repeat, there is an active shooter! We've trained for this! Be ready to engage! Let's move!"

He wheeled around and put on his siren.

Out on Holmberg Road, Deputy Perry said to Goolsby, "We better go in."

"All right, let's go," said Goolsby as they ran toward the north gate. Deputy Eason got into his car, "I'll secure the perimeter." He backed up and drove down Holmberg, past Deputy Katz, and turned the corner to head over by the baseball fields on the opposite end of campus.

Deputy Stambaugh watched them leave and slowly walked to the back of his cruiser. He opened the back hatch and began rummaging through his supplies looking for his vest. He found it, and slowly put it on, turning to see how Perry and Goolsby were faring.

Deputies Miller and Seward stood behind their cars, still off campus on Holmberg road, some fifty yards far from Stambaugh with their guns drawn, watching the windows of the third floor from a distance.

Deputies Perry & Goolsby awkwardly zigzagged their way to the north gate of the student parking lot. They were now on campus, but found the gate locked. "I got the key," said Goolsby. He fumbled for the key and radioed, "We have shots fired. I'm trying to get the fence open."

2:28 P.M.   9 MINUTES HAVE PASSED SINCE CRUZ'S ARRIVAL

As they neared Stoneman Douglas, the Dark Angel Sansa and Lynda saw sirens and students running away from campus; they were too late. Sansa zeroed in on Nikolas and saw he was in a room at the end of the third-floor hall. She pointed and raced downward taking Lynda with her.

She landed and grabbed Lynda by the shoulders, making eye contact. Lynda looked away, down the hall at the carnage and was suddenly frightened. Sansa was worried she was going to faint. "Lynda, Lynda, look at me. He is inside that room." She pointed, pleading, "You must stop him! You must! Please!"

Lynda looked again down the hall, then, in the eerie silence, turned to face the teacher's lounge door.

Suddenly the door opened, and Nikolas charged out. His face looked demonic as he gritted his teeth, tightly gripping the loaded AR-15.

"Nikolas!" cried Lynda as loud as she could.

Nikolas froze, his eyes showing shock. "Mom?"

"Nikolas, stop! Whatever you have done, it is over NOW! Do you hear me! Stop now!"

The Dark Angel Tira came up behind him, and her face too showed shock at seeing Lynda, "What are you doing here!" she screamed, "Nikolas, move! You have more to kill! Hundreds are getting away!"

Nikolas' mind slowed again, but this time in a different way, this time, it slowed toward reality, as his fantasy began to dissipate slowly. He looked down the hallway. He looked up at Tira hovering in the air over him with a stern look on her face. Then he looked again at his mom, and he started to shake. He was suddenly confused, suddenly afraid.

Lynda said sternly, "Nikolas, turn yourself in now. Do you hear me? Turn yourself in!"

Tira put her hands on her head, screaming, knowing at this moment her own fate was suddenly at stake! "NO NIKOLAS! Keep going! Start phase two! They all hate you!"

But Nikolas looked at her and glared. He then took his backpack off his back. He looked again at his mom who was staring at him with the tear-filled stern eyes he had seen most of his life. He lowered his glance, unable to face her. He bolted to the stairwell door, opened it, dropped his gun, backpack, and hat, and ran down the stairwell like a scared animal.

Just then the Angel Commander Rosie and Angel Jordan flew in, and Tira took off. Rosie ran up to Lynda, "Are you all right?"

"Yes," Lynda said through tear stained, mortified eyes. She looked around, devastated at what Nikolas had done.

"Where is Nikolas?" asked Rosie.

"He's gone. It's over."

Rosie looked down the hall, seeing the carnage, and she fell to her knees and began to weep.

Jordan looked around and suddenly saw her. It was Sansa laying on the floor in the corner of the hall, curled up, gasping for breath. He ran over to her, "Sansa, why? Why did you bring her? Why?"

She opened her eyes, and a small smile labored onto her face, "Because... I love you... and... I had to make up for my life."

Jordan started shaking his head, with tears rolling out, "Sansa, it is I who love you. You're going to be ok... The Lords will..."

She closed her eyes, mouthing the words, "I love you Jord..." She gasped one last shuddering breath and died.

Jordan screamed, "No, no! Rosie help me, please! Sansa! Wake up! No!"

Rosie knew it was too late, and she had no time to waste. She took Lynda and flew up to return her to the Land of Reform."

Outside Deputy Perry saw Coach Feis laying dead on the grass. He quickly maneuvered behind a nearby car, scanning the upper floor windows with his gun drawn, ready to shoot should he be engaged. Goolsby got the fence open and crouched nearby, taking a final look to see if it was safe yet.

Suddenly another transmission went out to them all. It was Peterson shouting, warning his fellow deputies, "Do not approach the 12 or 1300 buildings, stay at least 500 feet away at this point."

2:29 P.M.   10 MINUTES HAVE PASSED SINCE CRUZ'S ARRIVAL

Officer Burton of the Coral Springs Police Department arrives on the scene at the front entrance of Stoneman Douglas. No one from Coral Springs had been informed that the shooting was in Building 12. Security monitor Andrew Medina told Burton him to jump in the golf cart, and Medina raced him back toward Building 12. On the way, Burton immediately radioed his fellow officers, "He's in the 1200 building at the north end of campus."

2:31 P.M.   12 MINUTES HAVE PASSED SINCE CRUZ'S ARRIVAL

Six Coral Springs Police Cars raced up, and the officers jumped out. Within moments they charged Building 12, followed by only some deputies of Broward County.

Deputy Stambaugh watched them arrive, watched them charge away, got in his car, and drove away. Over by the distant baseball field, Deputy Eason heard the commotion on the radio. He looked over and saw Deputy Kratz still parked by the football field. Deputy Eason got out of his car, turned on his body cam, and approached some students. He pointed over toward the high school and asked, "Did you hear any shots fired?"

3:11 P.M.   **52 MINUTES HAVE PASSED SINCE CRUZ'S ARRIVAL**

Deputy Scott Peterson, having listened to the entire ordeal unfold from his hiding spot, only forty feet away, snapped the safety back on his weapon, and walked out to join the other first responders gathered inside and outside Building 12.

Chapter 122

February 14, 2018
Broward County Sheriff's Office

IT WAS 6:30 AT NIGHT AS NIKOLAS CRUZ sat in the white chair inside the interrogation room at the Broward Sheriff's Office. Detective John Curcio was charged with the interrogation. Tira hovered nearby, knowing she had to leave soon. The Angels of Heaven would be looking for who was responsible. Her plan to blame Sansa had failed. Her only hope lied in Legion's protection.

She wanted to hear what Nikolas would say, though, so she lingered a little longer.

Detective Curcio began the interrogation, "You say you've been depressed. Why?"

In a soft, gentle voice, Cruz replied meekly, "I'm lonely."

"Why?"

"I have no friends."

Curcio hated hearing any excuse, "You said there is a demon. Tell me about this demon?"

"It talks to me all the time."

"For how long?"

"Since my father died." Cruz was glad someone was listening. The detective appeared to believe him.

"Has it gotten worse?"

"Yes."

"Since when?"

"Since my mother died."

"What does this demon tell you?"

"To burn, to kill, to destroy."

"Burn, kill, destroy what?"

"Anything."

Curcio knew Cruz was playing games, but he had to play along. "When did you hear the voice last?"

"Last night."

"What did it say?"

"Hurt people."

"There is no voice, Nikolas. It's you."

"No, there is."

"The voice didn't tell you to take Uber."

"Yes, it did." Cruz pointed to his head, worried the detective did not believe him, "It's in here, it is always in here. But then this is me." He pointed to his chest. "The voice is up here," he said again, pointing to his head, tapping it. "But in here is just me, trying to be good." He pointed to his chest again.

"There is no voice. This is all you."

"No, it is real." He paused thinking, then his eyes widened, "It is... Tira!"

"It is what? Tearing?"

Tira smacked Nikolas, "Shut up, you idiot!"

Detective Curcio asked, "Nikolas, what did you say?"

"Nothing."

~ ~ ~ ~

At 11:30 at night, Nikolas Cruz sat alone in the jail cell wearing a straight jacket to prevent him from hurting himself. It was dark except for a light coming through a door at the end of the hall. He thought about his mother who he had seen, and he thought about what she said.

Something was suddenly missing. Then he realized what. It was Tira's presence, her voice. She was not there anymore. He called out, "Tira? Tira?"

He listened, but there was only silence.

"Tira? Don't leave me! Tira!"

Suddenly he began to feel fear like he had never felt. He felt closed in, trapped. He got up and ran to the cell door, slamming his head against the iron bars. He fell, banging his head in self-hatred against the floor of the jail. Then he began to cry, and he began calling out, "Mom, help me. Help me! Mom!"

He screamed into the darkness, "Mom!"

But there was nothing, only dark silence, and he shuddered, and whimpered, periodically banging his head into the floor until he fell asleep.

Chapter 123

February 15, 2018
1st Heavenly Realm, Sunrise Park – Dawn
The Day After

THE SUN PEAKED OVER THE HORIZON, casting its first rays across the sea and onto the faces of the seventeen people peacefully asleep on the warm plush grass in Sunrise Park. The park was located in a small valley, nestled between two hills, lined with blossoming flower trees. The park led to a small beach looking out over the Great Heavenly Sea. It was reserved for special events such as this, events where millions of people on earth had raised their voices to Heaven in grief. It was considered one of the most beautiful places in the Heavens.

The sea was perfectly calm, and the sky held a few clouds, but they were white, majestic clouds, the kind one could marvel at for hours.

In a wide array around the seventeen people, seventeen Angels were kneeling. Some of them were weeping as they had felt the anxious last thoughts of loved ones left behind. None of them had been aware of the yesterday's shooting until it started. Angels did not know the future. They were caught off guard as much as everyone else.

In the distance, the Angels looked up and saw a messenger Angel flying toward them. She landed quietly, and walked up in front of the kneeling Angels, whispering, "Visitors from the Throne Room are coming now." She turned and knelt with the others.

In a moment an illuminated cloud appeared over the sea, and it drew near, slowly lowering to the ground. The cloud dissipated on the edges and the seven Archangels of Heaven, dressed in white and gold trimmed uniforms, stood in a perfect array with their backs to the sea facing those about to be raised. To the right of them, a humble looking woman with a gentle smile, wearing a light blue tunic and a blue veil, stood with her hands folded.

A moment later the cloud dissipated completely, and in the center stood two men and a woman. They wore simple, yet royal looking gold colored robes, and had plant-like laurels on their heads.

No one spoke but only watched as the three slowly moved through the sleeping students and teachers, taking time to look down at each one of them. There were tears forming on their cheeks, and tight-lipped smiles on their faces, as each of the Lords knew how painful death was to the humans they had created, and yet they also knew how beautiful life forever in Heaven would be.

The woman in the blue veil signaled to one of the Lords, who walked over. She whispered something, and he nodded. He announced, "I am temporarily suspending their memory of the family and friends they left behind, so they may enter Heaven without sorrow." He waved his hand, and gold dust appeared and fluttered down upon all.

The older looking Lord turned to the Angels and asked, "Where is he?"

One of them stood, and walked over to one of those sleeping, and took a knee next to him, "Here, my Lord."

The three Lords walked over and joined the Angel. The older Lord kneeled on the other side of the sleeping man, and glanced up at the Angel, nodding. The Angel smiled and looked at the husky man wearing the same clothing he had put on yesterday morning before school. He took the man's hand and said, "Aaron? Aaron, it is time to wake up."

Aaron's eyes began to roll behind his eyelids, and suddenly he breathed. He opened his eyes, looking a little confused. He asked, "Who are you?"

"Aaron, I am Cameron. I am your Angel."

Aaron looked at the other man, and asked, "Who are you?"

"I am the Father, Aaron. Welcome home."

"Home?"

The Angel said, "You are in Heaven Aaron."

"Heaven? You mean... I'm dead?" His face grew sad and began to choke back tears.

The Father saw his dismay, so he placed his hand on Aaron's forehead, saying, "Peace be with you Aaron."

Aaron took a deep breath, as calm came over him. He asked, "What... what happened?" Even as he asked, his mind was working, vaguely remembering falling back on the grass in pain.

The Angel Cameron said, "You tried to save your students in a shooting, Aaron. You gave your life so that others might live."

Aaron now remembered being shot, and slowly the details of the horrific events began to form. He looked down at his chest and felt for the wound. He lifted his head and glanced at some others sleeping around him. "Oh, no! How many others are there?"

"There are 16 others who died Aaron. They are asleep, but we want you to help us wake them."

"Me, why me?"

The Father smiled, glancing up at the other Lords momentarily, "We heard you were the called the 'mayor' at your school, and we could think of no one more deserving as a man who loved others more than himself."

Aaron smiled for a brief second, but then his face grew somber. He sat up and looked around in both directions as a look of duty began to come over his face.

The Father stood up and reached his hand out to help Aaron stand. Aaron looked more closely at the others who were sleeping. He wiped a tear from his face, "There are so many."

The Father asked, "Who shall we wake first, Aaron,"

Aaron looked overwhelmed for a moment as he scanned the bodies, then he stopped. He looked down at the person closest to him, shaking his head. It was one of his favorite students. He pointed at the young man dressed sharply in his ROTC uniform, and said, "Peter."

Aaron and the younger looking Lord knelt on either side of the sleeping young man while the other two Lords stood over them. Aaron looked up for reassurance, then grasped Peter's hand, "Peter?"

Peter opened his eyes, squinting, "Coach?" He looked at the other man, "Where am I?"

Aaron said, "Peter, we are in Heaven." Peter stared off in the distance, suddenly remembering running away and being shot. He too, did not remember his loved ones as of now, yet he knew something was missing. He asked, "Is... Is Jaime Ok?"

Aaron suddenly began to choke up, he had already seen Jaime among those still sleeping. Peter sat up "It's ok coach. We are going to be all right."

"You think so, Peter?" asked Aaron, starting to choke up again.

"Isn't that what you always tell us?"

Aaron started nodding, taking in a deep breath, "Yes, that's what I always tell you."

Peter now looked at the other man, "Who are you?"

The younger Lord said, "I am Yeshua." Yeshua pointed at the others, "He is the Father, and she is the Holy Spirit."

Peter's eyes widened, "Wow, that is so cool!"

The female Lord smiled widely and looked at the others with a tear in her eye, "Well we haven't heard that in a while."

Yeshua helped Peter to his feet, "Welcome to Heaven, Peter. I saw your bravery today. We have a special job for you that you will learn about later. I can only tell you that it has to do with the Heavenly Army of Michael the Archangel."

Peter's eyes widened, "Really?"

"Yes, really!" Yeshua smiled inside. He was happy Heaven was that special place where after death, people could live a life full of joy, hope, and activity, getting to do the things their hearts desired on earth, but for whatever reason, they could not do.

Yeshua turned and waved for the woman in the blue veil to come forward. "Peter, this is Miryam, she is like a mother to many in Heaven. She is going to take you to some very special people." Yeshua turned and pointed to the top of the hillside. There was a group of about twenty people of Asian descent waiting for him. Miryam took Peter by the hand and she walked him up the hill.

Aaron looked at the next person nearest them and said, "Oh, no, not Meadow."

Aaron went quickly over to her and kneeled. The Father kneeled on the other side of her. Aaron always knew Meadow was going to be special, but he never imagined he would be waking her to life in Heaven. He gently called out, "Meadow?"

Meadow breathed, then opened her eyes, "Coach Feis?"

"Yes, it's me."

"Where are we?" she asked, looking around.

Aaron said, "Meadow... we are in Heaven."

"You mean... I... I..."

Aaron took her hand, "Meadow, you are alive forever now."

The Father said, "Meadow, we saw how bravely you acted today, when you tried to shield that girl who was so frightened. Heaven will always remember the courage you showed."

Meadow began to tear up as it all was coming back to her. Then, somehow the connection she had with her mom and dad was so strong it was breaking through the effects of the dust. "I want to see my mom and dad!" she exclaimed with a growing look of sadness on her face.

The Father nodded, and gently placed his hand on her forehead, "It's ok Meadow. You will see your mom and dad very soon. Shalom."

In an instant, Meadow felt a warm feeling of love she had never experienced wash over her, and suddenly she was no longer afraid. They helped her to stand, and the woman in the blue veil came over and gently took Meadow by the hand and walked her over to a group of her ancestors who were waiting on the hillside some fifty yards away.

As they drew nearer, Meadow saw the man in front and thought he looked familiar, and yet he looked much younger than she ever remembered. She called out, "Grandpa?"

He smiled widely, nodding, "Hello Meadow," he said, as they ran to each other and hugged tightly. "Meadow I've missed you more than I can say. Everything is going to be ok. Don't worry about anything. I've got a lot of people over here behind me who I've told all about you, and they can't wait to meet you."

Meadow looked behind him at all the smiling faces, and she suddenly felt like she was home.

One by one, Aaron and the Lords woke each of those who had lost their lives and took them to be with their families. When the last person had been awakened, the Father addressed them all.

"All of you will stay with your families today. Tonight, we have a very special place to go to."

Chapter 124

February 15, 2018
1st Heavenly Realm
Still the Day After

SCOTT BEIGEL SPENT THE DAY at a spacious villa overlooking a scenic valley filled with streams and peacefully flowing river. It was the home of his great-grandmother, who of course, he had never met. The day was fascinating for him and was amazed at life in Heaven. The thing he found the most amazing, was that he was able to have the most interesting conversations with people who lived in times only heard of in the history books. These were his people, people from his family tree who had gathered to support him. He still had no memory of those he left behind, only of the shooting itself.

In the early evening they all sat down to a sumptuous meal and when it was through, his great grandmother called him outside. His Angel, Edward, was also there waiting. "Hello Scott, we have something we need to tell you."

"Sure, what is it?"

"Well, when you died, you left some special people behind, and they are grieving for you."

"I did, who?"

His grandmother said, "Your mom, your dad, and your sister." Scott began to remember each of them, slowly, and he started to feel deep sorrow. His Angel Edward said, "There is one more very special person too, Scott... someone you loved very deeply."

Scott looked up through moistening eyes, "Who?"

"Your fiancée, Gwen."

"Gwen," he said, bewildered, starting to remember her. "Oh Gwen... oh no... she... she must be so sad." He turned away, now tearing up, "I can't believe it...."

He looked up and around, feeling lost, and with tear-filled eyes said, "She gave me a card that morning. It was on my car for Valentine's Day. I saw her face at the moment when I crossed over."

His grandmother hugged him tightly, "You will see her again someday, Scott. That is love's way. It is eternal."

"I know, I know that now... I need a few minutes." Scott walked away toward the setting sun and stared into the sky, wishing he could talk to her, hoping she might hear his heart suddenly aching for her.

After a while, he came back over to Edward and his grandmother, "Where are we going?"

"We are going to the candle light vigil in Parkland. We have to meet the others at Sunrise Park, where we were this morning, and we are leaving from there in a group."

Chapter 125

February 15, 2018
Legion's Villa – Southern Shores of Hell
The Day After - Evening.

LEGION ANGRILY PACED THE FLOOR OF HIS VILLA waiting for Vamorda. It was nearly nightfall, and he had already secretly spoken to her second-in-command, the Dark Angel Bronson. Bronson, along with several other Dark Angels, were waiting in the next room.

Vamorda landed on the portico and walked in. Legion turned to her with an angry look on his face, "This boy was supposed to kill hundreds! What happened?"

"It was Sansa, my Lord. She foiled the plan," said Vamorda, trying to stay calm, but her body betrayed her as her knees now trembled.

"Sansa!!! Why did you trust her!!!"

"My Lord, you told me to put her in charge!"

Legion replied in a loud angry tone, "No! You were in charge, Vamorda. Besides, Sansa is dead, but I will deal with you."

"My Lord, please, I have served you faithfully all these years."

Legion half smiled, and said, "Bronson?"

In a moment, Bronson and his Dark Angels walked in.

Legion glared at Vamorda, "Take her now and put her into the dark cage I have hanging outside."

"No, please!" she screamed, and turned to run, but the Dark Angels seized her and dragged her out.

Legion then said to Bronson, "Tira is waiting for me atop the cliff at Keem Bay in Achill Ireland. Go personally and inform the Angels of Heaven where she is. Tell them she is the one who was responsible for Cruz's actions."

"Yes, my Lord."

Chapter 126

February 15, 2018
Sunrise Park - Pines Trail Park
The Day After - Nightfall

ONE BY ONE, EACH OF THE SEVENTEEN NEWCOMERS to Heaven and
their Angels came to the park where they had awakened earlier that
morning. They had all experienced a wonderful day with a family
that they never even imagined meeting. They had enjoyed the warm
beautiful weather, spacious homes, and delicious foods, and yet now
all their faces held looks of sorrow, as all had been told about the
loved ones they left behind.

It was time to grieve, it was time to go back, it was time to mourn
their own loss, their loss of losing everyone they held close on earth.
They would not be grieving alone as their family in Heaven would be
helping them to grieve and adjust to their life in Heaven.

Tonight, they were going to the candle light vigil being held in
Pines Trail Park in Parkland.

When the last ones arrived, the whole group lifted into the air and
flew up through a thick bank of clouds, and suddenly they were in
the earth's atmosphere, flying toward Pines Trail Park. They landed
on the stage and stood at the back, so they could hear the speakers,
and still watch the crowd of thousands upon thousands of people
gathered in front of the wide stage.

It was a moving ceremony that brought tears to everyone. At one
point, Jaime's father got up to speak. He said, "I hope none of you
have to go through what we are going through. This should NEVER

have happened! My wife is at home, and we are broken. Don't tell me there is no such thing as gun violence. It happened in Parkland!" He paused, "I don't even remember if I told Jaime that I loved her yesterday morning. I don't remember." He went to sit down still in complete shock.

Jaime looked to her Angel. He nodded and took her by the hand. They walked over to where her dad was sitting, and Jaime whispered in his ear, "You told me dad. You did, and I will always know that you and mom love me! I am ok, please know this, and know that I will always love you." She kissed him and wiped a tear from her eye. Even though her dad could not see her, he felt peace for a moment, and more tears rolled down his face.

When they sat down, Jaime turned to her Angel with eyes wide, "I need a phone."

"For what? You can't call anyone."

"I know, trust me. I want to put out a tweet... from someone else's phone. Please!"

"A tweet!?" He looked at her, puzzled, but somehow knew he needed to trust her. He looked around and walked over and took some kids phone out of his pocket. He came back and handed it to her. Jaime quickly opened Twitter, and smiling, with a tear rolling down her face, typed, #NeverAgain, #StonemanDouglasStrong. She showed it to him as he quickly and carefully looked it over. He smiled, "Go ahead, but hurry."

She hit send. He quickly put his hand out and she gave the phone back and he went over and put it back in the student's pocket.

Near the middle of the ceremony, the Senior Class President, Julia Cordover came to the microphone and offered moving words to the crowd of thousands. "Home is where the heart is, and yesterday my heart was broken. This is our home, and this is where we will not be intimidated by evil. So now I am going to read the seventeen names, Carmen Schentrup, Meadow Pollack, Peter Wang, Nicholas Dworet, Mr. Christopher Hixon, Mr. Aaron Feis, Luke Hoyer, Alaina Petty, Jaime Guttenburg, Martin Duque, Alyssa Alhadeff, Helena Ramsay,

Mr. Scott Beigel, Joaquin Oliver, Cara Loughran, Gina Montalto, Alexander Schachter. As the last name was read, the cries of anguish echoed through the crowd.

Near the middle of the ceremony, they all left the stage, walked out among the crowd, and split up, each accompanied by their Angel. They walked around for a long time, silently observing the people gathered around the crosses that had been set up and surrounded by candles. They loved seeing their friends and wished they knew that they were ok.

Scott Beigel walked around for a long time too, aimless. Suddenly he turned to his Angel, "Please, you have to take me to see her."

"I can't do that. We were given special permission to be here. I am not allowed..."

Scott cut him off, "Listen, I won't tell anyone, but I HAVE to see her. I don't live far."

The Angel started to protest, but then sighed, and quickly looked around, "This way."

They walked to the back of the crowd and took off behind some trees and flew to Scott's home.

Inside, Gwen was alone, sitting on the couch with her head buried on her arm, weeping. Scott went in and kneeled next to her. He brushed her hair back, though she could not feel it, and he kissed her, though she did not know. He looked at his Angel, who waved his hand, opening her mind.

Scott said, "Gwen I love you. I will see you again someday my beautiful lady. Take care of yourself, for me, so that..." tears began to fall, "So that I know you are all right."

Gwen stopped crying for a moment, she looked up around the room at the ceiling, and she didn't know why, but she whispered, "I love you, Scott."

Scott's Angel gave them a few more moments, then said, "We have to go now."

Scott stood, and kissed her forehead, and said, "Goodbye, Gwen."

They turned and went back to the park to join the others. A little while later, they all went back to the ancestral homes in Heaven where they would spend the next few days with their Heavenly families before coming back for their funerals.

Chapter 127

February 17
Mountain Top overlooking Keem Bay, Achill Island,
Ireland

TIRA SAT ON THE HILLSIDE WAITING FOR LEGION to come. He had told her to come here to wait for him so she might receive her reward. She did not know what her reward would be, but she knew she had pretty much done all he asked. She could not help it if Sansa failed again.

Suddenly they were upon her. Four Angel guards from the Heavens seized her.

"Let me go!" she screamed.

One of the Angels stood before her and unfurled a scroll. He began to read, "Dark Angel Tira. You have been found guilty of heinous atrocities against the Human Race. You are sentenced to Seventeen years in a dark cage."

Tira's eyes widened, "No! No! No! It was Sansa! It was Legion! I can't! I can't handle it! NO!!!" They stuffed a black cloth into her mouth and quickly bound her hands and feet."

Tears streamed down her face as they lifted her and carried her to the place where the Dark Angels who had gone too far were serving their sentences.

She writhed wildly, trying to get free, as they opened the dark cage door filled with blackness. They thrust her inside and pulled the rag out of her mouth. She immediately pleaded and screamed, "Please!! PLEASE!! I'M SORRY!!!

The band around her hands, then feet were severed. "No! NO!!!!!"

The cage door was slammed shut and sealed, and she was hoisted up slowly to hang in the tree on the vast hillside that currently held 772 such dark cages, some that had been there as long as seventy years.

Chapter 128

February 16, 2018 7:00 A.M.
The White House, Washington D. C.

"SHE IS HERE, MR. PRESIDENT"

President Trump sat in the Oval Office with pictures of the 17 victims spread out on his desk. They were pictures depicting each of them during life, during days of happiness. Accompanying each picture was a small piece of paper with their name and age. The President had a tear in his eye, overwhelmed by the senseless tragedy, and overwhelmed to think the nation was going through yet another mass shooting.

He hit the intercom, "Give me a moment, Judy."

He took a Kleenex out of his drawer and dried his eyes, then stood up to look out the window for a few moments. He knew what was coming, and he hated the politics of it all. All of it defied common sense.

He took a deep breath and hit the intercom, "Ok, Judy, please send her in."

In a moment the door to the Oval Office opened and the House minority leader, Nancy Pelosi, came in.

"Good morning, Mr. President."

"Good morning, Nancy. It's a terrible time for our country."

"Yes, it is."

"Have you seen these pictures?"

She shook her head.

"Come and take a look."

Nancy stepped around the desk and looked at the pictures as Trump got up and moved aside by the side of the desk to give her ample room. It was a rare moment when politics did not matter. They were looking at innocent people whose lives had been cut terribly short. Pelosi looked up, and with her eyes tearing up. "It is truly overwhelming to see them all, Mr. President."

Just then a voice came over the intercom "Mr. President, Governor Scott is available now."

Trump motioned for Nancy to sit down. He also sat and put the phone on speaker.

"Rick?"

"Hello, Mr. President. I don't know what to say. It is a very sad day here in Florida."

"I know. It's senseless what is going on. It's a complete waste of precious young lives."

"Yes, it is Mr. President."

Trump glanced up at Nancy, and said, "Rick, I am here with Congresswoman Nancy Pelosi."

"Good morning Congresswoman."

"Good morning, Governor Scott. Our thoughts and prayers are with you right now. It is a very sad day for our nation."

"Thank you, Congresswoman."

President Trump then asked, "Rick, who is this Sheriff Israel?"

"I don't know him that well, Mr. President, but from what I am hearing, the Sheriff's Office down there really botched things."

President Trump said, "Very badly, I might add. It sounds like his people didn't do what they were supposed to do. I can't believe it. These poor parents, never being able to see their son or daughter again. I would be horrified. Losing those wonderful teachers too."

"I understand, Mr. President."

"It's very bad."

"I am afraid there is going to be more news coming out."

Trump looked up at Pelosi. "What could be worse than this?"

"Apparently, one of his deputies was actually on the scene. Instead of going in, he hid outside."

"Coward! Absolute Coward!" said Trump, looking at Pelosi who was shaking her head.

"Guys like this give Law Enforcement a bad name!" Trump said angrily.

Mr. President, there is something good to report though. These students down here are starting a movement, the likes of which I have never seen. There is a special light coming out of Parkland and I believe it is going to change things.

President Trump looked at Pelosi again. He was glad she was there. They both knew full well the politics involved, and yet, in this moment of mutual sadness, hearts were ready to listen.

Congresswoman Pelosi said, "I have been watching this unfold, Governor. It is indeed something special."

"Well, we will see if anything changes. I am afraid that is up to you all in Washington."

Trump said, "Scott, after Las Vegas, and now this, I believe things are going to change. Tell those kids to keep it up. They are the future."

"I will, Mr. President."

"Thank you, Governor Scott," said Nancy.

"Goodbye Congresswoman, goodbye Mr. President."

Chapter 129

February 18, 2018
Northwest Regional Medical Center, Parkland FL

"BRANDON HONEY, PLEASE WAKE UP. IT'S MOM."

Brandon heard his mom's voice and opened his eyes for the first time since the shooting. A tear fell down his cheek. "Mom."

"Oh Brandon, I love you," His mom leaned down and gently kissed her boy on the cheek.

"Where is Skylar?" asked Brandon.

"Who?"

"Skylar?" He closed his eyes again, thinking, remembering the final moment when they squeezed each other's hand "Skylar... she was shot."

Megan began to cry, "Oh Brandon, so many died. I'm sorry honey... I... don't know who she is."

Brandon closed his eyes and began to weep.

Megan got up and went outside to find his nurse. "Nurse... Brandon woke up!

The nurse picked up the phone, "Call the doctor, tell him Brandon has woken up." She hung up and went into the room. She looked at his vital signs and peered into his tear-stained eyes. "Brandon, how are you feeling?"

"Ok, I guess."

His mom asked her, "Do you have the newspaper?"

"Sure, I have it on my desk. What's wrong?"

Brandon's mom began to tear up, "Brandon is asking about someone who was shot... someone named Skylar."

The nurse said, "Hold on." She went out and returned 30 seconds later with the Sun-Sentinel and handed it to Brandon's mom who began to scan the list. She started to weep. Seeing the pictures and names of the victims, and knowing Brandon could have been killed was too overwhelming for her. She quickly brushed the tears away and looked again through all the names and pictures.

"Brandon, you said her name is Skylar. Are you sure?"

"Yes... I am sure."

"She is not in here, honey."

Brandon closed his eyes and began trying to calm his racing heart. His mom, too, began to weep, as the nurse turned and hugged her tightly, she too, overwhelmed in the moment.

Brandon began nodding with his eyes closed, "She's alive."

The nurse went out and returned a few minutes later. "Skylar is up on the fifth floor in ICU, but they said she is going to pull through."

Brandon exhaled loudly, "Oh thank God. I need to let her know that I am ok."

The nurse said, "I will get a message to her."

"Thank you," said Brandon. He turned to his mom, "Mom, she saved me."

His mom began to cry, hugging Brandon, "I can't wait to meet her Brandon. I can't wait."

Chapter 130

Feb 22, 2018
Church on the Glades, Parkland, Florida

AARON FEIS FLEW WITH HIS ANGEL toward the Church on the Glades in Parkland Florida. Today was the day of his funeral. He never liked going to funerals before, but today a myriad of emotions ran through his mind. He wanted to see all of them, all his students, all his friends and coworkers. But more than anything, he needed to see Melissa and Arielle one more time, and yet he knew he would not be able to compose himself.

Clearly, he had a new life beginning in Heaven, but he had left the most precious persons in his life behind. He had been told he would see them occasionally and be able to subtly communicate with their hearts, but this would never take the place of being a husband and father.

They landed in the parking lot and watched the Military Color Guard, along with several of his former lineman pick up his casket and begin walking into the church. Behind the casket walked his wife Melissa and daughter Arielle. Aaron walked behind them, though they did not know, with his wide arms around his two girls, shielding them, hoping for them, praying for them.

When they reached the front, Melissa took young Arielle and sat down. Aaron sat across from them, on the steps near the flag. His Angel, Cameron, sat next to him. Aaron marveled at the more than thousand people present, he scanned their faces, and wished he could tell them he was going to be ok. But he knew, though he was in

Heaven, in some way he would not be ok, until he could talk to them again, laugh with them again, encourage them again.

He listened to the beautiful words and the beautiful songs. When "How Great Thou Art" was sung, he cried, because he had now met the Lords, and he wished everyone there could know how truly wonderful, loving, and life giving they were.

At one point in the service, Arielle began to cry. Melissa teared up too and pulled her daughter close. Aaron looked over at Cameron who nodded, "Go to them Aaron, they will hear you."

Aaron got up and walked down the remaining two steps. He walked over behind them, putting his arms around them, and first whispered to his wife, "Melissa, I love you and I will always love you. Thank you for giving me a reason to live." He turned to Arielle, "Arielle, I am so proud to be your dad. Remember me and remember all that I taught you. Make me proud young lady!" He pulled them close, "I love you both and I can't wait to see you in Heaven."

The closing song played, and everyone filed out, but Aaron stayed on the stage, sitting on the steps. He looked over at his Angel Cameron, and said, "I don't know how, but I think I am going to be ok."

Cameron wiped a tear from his eye and nodded. "Are you ready to go?"

"Yes, let's go."

Chapter 131

March 17, 2018
3rd Heavenly Realm

ROSIE SENT A SECOND MESSAGE, then went on with her evening, making dinner, and writing various communications to those under her command. As the night wore on, she began to worry. This was not like Jordan. She had sent a message to him five days ago and received no reply. She knew he was grieving over the loss of Sansa, but she had not expected him not to reply. Now her second message was going unanswered.

Rosie decided to go see him first thing in the morning. She left at sun up and arrived at his home nestled between two hills overlooking the sea. She knocked on the door. There was no answer. She wondered where he might be and then it occurred to her, so she immediately flew to the mountain region that had been designated as the final resting place for Sansa. Rosie landed not far from the tomb and began to walk up the path. If Jordan were there, she did not want to startle him.

Within a few moments, she saw him, curled up in a fetal position, covered in a blanket, sleeping on the ground at the entrance.

She quietly walked up and saw him open one eye.

He opened his other eye, squinting at the morning sun, and asked, "Rosie? What are you doing here?"

"Jordan, are you ok?"

He quickly got up, and Rosie could instantly tell his eyes were reddened from weeping. She drew closer, "Jordan, how are you?"

"Not good Rosie, not good."

Rosie felt the sadness and hugged him tightly. "I'm sorry."

He shook his head with a forlorn look on his face. "I thought we had found each other again, we... we were falling in love again." He glanced over at the tomb entrance. "Now she is gone forever."

Rosie glanced over at the large rock sealing the entrance to the cave tomb. Jordan had neatly etched words into the stone, "Sansa, an Angel who gave her life so others might live, and who I will love forever."

Jordan watched Rosie read what he had carved, then asked, "Why does it have to be this way?"

Rosie shook her head, "I don't know, Jordan. Maybe it's time to resume your duties. Would you like to?

"No," said Jordan. "I am going to stay here."

Rosie flew for home upset and worried about her Host Commander. They had worked together for thousands of years, and she had never ever seen him so broken. She stopped in mid-air and changed course. She was too upset to go home.

Chapter 132

March 18, 2018
3rd Heavenly Realm

MIRYAM WALKED QUIETLY UP THE MILE-LONG PATH that led from her mountainside home to Yeshua's living quarters at Holy Mountain. She went in the large doors and started across the vast Throne Room floor. The sun was just rising in the east and shone its majestic golden morning light, creating a magical ambiance. Yeshua walked out of the living quarters and greeted her, "Good morning, Miryam."

"Good morning, Yeshua. I'm sorry to come so early."

Yeshua gestured, "Let's sit over by the eastern overlook."

"Our commander, Rosie came to see me," said Miryam as she sat down.

"Oh, is everything all right?"

"I'm afraid it is not. She said that the Angel Jordan is badly heartbroken. She's afraid he won't pull out of it."

"Is it because of what happened to the Dark Angel Sansa?"

"Yes."

Yeshua sighed, he already knew what she was going to ask. "I am sorry, I cannot."

"Yeshua, she gave her life to try to stop that boy. Isn't that worthy of something?"

"Of course, it is. But we can't allow Angels to transport people back to earth. It's against the entire order of Heaven. Besides, are you forgetting that she was personally involved in not one, but two major tragedies."

Miryam knew he was right, but still asked, "Are you sure you can't make an exception?"

"I'm sorry, Miryam. I absolutely cannot. I will go and speak with Jordan though, and I will try to encourage him."

She lowered her glance, and left, disappointed, yet also knowing she needed to trust her son's wisdom.

Chapter 133

March 20, 2018
Residential Home-Parkland

Brandon and his mom, Megan, slowly walked up the sidewalk toward the large house set slightly back from the road. They knocked and nervously waited. In a moment, Skylar's mom and dad opened the door, smiling. "Hello you two!"

"Hi!" Megan said, "I am Brandon's mom, Megan."

Mary Dunbar reached out to Megan, "Hi Megan, it is so nice to meet you finally. Come in."

Mary gave her a hug, and then warmly hugged Brandon. "Oh, Brandon, welcome."

They all walked in and immediately saw Skylar with a neck brace and a large cast on her leg sitting on the couch with a tray table, and crutches nearby. Brandon walked over, "Hi Skylar."

"Hi Brandon," she said, as a tear fell down her cheek.

"I really missed you, Skylar," he said, shyly.

She began crying, "I missed you too, Brandon. I am so glad you are ok. Here, give me those crutches and help me stand up."

Brandon helped her, and she stood up.

"There, that's better," she said, wiping another tear away.

"You were so brave," he said. He turned to her parents, "She jumped out of the closet to face him. She saved me. She was willing to die for me."

Skylar smiled, nodding, "Brandon, you tried to do the same thing, did you forget?"

"I didn't forget. I will never forget what happened." He reached over and they both hugged for a long tender moment.

Skylar's mom wiped the tears from her eyes, and said, "Come in and sit down over here. I have made us all some dinner, and we have a lot of 'getting to know each other' to do. I have a feeling we are going to be friends for a long time."

Chapter 134

April 14, 2018
3rd Heavenly Realm
Three Months Since Their Arrival in Heaven

COACH CHRIS HIXON WALKED ALONG a pleasant country path on his way to see his friend. He saw someone in the distance walking toward him. He recognized her, it was Meadow. He waved, and she looked to see who it was, and then began smiling and waving back. She picked up the pace half jogging to meet up with him, "Hi Mr. Hixon!"

"Hey, Meadow. How are you doing?"

"Oh, you know, good days and bad. Mostly good, but there are moments when I miss them all so much." A small tear fell from her eye.

Chris nodded, he knew exactly what she was talking about. No one was immune from their memories of their life on earth, or the memories of how they died, and especially the memories of those they left behind.

"So, what have you been doing with yourself?" he asked.

"Oh, just traveling some. My grandfather has taken me to meet every single one of his friends."

"Every single one?"

She laughed, "Yes, every single one. And a number of them twice already."

Chris started laughing, "That is very funny. I'm sure he is proud of you."

"Yeah, he is. So where are you going?"

"I was just about to tell you. I am going to see Coach Feis."

"Oh, really. How is he?"

"Well, you know Feis, he is already busy as can be. He's got lots of friends, and lots of people who need his help up here."

"Need his help?"

"Well, he is out and about his neighborhood helping with yard work, planting, home projects, and lots of other things. He's making himself useful to be sure."

Meadow laughed, "That is Coach Feis for you, always helping others."

Chris asked, "Where are you off to?"

"I'm going to visit Cara. She is staying with her great grandmother, who is cooking us a traditional Irish meal."

"Well, I hope you enjoy it."

"I am sure I will, Coach… but just between you and me, I think I'd rather have a traditional Italian meal."

Chris laughed, "Me too."

They both said nothing for a few moments, taking in the joy of Heaven.

"All right Mr. Hixon," said Meadow, as she warmly hugged him, "I'll see you later."

"Bye, Meadow. Say 'Hi' to Cara for me."

"I will. Tell Coach Feis I said 'Hi.'"

"I will."

Chapter 135

April 20, 2018
3rd Heavenly Realm

THE ANGEL JORDAN WOKE AS THE RAYS OF THE RISING SUN warmed his face. It had been over two months and he had not left the tomb. He knew he had to, but he could not see how he was going to walk away ever. Part of him wanted to stay forever. It was not supposed to end this way. It was never supposed to be 'never,' not in Heaven. He went down the path, away from the tomb entrance, to some nearby fruit trees and picked a few pieces. He heard a voice in the distance calling out to him, "Jordan?"

A man he did not recognize was walking across the green hillside toward him. He raised his hand, "Over here!"

The man nodded and kept walking, smiling now. Jordan now recognized him. It was Yeshua.

Yeshua came over to him, "Jordan, I have been looking for you. Your commander, Rosie, said you might be here."

"Good morning, my Lord," he bowed, "What are you doing here?"

"I wanted to speak with you."

Jordan lowered his glance.

Yeshua paused, thinking, he wanted to comfort Jordan, he wanted to choose the right words to help him to understand. But he asked, "You really loved her, didn't you?"

"More than I could ever say, my Lord."

"Let's sit down a moment. I want you to tell me about her Jordan. Tell me again what she did in the end."

Jordan sat down began telling him how they had met on the very first day of Creation. He told him about how they loved each other so long ago, and how much he missed her when she followed those who left Heaven.

He told Yeshua the whole story of their meeting again recently, and of the magical day they had spent together, and of their promise to love again. He also told him of the courage she showed by telling him the secret.

"You know, my Lord. She was so very brave. Telling me sealed her fate with Legion. I promised her that the Lords would have mercy on her. But then… then she had to decide… and she chose to give her own life. We were going to come later that day to see you and the other Lords. We wanted to ask your permission to love each other again and to ask you to show her mercy. I even wrote about it on her tombstone."

"I would like to see it," said Yeshua. "Will you show me?"

Jordan pointed up the hill, "Yes, it's over there."

They got up and began walking up the long path to the distant hillside, talking along the way. When they got to the tomb, Yeshua looked at the writing and watched Jordan tracing his fingers across the letters.

Hearing first hand of what Sansa had done, and seeing Jordan express such loving devotion, Yeshua suddenly felt overwhelmed. A tear fell from his face, and he turned and walked a few steps away, thinking.

He then called out, "Jordan?"

"Yes, my Lord."

Yeshua turned, "Roll the stone away."

Jordan looked at him with a look of concern on his face, but Yeshua slowly nodded. Jordan got to one side and pushed the stone aside.

Yeshua peered into the darkness and suddenly raised his hand into the air, "I am the Alpha and the Omega, the Beginning and the End." He paused, as a tear of joy rolled down his cheek, then shouted, "Sansa, come forth."

Jordan's eyes widened as they both stared at the dark entrance of the tomb. Suddenly Sansa walked out, her face and body still covered in the burial cloth Jordan had put on her. Jordan ran up, and unwrapped the cloth around her face, revealing her black hair and dark brown eyes. "Sansa, Sansa!" he yelled.

Sansa's eyes began tearing, "Jordan... I... I thought I would never see you again. Oh Jordan, I love you."

They both began to weep as they hugged each other tightly, refusing to let go even for a moment. Finally, they turned to look at Yeshua, but he was already far down the hill walking at a brisk pace across the hillside.

Jordan yelled, "Thank you, my Lord!"

Yeshua raised his hand, waving it briefly, and kept walking.

Sansa tapped Jordan on the shoulder, and he turned to face her. She smiled widely with deep love in her eyes, and said, "Listen here, mister. I think you owe me a kiss?"

The End???

No, it is only the beginning.

Last Scene

A PRIEST DRESSED IN BLACK AND WEARING a Roman collar walked into the Ft. Lauderdale jail and presented his credentials at the counter. He had been writing to Cruz for over a year and had finally been given permission by Cruz to be put on the visitor list.

"May I see your Bible, Father?"

"Sure," said the priest as he handed it across the counter. The deputy examined it carefully, thumbing through the worn pages. He then turned it upside down, and the priest said, "Careful, I have a tiny keepsake in there… from my late mother?"

"What is that?" The deputy asked. The priest reached across and opened to a certain page and pointed to a single strand of hair. "Just this, it is a strand of her hair."

The deputy looked closely, then closed the Bible and handed it back. "You are all set, Father."

"Thank you."

The deputy buzzed him in. As soon as the priest had gone inside the jail, another deputy asked, "Who was that going to see Cruz?"

The other deputy looked down at the paper again. "let's see… Oh, here it is. His name is Father Ricardo."

Epilogue
One Year Later In Heaven

ALYSSA ALHADEFF

Alyssa, now 15, has spent the last year attending the Angels Education Ministry with students from all over the world, including many of her classmates from Stoneman Douglas. She is known as one of the bright young female soccer stars in the 1st Heavenly Realm where she resides in a spacious home near the city. She is planning on trying out for the All Heaven soccer team in the Fall. Alyssa is planning on applying for early acceptance to the University of the Heavens next year. Her Angel says she has a good chance.

SCOTT BEIGEL

Scott now, 33, helps run the cross-country program for youth runners as part of the Angels Education Ministry for children who entered Heaven before reaching adult age. He runs every evening and frequently visits his ancestors, friends, and especially former students from Stoneman. Scott is still grieving over the absence of his partner, Gwen. He goes on hikes for days at a time spending his nights by a campfire under the stars of Heaven. Scott received a special award in Heaven in recognition of his heroic act to save so many students.

MARTIN DUQUE

Martin, now 15, has joined the central command staff of the Army of the 1st Heavenly Realm commanded by the Archangel Splendora. He also acts as a liaison with other realms and travels between the Seven Heavenly Realms every month. Martin attends the Angels Education

Ministry as often as he can though his priority is his position with the Army. During his free time, he goes to see plays and movies that play throughout the Heavens. He spent three separate evenings with a group of fellow Star Wars lovers at the home of Carrie Fisher where during screenings of her favorite Star Wars movies, she treated the group to the back story of each movie. Martin also visited Yeshua's mother, Miryam, and was given the first-hand account of the story of Juan Diego and Our Lady of Guadalupe.

NICHOLAS DWORET

Nick, now 18, is thriving in Heaven. He keeps a whiteboard in his home where he still lists his goals and motivations. He swims twice a day in the Great Heavenly Sea that is next to his home in Gabriel's 5th Heavenly Realm. Nick is hoping to make the team that competes in the annual All Heaven Games. He has a deal with his Angel to smuggle a pack of Oreo cookies into Heaven once a month as one of his motivations. Nick is still unattached, but there are some young females who have their eye on him.

AARON FEIS

Aaron, now 33, is still getting adjusted to his life in Heaven. More than anything he misses his wife, Melissa and his daughter Arielle. He frequently visits a viewing room to see how they are doing. He decided to move to the 4th Heavenly Realm because there was a teaching position available and because there was a house available looking out at the Great Heavenly Sea. He lives in a small community tucked away in a valley where about 1,200 people from all over the world now live. Aaron is out and about, daily, helping people and helping to make sure everyone is happy. He has been nicknamed 'the mayor.'

JAIME GUTTENBERG

Jaime, now 15, is considered a very funny person in Heaven. She hit the ground running and joined a dance group near her home near a scenic mountain in the 1st Heavenly Realm. She loves how there are formal dances all the time in Heaven as it is a favorite pastime of many. Jamie has also gotten involved with the Guardian Angel anti-bully ministry to help them understand what kids go through, and more importantly what kids should be trained to do about it. She laughs when they ask her to show them her patented kangaroo kick. She has two dogs that she loves, and two different suitors currently. Jaime pins an orange ribbon to her lapel every chance she gets in solidarity with her mom who she is anxious to see again.

CHRIS HIXON

Chris, now 33, was recognized with a special Hero's award as the first teacher to try to save his students at Stoneman Douglas. He is enjoying his life in Heaven and yet misses his wife Debra and his children Corey and Thomas more than he can say. Because of his military training, he has been recruited to serve on the home defense committee for the 6th Heavenly Realm. Chris goes sailing every week and spends a lot of time scuba diving. Since getting into Heaven, he is enjoying being younger again and feeling very strong at his new permanent age of 33.

LUKE HOYER

Luke, now 16, lives in the 2nd Heavenly Realm and is attending the University of the Heavens there. He plays pickup basketball every weekday at lunchtime with other students from all over the world. He is quiet, and always smiling, and generally very happy, though he misses his family more than he can say to others. He visits the viewing room once a month to see them. Out of respect for his dad,

Luke went to visit former Clemson great C.J. Fuller who entered Heaven several months ago.

CARA LOUGHRAN

Cara, now 15, is a friend to many, though she has only been in Heaven for a year. She has traveled the Heavens and met some of the most famous Irish dancers in history. She even spent an afternoon with St. Patrick at his home on the rocky western coast of the 6th Heavenly Realm and was introduced to several men and women who originated Irish dancing. Cara has also spent time surfing and was invited by Yeshua himself, on two different occasions, to join one of the frequent groups of 100 students he hosts throughout the year at his Seaside Villa. She rode his horse Hunter on one of the days and says it was the greatest day of her life so far. Cara also attends school at the Angels Education Ministry.

GINA MONTALTO

Gina, now 15, loves her life in Heaven. She is very active in all kinds of sports including playing tennis four times a week. She lives in the 4th Heavenly Realm governed by the Archangel Raphael. Gina volunteers working with the Angels and other people on Saturday mornings in the Land of Toddlers where children who died before the age of three are lovingly cared for until one of their parents arrives in Heaven. It is a very fun place, and Gina is thinking of adding Sundays to her schedule. She is also on the welcoming committee in her neighborhood charged with helping new arrivals to have a wonderful experience in their new homes.

JOAQUIN OLIVER

Joaquin, now 18, has been accepted to the University of the Heavens but has decided to first take a year off for travel. He plays pickup basketball three times a week and plays soccer with a group of men from Venezuela every Saturday and Sunday afternoon. He received special permission to watch his favorite movie "The Godfather" but his Angel insists he keep it under wraps. Joaquin has met a young lady from Sweden who entered Heaven at the age of 18 just four months ago. Joaquin has asked his Angel to call him 'Guac,' and the name is catching on.

ALAINA PETTY

Alaina, now 16, works alongside Martin on the central command staff of Splendora, commander of the Army of the 1st Heavenly Realm. She has become an exceptional swordsman and is being personally trained by the renowned Angel, Michael the Swordsman who she also has a secret crush on. Alaina attends the Angels Education Ministry and volunteers alongside Gina at the Land of Toddlers on Saturdays. In her free time, she likes to swim and go on hikes with her two new dogs she has named Diego2 and Leo2.

MEADOW POLLACK

Meadow, now 19, is enjoying her life in Heaven, though she misses the team effort at the life she shared with her brother. She goes on hikes daily and rides her bike. She has immersed herself in history and has spent the last year traveling to meet historical figures who actually made history, allowing her to understand firsthand what really happened. Missing her boyfriend of three years has been hard but of late Meadow has met some interesting young men she enjoys spending time with.

HELENA RAMSAY

Helena, now 18, lives in a quiet valley of the 7th Heavenly Realm and also attends the University of the Heavens. Her home is next to a creek and has an open-air kitchen that leads to a private garden. When she is not traveling, she and her neighbors all share a large community garden that she tends to for an hour each morning. She has three cats and has become known as the person who will babysit someone's cat should they be away. Helena frequently travels throughout all the Seven Heavenly Realms and recently met a special young man from Paris who was also seventeen when he arrived in Heaven last year.

ALEX SCHACHTER

Alex, now 15, was reunited with his mother Debbie in Sunrise Park on the day they awakened him into his life in Heaven. He now lives with her and attends the Angels Education Ministry School, a prep school for the University of the Heavens. He enjoys school and arranged for his Angel to smuggle two University of Connecticut hoodies into Heaven. He has one, and he gave the other one, a light blue version, to his mom.

CARMEN SCHENTRUP

Carmen, now 17, is having the time of her life in Heaven. She was granted special permission to spend two days visiting William Shakespeare who told her the back story to all the plays. She still reads a lot but also visits famous historical persons. She is thinking of becoming a writer of historical fiction as she believes she can now bring a new insightful angle to it. In honor of her acceptance as a National Merit Finalist shortly before entering Heaven, she has been accepted for early admission to the University of the Heavens and begins in the Fall. She currently has a crush on a young man in her swim club.

PETER WANG

Peter, now 16, is the youngest serving member of the command staff of Michael the Archangel's 3rd Heavenly Army. Peter is thriving in the military but has lots of free time. He has obtained permission from his Angel to listen to the Houston Rockets games once a month, a privilege that only a few share as long as he keeps it under wraps. He visits his ancestor's homes weekly and is learning about ancient Chinese history from the people who lived it. Peter has also visited

George Patton and spent an afternoon swith Napoleon Bonaparte to discuss their views on military strategy. He said it was the most fascinating day of his life so far.

A Note from the Author

I hope you enjoyed this novel.
Please post a review on Amazon.
And tell others about this book.

What's Real? What's Fiction? And why?

Visit www.dpconway.com to see our research and get your answers.

Audio Book Coming Soon

Join our Email List at
www.dpconway.com

Also Available by D.P. Conway

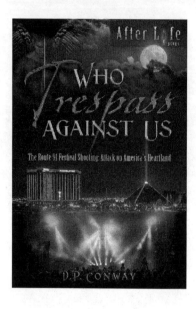

The Untold Story of the Life, Death, and Judgment of the
Las Vegas Shooter.

Available at Amazon and in audiobook at Audible

Coming Soon from D.P Conway

After Life, the 12 book series.

The Greatest Story, Never Told… Until Now

See how it all began and find out how it will all end.

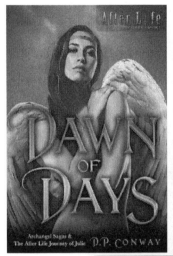
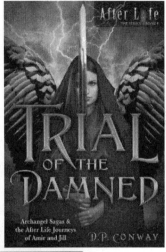

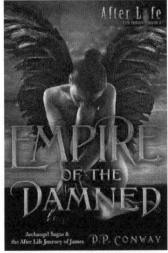

12 Novels in all coming in 2019 and 2020.

Acknowledgments

For Marisa, your patience, encouragement, and love made all the difference.

Contributing Editors, Colleen Conway Cooper, Ed Markovich, Peggy Stewart, Mary Egan, Connie Swenson, Patrick Conway, Christopher Conway, Final Editor Connie Swenson
Cover: Nate Myers, Colleen Conway Cooper, Mary Egan

After Life Series Acknowledgments

For Marisa, my wife, your patience, love, and encouragement, made it possible for me to write this series. *Cara Mia, Io ti amo. Solo tu femmina.*

For Carla Reid, who with her strength and flare inspired the Archangel Splendora in the upcoming After Life series. Carla, the joy I receive from your wonderful friendship can never be measured.

For Sadie Sutton, who inspired the Angel Sadie, the lead character in the upcoming After Life series. Sadie, you really must be an Angel, because meeting you changed me forever. Always… my friend.

For Colleen Conway Cooper, what a wonderful job you did in supporting me though you were so busy. Daughter, you're so very talented. Love, Dad.

For Ed Markovich, our associate, who has been a rock since the beginning, and who asked me to consider writing *Who Trespass Against Us.*

For Reda Nelson, our long-time associate, who helped keep the ball rolling, and moving through five long, difficult years.

For Mary Egan, our dear friend, who has insisted on rewrites and asked the right questions and offered great ideas.

For Megan Franciscus who was a major force for shaping and editing half of the books in the series during the first three years.

For Peggy Stewart, who gave much needed encouragement throughout and has always provided helpful insights.

Also, thanks to Jocelyn Caradang, Rosie Queen, Mary Greene, Angela Rabbitts, Annette Joseph, Bridget Mae Conway, Patrick Conway, Christopher Conway, and all 50 or so test readers over the last five years.

Thank you!

Made in the USA
Lexington, KY
13 April 2019